Love Muffin And Chai Latte

ANYA WYLDE

DEDICATION

For John

CONTENTS

ACKNOWLEDGMENTS

A big thank you to John, Camille, Margie, Shelley and Arya for all the help.

And finally, thank you, Asha, for always being a phone call away.

.

Chapter One

It all began on a dreary June day.

The morning started off with Tabby watching a willowy, blonde weather girl cheerfully point at spots on the map and announce that heavy rain and wind was going to sweep across Britain later in the day. She went on to gleefully add that the onset of an unusual cold snap would see temperatures plummet overnight. She further infuriated the viewers by suggesting that they should settle for a hot toddy and a cosy night at home.

"A thunderstorm," she shot the camera a sultry look, "is fast approaching."

By mid-afternoon, the weather girl was proven right when the lovely warm breeze turned chilly and began zooming around like a bratty child on a sugar high.

Tabby squinted at the sheet of dark clouds rolling across the sky. The nip in the air was welcome since it allowed her to hide under the king-sized duvet, but the rain would ruin not only the duvet but also the purple leather couch she was currently lying on. She wondered if her stuff would stay waterproof in the black garbage bags—

"Tabitha Lee Timmons, will you marry me?"

Her small ears quivered under the heavy quilt. She recognised the voice, and it certainly did not belong to the exceptionally seedy, penniless wanderer she had befriended a few months ago.

The same exceptionally seedy, penniless wanderer that often ran into her on the street. She would give him a couple of bob, and in return he kept his dodgy peers out of her way. A mutual symbiotic relationship had sprouted up between them. And just like an Ocellaris Clownfish relaxes under the poisonous tentacles of a Ritteri Sea Anemone, she, too, now moved under the protection of the local bum lord.

No, the proposal had come from a dark man. A man with attractive, boyish features and a mop of thick hair that was always painstakingly gelled to look as if pointy liquorice sticks were enthusiastically sprouting from the top of his head.

They had met a year ago when she had been working in an upmarket shoe shop. He had strolled in one wintery evening, his muscular form had turned in her direction, and his dark eyes had lit up.

She had openly ogled his attractive head thinking he was eyeing the striking blonde managing the till behind her.

He had proven her wrong by slipping his phone number into her sweaty palm.

He was handsome, wealthy and sane, and yet he had continued to date her after that for an entire year.

It was positively thrilling. No one would believe it back home.

"Will you marry me?" Chris repeated holding out a Styrofoam cup and a muffin towards her.

She reluctantly pushed away the quilt. She didn't trust herself to speak yet. Mainly because she wasn't sure how smelly her breath was.

"Scoot," he said.

She unpeeled the back of her thigh from the purple leather couch with a loud purrp and shifted to make room for him.

He sat down at the end of the sofa.

"So?" he prompted impatiently.

She took a sip of the drink. The taste of strong, bitter coffee hit her tongue. Great. She despised coffee, always had. She quickly took a bite of the muffin. It was white chocolate. Gross.

He jerked his chin towards the cup. "I hope I put enough sugar for you."

"It is perfect," she said brightly.

"The muffin should be good. I got it from Café Blue Glace."

She smiled in what she hoped was a grateful fashion and took another quick sip. The motion dislodged the quilt that had lain under her neck, and it slipped past her shoulders, pooling at her waist.

He frowned. "I thought we spoke about this. You promised to stop dressing up like a theatre group reject."

She guiltily tucked the quilt around her chest. She was wearing her mother's dress. It was a floral retro-style summer dress with a fitted bodice and a full circle skirt. And in a cleverly hidden pocket of the skirt she had placed a maroon pipe. She remembered her mother smoking it with her head hanging out of the kitchen window away from father's disapproving eye.

Over the dress she had added a striped mint apron that smelled like a delicious concoction of tobacco, vanilla and freshly baked bread—her mother's essence—and sometimes when she least expected it, the scent would float up and tickle her nostrils.

She supposed the entire outfit would have been pretty in a classic vintagey way if she hadn't added the round, Gandhi style glasses that had once belonged to her elder sister, Maryanne, or the long white scarf covered in plastic googly eyes.

She removed the glasses and stuffed her mouth with the muffin to avoid an argument. The dry texture of the overly sweet muffin sat like a big lump on her distressed tongue, refusing to moisten and slide down her throat. She chased it down with the coffee.

"I was taking a nap before you arrived. I need a moment," she croaked, "to wake up."

"Sure," he shrugged and took out his phone.

She watched him tap away for a few minutes before taking another cautious sip of the coffee. She quickly bit into the muffin to cut through the bitterness. The coffee and the muffin mixed together and turned into a delicious pudding in her mouth. Her eyes widened, and her face lit up in delight.

Her sister had always teased her saying that people who drank tea were boring, but the ones who drank coffee were cool. It had been childish and silly and yet the thought had stuck with her.

She looked at her dark, handsome boyfriend and the now empty coffee cup and grinned. She, Tabby Timmons, was cool—How wonderful was that!

"Tabitha, you have not answered my question." He squeezed her toe to get her attention.

She snatched back her foot. She was awake now.

"For the last time, Tabby, will you marry me?"

She straightened up on the couch and looked around suspiciously. "I'm on that show. What is it called? Funked? Thunked?"

"What?"

"Are you pranking me right now?" she clarified.

His mouth twisted in distaste. "Pranking you?"

4

She narrowed her eyes and squinted at a suspicious looking fluffy thing poking out from behind an oak tree. "That looks like one of the sound mikes. They have that furry thing on top. What is it called? Dead cat."

He eyed her with concern, "It is a squirrel and it is alive. Tabitha, are you all right?"

"This is some elaborate joke, isn't it?"

"How is this even remotely funny? You should know me by now. I don't play stupid pranks."

She crushed the Styrofoam cup between her hands.

He sighed. "I know this is not an ideal proposal, but considering the situation—"

"Is this a pity proposal?" she asked in a small voice.

"Why would you think that?"

"Maybe because I'm sleeping on a sofa that happens to be lying on the street instead of inside the spacious apartment behind me."

"Look—"

"And I have lost my job at the bakery," she continued glumly. "I left the bread in the oven too long and part of the kitchen went up in flames. The new apartment I was meant to move into didn't work out at the last minute. And now I'm stranded on a fairly busy London street with only the neighbour's Pomeranian to keep me company. I'm, in short, a hobo."

"What Pomeranian?"

She twitched the blanket aside to show a furry creature sleeping next to her.

He quickly slid to the other end of the couch away from the dog. "I admit seeing you like this forced me to speed up my plans, but I was going to ask you to marry me tonight anyway. I had the table booked and roses ordered—"

"I don't believe you."

"I had the ring in my pocket, Tabby, trust me. I had already bought it." He pulled out an expensive looking brown wallet from his back pocket and rummaged around until he found what he was looking for. "Here is the receipt for the ring. It clearly states that I bought the ring two days ago."

She peered at the paper. The amount he had spent on the ring made her gasp, and the date imprinted on the slip proved he was telling the truth.

"So you honestly want me to marry you?" she asked in amazement.

"Yes!"

"Me?"

"Yes, you, Tabitha Lee Timmons, I want to marry you."

"You want to wake up to my moody brown hair, funny little nose and pale, freckled skin every single day for the rest of your life?"

He nodded.

"Oh."

"Well?"

"Yes, well . . ." she took a deep breath. After the horrible day she had had and now this proposal, she wasn't sure what she was feeling. "Where is the ring?" she asked trying to buy some time.

"About that."

"Hmm?"

"You ate it."

"What?"

"You ate the ring."

"What do you mean I ate the ring?"

"I shoved it into the muffin before giving it to you. I didn't think about it. It was spontaneous. I saw you sleeping on the purple couch, and I thought that it would be more romantic if I proposed to you off the cuff. Everyone does the fancy dinner and wine thing."

"Off the cuff?"

"In the moment sort of thing."

"I see, and I swallowed the said muffin."

"And the ring."

"Will I die?"

"Hopefully not."

"What was it like?"

"It had a big square diamond with little diamonds on a platinum band."

"Sounds nice."

"It was . . . is nice, I mean."

"Where did you buy it?"

"The quaint little antique store we found last month. You remember when went to Brighton?"

"It was a lovely little place."

"Yes, pretty."

"The ring . . . it was expensive. I saw the price on the receipt."

He bobbed his head. "The contents of your stomach are currently worth more than my car."

"The shop was horrendously pricey."

"True, but worth it."

She nodded. After a moment, she asked, "Did it have sharp edges?"

"The shop?"

"No, the ring."

"I think it had a few pointy bits."

She sat up on the couch with a sigh. "I suppose we'd better go to the hospital."

"Right, I'll get the car.

Chapter Two

The storm arrived in full force. The windows rattled and rain crashed on a tin roof somewhere in the neighbourhood.

Tabby was tired and gloomy. It had been such a long day. She was at Chris's mercy, most of her stuff was soaked through and probably destroyed, and her bank balance was running frighteningly low.

She wished she was back home in America staying with her dad, taking care of him, back in her old room with its slanting roof, walls covered with posters and stickers and mismatched furniture. Nothing had been expensive in her room, but it was familiar . . . comforting. Why couldn't someone hurry up and invent teleportation? She could zoom her way to America or have her family over or her best friend Becky . . . She jerked up into sitting position, pulled out her cell phone and dialled a number.

Becky picked up on the first ring.

They both automatically switched on video chat.

"Hey, Beckster."

Becky's heart-shaped face framed by bouncy golden curls appeared on the screen of her phone. "Tabby, hold on a moment . . . Louise, don't disturb me for the next twenty minutes."

"But Miss Penrose, your next patient will arrive any moment."

"Is this patient planning to jump off the roof?"

"No, but—"

"Then ask him to wait."

"But, Miss Penrose, he is one of your wealthiest clients."

"Mr Adams?"

"Yes."

"Damn. He is cute . . ."

Tabby watched her childhood friend bite her lip indecisively.

After a moment, Becky closed her eyes and continued with a sigh,

"Louise, ask Mr Adams to wait. I know, I know, but currently I have something far more important to see to. Close the door behind you."

"Thanks, Becks," Tabby said.

"Now, tell me what's wrong?"

"It's not that important. You can finish your appointment. I will call you later."

Tabby heard Becky's heels click on the glass as she lifted her legs up to rest her ankles on the table.

"Tabs, I have known you since you were three. Plus, my phone has sixteen missed calls from you in the last two hours. Now, out with it."

"Promise you won't talk to me as if I'm your patient. I don't need a psychiatrist, I need a friend."

"Sure," Becky said and pulled open a pack of gum and popped one in her mouth.

"Mr Adams must be a hottie," Tabby remarked watching her friend chew furiously.

"So is Chris," Becky replied.

"About that. He asked me to marry him."

"He what!" Becky spat. The green gum flew out of her mouth and attached itself to the phone screen. "Tell me everything. Quick," she demanded, extracting the gum and hurriedly wiping away the droplets of saliva splattered on her phone.

Tabby took a long gulp of her drink. "It's a long story."

"I'm all ears,"

"It all started last evening. I had packed everything up to move to my new place, Chris was going to help me transport my stuff in his car, and everything was in order. Then the hobgoblin—"

"You mean your landlady?

"Right. So, the hobgoblin arrived on my doorstep. She wanted to see how clean the apartment was and inspect the damages that I had done after living in it for two years. Well, all the anger I had bottled up inside me against the woman erupted, and unfortunately I yelled at her. I told her that I still had a day left on the lease, and she had no right to barge in when she pleased. It was against the law and whatnot."

"You finally read the rights of a tenant that I emailed you," Becky grinned.

Tabby did not smile back. She took another long gulp from the glass, making a disgusted face as the contents slid down her throat. "I was at a point where I was certain nothing else could go wrong."

"And then it did," Becky remarked knowingly.

"It did. My boss called me to say I was fired."

"Dang!"

"It wasn't over. The next morning I received a call from my new landlady—"

"The sweet old flighty one? I thought you adored her."

"Let us amend the sweet and replace it with the word senile. She called me to say she had a bit of a problem. She had decided not to rent out the place since her son had chosen to return from Norway and live in England for a while. She was going to give him the apartment that I was meant to move into."

"She can't do that." Becky gasped.

"She can. I had not yet signed the lease agreement. And the worst part is, I'm the one who delayed signing it. I was saving up for the deposit."

"I see."

"Then, my old landlady arrived at nine in the morning with two men. She said she needed to fumigate the entire place before the new owners could move in. She said she suspected the house was infested with bed bugs and fleas. My request for one month's extension on the lease was giggled off. Next thing I know, I'm on the street surrounded by my stuff . . . a homeless person."

"Then?"

"Chris arrived and proposed. Convinced me he was dead serious and that he had been planning to ask me for a while."

Becky popped a second piece of gum into her mouth and chewed thoughtfully. "He had to convince you? Didn't you believe him?"

"Becky, he is sooo good looking."

"And you are not?"

"I have been called cute a few times in my life. A rabbit should be cute, not a full-grown human being."

"You are being pathetic."

"I think he is dating me for my scintillating personality."

"That's more like the Tabby I know."

"I make him laugh, but I'm not glamorous. He is the type of man who should be with a glamorous, modern woman. Someone who knows the right people, wears the right clothes, lives on lettuce and air—I just don't fit it."

"Tabby, you don't understand your own charm. You are like durian, caviar or fermented camel's milk. You are an acquired taste. It takes a couple of meetings for you to grow on people."

"Like mould," Tabby said unhappily. "I grow on people like blobs of green mould."

"Just because Luke—"

"No analysing," Tabby warned.

"Right . . . Do you want to marry Chris?"

"He brought me coffee and a white chocolate muffin."

"Ouch."

"Precisely. After one year of dating him, he still does not know my taste."

"I hear a but . . ."

"But when I bit into the muffin and chased it with a sip of coffee, it was delicious."

"Are you trying to find some spiritual meaning in that?"

"How did you know?"

Becky rolled her eyes. "I know you better than anyone in the world."

"True."

"You always wanted to get married, have a dozen children, a big house and a cucumber patch in the garden. Ever since you were ten years old."

"Hmm."

"And you would have been married a long time ago if—"

"My elder sister had not married my fiancé leaving me with no choice but to leave America and move to England," Tabby finished. "It was the one and only time I did anything brave in my life."

"Your sister is a twit," Becky responded loyally.

Tabby nodded. "As for Chris, I really like him. He makes me happy. In the past year, we have met almost every weekend . . . But rarely alone. He is always surrounded by people. Even if we go for dinner, someone or the other always comes up to our table to chat, and then we are off to a friend's party or a new nightclub. What if. . . ." She trailed off.

"You are wearing your mother's dress," Becky remarked suddenly. "It is her birthday today, isn't it?"

"He proposed to me on my mother's birthday," Tabby nodded.

"Is this a sign? Are we meant to be?"

"Perhaps."

They felt silent, pondering on the importance of signs and omens.

"I saw a single Magpie while I was with him in the car," Tabby recalled.

"Bad omen," Becky responded.

"But he proposed on my mother's birthday."

"Good omen," she conceded. "Does that mean they cancel each other out?"

"I'm not sure."

"So you like him."

"Yes."

"And you want to get married, right?"

"I feel lost . . . Everyone seems to be busy focusing on their careers or getting married and having babies, while nothing seems to be happening in my life. I just need something to work on, something to look forward to. I want to stop being a weedy, stagnant pond and flow free like a river—"

"Tabby, you are losing it," Becky observed.

"Suppose so."

Becky took a deep breath, "Why don't you get engaged and see how things go? It is not like you are walking down the aisle tomorrow."

"He wants to get married in November."

"This November," Becky shrieked.

"Precisely. It is happening so fast, I don't know what to do. I'm already staying at his cousin Dinky's holiday home. It looks like an apartment out of one of those fancy magazines. He has all these expensive things; an antique gold-plated turtle shell, an old Japanese sword, a hundred and one laughing Buddha's in jade, creepy stuffed birds—"

"Tabby," Becky said firmly steering the conversation back to important matters. "Chris is rich, good looking and generous. What more do you want?"

"My family barely speaks to me, you are my only friend, and even my employers keep firing me. I don't think I'm lovable," she confessed in a small voice. "And I want him to love me."

"He wouldn't have asked you to marry him if he didn't love you," Becky said gently. "And don't be a silly goose. Of course, he loves you. Some people are not very good at showing affection. One of my patients only managed to tell his wife of forty years that he loved her after he had stabbed her to death. I found him blubbering over her body in a freezer."

"Why did he stab her?"

"He read Othello and was inspired."

"I suppose you are right," Tabby mused after a moment, and then straightened up and said in a firmer voice, "Scratch that, I'm sure you are right. This is what I want, what I've always wanted."

"To be inspired by Othello?"

"To marry and have children . . . Becks," her voice barely trembled, "I'm going to marry him. He is sweet, generous, caring, wealthy, good looking—I could go on. I would be a fool to say no."

"Yay," Becky squealed.

"Woo-hoo," Tabby responded feeling an inkling of excitement for the first time.

"Don't shop for the wedding dress without me," Becky warned.

"Eeek, I get to buy a wedding dress." Tabby bounced in her seat.

"Miss Penrose," the plaintive voice of the secretary floated into the room. "I just noticed Mr Adams take out a bag of what looks like sleeping pills."

"Five minutes. Show the man in." Becky's feet hit the floor. She spat the gum out into a wad of tissue paper and aimed it at a bin. "Before I go, Tabs, show me the ring."

"What ring?" Tabby asked, watching her friend adjust her bra, smooth her white silk top and apply a pale pink lipstick.

"Your engagement ring, dummy."

"He had jammed it in the middle of the muffin, and I ate it." Tabby shook the glass in front of the screen making the purple contents slosh around. "Which is why I'm drinking prune juice."

Becky's hand froze, her mouth dropped open, and she slowly rotated her blonde head where the comb lay forgotten in the middle of her curls. She passed the test of friendship when she did not laugh. "If that is how you got engaged, I wonder what your wedding will be like."

Tabby shivered at her friend's ominous tone. She downed the rest of the drink and slammed the cup down.

Surely things couldn't get any worse than having her stunning engagement turn into the poo ring?

Chapter Three

Two seconds after Tabby finished talking to Becky, her phone lit up again and the song 'Don't worry, be snappy' started echoing around the large apartment.

"Yellow," she said.

"Can't you say hello like a normal person? You are not five, Tabby," Chris groaned at the other end of the line.

"Mellow," she amended.

"Never mind," he said. "What's the situation?"

She could hear the smile in his voice. "The apartment is lovely. Thank you, I really appreciate you doing this for me."

"You are my fiancée," he replied. "It is the least I can do."

She remained silent. It was a pity he lived with his parents. She would have liked a chance to move in with him before getting engaged.

"But I was asking about the ring," he continued. "Is it out yet?"

She wrinkled her nose. "A pint of prune juice and a tablespoon of flaxseed later, I'm unhappy to report that nothing has moved forward."

"I don't need to know the details," he muttered.

"Oh, wait, I think I feel a little rumble."

"Sounds promising. Let me know when you—"

"—Poop it out," she finished for him. "I will call you immediately."

"Before I forget, I have booked a table at the Plaza for eight-tomorrow evening. I will pick you up at half seven. I hope to God you have the ring by then."

"I'm about to commence eating a bag of oranges. It always works. Stay positive and pray to the gods of digestion to quicken the process."

"You are really strange."

"I prefer adorably weird."

"Right, I will talk to you later before you start becoming any more descriptive."

She didn't reply, for a sudden roar in her stomach reminded her that the time had come. She tossed aside the phone and raced to the bathroom.

Five minutes later an old man in the neighbouring apartment heard her shout, "Woo-hoo, I did it!"

"Bless her," he smiled to himself. "She must have achieved something truly wonderful to sound so happy."

After pooping out the ring, Tabby fell asleep.

She woke up the next day to find that the storm was over, and, just like a nasal passage cleaned out after an aromatic steam inhalation, London, too, appeared refreshed, bright and perky.

But all good things have the opposite of a silver lining. The storm, in its final burst of excitement, had caused a tiny bit of damage. She could see from her bedroom window that a large oak tree had collapsed on top of a red Mercedes, leaving a sizable dent on the roof. She hoped no one had been hurt.

After a quick cup of tea, she rushed to unpack the boxes that had gotten wet. She discovered that all her winter clothes were soaked and smelling funny. She laid them around the apartment to dry out as much as possible.

Her beloved blue silk clutch was ruined beyond repair. She placed it reverently on the coffee table and shed a few tears. It would be a long time before she would be able to afford anything that expensive again.

She spent the rest of the day calling a few job placement agencies. She also called a few people she had worked with before to see if they could be of any help.

What with all the unpacking, sorting and worrying, she forgot about her dinner date with Chris. So when he called to tell her he would be leaving shortly, she panicked.

She had less than an hour to find something suitable to wear, shower, shave her legs and eat a quick snack before he arrived to pick her up.

She flew towards the boxes, upturned the one marked 'kitchen' and grabbed the first thing that fell out. It was an instant ramen noodle packet. She ripped it apart and poured it into a saucepan—Expensive restaurants, she knew from experience, never gave you enough to eat.

The apartment had a fancy kettle that changed colours as it boiled water. She wasted a few precious seconds watching it go from red to blue to green.

Next, she attacked the box labelled dresses. A giant pile fell out, but most of it was wrinkled. With a fork in her mouth, she grabbed a green dress in jersey material which was comfortable and yet fancy enough for a date. More importantly, it had the least wrinkles and was dry.

Swallowing the rest of the half raw, piping hot noodles, she hurtled over to the bathroom.

She had a cold shower, since she couldn't figure out how to turn the heat on, brushed her teeth and slipped into the dress. Makeup consisted of some concealer, mascara and a nude lip gloss. She had just run a brush through her long brown hair when the doorbell buzzed.

"You are not coming out with me looking like that," was the first thing out of Chris's mouth.

"I thought you would like the dress."

"It is the coat that I'm objecting to. You look like a bare-shanked screech owl."

Tabby stroked the brown feather coat in surprise. "Really?"

"And what you are wearing is clearly a winter coat."

"I was cold."

"You are always cold. Change the jacket, add a belt or something and tie your hair up. I don't like it hanging around your ears like a cocker spaniel."

She didn't want to argue so she did what he said.

He shot her a sepulchral look when she returned. "Is that your father's jacket?" he scowled.

"You didn't like the feather one, and this is the only other jacket that was dry—"

"We are getting late. You can leave the jacket in the car," he ordered. After a moment, he leaned over and kissed her cheek. "Sorry, I am grumpy today."

She stuck a tongue at his back as she traipsed after him.

16

"The ring?" he asked the moment she had buckled herself in.

"Safe in my handbag."

"Good," he replied, looking relieved.

They drove for a few moments in silence.

"I disinfected it," she suddenly announced.

"What?"

"The ring."

He eyed her from the corner of his eyes. "I am sure you did."

"Three times," she comforted him.

"I see."

"I also sprayed two different perfumes on it."

"You shouldn't spray perfumes on jewellery," he said. "Mother says so."

"Both were a complex floral with undertones of jasmine and ylang ylang."

"Huh." He revved his engine and quickly overtook two cars.

"I was talking about the scents," she clarified.

"Why don't you put the ring on?" he asked.

"Put the ring on?"

"Yes."

"What ring?"

"The ring I gave you. The ring we have been talking about all day. The very ring you had such pleasure describing to me how it passed through your intestines. We have an x-ray of the said ring lying in the back seat—"

"That ring," she giggled nervously.

He didn't laugh.

"Shouldn't put it on my finger?"

"I have to touch it?" he asked looking horrified.

"Oh yeah," she answered happily. "Or it won't feel like an engagement ring."

❖ ❖ ❖

"Here we are," he said, smoothly backing into a parking space.

"How do you always manage to park so perfectly?"

"Because I am perfect," he replied looking smug.

She rolled her eyes and got out of the car.

A thrill went through her as she walked into the beautiful oriental-themed restaurant with its gold and red décor. Her heels clicked on the black tiles flecked with gold.

This was it, she thought, as she sank into the dark velvet seat. The proper engagement.

She wondered if the ring would fit.

The moment Chris sat down opposite her, he started scanning the restaurant, his right leg bouncing up and down under the table.

"I think that is Mark," he said after a moment. "Don't turn your head. I don't want him to come over. Once he starts talking, there is no stopping him. He will insist on joining us for the entire evening."

Tabby tuned him out. She knew for the next ten minutes he would eye every person in the restaurant in an attempt to figure out how many of them he recognized, and he would recognize a whole lot of them. Chris was a friendly soul, the sort that dragged the painfully shy wallflowers out from the shadows and got them drunk and merry and singing patriotic songs by the end of the night. Whenever they went out, it was always with a group of laughing, glittering, confident people.

She eyed him fondly. He was so like an attention seeking foxhound puppy—a very well-groomed foxhound puppy in a designer suit. Sometimes she thought he would flip over on his back, yank off his shirt and present his belly for a scratch.

She, too, enjoyed it. Not the flipping over and scratching the belly bit, but the heady London nightlife. She loved hopping from nightclub to nightclub, rubbing shoulders with famous people, tasting the sort of upper-class lifestyle she had never imagined she would ever have been part of.

It fascinated her.

And yet, she wished she could spend some quality time with Chris over pizza or coffee, sharing hopes and dreams like an old-fashioned couple. Meeting for a few hours every week in a noisy, chaotic environment where you can barely speak to each other—forget exchanging confidences—was not a very good foundation for a marriage. She wanted to know him. To learn his likes and dislikes, his various moods, his faults, the location of all his moles and warts. . . .

Her stomach grumbled snapping her out of her gloomy mood. Her eyes glazed over as a plate of wings sailed by her hungry nose and landed at the table next to theirs. Soon bowls of salads, fried rice, steaming vegetables, meat swimming in gravy, and baked fish on a bed of pak choi followed. She watched enviously as a little girl was presented with a burger.

A burger in an Oriental restaurant.

Tabby sighed. She would have liked to sink her teeth into a juicy burger. But she knew that was unlikely. She couldn't possibly order from the children's menu, besides Chris would never let her choose a main dish. In fact, he never ordered mains. It was always one portion of every starter on the menu, even if it meant that their table was littered with fifteen different dishes.

In the beginning, she had enjoyed the experience. He had excellent taste and the places they visited were fancy, often having exotic dishes whose names she couldn't pronounce. But sometimes when she was feeling a little apprehensive like today, she would have liked to eat something comforting.

She turned her head away from the sight of an old woman putting in her dentures and focused on Chris.

"I am sure the bartender would know," he was telling a waitress with a charming smile.

The waitress wearing a black silk kimono with a tiny gold dragon woven into the front pocket almost toppled into his lap. "Yes sir," she blushed and sashayed away.

Tabby turned to Chris. "Love Muffin, what did you order?"

"Don't," he frowned, tossing aside the menu. "I have told you before not to call me mushy names in public."

"You called me chicken liver in the supermarket last week," she reminded him.

"That was a slip of the tongue."

She changed the topic. "What did you do after you dropped me off?"

"Went to the club, swam, worked out, the usual—Where is the ring?"

"Here," she said, patting her beige purse.

"Show me."

She pulled it out, blew off the grey fluff that was stuck to it and held it towards him.

After a brief hesitation, he took the ring.

"Miss Tabitha Lee Timmons, let us try this again," he said, his eyes glittering in the candlelight like dark jewels. "Will you marry me?"

"Can I ask you a question first?

A flash of emotion crossed his face. He carefully smoothed it out before she could interpret it and said, "Go ahead."

"Do you love me?"

He stared at her as if she had sprouted horns on her head.

She leaned forward and held his large hand. She noticed he had long, dark curly hairs on his fingers. "I want to marry someone who loves me," she said in what she hoped was a low, throaty, meaningful tone.

"You are coming down with a cold," he told her. "You sound snotty."

She dropped his hand. "You don't love me."

"I never said that," he protested.

"So you do love me?"

"I guess," he responded.

Somebody growled above their heads. The waitress was back. She slammed the dishes on the table and flounced off.

I guess, he had said. Tabby wondered what that meant.

He reached over and caught her hand. He slipped the ring into place before she could come up with any other objections.

The poo ring was slightly loose but wearable.

He gazed deep into her eyes and smiled roguishly. "Soon you are going to be Mrs Chandramohan Mansukhani. It is a new beginning for us."

"Who is Chandramohan?" she asked, gazing back lovingly.

"Very funny," he said with a soft smile.

"No truly, who is Chandra-whatever you said?" she asked.

"I am Chandramohan, sweetheart." He ran a finger over her knuckle. "Chintu for family, Chris for my friends. Love muffin," he murmured, "for you."

She paled, "Your name is Chandramohan."

He dropped her hand. "You didn't know?"

She grabbed the glass of wine lying next to her and downed it. Inside she was screeching in shock.

Chandramohan?

She was now engaged to a man whose first name she had not known. This did not sound like a very good beginning. She felt that familiar urge rising in her, that intense urge to bolt or do something so horrendous that he would be the one hurtling out the door.

She forcefully buried that part of her. However tempting moving to Surrey and owning a dozen cats suddenly seemed, she would stick by her decision and marry the man.

"You didn't know," he spluttered. "Do you know anything about me? About my family?"

"Yes," she hastily soothed him. "You have a mom, a dad—"

"Everyone has that," he cut in.

"You live with your parents, and you have a sister," she went on. "You are Indian."

"You should know something more about my family, the way we live, our culture. Now that you are my fiancée, we have hardly any time and so much to do. . . ."

"Huh?"

He clicked his tongue impatiently. "We are engaged, but that is only a very small step. Now you have to impress my parents and my aunts in England as well as my grandfather, and the moment that is done, we can start planning the wedding."

"What?" she squeaked.

"Don't worry, you will do fine. It is only a matter of learning a few Indian rituals, amongst other things. Maya will teach you everything. She is whizz at stuff like that."

"Maya, your sister?"

"That's me," a tall lithesome creature said floating towards the table.

Tabby eyed the skin tight electric blue dress, designer bag and manicured nails and gulped. It seemed that deciding on the wedding dress and cake was the least of her hurdles.

"Hello," Maya purred and kissed the air above Tabby's head. "Aren't you a sweet little thing, but the clothes—"

"I know," Chris nodded. "She needs a complete makeover."

"Ask me whatever you want to know," Maya said in a voice that sounded like she had just consumed a pack of cigarettes.

"I have watched a few documentaries on India," Tabby began confidently. "You have elephants, tigers and snake charmers. Right?"

"Yes, in fact, I used to go to school perched upon a tiger. They are just like cats," Maya replied, rotating the straw in her drink. "If you see one strolling by, you must pet it."

Chris made a warning noise in his throat.

Tabby hurried on, "Your country is exquisite, imbibed in culture with a rich history—"

"I am yet to find a country without any history or culture," Maya snorted.

"You wear saris," Tabby went on, "and pray in temples and speak Hindi—"

"Indians also wear jeans, skirts, dresses, pray in mosques, gurdwaras and churches and speak hundreds of languages—" Maya snapped.

"I get your point," Tabby snapped back. "India is multi-faceted and you have a tough time ahead of you if you have to teach an ignoramus like me anything in such a short period."

Maya leaned back on the chair, her dark, red lips pursed thoughtfully. "This one," she said to her brother, "is smart. Uses big words, unlike your other exes who couldn't think beyond awesome, like and amazeballs."

Chris grinned. "I know. A keeper, eh?"

"What have you taught her?" Maya asked, poking a finger into her brother's arm. "You must have told her something about us considering you guys have been dating for a year."

"How to keep me happy," Chris replied promptly.

"Chauvinist pig," Maya purred. "By the way, Bro, your ears are looking bigger than usual. You shouldn't gel your hair back like that. Also, I suspect mother picked you up from a dustbin. "

"I do not have big ears," he drawled.

"Try and wriggle your ears really fast. I am sure you would shoot off your seat and fly up into the air. Try it," Maya dared him.

Chris turned his back on his sister. He asked Tabby, "How do I like my coffee?"

"A shot of espresso, a shot of hazelnut liquor, a little bit of almond milk, lots of froth with a fine dusting of cinnamon on top," Tabby replied, feeling her cheeks burn.

"See what I mean," Chris said, waggling his eyebrows at his sister. "I taught her all the important stuff."

Maya turned towards Tabby, "Honestly, what in the world do you see in my brother?"

"Stop bullying her and get on with the teaching," Chris ordered.

"Chris used to sit in the fridge with his pants down in summer," Maya announced.

"What the hell!" Chris yelped.

"And poof," Maya grinned, "smug look on a man's face gone."

"I do have a lot to learn from you," Tabby grinned back.

Maya handed her a beautifully beaded green diary and a silver pen. "Make notes."

Chapter Four

Tabby sat crossed-legged in the middle of the four-poster bed. The poo ring on her finger glittered in the light cascading down from the chandelier above. She held her hand up and inspected her fingers. The large diamond sat awkwardly, tilting to one side like a drunken man. The chipped nail didn't help.

Maya's hands had looked beautiful adorned with plenty of rings and jingling bracelets. Her nails hadn't been chipped but buffed, filed and painted in a lovely shade of coral.

Tabby wondered if after marrying Chris she would also look just as graceful, wealthy and stylish.

The thought was a pleasant one.

She tilted backwards until her head landed on the soft pillow. A life of luxury, travel, shopping and no stress. She would never have to worry about rent or bills.

And if she broke off the engagement? The peeling purple couch on a busy London street loomed large in her mind.

She turned over on her side and crossed her arms.

She had been lonely when she had first moved to London. Frightened, naive, and friendless. Chris had walked into her life and brought friends, comfort and security. He had been her world since then, his friends were her friends and his interests had become her interests . . . but, she wondered, was she in love with him or dependent on him?

She clicked the light off, plunging the room into darkness. It was natural to feel anxious, confused and a tiny bit scared. After all, marriage was a big decision. Tomorrow, she was certain, the whole thing would sink in and she would consider herself the happiest girl in the world.

She didn't sleep a wink the whole night. She tried counting sheep, but the woolly creatures kept running down the hill instead of leaping over the fence, and then she would feel sorry and chase after them to make sure they were all right. The mental acrobatics that followed left her more invigorated than tired.

Predictably, the minute the warm, bright sun popped up, she fell asleep. An hour later, Maya and Chris burst into the apartment ready to drag her out to the shops.

Tabby eyed them morosely. She was exhausted, irritable, and in no mood to leave her deliciously cosy bed.

Brother and sister peered down at her with identical expressions of horror. Clearly they couldn't believe someone could look so gruesome upon waking up.

Tabby glanced at the mirror hanging on the opposite wall and winced. She looked like a hungry vampire with dark circles whose hair had been electrocuted sometime during the night. Reluctantly, she rolled out of bed, fell into a pair of jeans and a t-shirt, crawled into the car and then crawled back out when they reached a street riddled with colourful shops and cafés.

"We have booked an appointment for you at the White Spring Spa," Maya informed her. "Chris and I are going to go shop for your clothes while you go get a haircut, facial, waxing, threading, manicure and pedicure to begin with. We will look into bridal beauty packages some other time."

"Tea," Tabby begged in response.

"They will give you a cup of tasty detox tea," Maya said, pointing at something behind Tabby's head.

Tabby turned to find herself facing a gleaming black glass door. It had a large silver plaque hanging on the door knob with 'White Spring' written in pointy handwriting. By the time she turned back around, Maya and Chris were already racing away towards a shop that looked more like a nightclub than a clothing store.

Tabby had been to salons, but nothing like the one she entered. It was decorated like the inside of a rocket ship. The walls seemed to be made of some sort of hammered metal. In fact, everything was silver including the swivel chairs, curling tongs and blow dryers.

The reflective surfaces, the mirrors and the bright white lights made her tired eyes water. She squinted and lurched towards what looked like a reception area.

The receptionist was an orange-hued, blonde young woman wearing an unfortunate salmon-pink chiffon blouse with a large bow in the same material knotted under her pointy chin.

Tabby bared her teeth in what she hoped was a pleasant smile.

"Yes?" Blondey asked, eyeing Tabby's scuffed runners and wrinkled t-shirt doubtfully.

"My name is Tabitha—" Tabby began.

"—Lee Timmons?" the girl cut in.

"Err, yes," Tabby said and reeled back at the blinding smile that was suddenly directed her way. She moaned inwardly. It was too early in the morning for such blatant chirpiness.

"We were expecting you," the receptionist smiled even more broadly, showing a row of startlingly white teeth and a bit of healthy pink gums. "Maya told me you wanted the best, and that means Lily."

Lily turned out to be a large, muscular man with half his head shaved off. The rest of it was pink and spiked.

She followed him nervously to one of the swivel chairs and sat down. She could smell nail paint, bleach and burning hair.

Lily picked up a strand of her brown hair and scowled. He didn't ask what she wanted and reached for the scissors.

Maya must have told him what to do, Tabby thought nervously as the scissors inched closer to her head.

He chopped off eight inches without ceremony. Her hair that had been long enough to hit the top of her hips a second ago was now tragically a little longer than shoulder length.

He went on to give her a fringe, a thing she had never had before, then added layers and blow dried it until she resembled a poorly groomed Lhasa Apso. The fringe, she realised after a moment, was so thick and so long that it completely covered her eyes rendering her blind. How in the world was she supposed to see anything?

Lily used a giant brush with soft, dense bristles to whack all the bits of hair off her back and neck. A man arrived with a broom and swept away the swirls of brown hair that had once been part of her head.

Tabby closed her eyes and promised herself a good cry later.

Sometime during the morning, she was offered the detox tea. It was just as she had expected. Caffeine free and god-awful. She swallowed it. After that, she was taken into a little cubicle where every bit of hair was ripped off her body with itty bitty waxing strips. That woke her right up.

"You look cute," the pedicurist comforted her.

"Adorable," the manicurist agreed, poking at the dirt under her nails.

Sexy, was the transformation Tabby had been hoping for, but adorable as a compliment was not too bad.

"You will be spotty after the facial," the receptionist warned as Tabby paid the astronomical fee. "So don't plan anything important for at least a week."

Once outside, Tabby stretched luxuriously. She was almost broke after the extravagant makeover, and yet she felt light as a feather. She floated down the sunny street, enjoying the freedom after being cooped up for so long in the spa. She felt like a Labradoodle who had just been given a bath, blow-dried, fluffed up and then set free.

She skipped up to Chris when she saw him, her eyes shining.

"You look cute," he said giving her a brief kiss and handing her a dozen plastic bags. "Here are your clothes. We will go back to your apartment and you can try them on for us."

"I think the blue," Maya told Chris as they walked back to the car.

"I prefer the *salwar kameez*—" Chris objected.

"She may come across as trying too hard," Maya replied stubbornly.

"Whatever looks best," Chris conceded.

"Who are you talking about?" Tabby asked.

"You," Maya responded. "Hurry now, we have only a few days to go, and you have a lot to learn."

"Few days for what?" Tabby pulled open the car door and slipped into the back seat.

"For the meeting with the family. You are invited to dinner this Friday," Maya said, dumping the bags in after her.

The first dress that Maya handed over to Tabby to try on was carefully wrapped in a thick white glossy paper embossed with silver swirls and tied with a big, fat grey bow.

With great care, Tabby untied the bow and parted the paper.

Her breath caught in her throat.

The dress was made up of masses of mint green chiffon, lace and silk. Maya had given her a soft black leather jacket and gold hoop earrings to pair with it.

Tabby spied a dark green satin slip nestled at the bottom of the box. She pulled that on first, and the dress followed.

She stared at herself in the full-length mirror that was glued to the back of the bathroom door. A hint of lace peeked out over the sweetheart neckline, and the hem fell just shy of her knees.

"Does it fit?" Maya called.

"Yes," Tabby breathed out in delight. She had never worn anything so beautiful in her life. This, she thought, was a transformation. She turned to see the back and found she wasn't fully zipped up fully.

"Come out, we want to see," Maya said from the bedroom.

"A moment," Tabby responded trying to pull the zip up. She was scared of using too much force in case she ripped the dress. "How long can I keep it for?" Tabby asked.

"It's yours," Maya replied.

"The dress is mine to keep?" Tabby's fingers froze on the zip.

"Yes."

"Truly?" Tabby asked.

"Tabby, you sound as if Chris has never given you a gift," Maya said waltzing into the bathroom. "Oh, stop being so shy and turn around and let me do you up. It's not like your bits are any different from mine."

Once she was dressed, they walked out into the bedroom to show Chris the whole effect.

Chris jerked to sitting position the moment he saw her. "Perfect for a night out with my friends," he said, his eyes wide and appreciative.

Tabby grinned and twirled on the spot.

Maya thrust a pair of pinstripe cigarette pants, white shirt and a beautifully-cut black blazer at Tabby and made shooing motions.

Tabby disappeared into the bathroom once again.

"The most important person in our family," Maya spoke, through the slightly ajar bathroom door, "is our grandfather. We call him Daaji."

"He owns Pick and Flick, the largest toothpick factory in India," Chris said, handing Tabby a pair of fuchsia high-heeled pumps through the door. "And everything in our family happens according to his wishes. Think of him as an old-fashioned, smug little landlord and we are his oppressed tenants."

Tabby came out of the bathroom and teetered up to the full-length mirror. She wondered if Chris and Maya were aware of how their voice had dropped to hushed tones when they mentioned their grandfather. "Why do you have to listen to him?" she asked turning to inspect her profile.

Chris answered Tabby's question, "Daaji has three sons, the middle one being my father. The sons run the company and get paid directly by him."

"The eldest son doesn't," Maya corrected him. "He walked out, remember? Wanted to work in the theatre as an actor. Daaji cut him off clean. Taught us all a lesson."

"And now dad will do nothing to displease him," Chris agreed. "Otherwise we lose not only our source of income but a large inheritance as well. Come here," he patted the empty space next to him on the bed. "I want to show you the family picture."

Tabby wobbled up to him. The shoes pinched, and the heels were higher than she was used to. She sat down on the bed and peered at the picture on the phone.

It was an old, sepia-coloured photo that had been crookedly scanned in. It showed a middle-aged Indian man wearing long flowing pyjamas and a Nehru-style shirt. He was sitting right in the centre, his spine straight, and a cold, arrogant look on his angular face, with his arm, stuck straight out in front of him holding what looked like a walking stick.

Behind him stood three young men, all in their twenties, wearing clothes similar to those of their father.

"This one," Chris pointed, "is my father."

The man he had indicated was the first one on the left. He looked remarkably like Daaji. He, too, sported the same superior expression, as if someone had stuck a smelly sock under his nose.

"This is Tayaji, my father's elder brother. The one who has been cut off," Maya said, her voice warming. "He is nice. We don't meet him often, though. He never comes to any family gathering if Daaji is present."

Tayaji, as Maya called him, stood right in the middle. He was clearly the best looking. His face was softer, his physique broader, and his dark eyes sparkled with mischief. He stood with a certain confident, relaxed stance that gave him a star-like quality. Tabby could easily imagine him romancing on the silver screen.

"This one is the youngest son," Maya continued. "We call him Chachoo."

Maya didn't say anything more, and Tabby could guess why. He seemed insignificant next to Daaji and Tayaji. He was the shortest, and with his shoulders hunched and his expression vaguely panicked, he looked out of place, as if someone had decided to Photoshop him into the picture at the last minute.

Tabby didn't recall her own grandfather, and as for the rest of her extended family, she had barely met them. She wondered why she had never made more of an effort to stay in touch with them all.

She plucked the next set of clothes from Maya's hand and once again retreated to the bathroom. "Your factory is in India, isn't it?" she called out, slipping into a copper paisley print skirt. "Then how come your family lives in London?"

"Father's job is to expand the toothpick factory business. He runs the global office from London," Chris replied. "And I help him."

"So, all of you depend on him financially?" Tabby asked, shuffling back into the room.

Maya shook her head at the long trailing skirt, shoved a flowery gypsy dress at her, and sent her right back into the bathroom.

"We depend on him completely," Chris concurred. "Tabby, if we are to marry, you have to impress him."

Tabby paused in the middle of trying to stick her head into the armhole of the dress. "And if I can't?" she asked, her voice muffled by the soft cotton.

"Then the wedding is off," Maya's voice floated into the bathroom and bounced off the cold, tiled walls.

Chapter Five

Tabby woke up starving at five in the morning. She turned onto her side and adjusted her pillow and tried to fall back to sleep, but her dreams of pancakes, bacon and many-layered cakes continued to linger. And no wonder. After Maya and Chris had departed last evening, she had fallen asleep without eating her dinner.

She sighed, got out of bed and padded towards the kitchen. She popped in some bread to toast and started pulling out ingredients for a Victoria sponge cake. She had learned a few tricks on the job she had had with the bakery to make the sponge light as air, and she wanted to try the recipe in a home environment. If it turned out all right, she could make it again on Friday for Chris's family get-together.

She hummed to herself as she set about buttering the tins and turning on the oven to pre-heat. She spent the next few hours sifting, flouring, mixing, and icing.

"Good morning," Maya strode into the kitchen.

"Crap," Tabby exclaimed as a blob of white paste spurted out of the icing bag and onto the centre of the cake.

"You can bake?" Maya asked, sniffing appreciatively.

"I didn't hear the bell ring. How did you enter?" Tabby asked, carefully lifting off the icing with a butter knife.

"Chris gave me the other set of keys. He said you wouldn't mind."

"I don't." Tabby wiped off the tip of the icing bag and stood back to admire her handiwork. The cake had four layers slathered with black cherry jam and cream. She had smoothed the top with vanilla frosting. "Would you like a slice?" she asked feeling mighty pleased with her morning's hard work.

Maya admired the large white rose Tabby had added to the centre of the cake, "Sure. Looks good. I brought coffee."

"I don't drink coffee," Tabby replied. "Only tea when I'm at home or chai latte if I'm in a cafe."

"But Chris told me you adored coffee. Milky with lots of sugar."

"He is mistaken," she said shortly.

"I see."

Tabby smiled a little too brightly and pushed a generous slice of cake and a bit of banana bread towards Maya.

"We have to return the clothes to the shops today and look around some more." Maya took a bite of the cake. A shadow crossed her face, and her shoulders dropped.

"Something wrong?" Tabby asked. "Did you bite into an eggshell?"

"No. It's not that. The cake is delicious . . . It's him."

"Him?"

"He is going to be there," Maya muttered.

"Who is going to be where?"

"Cuckoo is going to be there on Friday at our place. That hideous creature crawled all the way to London from Ludhiana to shop for the wedding."

"What wedding? Who is Cuckoo?"

"I will be Cuckoo soon enough," Maya responded irritably. "Rather, Mrs Cuckoo Singh."

"You are getting married?" Tabby squealed.

"I am going to be Mrs Cuckoo Singh in two months. Is that something to be excited about? Would you like to be called Mrs Cuckoo all your life? His mother has started calling me Cookie already. Cookie Singh." She shuddered.

"How come Chris didn't tell me about it?" Tabby asked, feeling a tad hurt.

"We try and pretend it isn't happening. It was another of Daaji's whims. He met Cuckoo on a flight, found out he owned a toothpaste factory. And bam! Daaji took it as a sign and decided to get him married to me."

"A sign?"

"He owns a toothpaste factory, we own a toothpick factory, which automatically equals a match made in heaven."

Tabby pressed her lips together to keep from giggling.

"You will see what a slimy blob he is on Friday," Maya continued gloomily.

"Why don't you tell Daaji you don't want to marry him?" Tabby asked.

"Because Daaji has promised to present me with a quarter of a million pounds on my wedding day if I marry him before December. I thought you knew all about that."

Tabby let out a slow whistle. "Daaji is that rich?"

"Lots of Indians use toothpicks," Maya replied with a slight frown.

They fell silent pondering on the benefits of flossing versus toothpicks and what one would do with a quarter of a million pounds in the bank.

Maya finally stood up. "Also this Friday is grandfather's birthday. We will be celebrating that as well."

"But Chris told me that your grandfather lives in India," Tabby said.

"Yes, but we video chat with him on that day. He likes seeing us celebrate his birthday even in London." Maya paused near the door. "Where are the bags with the clothes that needed to be returned?"

"I'll get them," Tabby said. Once in the master bedroom, she dusted off the flour from her face and hair, applied a lip-plumping clear gloss, grabbed the bags lying on an antique chair and rushed back out.

She found Maya punching the security code for the house alarm.

Worried the house alarm would go off if she lingered any longer, Tabby snatched a pair of shoes lying near the entrance and raced out after Maya. She hopped over hot cobblestones, her toes shrieking in protest. She dived into the passenger seat, grabbed her poor smoking toes and blew on them.

Maya sent her a cold look and started the car.

"What does Cuckoo Singh look like?" Tabby asked, hurriedly slipping on the orange and green canvas shoes over her burning toes.

"Like a hairy walrus with a sleazy, oily moustache."

Tabby changed the topic. "Thank you for doing this. Helping me, I mean, with the clothes and things."

"I am not doing you guys a favour. Chris is paying me, it helps distract me from my own impending wedding, and I want to be a fashion designer and currently I am using you as a lab rat to try out my styling ideas. When I get the money from Daaji, I am planning to open a store."

"I see."

"Before I forget," Maya said. "The cloth bag lying near your feet is for you."

Tabby peeked into the bag, "What's this?"

"Bollywood movies and copies of Indian soaps with English translations. You will learn everything you need to know about India from this."

"This is amazing—"

"Not really. They are full of stereotypes, but they will give you a fairly good understanding of how things work."

Tabby couldn't help herself. She leaned over and gave Maya a quick warm hug.

"Yeah, well, you are welcome." Maya changed gear and skidded out of the parking space, sending Tabby flying back into her seat. She turned right and headed towards Selfridges.

"The woman at the parlour said I shouldn't plan anything important this week. My skin will be purging itself," Tabby said. "What if I have a zit or many zits on Friday?"

"You won't have a zit," Maya responded. "I never do after visiting that spa."

"But what if I do?"

"You won't."

"But if I do?"

"I am telling you, you won't."

"I can feel it under my skin waiting to erupt," Tabby said touching her chin in concern.

Maya turned up the volume on the radio.

The next morning Tabby rolled out of bed, put on a pair of old jeans and a t-shirt and headed to the kitchen.

She switched on the radio and pulled everything out of the cupboards. Singing at the top of her voice, she cleaned and mopped and scrubbed and wiped every inch of the kitchen.

With a few badly executed dance steps, she twirled her way into the dining area.

She didn't like the fact that Chris's cousin had refused to take rent. The only way she could think of repaying him in some small way was to leave the place sparkling.

In the afternoon, she turned on her laptop and searched for

apartments and applied for jobs. In the evening, she took the tube and went to see the three places she had found available for rent that fit her budget and were not too far off.

The places were tiny, dark and depressing. Still, she didn't have much choice. She gave them her number, indicated an interest and returned home.

The next day was almost a repeat. She finished cleaning up the apartment, applied for still more jobs and went and looked at a few more apartments.

She had been so busy in the last two days that, along with the fact that she no longer had a job, she lost track of what day it was.

Which was why when Friday morning came around and Maya called to say she would pick her up at five in the evening for dinner, Tabby was horrified.

She was far from ready. She had not watched any of the Bollywood movies, read up anything about Indian culture, or painted her nails. She didn't even have the time to bake a cake.

She pushed aside her toast and raced to the mirror in the bathroom.

Her nose was red, eyes hot and puffy, and she was wearing her favourite, though unflattering, long white t-shirt that said 'Love Muffin and Chai Latte'. Also, she had four giant zits on her face.

One pimple was the size of a planet, bright red and sore and perched on her upper lip. It looked demonic, filled with puss, and she had this strange feeling that if she asked it a question, it would respond.

She blinked, turned on the tap and splashed her face with cold water.

That helped somewhat.

She wiped away the droplets with a fancy white face cloth that lay by the sink in a wicker basket and inspected the other three zits. They were all on her forehead and if she styled her hair right, she could conceal it behind her fringe.

She applied a mud mask to her face hoping it would dry out the spots, slathered her hair with olive oil, and went back to the kitchen to make herself another cup of tea. She had discovered the switch that turned on the heat in the bathroom when she had been cleaning. She switched it on now since it would take at least fifteen minutes for the water to be hot enough for a shower.

She was half way through her cup of tea when her phone rang. It was Chris.

"Hey," he said. "You are on speaker. Maya is with me."

"Hey, Love muffin," Tabby responded. Her face mask had dried, and she could barely move her lips. Her voice came out all funny.

Maya laughed.

"I told you that you were on speaker phone and that Maya was with me for a reason," Chris said in exasperation.

"I'm sorry," Tabby said. "I didn't think."

"Do you ever think?" he asked.

"Squabble later," Maya interrupted. "Now, Tabby, did you watch the movies that I gave you?"

"Hmm," Tabby replied.

"Is that a yes?" Chris asked.

"Hmm," Tabby said again.

"I am taking that as a yes," Chris threatened.

Tabby chose to stay silent.

"Now, since you have watched them," Maya waited for Tabby to refute her assumption, and when she didn't, she continued, "we don't have much to say. You must know everything by now."

"What did you learn?" Chris asked.

"Spirituality is big in India, isn't it? Lots of spiritual people meditating and doing yoga—" Tabby began.

Maya chuckled. "That's right, Tabby. All Indians party with levitating gurus in the Himalayas."

"You didn't watch the movies," Chris said, through clenched teeth.

Tabby closed her eyes, crossed her fingers and lied, "I did."

"Do you have any questions?" Maya asked.

"What do I wear?"

"The lilac and pink floral print tunic in crepe, along with the tapered cream pants, nude pumps and a pink scarf. Don't carry a handbag since the one you have looks like a dead woolly mammoth," Maya replied.

"The nude pumps are too high—" Tabby began.

"You won't be standing for long," Maya responded.

"And jewellery?" Tabby asked.

"Your engagement ring should be fine," Maya said.

Chris cleared his throat. "If the two of you have finished, can I say something?"

"Yes," Tabby responded.

"Stick to one-word answers until you get used to us all," he suggested.

"Everyone in the family loves talking, and no one enjoys listening," Maya agreed. "The less you speak, the more they will like you."

"And one more thing . . ." Chris paused briefly. "Don't mention that you used to work in a shoe shop . . . or at the bakers or that shady beauty parlour. In fact, don't mention any of your workplaces."

Tabby felt her face burn. "I don't mind—"

"Nor do we," Maya hurriedly put in. "But Daaji, Dad, and the aunties are old fashioned and don't understand that work is work."

"And you won't be lying," Chris said soothingly. "After all, you are not working anymore."

"What am I supposed to say I did then?" Tabby asked.

"How about saying you do what one of your friends does," Chris said, "your best friend, what's her name?"

"Becky . . . Rebecca Penrose. She is a psychiatrist, and that is a very hard thing to lie about," Tabby said curtly.

"Say you are a writer," Maya mused. "Carry a book around and scribble in it now and then. In a year or two no one will remember or care what you said you did. You would be part of the family by then."

"But I can't write. And I'm not sure about lying—"

"It is such a small thing, Tabby. We have to make certain compromises," Chris admonished.

Tabby frowned. "This is all sounding so wrong. I don't understand the need for lies and pretence."

"When you meet Daaji and the family, you will know what we mean," Maya said. "I will stay with you the whole time." A hint of concern laced her voice. "You will be fine, Tabby."

I'm not a very brave person," Tabby said honestly. "Leaving my hometown in America and coming to England was the bravest thing I have ever done. And even after two years, my legs still turn to jelly when I think of the moment I got onto the flight—"

"You will be going across town, not flying across oceans," Maya cut in.

"You will be fine," Chris repeated, "and don't forget that I will be around to help you."

Chapter Six

Tabby agonized over her fringe. She had swept it to one side and pinned it up. She wondered if the style left her looking too young, or silly, or—

The doorbell pinged.

Tabby took a deep breath, smoothed the front of her silk tunic and opened the door.

"You look nice," Maya said, surprised, "apart from the leprechaun hat."

"And you look beautiful," Tabby responded sincerely. "I'm wearing the hat for luck."

"Hey," Chris said, giving Tabby a light peck on the cheek.

Tabby smiled weakly and clutched the doorknob in a deathly grip.

"Let's go," Maya said. "Dad will be pissed off if we are late."

Tabby forcefully detached herself from the doorknob. She paused to put the house alarm on and lock the door behind herself. She noticed Chris lingering next to her.

She raised an eyebrow enquiringly. In reply, he pulled her into his arms and hugged her.

"What's this for?" she asked, her face squished to his shirt front. A button was trying to lodge itself up her left nostril. She didn't dare adjust her position in case it ruined the moment.

He cuddled her closer. "I have been testy, nervous and grumpy. I haven't behaved fiancé-like since the day I proposed. Thank you for understanding, for doing this for me . . . meeting my family, trying to please them . . . Thank you for being you."

"You are welcome," Tabby said, feeling touched. The warmth in his voice strengthened her belief that she was doing the right thing by agreeing to marry him.

They stood together for another few moments, and finally he gave her a big squeeze almost lifting her off her feet. She squealed in delight.

"Aww," Maya said coldly. "Are we being mushy and disgusting in public? How cute. Now come on before I stab myself to end this vision from hell."

Tabby reluctantly let Chris go and began walking towards the car. She wobbled on her high heels.

Maya threw her a wary look. "You are not going to throw up are you?"

"I hope not," Tabby said, turning green at the thought.

"Have gum," Maya said, offering her a stick.

Tabby popped it into her mouth and chewed. It helped ease the sick feeling in her stomach.

Maya hopped into the front seat of the car while Tabby slid into the back.

"Relax," Chris said looking at her through the rear-view mirror.

"How was work?" Tabby asked, thinking now that she was his fiancée she should start behaving in wifely manner.

"I wasn't in the mood to go in today," Chris responded.

Maya chuckled, "If Chris ever ends up in the office two days in a row, then mum will pack her bags and set off on a pilgrimage to thank the gods for the miracle."

"Shut up, Maya," Chris muttered.

"Shut up, Chris," Maya mimicked and blew a raspberry at him.

The rest of the drive was spent in silence until they drove into the heart of London and turned onto a broad street lined with majestic trees.

"Almost home," Chris warned. "Take the hat off now just in case you forget to later."

Tabby obliged him and eagerly scanned her surroundings. The winding road they were now on was eerily quiet after the congested traffic they had left behind. She felt as if someone had turned down the volume of a noisy television set.

Her nose twitched, and she could almost smell the stacks of money and musty antiques stuffed inside the tall, old-fashioned houses looming on either side of the street. She wondered if the houses had safes or one of those steel vaults complete with a dial and a complicated numerical password. The sort she had seen people rob in movies.

The car slowed down and paused outside large electronic gates. Chris called someone from his mobile and asked them to let him in. Like magic, the gates swung open and they drove in.

The meandering driveway was wide and long with a border of fragrant lavender flowers that ran all the way from the entrance to the front door of the house. On either side of the driveway were sprawling emerald-green lawns bursting with white and pink peonies, Canterbury bells, Freesia, dark red hydrangeas and masses of Queen Anne's lace.

They turned a corner and a handsome Victorian-style house came into view. It was painted dark grey and had a number of white trimmed balconies along with large French windows that glittered invitingly in the sunlight. A pebbled pathway led up to wide, marble steps, and Tabby was certain that somewhere behind the building lay another garden complete with cupid statues and tinkling fountains.

Some cars were already parked outside, and the old-fashioned green door with a dull gold lion-head knocker was closed. She glanced upwards and found five medium sized gargoyles peering down at her from the rooftop. They looked disapproving and more than a little menacing.

Tabby drank in the sight. This could be her new home in a couple of months.

"The family is here," Chris remarked.

Tabby felt a lump in her throat. Family. It had been a while since she had felt part of any family, and now that she was engaged . . . She swallowed hard.

"Good luck," Maya said to Tabby and squeezed her hand.

They exited together and went up to the door.

Tabby recalled the gum in her mouth. She hurriedly spat it out into her left hand.

"Mum's sweet," Maya comforted Tabby. "Just don't say anything. Do everything I do. And don't forget to touch everyone's feet—"

"Wait, what?"

Maya's hand paused on the doorbell. "I thought you watched the Bollywood films . . ." At Tabby's confused look, she continued, "Every time you are introduced to someone, dive towards their feet and touch them. If the feet look terribly unpleasant, then you can cheat the act by waggling your fingers close enough to it or touch the ground instead of the toes."

"Huh?"

"Just watch me," Maya ordered, and her French tipped nail dug into the doorbell.

A sad tune began playing.

"The bell, it is an old Bollywood song. Ma's favourite. Dad put it in as a romantic gesture," Maya said, noting Tabby's expression.

Tabby was too nervous to smile. Someone was opening the door.

"Hello," said a plump woman in, what Tabby guessed to be, her late fifties. She wore a striking gold and cream *salwar kameez* and lots of pearl and gold jewellery, including a dozen or so gold bangles that jingled on her wrists. Her warm brown eyes were lined with kohl while a red dot gleamed on her high forehead.

"Ma," Maya said. "Has everyone arrived? Sorry, I am late. Oh, and this is Tabby."

Tabby pasted a polite smile on her face and stepped forward. The heel of her brand new pumps firmly settled into the coir mat. They settled in so well that they refused to detach.

Tabby panicked. She needed to take the next crucial step forward to be close enough to shake hands with Mrs Mansukhani.

Mrs Mansukhani smiled and nodded encouragingly, her hand stretched out in welcome.

Tabby gritted her teeth and yanked her foot.

Nothing happened. Tabby's shoe remained stuck, and Mrs Mansukhani's bright smile began to dim.

Tabby pulled again, this time using all her strength. It worked. Sort of. The shoe remained stuck, but her foot was free and she lurched one-legged into the air.

Time seemed to stand still as Tabby oscillated in mid-air for a moment like a moody pendulum.

And then slowly she began tilting forward.

Mrs Mansukhani's paled, and she raised her arms to protect herself.

Tabby fell into those very arms knocking the small, round and not very strong woman off her feet.

Mrs Mansukhani landed on her back with a shriek, and Tabby collapsed right on top of her. Mrs Mansukhani jerked her neck to one side in an attempt to get up and banged her forehead against a giant potted plant lying near the entrance.

Someone began shouting. Tabby looked up to find what appeared to be Chris's entire family peering down at her.

When she looked back down, it was to find that Mrs Mansukhani's eyes were closed, and a trickle of blood was leaking from the spot on her head where she had banged it.

Tabby stared down at the pale face in horror. Good lord, she had just killed her future mother-in-law.

Chapter Seven

"She killed my sister, waaah!" howled a voice somewhere above Tabby's head.

Tabby didn't get a chance to panic for right then Chris wrapped his hands around her waist and hauled her off his mother.

"Get a glass of water." Mr Mansukhani arrived to take control of the situation. He was reed-thin all over except for his beautifully rounded pot belly. His designer blue suit strained against his stomach ready to pop its buttons at any moment. A red silk scarf threateningly peeped out of his breast pocket while a gold watch gleamed condescendingly on his wrist. And if you stood at a little distance and eyed his entire form, you would be forgiven for thinking that he looked remarkably like an Anaconda who had just swallowed a small animal and was in the process of digesting it.

"Dad, we need to take mom to the hospital," Maya shrieked.

"Get the car," Mr Mansukhani roared.

Chris raced to do his bidding.

The water arrived and Mr Mansukhani sprinkled a few drops on his wife's face.

"Please be alive, please, please, please," Tabby prayed.

With a low moan, Mrs Mansukhani came to.

Mr Mansukhani spoke to Mrs Mansukhani in what Tabby presumed was Hindi. Mrs Mansukhani was shaking her head adamantly, but Mr Mansukhani snapped out another order.

Eight pairs of hands arrived to lift Mrs Mansukhani up and began carrying her towards the car that Chris had brought around and parked right outside the door.

They were taking her to the hospital Tabby realised. She followed close behind and slipped into the car boot which had two foldable rear seats. Mrs Mansukhani was laid into the back seat with her head resting on Mr Mansukhani's lap while Maya sat in the front.

In the confusion, no one noticed or objected to Tabby's presence.

"She is dead," howled someone as the car started up again and moved down the driveway.

"She was speaking when they lifted her," someone else soothed.

"My sister is dead," insisted the first voice, shrieking tragically as the car accelerated.

Chris drove like the devil, breaking at least two traffic signals. They reached the hospital in record time.

Mrs Mansukhani was quickly laid out on a stretcher even though she insisted she could walk. No one listened to her.

Twenty minutes later Mrs Mansukhani was being seen to in a private ward. The rest of them sat in the waiting room, silent and brooding.

Mr Mansukhani picked up a copy of the Sun and began to read. Maya sat next to him reading Cosmopolitan turning the pages with bright pink tweezers. She advised her father to do the same. "Hospital germs," she explained meaningfully.

"Tabby," Chris growled in her ear.

Mr Mansukhani briefly looked up, eyed Tabby with no particular expression and then dipped his head to the paper again.

Tabby reluctantly got up and followed Chris out to the front of the hospital.

"How could you?" Chris roared, the moment they were outside in a fairly secluded corner by a dustbin.

She dropped her eyes to the ground and stared at the cigarette buds dotting the pavement.

"If anything happens to my mother, I will never forgive you," he continued. "How could you be so bloody stupid?"

"I'm sorry," she mumbled. She was feeling terrible and a little bit scared. What if something did happen to Mrs Mansukhani? She had read about a man once who had knocked his head on a door . . . or was it a tree . . . Anyhow, the man had been fine all day and then suddenly fell into a coma at night and died two days later. What if the same thing happened to Mrs Mansukhani? Would she be charged with murder?

"Sorry is not good enough," Chris said coldly.

"It wasn't her fault," Maya said. Tabby had not heard her come up. "We forced her to wear those heels, Chris. She told us she wasn't comfortable in them."

"What sort of a woman can't walk in heels?" Chris snapped.

"Chris, it was a small cut," Maya soothed. "Ma will be fine."

"And if she isn't?"

"You are being overly dramatic," Maya sighed. "Both you and dad overreact whenever Ma has so much as a headache."

"She fainted, Maya," Chris reminded her. "And you are worried as well. I can see it on your face."

"I don't want to fight. Come inside, the doctor will be with us soon," Maya said, turning on her heel.

Chris and Tabby followed, walking as far apart from each other as possible.

Mrs Mansukhani was sitting in the waiting room.

"What did the doctor say?" Chris asked, racing up to his mother.

"Nothing is wrong," Mrs Mansukhani smiled. "He said I should go on a diet. Other than that I am in good health."

"The cut?" Maya asked, her voice slightly wobbled in the end.

Mrs Mansukhani took Maya's hand and patted it. "Nothing a bit of antiseptic can't heal." She looked up at Tabby hanging back near the water cooler. She gestured for her to come forward.

Tabby came up to her and took a deep breath ready to apologise.

"Don't apologise," Mrs Mansukhani said. She patted the seat next to her and Tabby obediently sat down. "It was an accident. You didn't mean it. I wish our first meeting hadn't gone so badly. I was looking forward to giving you a proper welcome and introducing you to the family."

Tabby had expected Mrs Mansukhani to order her to get out of her son's life and tell her that she wasn't good enough for her son. But hearing the warmth in the old woman's voice tipped her over the edge. The tears she had been keeping in check all this time erupted. A sob escaped her and then another and another until finally she was bawling with snot running down her nose.

"I'm sorry. I didn't mean to," Tabby wailed. "And I stuck my chewing gum in your hair—"

"I needed a trim," Mrs Mansukhani hastily soothed her.

Maya shoved a few tissues into Tabby's hand.

Tabby blew her nose. "I never cry, but you are so nice and I'm so sorry. I don't wear heels and then the coir mat—"

"Don't worry," Mrs Mansukhani patted her back. "It is the mat's

45

fault. I will throw it out as soon as I get home."

Tabby wiped her eyes and noticed Mr Mansukhani arrive back into the waiting room. He took one look at Tabby's face and scurried back out.

"Goober, goober," Tabby said and began howling all over again.

"Yes, yes, that's right," Mrs Mansukhani said. "Drink some water. Now be a good girl and stop crying. We have wasted an hour over this nonsense. We have the whole evening to celebrate and you can still meet everyone. All is not lost."

"They saw me knock you down," Tabby blubbered. "Your sister thinks I killed you."

"My sister would be the happiest person on earth had you truly killed me. She would have married you off to her own son in joy," Mrs Mansukhani informed her. "Now, go along with Maya, fix yourself up and come and meet us in the car park."

Tabby stood up with a loud gulp and took a shuddering breath. "I won't take long," she said, her voice still thick with tears.

Maya led Tabby to the hospital bathroom, which reeked with the smell of disinfectant.

Tabby splashed her face. The cold water calmed her down.

Tabby had not carried her handbag, and Maya's concealer stick was too dark for her, but Maya did have some pink lipstick and mascara. Tabby applied both and looked back at herself.

"You look far too young without the makeup," Maya commented. "Your face is all red and blotchy, but hopefully that will settle down. Once we are in the house, I can sneak you up to my room and fix the rest of you. I think I have something that matches your skin tone."

"I still feel like a fool," Tabby said.

"Chris was frightened," Maya said.

"I have never cried in front of him," Tabby said.

"I enjoyed the drama," Maya confessed smoothing her own hair back and tucking an escaped strand behind her ear. "We have never had such a memorable start to a family gathering."

Tabby was too shook up to see the joke yet. She soberly walked back to the car and got in the back.

It was an uncomfortable ride back to the house, what with being squished in between Mr and Mrs Mansukhani.

Chapter Eight

They arrived back at the house.

"Wait," Mrs Mansukhani told Maya while she held on to Tabby's hand. "I need to talk to the two of you before we go in." She turned to her husband. "You and Chris go on ahead."

Once the men departed, Mrs Mansukhani said, "Maya, take Tabby in through the back and up to your room. Help her redo her makeup and hair. I don't think the quick wash in the hospital helped much. I can still see streaks of mascara on her cheek."

"Ma," Maya raised a quizzical brow, "we don't have an entrance at the back."

"Get in through the kitchen window, like you always do when you come home late from a party," Mrs Mansukhani said.

"You know?" Maya asked in amazement.

"I am your mother," Mrs Mansukhani replied as if that title provided her with super powers. She swirled her scarf around like a cape and headed towards the main door.

Maya and Tabby crouched low and scuttled past the living room window and around to the back.

They arrived near the kitchen window. Maya expertly hauled herself up and disappeared into the kitchen. Tabby raised her hand and was not surprised to find that her fingertips did not even brush the edge of the window sill. She was too short to accomplish this.

"Maya," she called softly.

Maya's head popped out.

"I can't reach the sill, let alone haul myself up," Tabby said, lifting her hand up to demonstrate.

Maya scowled. "Oh, all right." She jumped back down and catching Tabby up by the waist lifted her up.

Tabby grabbed the windowsill and heaved herself up until her head emerged into the kitchen. Her waist followed, but her hip got stuck.

"Hurry up," Maya growled from below.

"I think," Tabby gasped, "I'm stuck."

Maya muttered something rude under her breath. After a few deep breaths, she said, "I will have to come and yank you up by your hands. Pushing from this end is getting us nowhere."

While Tabby waited for Maya to appear, she looked around the slate grey and silver kitchen. She was admiring the largest fridge she had ever seen when footsteps sounded nearby.

Suddenly Tabby panicked. What if the footsteps did not belong to Maya? What if it was a relative? No, it must be Maya. Mrs Mansukhani would be keeping the rest of them busy. But if it wasn't?

It wasn't.

A sharp-faced woman entered the room. "Thief?" she asked curiously.

"Hello," Tabby squeaked. "I'm Tabby."

"Chris's girlfriend?"

"Yes."

Mrs Mansukhani came charging into the kitchen. "Gayatri," she said. "This is Tabby."

Tabby obligingly waved from where she was half hanging out of the window.

"We met," Gayatri said. "I am Mr Mansukhani's sister. You can call me Aunty."

Tabby was surprised. She knew Mr Mansukhani had two brothers, but Maya had not mentioned any sister.

Two teenagers entered the kitchen now.

"This is Bunty and that is Smita," Gayatri said. "My kids. Say hello to Aunty."

"Hello, Aunty," the kids said sourly.

"My name is Tabby."

"Hello, Aunty Tabby," the kids chorused obligingly.

"We address everyone older than us as aunty and uncle even if we are not related," Mrs Mansukhani explained.

Just then, another woman in a flurry of pink, white and silver zoomed into the kitchen. "Thief?" she asked looking at Tabby.

"This is Tabby," Mrs Mansukhani said hurriedly. "Tabby, this is my sister, Meena. You will get to meet her properly in a bit. Why don't you—"

"Ah, the one who almost killed you? You can call me Aunty," Meena giggled. "Why are you hanging out of the window?"

Tabby wriggled her butt discreetly trying to dislodge herself. "I, errr—"

"Have you tasted the *biryani?*" Mrs Mansukhani asked, lifting the lid off one of the dishes lying on the counter.

Meena, it seemed, could be easily distracted.

Tabby heaved a sigh of relief and then noticed Gayatri's glittering eye on her. She swallowed nervously and focused on the butter knife. She prayed no one else would arrive to witness her humiliation.

Her prayers were not answered. A dark face with cheeks that hung loose appeared near the door. Between the cheeks and over a thin, dark upper lip was draped a long, sad moustache that had been carefully oiled and formed into sharp points at the end.

"Cuckoo ji," Mrs Mansukhani said planting herself in front of this new arrival. "Did you need anything?"

Cuckoo Singh peered over Mrs Mansukhani's head. "I just wanted a glass of water." He stood up on his toes, his attention riveted on Tabby.

"I will bring it to you in the living room. Why don't you join Maya's papa and I will—"

"No need, no need," Cuckoo Singh said as he nudged Mrs Mansukhani out of the way.

He came and stood in front of Tabby, his eyes glued to the valley between her breasts. Her unfortunate position had made the tunic slip off her shoulders, exposing more than she liked.

His moustache quivered lustily.

Mrs Mansukhani planted herself in front of Tabby. "Here," she said handing him a glass of water."

Tabby hurriedly adjusted her top while he was busy gulping the water. He wiped his upper lip carefully with a napkin and turned back to Tabby.

"Your good name?" he asked.

"Eh?" Tabby scrunched up her forehead.

"Your good name?" he repeated.

"Tabitha," she replied, hoping that was the right answer.

It apparently was. He nodded his head importantly. "My name is Cuckoo Singh."

Tabby was holding her top closed together. She didn't want to let go to shake his hand. So she smiled politely.

"This position," he said gesturing to her stuck behind. "Yoga?"

"Yes, yes," Mrs Mansukhani answered for Tabby. "Yoga. New age yoga."

"Airing legs, eh?" he asked gravely.

"Airing legs," Tabby agreed.

"I own a toothpaste factory," he told her proudly.

Tabby tried to look suitably impressed.

He rested his hip on the counter, apparently settling in for a good long talk. "Rub, scrub and twinkle is our motto. Here," he said rummaging around in his jacket pocket and producing a long white tube with pink flowers. "This a full sized tube of Blooming Fresh, the toothpaste from my factory. Complimentary. You can keep it."

Tabby carefully extracted one hand while the other continued to grip her top together and took the toothpaste.

He watched the entire procedure with utmost interest.

She extended her hand, and when her top failed to slip again, she could have sworn he looked disappointed.

He pulled out a toothpick from his front pocket and put it into his mouth. He then proceeded to chew on it and occasionally rotate it from one side of his mouth to the other. He seemed to be waiting to see how she was going to extract herself.

Maya poked her head in from the doorway. She gestured to her mother to get Cuckoo Singh out of the room.

Mrs Mansukhani wrung her hands helplessly. She finally blurted out, "Gayatri, Meena, why don't you take some of these snacks to the table? Oh, I think I just saw Maya go by. She is home."

Maya ducked out of sight and presumably ran and hid.

Cuckoo Singh tilted his head like an alert owl. "She is here, excellent. We will meet again," he threatened Tabby before leaving the kitchen.

The moment footsteps receded, Mrs Mansukhani rushed towards Tabby and tried to yank her into the kitchen. Maya arrived shortly after that to help her mother. The two of them caught Tabby's hand and pulled. When that didn't work, they grabbed the waistband of her jeans and tugged.

The motion gave Tabby an unpleasant wedgie, but it freed her. It was Maya's strong arms that caught her just in time to save her from bloodying her head on the granite floor.

"Now to repair the damage," Maya grunted.

Maya had done a remarkable job, Tabby thought, staring at herself in the mirror. Her skilful hands had concealed most of the red blotches, and the expensive mascara made her lashes look longer and darker than they ever had. Maya's trick of applying red lipstick and then wiping it off, gave her lips a cherry stained finish which made her appear young, fresh, and dare she say . . . pretty?

Maya made a frustrated sound and flung the hairpin she had been trying to stick into her hair. The pin flew into the air and pinged as it hit the glass dresser.

Tabby sent Maya a wary look. "Err, did I do something?"

Maya took a breath and exhaled audibly. "Never mind. Let's go. It's almost dinner time."

Tabby frowned, but Maya's set jaw clearly indicated an end to the topic. They headed down the wide theatrical staircase in silence. The moment they reached the bottom step, a roar erupted above their startled heads, loud enough to make the chandelier in the hallway sway alarmingly.

Tabby clamped her hands over her ears. "What is going on?" she yelled in fright.

"It is a helicopter," Maya yelled back. "We have a helipad on the rooftop. Dev must have arrived."

"Dev?" Tabby asked.

The noise of the helicopter suddenly shut off, and at the same time she spotted Chris emerging from one of the doors on the right.

"Chris," Tabby ran up to him.

"Tabby," He extracted himself from her hug, "please don't touch me in front of the family. They won't like it."

Tabby's shoulders drooped. "I was looking for you."

"I have been playing chess," he said, carefully tucking a striped silk scarf inside his shirt. He looked into a giant wall mirror and tweaked a few strands of hair into perfect points atop his head. His eyes suddenly narrowed and his head tilted towards the top of the stairs as if he knew someone disagreeable was about to walk into his life.

A dark figure appeared on top of the stairs. The chandelier swung towards the figure briefly lighting up a man's rugged features before swinging back and leaving it in shadows.

"Dev," Maya grinned in delight. She let out a whoop, raced up the stairs and flung herself into the man's outstretched arms.

Dev met Maya halfway down the stairs and engulfed her in a bear hug, lifting her off her feet.

The chandelier brightened, emitting a golden light that blazed through dozens of sparkling crystals and finally illuminated the harsh planes of Dev's face.

He was a tall man and the colour of toasted almonds. His muscular frame and height dwarfed even Maya, who stood six feet tall in her four-inch heels.

He laughed as he lifted Maya higher in the air playfully threatening to toss her like a doll.

He was also surprisingly gentle. His muscles rippled beneath his white shirt as he carefully set her back down. He kissed her forehead and then as if he realised he was being watched looked down towards them.

Tabby felt his gaze as surely as if he had physically touched her. She wrapped her arms around herself, her eyes wide and unblinking.

He was the handsomest man she had ever seen. His face was dark, sculpted, and oh, so masculine. His eyes were heavy-lidded, sleepy and framed by thick, long, dark lashes.

As they continued to gaze at each other, oblivious to the world around them, her heart began beating painfully against her ribs. She hugged herself more tightly, trying to quell the urge to launch herself like Spiderwoman and wrap her web around him.

She had never felt like this before in her entire life. Never felt this kind of wild attraction. She was afraid the heat unfurling in the pit of her belly would erupt at any moment. Her hands curled into a fist and her body swayed forward

She had heard of love at first sight, but this . . . this was clearly lust at first peek.

"He is our cousin."

Tabby blinked. She hadn't noticed Maya come back down the stairs. She forced her eyes away from Dev, feeling horribly guilty for thinking naughty thoughts while standing right next to her fiancé.

"He is also my best friend," Maya continued.

"Show off," Chris scowled, watching Dev descend the stairs with an easy grace and head towards the living room

"You are just jealous," Maya said.

"Of a criminal?" Chris asked.

"He is not a criminal," Maya growled.

"He just got out of an Indian jail, didn't he?"

Tabby's eyes widened. "Is that right?" she asked Maya.

"Yes, but he wouldn't hurt a fly—"

Chris snorted. "He has spent nights with hardened criminals. We don't know what he is capable off."

"Don't be so melodramatic," Maya rolled her eyes.

"Sis, people change as they grow older." Chris turned towards Tabby, "Maya still thinks of Dev as her childhood playmate who can do no wrong. But I know the man is dangerous." He added in a low, sinister tone, "And if you ever find yourself alone with him, get away as soon as possible."

"Oh, please!" Maya scoffed. "This is Dev we are talking about. He is kind and gentle and—"

"Why was he in jail?" Tabby hastily intervened, since Chris looked like he was going explode if Maya continued lauding Dev's virtues.

Chris knocked back the whisky, wiped his mouth with the back of his hand and drawled, "He killed someone."

Chapter Nine

He killed someone.

The words that Chris had thrown at her so casually sent a chill down Tabby's spine.

She shivered as she recalled Dev's dark, arrogant face. It was possible that he had a cruel streak. His lips had hardened into thin lines when he had looked at Chris or was her imagination getting the better of her?

"Mum's waiting," Chris broke into her thoughts. He placed the empty whiskey glass on a side table and touched her arm. "Come on."

They entered the living room together.

Peacocks seemed to be the dominating theme of the spacious room.

Large peacock feathers were placed in giant vases as decoration, the cushions dotting the sofa were made of matching blue-green silk, and even the walls had oil paintings of peacocks hanging on it.

The men were sitting on comfy looking sofas, drinks in hand, while the women had congregated near the dining table.

A few faces turned towards them. Inspecting, analysing, but giving away nothing.

"Chintu," Cuckoo Singh squealed and gestured at Chris.

Chris headed towards him, leaving Tabby to squirm near the door all alone.

Maya approached her. "Chintu is Chris's pet name at home. I think it means small . . . like a hobbit."

"We used to call you Pinky," Mrs Mansukhani said, wobbling up to them. "Then one day you threatened to jump off a building until we promised to never call you that again."

"You must have been a naughty child," Tabby said politely.

"This happened last year." Mrs Mansukhani clarified.

Mr Mansukhani oozed over and stood next to his wife. His expression was guarded. "Hello," he said to Tabby.

"Touch his feet," Maya whispered in Tabby's ear.

Tabby gaped at her.

"It is a sign of respect, and he will protest but ignore that. It will make you look good in front of the others," Maya hissed. "Now hurry up, ask questions later."

Tabby pasted a smile on her face and dived towards Mr Mansukhani's feet, frightening the life out of him.

He leaped back a foot, avoiding Tabby's eager fingertips.

Tabby did not give up. She followed his feet, her head bent low. The brown leather shoes would not escape her.

The shoes scuttled back. Tabby chased them.

Mr Mansukhani's feet quickened in pace, scampered back and jumped on top of the sofa.

Tabby pitched forward at lighting pace and grabbed his ankles.

"Dad," Maya said, in a strangled voice, "She is only trying to touch your feet for *ashirwad* . . . blessing."

"Oh, no need, no need," Mr Mansukhani's relieved voice said above her head.

Tabby triumphantly touched the tip of the shiny leather shoes and stood up.

Mr Mansukhani jumped down from the sofa looking a little strained.

Maya whispered in her ear. "He is pleased. Now, do the same to everyone else you are introduced to . . . but hold back the enthusiasm a tad bit.

"This," Mr Mansukhani said to Tabby, "is my cousin brother, Mintu Singh, from my mother's side. This is his wife and those two are his little children."

Tabby touched the round and red Mr Mintu Singh's feet and then turned towards his wife. Mrs Mintu Singh was hidden behind a thick veil and was wearing silver rings on her fat toes. The two little children turned out to be giant sized teenagers. She touched their feet as well and a loud guffaw erupted around her.

"Only touch the feet of people who are older than you," Maya explained apologetically.

Once the mirth subsided, the introductions continued.

"This is my eldest cousin, Honey, from my father's side—"

Honey was a tall man with a thin moustache. His wife was also a tall woman with a thin moustache.

"This is my sister's husband, this is my younger sister's husband's friend, and this is the son of my father's best friend from school. This is Maya's second cousin's second child, this is Chris's third cousin's second wife . . ."

And so on the introductions continued. Finally, Mr Mansukhani turned to Tabby, "And this everyone is Tabby. Chris's girlfriend."

A few children snickered at the girlfriend bit.

"Toby is a boy's name," one man, whose name she had forgotten, remarked.

"Not Toby, Tabby," she clarified. "Short for Tabitha."

"Tubby? Ah, I see, pet name. Tubby. Don't worry, we like tubby women. Skinny, no good."

Another man with grey hair and suspiciously red eyes slurred, "Tubby means juicy. Very, very juicy."

She raised an eyebrow.

"Yum," he replied underlining his point.

"We call him sleazy uncle," Maya whispered in her ear. "And that one is whisky sour. He is always drunk."

"How am I going to remember everyone?" Tabby asked, feeling overwhelmed.

"We call all older men uncle and all older women aunties, irrespective of whether they are related to us or not. Calling them by their name is considered impolite, so don't worry."

After that Maya led her towards the dinner table, and they sat down on the only two available chairs.

A sari slipped off one stocky, muscular lady revealing a blue skull and roses tattoo. The woman discreetly lifted the sari back up.

Mrs Mansukhani came up to Tabby. "You have already met everyone, but let me introduce you again. I am sure you can't possibly recall of them."

"Not again," Maya muttered under her breath.

"This is my husband's elder sister," she began. "Mrs Malhotra. You can call her Gayatri Aunty."

Tabby recognised her from the kitchen debacle.

"Hello again," Gayatri Aunty said in a posh English accent. She had a narrow face and a stick thin figure that was tightly wrapped in a steel grey sari. She didn't wait for Tabby to respond. "Is this really the girl Chris chose?" she asked turning to Mrs Mansukhani. "I thought she was one of Maya's wayward friends. Do we know anything about her background?"

"Call her demon Aunty in your head," Maya hissed under her breath.

"Don't start now, Gayatri," the Aunty with the tattoo piped up. "My dear, don't mind her, she is sexually frustrated."

Everyone tittered at that. Tabby blushed.

"Mrs Charu Dayal," Mrs Mansukhani introduced Tabby to the tattooed woman. "She is a family friend. Call her baby Aunty. Everyone does."

Tabby thought the woman looked anything but a baby. She sniggered in her head.

"Baby aunty," Maya whispered in her ear, "is nice. She adores motorcycles and hides a bright blue Mohawk under that wig."

Mrs Mansukhani continued with the introductions, but Tabby concentrated on listening to Maya instead.

"Meena is mom's sister. She is silly and sweet and wants to be fashionable and cool. Call her social networking Aunty. That one is Aunty gossip queen. Has all the insider dirt on Bollywood actors. She is popular at kitty parties—"

"Kitty parties?" Tabby interrupted.

"Where women get together and gossip once a month. Like a woman's club."

"I see."

"That one gets horrified easily. We call her soap opera Aunty. Adores her soaps, dresses like them and is overly dramatic."

And as if to prove Maya's point, soap opera Aunty burst into tears. "I am so happy," she howled. "So, so happy that Chris is now engaged. I remember how I used to come to the house and watch him crawl around in his diapers. And when," she hiccupped, "he grew a little older I remember how he refused to wear pants. He used to zip around the house without his pants on while all the servants would grab a handful of underwear and chase him. Oh, those were the good old days. . . ."

"Someone take her gin and tonic away," Gayatri Aunty said coldly.

"Have I come at wrong time?" Cuckoo Singh asked, slithering up to their table.

Maya quietly slipped away.

"No, no," Mrs Mansukhani fluttered up to him. "You are welcome to join us."

He sat on the seat that Maya had just vacated. It happened to be right next to Tabby's chair.

"Why are you wearing sunglasses inside the house?" Gayatri Aunty asked Cuckoo Singh.

Cuckoo Singh let out a hesitant giggle clearly at a loss as to how to respond to the question.

Gayatri Aunty refused to giggle along with him.

"It's hot, no?" he asked finally. He seemed a little surprised that not everyone was willing to fall over themselves to please him.

Mrs Mansukhani leaped up from her chair and turned on a large standing fan that rotated from side to side.

Tabby sighed in pleasure as the cold air hit her face. The next moment she stifled a screech when she felt a hand grab her knee.

She looked down to find Cuckoo Singh's fingertips dancing on her leg while he munched on a *samosa* with his other hand.

"What do you do?" Gayatri Aunty chose that moment to boom across at Tabby.

"I'm a writer," Tabby squeaked. She tried to prise Cuckoo Singh's hand off her leg under the table. He gripped harder.

"What do you write?" Gayatri Aunty asked.

"Books," Tabby gasped. She managed to dig her nails into Cuckoo Singh's hand, who immediately loosened his grip on her thigh. She shot up before he could latch on again. "I think I should help Mrs Mansukhani with the dinner."

Gayatri Aunty scowled and looked away. Taking that as permission to leave, Tabby hurried out of the room.

Once she was in the hall, she realised she couldn't remember where the kitchen was. She began walking down a corridor, wondering how long she could linger before going back to the living room.

"I don't want to marry him," Maya's voice floated out from one of the rooms.

Tabby froze.

"I can give you the money. You can continue living in London and attend a fashion school." The voice was deep, rich, warm . . . It sounded like Dev.

"I am not going to take your money, nor am I going to marry Cuckoo. You have to think of a way out."

"I will not speak to Daaji."

"Please. No one else can face him."

"No." His voice softened. "What is more important for you, Maya? Your independence or Daaji's money?"

"Why can't I have both?" Maya growled.

Tabby didn't want to eavesdrop any longer. She stepped forward to alert them to her presence when her cursed nude pumps snagged on the edge of the white lace curtains hanging in the doorway. She shrieked and lurched forward.

A warm hand caught her waist before she hit the ground.

Her breath sped up when she realised that the hand clutching her stomach belonged to Dev.

She peeked at him from beneath her lashes, feeling his warm whiskey breath fan her face. His jaw was faintly shadowed, and the top two buttons of his shirt were open exposing his throat. Heat emanated from him like a furnace, and she could feel the intoxicating warmth wrap around herself.

His dark eyes glittered down at her. His fingers dug into her waist signalling her to straighten up.

Dear God, she thought in utter confusion, why didn't she want to let his neck go? She was clearly gripping his throat too hard. In fact, one could say from his increasingly pained expression that she was strangling him.

"Gack," he wheezed as if confirming her thoughts. He was about to choke to death.

She was going to murder a murderer, she grinned inwardly. The smile fell away and her eyes widened in horror. He was a murderer. She was touching a murderer. Not just touching him, but pissing him off as well.

She snatched her hand back and straightened up like a spring.

"I'm sorry," she stammered.

"How much did you hear? Did Chris send you to spy on us?" Dev thundered while his long, masculine fingers massaged his neck.

Tabby tilted her head way up to look at him while her feet scuttled closer to Maya.

"Dev, I don't think she was deliberately eavesdropping," Maya said.

He didn't look like he trusted Tabby one jot. "Whatever you heard, keep it to yourself," he warned her.

Tabby nodded fervently.

"Chris wants this wedding to happen," Maya added bitterly.

"He grabbed my knee," Tabby blurted out. "I mean, Cuckoo Singh grabbed my knee. If you want me to help you get out of this wedding, then let me know. I can try and convince Chris—"

"No! Don't you dare say anything to Chris. Promise me you won't," Maya exploded.

"I won't," Tabby swore, though her forehead scrunched up in confusion.

Maya's shoulders sagged. "I wish I had a plan."

Tabby touched Maya's shoulder. "Why don't you get Cuckoo Singh to break off the engagement? Daaji won't blame you, and he might even feel sorry enough to give you the money. Or it will buy you time to find someone you really like while remaining in Daaji's good books."

Both Maya and Dev turned to look at her, their expressions comical.

"So simple," Maya whispered.

"It won't work," Dev said at the same time. "I think you should speak to your mother and if she continues to disagree, then forget the money and find a job like most people—"

"I can't believe this cute little button of a thing has found the perfect solution. Why in the world didn't I think of it?" Maya murmured thoughtfully.

Dev frowned while Tabby grinned in pleasure.

"Now all I have to do is annoy Cuckoo Singh until he breaks off the engagement. Daaji can't blame me if the groom backs off." Maya's eyes began to dance. "This is going to be so much fun." She turned to Tabby. "And you, my new best friend, are going to help us."

Chapter Ten

Tabby returned to the living room and sent Chris a guilty look. In all the time they had been dating, she had never so much as looked at another man, and here she was drooling over his murderous cousin as well as keeping secrets from him.

She schooled her face and went to help Mrs Mansukhani lay the table.

An argument was going on at the other end of the room. Mr Mansukhani was attempting to call his father on the computer while a few smug young men were giving him plenty of unhelpful advice. After a few minutes of *'not like this, can't hear, the microphone is switched off, where is the microphone, Daaji move lower so we can see your face'* finally everything was set up.

First, everyone went up to the computer one by one and wished Daaji a happy birthday.

The line kept dropping, but the call was made over and over again.

Then, Tabby was called to talk to Daaji.

Mrs Mansukhani scuttled up to Tabby and covered her head with a scarf. She nervously patted her hand. "You will be fine. Smile and keep the scarf on your head and your eyes on the floor," she advised.

Tabby bared her teeth in some semblance of a polite smile and walked towards the chair placed in front of the laptop. She felt someone's eyes on her and slid her eyeballs sideways to find Dev watching her.

He had an odd expression on his face. Was it pity? She nervously licked her lower lip. He knew nothing about her . . . then why feel sorry for her? Was Daaji that terrifying?

She quickly sank into the seat, her hand clutching her queasy stomach. She felt as if she was sitting for an important exam.

A white-haired man with plenty of wrinkles stared at her through the laptop screen.

She dropped her lashes.

"What's your name?" he asked in perfect English without a hint of an accent.

"Tabitha Lee Timmons," she told her ankles.

"You are engaged to my grandson, Chris?"

"Yes." She wanted to add sir.

"What in the world do you see in that fool?"

She quickly looked up. "He is not a fool."

"I think he is."

"I don't think so," she bristled and then looked horrified. He was his grandfather. He could call Chris a dweeb if he wanted to.

Daaji's already thin lips disappeared entirely. "You are loyal with plenty of spirit. I am not sure about the latter bit."

She ducked her head trying her best to look demur.

"I am not sure if. . . ." he trailed off.

She peeked at him. He appeared to be thinking deeply.

He spoke slowly as if he was carefully weighing his words. "I suppose if you want to marry him, then I can't stop you. But if you and Chris would like my blessing then I would like to suggest something."

"That is?" Tabby asked trying not to sound too eager. His consent was important. Very important. Without it Chris would be cut off, he would lose his job, his financial support, and they wouldn't be able to marry.

"Babaji," he replied, stroking his white stubbly chin.

"Eh?"

"You will have to get Babaji's consent. I never do anything in my life without his approval. He is my guru. If he agrees to your union, then you will be welcomed with open arms."

Tabby remained silent, unsure of what to say. She had never heard of this Babaji.

"So, the question remains," he went on. "Will you be willing to meet Babaji?"

"I will," she said promptly. It couldn't hurt.

"I mean Chapal Wale Babaji," he pressed.

"Yes," she said more firmly.

"Wonderful. I will expect you in India next week. If Babaji approves, then you can stay for Maya's wedding. It will be an excellent way of introducing you to the family."

A small hand tugged at Tabby's sleeve. Dazed, she looked down to find a little girl smiling up at her.

"Hello," the girl said.

"Hello," Tabby replied mechanically.

"I lost my front tooth."

"Didn't the tooth fairy give you any money?" Tabby asked.

"Only a pound. You should spend more to get quality stuff. That is what mommy says to Daddy when he is a *kanjoos*."

"*Kanjoos?*"

"It's Hindi for cheapskate."

"I see."

"Would you like to know what else I am thinking about?"

"Sure."

"Cauliflowers. Also that you have been chatting with Daaji long enough. Now my turn."

Tabby stood up and walked over to Maya.

"You look ghastly," Maya muttered. "What did he say?"

"He said I have to meet Babaji."

"Chapal Wale Babaji?"

"Yeah,"

"You agreed?"

"I did."

"But he lives in India."

"So I learned."

"Bloody hell."

"Precisely."

As soon as everyone learnt that Tabby was going to India in a week, they swarmed around her bursting with advice.

"Take proper clothes."

"Carry a litre of sunscreen."

"It is July, monsoon season. You will have to get shots for malaria—"

"And typhoid."

"Don't pet the dogs on the street—"

"Or the squirrels."

"They have rabies."

"Don't drink the water from the tap. Always drink bottled water."

"Never eat salads. They wash it with bad water. It can kill you. So can the mosquitoes, spiders, scorpions, snakes, wild elephants—"

"You are lucky. All of us are going to India next week and you can travel with us."

"We will be going to Delhi and from Delhi to Dehradun where Babaji is."

"Ooh, what fun," one of the children squealed.

"You will see camels and elephants and cows and all sorts of birds," a little girl told her importantly.

"From Dehradun we will go to Punjab. We have a lovely ancestral home where Maya's wedding is going to happen."

"Oh, you are going to love it!"

"Chapal Wale Babaji," Chris whispered in her ear, "is easy enough to deal with. I will make sure he gives you his consent."

"But he gives his blessings by whacking you on the head with a slipper," Maya whispered in her other ear. "That is where he gets his name from. *Chapal* means slipper.

Tabby took a deep breath. "I'm not sure I'm ready," she began.

"You are," Chris said. His hand squeezed her tensed fingers under the table. "I will take care of you."

She felt some of the stress evaporate. He would be with her in India and so would Maya and Mrs Mansukhani. She wouldn't be alone. She could do this. She felt a hint of excitement brewing in her tummy. She had never been anywhere so exotic.

"Is dinner ready?" Dev asked, coming up to the table.

The women shot up and began laying the table.

"The food is mild here," Maya said. "But in India, everything is spicy. You will have to be careful when you are there."

When I am there, Tabby thought with a thrill. In one week exactly she would be India.

The week went by in a whirl of preparation. Tabby bought a few travel books, googled what sights to see, things to buy and food to try. The more she read, the more excited she got.

Maya helped her apply for a visa to visit India. After that, they spent the next few days shopping. The aunties joined them, and they spent hours in vibrant Indian wear shops.

Tabby's heart lurched as she paid for the emerald and gold, intricately embroidered *kurta* set. The prices were ridiculously high.

She had never spent so much money on clothes before. But she was told she would need something to wear when meeting Daaji and Babaji. They would prefer her in Indian wear. Also, she needed a ton more things for Maya's wedding. They would have at least five functions and dozens of get-togethers.

It was in these brief moments that she realised how different her world was from theirs. No one else seemed to think twice before spending hundreds of pounds. When they casually spoke of buying an emerald or a ruby set studded with diamonds to match their sarees, she had trouble keeping her face neutral.

She felt as if a tidal wave had hit her and was now carrying her along at a great rushing speed. Her dull, dreary life was suddenly filled with colour, excitement and lots and lots of people.

Aunties were handing her their cell phones telling her to talk to people she had never met but were now somehow related to her. Uncles were offering to carry part of her luggage to India if her own bags became too heavy, and random wailing babies were being thrust into her confused arms.

She even had new names. She was now someone's bhabhi, maasi, chaachi, aunty, didi . . . and she had no clue what any of it meant. She smiled and nodded and blindly waded through the family dinners that she found herself at every single night.

It was during these dinner parties that people told her horrific travel stories. Maya mentioned how a cousin had died a few years ago in Calcutta after contracting malaria. Someone recalled the day a tiger had eaten up an entire family when they were visiting Sunderban. An aunt told her that a leopard had jumped into her backyard and taken away her little white Pomeranian called Tutu.

The stories added to her wonderment, and she felt as thrilled as a child off on a summer holiday.

It was on Saturday morning that Chris presented her with the tickets to India.

Tabby stared at the glossy white and red business class ticket and realised her bank balance was dangerously low. She had spent a lot more than she could afford to spend. If things went wrong with Chris or Babaji said no, then she would be in big trouble.

"I will need some time to pay you back for this," Tabby said, flushing red in embarrassment.

"My dad paid for it," Chris shrugged indifferently.

Tabby squirmed, feeling even more uncomfortable. "I can transfer the money to his account in a few days if it's all right." It would completely clean out her bank account she realised in panic.

"No need," he said, admiring his reflection on the back of the coffee spoon.

"But, I can't let him pay for my flights," Tabby objected.

"You can," Maya said. "You are part of the family now, Tabby . . ."

Part of the family. Tabby felt the familiar lump form in her throat. It took her a few moments to compose herself and focus on Maya once more.

" . . . Besides, Daaji asked you to come down, and it is only fair that he pays for your flight."

After another ten minutes of argument, Tabby reluctantly agreed.

Chris smiled at her. "I bought you a notebook. Start scribbling in it." At Tabby's confused look, he clarified, "to keep up your image as a writer. Get used to it. Everyone's eyes will be on you throughout this trip."

She ducked her head and flipped open the flight ticket. She stared at the date and her stomach flipped over. This was truly happening.

She was flying to India the next day.

Chapter Eleven

"I'm leaving for India in an hour," Tabby announced.

"Don't lie," Becky squawked at the other end of the line.

"I swear," Tabby replied.

"Tabby, I'm in a middle of a conversation with a man who is threatening to drink pine scented floor cleaner. I can't handle jokes right now."

"I'm not joking. Everything has been happening so quickly that I had no time to tell you."

"One moment," Becky said and put Tabby on hold.

Tabby pulled the suitcases closer to the main door while she waited. She fished out her packing list and ran an eye over it.

"Sorry," Becky said coming back on the line. "He only took a sip of the cleaning stuff. His family is with him now."

"So you can talk?"

"I can talk," Becky confirmed.

"I'm going to India to meet Babaji. If Babaji gives his consent, then I will stay for Maya's wedding."

"Who is Babaji?"

"Chris's grandfather's guru. He doesn't do anything without his consent."

"I am confused."

"Never mind. The point is I'm going with Chris's entire family, and if all goes well, I won't be back for over a month. I won't have my phone with me, but I will email you every chance I get."

Becky took a moment to digest that. She finally asked, "How is your sex life with Chris?"

"Err—"

"You still haven't? It's been a year, and now that you are engaged—"

"Maybe he is conservative in that area. I mean his culture is different—"

"But what if his thingamajig doesn't work."

"Becky!" she scolded, her face flaming with embarrassment.

"I'm serious."

"I'm sure it works."

"What if it is itty bitty?"

"It won't be."

"Does he kiss well?" Becky coaxed.

"Like an electronic toothbrush."

"What?"

"He kisses like an electronic toothbrush. His tongue whizzes all over my teeth and it's all over before I know it."

A short silence followed this confession.

"Tabby, did you ever want to fly across the table and kiss the hell out of your ex?"

"You mean Luke? Initially when we started dating in high school—Am I frigid? Is that why Chris—"

"Nothing is wrong with you," Becky cut her short. "I'm a professional. I know these things."

"Then?"

"Are you sure you love Chris?"

"Well, angels don't sing and rose petals don't fall from the sky when I see him, but I think I love him. Love is such an abstract emotion . . . How can you know for certain that you love someone or that he is the one—"

"Tabby, who is the most important person in your life?"

"You," she replied promptly.

Becky's face scrunched up for a moment, and then with visible effort, she smoothed out the lines. "You almost made me cry. Now apart from me, who do you care about the most?"

"My father," Tabby said, her throat feeling as if something was caught in it.

"And?"

"My sister, I suppose. I know what she did was wrong but still . . . she is my sister."

"And?"

Tabby tapped her lips thoughtfully. "I adored my English teacher in high school and then the old cook at café Rose I worked with around the corner from my house when I was eighteen. You remember—"

"Tabby, if you loved Chris, *his* name would have been number one on that list not mine."

"I care about him, too," she replied defensively.

"Yeah, right after your English teacher from ten years ago."

"How do you know if you love someone?"

"You just do. Next time, notice how you feel when he talks to another woman. Do you burn with jealousy? Does seeing him smile make you happy?"

"I do love Chris."

"You compared his kisses to an electronic toothbrush."

"No relationship is perfect. Emotional attachment is more important than physical attraction. "

"It can be imperfectly perfect."

"I thought you wanted me to marry Chris."

"He sounds like a nice man. Wealthy, good-looking, but I have never met him. My opinion is made from what you have told me—"

"Don't you dare. You agreed that getting engaged was the right thing to do, and now at the last moment—"

"Just remember, I love you no matter what. If you want to run away on the wedding day, I will not only support you but plan the entire thing as well. If you want to come back to America, my home is as good as yours. Don't worry about finances. I make more than enough, and if I can't help my friend, then what's the point of it all—"

"Stop," Tabby half laughed, half sobbed out. "I get it. And thank you."

"Call your father and tell him." It was a habit of Becky's. Switching topics without warning.

That wiped the smile off Tabby's face. "He doesn't know about Chris."

"It's time he did. You can't keep behaving like his mother. He is the one who should be taking care of you. You have suffered through enough on your own. He should have taken care of you when you needed him most. Instead, he bought you a flight to London—"

"Stop. You know he is not . . . he is not good in such situations. It was best for everyone that I left. And . . . and I can't tell him about the engagement."

"To protect yourself this time," Becky remarked shrewdly.

"What if my engagement ends again? I can't let anyone know."

"At least tell him about the trip."

"I will."

"Call me before you board. Text me as soon as you land."

"I will."

Tabby disconnected the call and before she could lose her nerve dialled her father's number.

"Dad," Tabby said, her voice came out a little choked.

"Hey, my little Tablet. How are you?" He sounded happy.

"Have you been taking your medicines? Is your cholesterol any better? What were the numbers?"

He chuckled. "You have even perfected her scolding tone."

Tabby knew that by her he meant her mother. She had been fifteen years old when she had died. Her father had fallen apart. Her elder sister had started sniffing glue and wearing garbage bags, so it had been up to Tabby to mimic her mother as best as she could to keep the family together.

"Dad, can you feed Gerry?" someone called out.

"A moment," he yelled back. A door shut with an unmistakable click. "What were you saying?" he asked Tabby.

"That was Luke, wasn't it?" Tabby asked.

"Yes. I'm staying here now . . . Your sis . . . They insisted. It helps them out," his voice sounded artificially cheerful laced with guilt.

"I don't mind if you spend time with them or your grandchildren, Dad."

An awkward silence fell after that. Tabby realised that if things had gone according to plan, then the wailing children in the background would have been hers and Luke's.

"How is she?" A hesitant voice asked in the background.

The sympathetic tone irritated Tabby. Her sister must have followed Dad into the room.

"I'm good," Tabby snapped. "I called to say I'm going to India to attend my boyfriend's sister's wedding."

"You are going to India? You never told me you were dating anyone?" her father said sounding hurt.

Her sister gasped in the background. It was a satisfying sound.

Tabby felt her lips quirk upwards and her spirits lifted." I'm leaving in an hour. I have been dating Chris for a year, and I didn't want to say anything until things were serious."

"I see," her father said sounding pleased. "India, eh? You are travelling the world, becoming all fancy. Take lots of pictures and keep calling me. I know you can take care of yourself, but I can't help worrying."

"I will be fine, Dad."

After a few more minutes of general chit-chat, Tabby put the phone down.

She was glad she had called him. It made her realise two important things. Firstly, when she had heard Luke's voice for the first time in two years, she had felt nothing. No hurt, no anger, no bitterness. She was well and truly over that man. Secondly, she no longer wanted that life. If she had married Luke, she would have lived her entire life in a dull little town, produced lots of kids and never discovered the world outside.

For the first time, she was ever so grateful that her glue sniffing sister had married her no-good boyfriend.

Somewhere in her heart, an angry wound healed and closed over.

She hugged herself, feeling a sudden surge of joy. A small town girl like her was going all the way to India. She was seeing the world. Learning new things. This was far, far more exciting than being a certain Luke Hogwood's wife.

This was the life she wanted.

Chapter Twelve

Maya, Chris and Tabby arrived at the airport on time. They strolled into Heathrow and waited for the rest of the relatives to join them. Tabby learned that most of the first class and business class seats on their plane had been booked by Chris's family.

Chris's mother and father arrived late, and the moment they were spotted, everyone began pelting towards the security check-in. The flight had already started boarding when they arrived huffing and puffing at their gates.

What with all the last minute chaos, Tabby found herself lodged in a window seat, chewing gum and staring at an in-flight magazine before she knew it.

Chris sat next to her.

"It's going to be a long flight," Chris said when they were airborne.

"Nine hours," Tabby sighed. She had barely slept the night before, and she doubted she would get any sleep on the plane either.

Chris adjusted his neck pillow and pulled out a lavender scented sleep mask.

"What did you just spray?" Tabby asked him.

"Magnesium oil. It helps you sleep. Do you want to try it?"

"No, that's all right."

He unzipped a small black leather case and pulled out a moisturiser. He began applying it as he spoke. "When I had gone to the doctor about my foot, he had recommended the spray. He said to try a high dose if I have trouble sleeping."

"What's wrong with your foot?"

"Plantar fasciitis," he replied, puffing up like a proud little bird.

"What's that?"

"The sole of my foot feels like I am walking on glass in the morning. Becomes better once stretched."

"I see. I hope it doesn't bother you too much."

"Sometimes it's bad, sometimes it's not that bad."

"What's the reason for it?" she asked. Her eyelids started feeling heavy and dry. She blinked rapidly.

"Only started this year, so it is probably something recent."

Tabby pursed her lips. "Do you know I call toes feet fingers. I always have . . . I don't know why. . . ."

He wiped his hand on a tissue paper, put away the mask and flipped open his laptop. "The tendon at the sole of the foot is too contracted. Stretching the calf, Achilles and soleus three times a day makes a massive difference. Here, I have a diagram that I downloaded from the internet explaining the entire thing."

She hid a yawn.

"The doctor said it normally shows up as a foot injury in adults, probably due to poor shoe choices as kids. Wrong shoes with the wrong type of support . . . Anyway, I start the stretching for the calf, Achilles and soleus three times a day for about two minutes each. I set an alarm on my phone. The foot has improved dramatically, but the doctor wants me back. He wants to see it in person before he can give a permanent solution."

Tabby forced her lids to stay open. She nodded dazedly.

He stared out at the clouds floating by. "The Calf and the Sole. That could be a pub with a terrible secret or a shoe shop, even a restaurant. Because calf and sole you know?"

That was the last thing that Tabby heard before nodding off. She only woke when the plane touched down on Indian soil.

It was four in the morning by the time they got through security and arrived at the baggage claim area at the New Delhi airport which, incidentally, was much like any other airport. It had the same metallic look, air-conditioned environment and funny airport smell.

Tabby was wide awake and buzzing with energy. She bounced on her toes while she waited for her battered silver suitcase to appear on the luggage carousel.

She spotted it soon enough as it as it slid under the flap and on to the revolving band.

She panicked and looked around for Chris. How was she meant to pull the heavy suitcase off on her own?

He was nowhere to be found. Maya was busy wrestling with her own bag, and Tabby didn't want to ask Mr or Mrs Mansukhani for help.

Her bag was getting closer and heading her way pretty fast.

She had no choice but to attempt pulling it off on her own. With a deep breath, she leaned over, curled her fingers around the handle and yanked.

The bag didn't move, but she did. She almost fell on top of the carousel. She let the handle go and scrambled back up in embarrassment.

A strong brown hand reached over and effortlessly lifted her suitcase off and placed it on the trolley.

"Thank—" She stopped, her eyes widening.

Dev, wearing a soft, grey cotton shirt and blue jeans, stood in front of her.

Her mouth turned dry and her heart began thudding in what she assumed was fright.

"Do you have another bag coming?" he asked when Tabby continued staring at him mutely.

Tabby grabbed the trolley and hurried away without saying a single word. She looked back once to find him staring at her with a baffled expression.

Tabby walked through the automatic glass door and was immediately doused by the monsoon rain cascading down like a giant waterfall. The warm and heavy droplets were welcome, since they effectively washed away the airport chill and stench.

She took a deep happy breath and looked around.

Droplets were sparkling and bouncing off the steel railing on either side of her, and wherever the lamp-light fell, a film of rainwater shimmered like black glass on the ground.

Chris's family had already walked on ahead and were gathered under a street lamp with some relatives who had arrived to meet them.

She heard the family's collective laughter through the thundering rain and began pushing the airport trolley towards them.

Something was wrong with the left wheel of her trolley. It kept veering right instead of going straight. She blinked rapidly, almost blind from the wind whipping strands of hair into her face.

At a distance, Chris's family seemed to be having a better time. Drivers wearing white uniforms had materialised by their side and taken control of their trolleys while they strolled towards the parking holding big black umbrellas.

She tried to hurry and catch up with them, but the ground was slippery and her trolley was continuing to misbehave.

Had they forgotten about her?

"Chris, Maya," she called. The wind, rain and a roaring airplane getting ready to land snatched away her words.

She sped up, pushing with all her might.

The trolley hit the curb, jarring her, and the suitcase slid off landing with a thud on the ground.

Heart pounding, she grabbed the handle and tried to lift it back up. It wouldn't budge.

In part panic and part exasperation, she took a deep breath and pulled. She thanked the sudden rush of adrenaline when the suitcase lifted and slid back on the trolley.

With renewed determination, she once again made her way towards Chris. Gripping the handle, she threw her entire weight on the trolley and pushed. It seemed to work.

"Tabby!" Maya spotted her and waved.

Tabby could see his family huddled together in the car park while the drivers were loading the luggage. She straightened her back, feeling pleased with herself. She had arrived without needing anyone's help.

The seat of the car was covered in plastic. Good thinking, Tabby applauded silently, considering how drenched they all were. The umbrellas had been unable to keep anyone dry.

She chose a seat next to the window and eagerly stuck her head out. She noted the landscape as the car slowly left the airport area and moved onto to a large, wide road. It was half four in the morning and pitch dark outside, and in spite of the many street lamps dotting the sides of the road, the rain made it hard for her to see anything clearly.

Dark shadowy trees swayed in the distance while bright yellow lamps lit the dark bumpy road that was flooded in many places. A few cars whizzed by them, but even through the familiarity of it all, she could sense the otherness.

A hint of fear and excitement crept into her heart.

Their own vehicle felt small and vulnerable on such wide, empty roads. Like a tiny boat bobbing along on a vast, roiling ocean that had hundreds of unknowns hidden within its depths.

She couldn't see much, but she could feel that she was no longer in England. The air wrapped around her body felt different—warmer, more humid and heavy.

It smelled familiar, though, like the scent of earth after a thunderstorm but a hundred times more intense. As if you could squeeze the wind laden with the earthy, watery perfume and fill bottles with the potent extract.

She rubbed her arms. Her wet clothes had chilled in the breeze blowing in from the window, but she did not have the heart to wind the glass up.

It was all so different, and she hadn't even begun to scratch the surface yet.

"Finally," Maya sighed when twenty minutes later the car drove in through the gates of a guesthouse. "I am all icky. I need a bath."

Tabby would have liked to linger outside a little longer, but she knew everyone was exhausted after the long flight, so she obediently trooped after Mrs Mansukani and Maya.

Welcome to Nirvana

The metallic gold words shimmered above the door of the main entrance.

The lobby was decorated in black and white, sleek modern style complete with oil paintings nailed to the wall. The paintings were the bewildering sort that left you wondering which way was up and which way down, and if you figured that out, then you spent another hour wondering what it all meant.

It was also air conditioned. The slight chill she had felt in the car increased threefold, and she had to concentrate on not shivering like a newly shaved Welsh mountain sheep.

No one was in a mood to talk anymore. Everyone stood around grumpily while the manager took signatures in his log book and handed over keys to the rooms.

Tabby almost snatched the electronic card out of the manager's hand in her hurry to get to her room. She scrambled up the stairs to the second floor instead of taking the elevator and swiped the card in the door with trembling hands.

The bellboy arrived right on her heels and deposited her suitcase inside the room. She tipped him generously, and the moment he departed she tore off her clothes and began rubbing her skin raw with a clean towel she found rolled up in the bathroom.

After that, she crawled into bed and snuggling deep under the soft blankets fell fast asleep.

Sometime early in the morning when the sun had forced its way back up in the sky, Tabby began dreaming a very strange dream . . .

She was racing down a seedy street. Slap, slap, slap her old, trusty sneakers echoed in the eerily silent night as they rhythmically hit the ground. Plastic crunched under her feet as she stepped on a discarded packet of chips. A giant rat sped past her, making her heart pound harder than it already was.

A black shadow loomed in front of her. She hissed in fright.

No, he couldn't be so close.

She forced her feet to move more quickly.

A finger slipped into the back of her t-shirt and tugged. She didn't stop running but let the cloth rip. She felt icy wind race over her bare back.

The street seemed to never end.

The buildings looming on either side of the street looked old. The paint was peeling from the walls and the windows were boarded up.

The mist suddenly swirled onto to the road, thick and grey, plunging the world into darkness.

She stumbled, her eyes desperately searching for a glimmer of light. She tilted her head up and found a yellow neon sign saying 'Lotus Town' flickering half-heartedly atop a dilapidated building. She slowed down and made her way towards that bit of light.

Warm breath brushed the nape of her neck.

Stifling a gasp, she picked up speed, impervious to the mist and the darkness. She didn't care if she banged into a pole or tripped over a garbage bin.

Only that he shouldn't catch her.

She reached the base of the building, above which the neon sign was hanging. The door was locked, but she could see the beginnings of a scaffolding within her grasp. Without wasting a moment to think about it, she grabbed the lowest board and pulled herself up. She hoped he didn't know how to climb or better still that the boards would turn out to be weak, unable to carry such a heavy man.

A cloak flapped below her.

He could climb.

Tabby's eyes shot open under the quilt. She blinked in confusion.

What in the world was that?

She slowly sat up in bed, her cheeks still flushed from sleep. She rubbed her eyes, trying to wipe away the nightmare.

It was freezing in the room. She looked around blearily, hoping to spot the remote for the air conditioner.

A shaft of sunlight fell on something white peeking out from behind the bedside table lamp. It was the remote. She lunged towards it and stabbed the off button in relief.

She debated going back to sleep, but her eyes fell on the dark blue suede notebook that Chris had given her. It was poking out of her handbag bag that lay on the edge of the bed.

She reached over and pulled the notebook closer to herself. She opened to the first blank page and pulled out a pen.

25th June

I have arrived in India . . .

She chewed the back of the pen, at a loss as to how to continue. The nightmare loomed up once more in the mind. Vivid in detail. She could once again feel the scaffolding under her palm and the danger gaining steadily closer. A strange urge took hold of her and the pen moved on paper.

Fifteen minutes later she closed the notebook and stared at her ink-stained hands. She had written the entire dream down as best as she could remember it and she had no idea why.

Her first morning in India had begun on a very odd note.

Feeling a tad foolish, she flung aside the blanket and headed towards the shower, brimming full of plans and a hope that the rest of the day would be less of a tangle.

Chapter Thirteen

Tabby didn't want to get out from under the shower. The warm water beating down on her sore back felt wonderful. She wanted to spend a good ten minutes longer letting the powerful spray massage the tension out of her neck . . . but she had a long list to get through. Reluctantly she turned the tap off, towel dried herself and walked back into the bedroom.

A quick glance at the clock on her bedside showed that it was already eleven. She changed into a short yellow sundress and rang the reception. They promised to send up a pot of tea and some toast and fruit for breakfast. The manager also gave her Maya and Chris's room number but said that both phones were on *do not disturb*.

She scanned her list of things to do as she ate her breakfast. Qutub Minar, Red Fort and the mysterious rust-resistant iron pillar of Delhi were on her agenda of sites to see for today. She would have to ask the manager how far they were and the best way to get there. She doubted Maya or Chris would want to come along.

She opened a travel book on India and turned towards the map of New Delhi. She paused in the middle of searching for the Lotus Temple and frowned at the toast in her hand. It tasted strange. Almost rancid. She grabbed the cup and took a gulp of hot, sweet tea washing away the aftertaste.

Feeling slightly uneasy, she picked up her handbag and left the room. Fresh air, she hoped, would make her feel better.

"How far away is . . ." Tabby paused as she flipped open her list and showed the pretty receptionist the name of the place.

"Qutub Minar," the receptionist smiled, showing a row of even white teeth. "Half an hour by taxi."

"And the Red fort?"

"Forty to fifty minutes by taxi. It depends on the traffic, Madam."

The manager came up to them. "Can I help you, miss?"

"Where can I get a taxi?"

"I can order one for you," the manager replied. He was staring at her legs.

Tabby crossed her arms. "I will let you know," she said sharply.

His eyes lifted to her face. He smirked.

Tabby turned around, her fists clenched at her sides. She wanted to punch his sleazy face.

She took a steadying breath and decided to walk around outside and leave the sightseeing until Maya and Chris were awake. She didn't think they would be too happy to find her gone for hours without informing them.

She stepped out into the sunshine and found everything bone dry, which was remarkable considering the heavy rainfall last night. The sun was blazing hot and the air humid, still and heavily perfumed with the scent of Indian Magnolia.

Sniffing appreciatively, she walked down the driveway and out the gate that had an armed guard posted next to it. Adjacent to the guest house was a fancy looking residential house that loomed up behind black iron gates. That, too, had a guard posted outside it.

She continued walking past many more grand homes with the sound of traffic humming softly in her ear.

A cow mooed somewhere and temple bells began ringing frantically in the distance.

She quickened her steps. The bells had sounded close enough to warrant an investigation.

The sun beat down bright and hot on the narrow road, and she wondered how the lush plumeria, neem and guava trees dotting the sidewalk did not spark and burst into flames from the heat. Further on, she spotted some sort of dark purple juicy fruits, the size of her thumb, fallen on the ground. Most were half eaten by birds and animals with dark juices oozing out and staining the ground. She had never seen fruits like that before.

She finally arrived at a junction where the road broadened on one side. Here the atmosphere felt different. It was dusty, the trees were scant and the grass grew in uneven clumps. The road had far more potholes and rubbish littered the streets.

An abandoned bullock cart with a broken wheel rested against a wall which was covered in bright peeling posters. The posters asked people to vote for a man whose face had been ripped off leaving only his bald sparkling head visible.

Still farther, a pile of stinking garbage lay abandoned with hundreds of happy flies buzzing around it.

The sun crawled up higher in the sky, and the sharp rays began to burn through her clothes, the piercing bright light giving her the beginning of a headache. She swallowed, trying to moisten her dry mouth. She desperately wanted water.

A small shop stood a few of feet away from her. Small, shiny metallic packets attached to strings dangled in front of the shop while glass jars full of sweets sat in front of a shopkeeper whose mouth was stained with betel juice.

She was about to take a step in the direction of the shop when suddenly a devious little monkey popped out of a scraggly bush and blocked her path. . . .

Tabby burst into the reception area and collapsed on the floor in front of the manager.

"Talking monkey tried to eat me," she panted. "This big, huge, size of a yeti—"

"Excuse me?" the manager frowned.

"Out there. It followed . . . dangerous . . . ." She gulped in air.

"Talking monkey?"

Tabby nodded frantically.

The manager cocked his head to one side. His beady eyes took in the bruised knee and the tiny little red scratches on her pale calves.

"Madame," he bobbed his head from side to side, "what happened? Can you be more clear only?"

Tabby waited until her breath had steadied and the panic had receded somewhat before launching into the story. "I left the guest house, turned right and walked to the very end of the road. I took another right and came upon a street. It was different. Not as clean. I spotted a shop at the end of this street and started walking towards it. I wanted to buy a bottle of water." She paused, took a breath and continued, "And that was when the monkey landed in front of me."

"Monkey," the manager nodded indulgently. "Brown monkey?"

Her head snapped up and her eyes blazed at the manager's condescending tone. "Big as a two-year-old, brown, with a pink furless face. It had a long swishy tail and sharp pointed teeth."

"And then?"

"Another monkey joined the first one. When I looked around, I realised I was surrounded by dozens of the wild creatures inching closer and closer to me."

The manager, in spite of himself, was intrigued. Even the receptionist standing behind the counter leaned forward to hear her tale.

"The monkeys," Tabby continued in a hushed voice, "seemed unafraid. Their eyes were glued to my bag."

"They wanted food," the receptionist spoke up.

Tabby nodded. "But I didn't have any food to give them. I didn't know how to distract them. I had never been this close to a monkey before in my life. My heart was thundering in my chest and the sick feeling in my stomach was growing worse. I looked around desperate for someone to come by and help me. And—"

"And?" the manager prodded.

"I saw him. The shopkeeper. He was looking at me with a fearful expression. He shouted something, but I couldn't understand his language. I gazed at him hopelessly, willing him with my eyes to leave his spot and come and help me. That was when the first monkey touched my leg."

"One kick would have sent the monkey flying and then you could have easily escaped," the receptionist scoffed.

Tabby's eyes narrowed, "I would have done that had something else not occurred. If you would let me finish, I will get to the good bit in a minute."

"Go on," the manager said.

"Where was I?" Tabby asked.

"Monkey touched your leg," the manager replied. For a moment, his eyes glazed over and he looked as if he envied the monkey.

"Right," Tabby said. "A furry paw with sharp claws touched my leg. I screamed and stopped breathing altogether because—"

The manager tensed, knowing the climax of the story had arrived. The receptionist leaned even further on the glass-topped table, now lying almost horizontal as she waited for Tabby to continue.

And after a short dramatic pause, Tabby spoke again in a hushed, breathy voice. "And then from the corner of my eye I spotted him. A large grey monkey with a black face, and a long, stiff tail. He was as tall as I'm, if not taller. He stealthily approached me from my left. I thought I was hallucinating, having a nightmare or suffering from a sun stroke. Monkeys this big do not exist. My head swam and my vision blurred. The grey monkey came closer. It was a huge, monstrous, colossal cryptid, as big as a yeti. I felt as if I had walked through a portal and landed in the Mesozoic era and at any moment a pterosaurs or a cynodont would come stomping around the corner."

The receptionist's eyes were now as wide as saucers.

"The grey monkey lifted its paws and roared," Tabby said in a sudden sharp voice that made her audience jump. "The smaller monkeys screeched and scattered. The grey monkey stopped roaring as soon as the last tail disappeared. And then he turned his attention to me." Her voice fell to almost a whisper. "I couldn't kick this giant and get away. I began to tremble . . . And then he spoke."

"Who spoke?" the manager asked in a hushed voice.

"The grey monkey spoke," Tabby replied.

"What did he say?" the receptionist asked enthralled.

"'Madam?' He queried with his giant paw lifted up in the air," Tabby replied.

The receptionist gasped.

Tabby continued in a soft, brave voice. "I froze, wondering if the monkey had truly spoken. And then he repeated himself and said 'Madam' in a clear high pitched voice. I knew then that I hadn't been mistaken that first time. He took another step, and now only a foot away opened his mouth with an expectant look in his eye as if he wanted to say something else. But I didn't wait to hear it. I screamed in terror and began running and did not stop running until I arrived here."

After a few minutes of thoughtful silence the manager spoke. "We do not approve of guests taking drugs, Madam. I am afraid I will have to call the police."

Tabby spluttered in shock.

"What is going on?" Mrs Mansukhani asked, appearing behind the manager. She spotted Tabby sitting on the floor with her head resting against the leg of the reception table. "Tabby? Are you all right—"

The manager flicked a disgusted glance at Tabby." This young lady has been doing drugs."

"No." Tabby desperately shook her head and moaned when her head hurt from the action.

"I have to inform the police," he went on.

Mrs Mansukhani stared down at Tabby. "Did you take drugs?"

"No," she repeated more firmly this time. "But I did see a talking monkey and it chased me. I'm not lying!"

Mrs Mansukhani bit her lip and thought for a moment. "Let me make a call. I am certain this is a misunderstanding."

"But—"

"One call," Mrs Mansukhani begged.

The manager scowled. "I am an honest man. Even if the prime minister comes and asks me to let her off, I won't."

Gayatri Aunty swayed up to them. "What happened?"

The manager told her.

Gayatri Aunty grinned in delight. "Chris wants to marry a loon?"

"Gayatri, stay out of this. " Mrs Mansukhani turned back to the manager. "You will look like a fool if this girl turns out to be telling the truth. And you will lose a lot of customers. Our family has booked fifteen rooms." She let the threat hang in the air.

He smirked. "How is she going to produce a talking monkey?" The receptionist standing next to him whispered something in his ear. He frowned and said, "One call, and if I am right, then I will call the police."

Mrs Mansukhani quickly punched in the number on the phone.

"Dev, I need your help. I am in the lobby," Mrs Mansukhani barked into the receiver.

The manager wilted. "You know Mr Dev?"

"My nephew," Mrs Mansukhani replied.

"Look, we can talk about this," the manager said with oily charm. "No need to involve him—"

"Too late," Tabby whispered.

The elevator pinged open and Dev strode out.

"What's going on?" he demanded.

"The manager suspects Tabby has taken drugs. He is threatening to call the police."

"Sir, if I knew she was your family friend, then I would have never questioned her."

Dev ignored the manager. He stooped next to Tabby and tilted her face up. His warm, cinnamon scented breath fanned her face as he checked her pupils and her pulse.

"Sir, if the young lady wants drugs, she can have drugs," the manager pleaded.

Dev glared at him.

"Sir, I will provide the drugs, sir," he continued babbling. "I will find the very best, sir."

Dev's face turned thunderous. "What did you say?"

The manager closed his mouth.

"What happened?" Dev asked, turning back to Tabby.

So Tabby told him. She told him about the small monkeys and the arrival of the big monkey. She swore up and down it was all true.

Dev's lips twitched when she finished the story. "I will be back in a moment," he said and walked out of the main exit.

Tabby grabbed the edge of the table and heaved herself up. She swayed slightly.

"You don't look well," Mrs Mansukhani commented worriedly. "Get her some water."

The manager scuttled away to do her bidding.

By the time Dev returned, Tabby was sitting in the coffee shop sipping from a tall glass of icy lemonade.

Dev had not returned alone. He had the grey monkey with him.

Gayatri Aunty took one look at the monkey and began laughing. The manager scowled, and Mrs Mansukhani permitted herself a small smile.

"Madam," The grey monkey pulled his monkey head off and revealed a human head, "I am in charge of chasing away the small monkeys."

Tabby blinked in confusion.

"Monkeys are a nuisance here," Mrs Mansukhani explained gently. "They steal and attack people, and since killing them is not feasible, men dress up in costume and frighten them away. It is his job."

"You couldn't tell it was a costume?" the manager snapped in irritation at Tabby. He wanted to add more, but Dev's warning glance stopped him.

Now that Tabby looked, she couldn't understand how she had missed it. The costume was poorly made and looked cheap and fake. Her cheeks burned with embarrassment.

The manager rolled his eyes clearly thinking Tabby was stupid.

Embarrassment was replaced by rage. Tabby wanted to fly across the table and repeatedly whack the manager on his head. She froze, wondering where that violent thought had come from.

Mrs Mansukhani exchanged a glance with Dev. He dipped his

head so slightly that Tabby almost missed it.

"Sir, photo," the grey monkey begged Dev.

Dev smiled obligingly as the monkey man took a picture with him.

Once the monkey man had thanked Dev a million times for the photo, he departed.

Dev now turned towards the manager. He spoke quietly in clipped even tones. "Your hospitality is deplorable. I am going to speak to the owner about this. You should have heard this young lady out, treated her with respect until the truth was discovered. Everyone is considered innocent until proven guilty."

"Yes, sir you are right, sir—"

"You should have warned her about the monkeys," Dev continued coldly.

Mrs Mansukhani caught Tabby's hand and gestured her to follow.

"Sir," the manager whined, "I am your fan, sir—"

"I don't care if you are a fan or a thirty watt light bulb," Dev replied.

"The monkeys are harmless—"

"A man was killed two years ago, a child mauled because of these very monkeys. And you are aware of the diseases these creatures carry—"

"That's why the man dressed as a monkey sir. We pay him—"

"So you knew about it and understood what that girl was saying and yet you continued to harass her?"

Tabby walked towards the elevator, and the sounds of the argument faded away.

"See, you have nothing to be embarrassed about," Mrs Mansukhani soothed her. "Monkeys are dangerous. If, God forbid, one of them had a disease and bit you . . ."

Tabby nodded, no longer feeling quite so silly.

Mrs Mansukhani touched Tabby's wrist, "I think you have a slight temperature, I am afraid you have a sunstroke or . . . Did you brush your teeth with tap water?"

Tabby nodded.

"I forgot to warn you to use only bottled water even while brushing. I have a feeling you are going to get the Delhi belly by this evening. You are already looking pale. Are you queasy?"

Again, Tabby nodded.

Mrs Mansukhani made a sympathetic cluck and led her into the room. "Eat something now. I suspect you won't be able to keep anything down in a few hours. I will sit with you and share a pot of tea, and then you should go to sleep—"

Tabby cut her off by leaning over and hugging her tightly. She couldn't help it. Mrs Mansukhani was just so . . . motherly. A lovely concoction of jasmine and sandalwood drifted up to her nose, and after a moment, she reluctantly let go.

"I will order the chai," Mrs Mansukhani said, looking pleased. "You will like it. We call it *masala chai*, similar to chai latte in England."

"My favourite," Tabby smiled.

Mrs Mansukhani ordered a slice of chocolate cake and sandwiches, along with the *masala chai*, which arrived speedily enough.

They shared the food while Mrs Mansukhani kept up a mundane, yet comforting chatter all throughout.

They drank the pot dry. Finally, Mrs Mansukhani got up to go. "If you need to call your mum, you can use my cell phone. It will be cheaper than making a call on the guesthouse phone."

"Thank you," Tabby replied. "But my mum . . . she is no longer . . . She is—"

"How old were you?"

"Fifteen."

Mrs Mansukhani patted Tabby's head and didn't offer any empty words. "Go to sleep," she said instead and left the room.

Chapter Fourteen

Tabby had the Delhi Belly. She spent the next two days closeted in the bathroom. Word spread, and relatives began appearing outside her bathroom door. They huddled outside like sympathetic chickens offering plenty of unhelpful advice. They admonished her for brushing her teeth with tap water and asked her to drink lots of lemonade to keep herself hydrated. All sorts of medicines were offered to her from charcoal tablets and Imodium to homemade healing concoctions such as warm water mixed with turmeric, pounded herbs mixed with carom seeds, and *khichdi*—a bland lentil and rice dish.

They asked her how much she had slept, what did her poo look like and how many times had she spewed her guts. Then they discussed the reluctantly given answers and assured her that it all sounded positive. She would be better in no time. No time at all.

It was a novel experience. She had been so used to taking care of herself whenever she was ill that suddenly having so many people worrying about her was touching and at the same time overwhelming. She wondered if Chris and Maya knew how lucky they were to have such a close-knit family.

It was on the third morning that Tabby felt well enough to put on her father's old grey jacket and mother's white dress and crawl downstairs to join everyone for tea.

Chris and his family were sitting on the balcony drinking *masala chai* and eating *pakoras*. It was raining again and everyone was talking about how wonderful the weather was

They were not being sarcastic.

Apparently, the rainy season was celebrated in India since it brought relief from the scorching summer heat and was beneficial for agriculture. Bollywood had further romanticised the monsoon season with its depiction of lovely young women prancing around in soggy saris.

Tabby took a seat next to Mrs Mansukhani and scowled at the cloudy sky. She didn't think she would ever love a rainy day. She had enough of it in England.

The sky darkened as if mocking her. Thunder roared and lightning flashed. A waiter brought over a few candles and placed them on the table.

"This is disgusting." Chris shook his half empty glass of what look like iced tea at the waiter. "Get me a cappuccino instead."

The waiter, who looked no older than seventeen, nodded apologetically.

"Also, ask someone to take a look at my room. The air-conditioner doesn't cool properly," Chris continued irritably.

Tabby frowned. Chris was never rude to the staff in England. What had gotten into him?

Chris caught her watching. He made a face. "It's miserable here, isn't it? I can't wait to get back to London. The food is terrible, the service rubbish and all these bloody mosquitoes will eat me alive."

"I like it here," Maya said, her eyes flashing in annoyance. She opened her mouth ready to argue further—

"Has the bus been booked?" Baby Aunty cut in. "And isn't Chapal Wale Babaji famous? I heard you have to stand in line for hours and hours to meet him."

"Babaji has a special relationship with our family. He has put an hour aside for us from his busy schedule. We will meet him in the VIP room. We won't have to wait," Mr Mansukhani replied.

"The last time I took my friend Shreya to meet Babaji," Mrs Mansukhani recalled, "he took one look at her and told her that she would meet her fourth husband within forty-eight hours. And sure enough she met him on her flight back home to Calcutta."

"I remember when I met him for the first time," Meena Aunty said. "He told me to call my cousin and ask him not to take the flight. I didn't know what Babaji was talking about, but I did as he asked. I called my cousin and found out that he was going to leave for a holiday that night. I convinced him to delay his flight by a day. And thank God I did because the flight he was going to take crashed into the Pacific, killing everyone on board."

Tabby felt a shiver run down her spine.

"Babaji told me that I would die at the age of fifty," Gayatri Aunty announced. "I am now sixty-one."

"You are a ghost?" Meena gasped.

"You are an idiot," Gayatri Aunty responded.

"How are you feeling?" Baby Aunty asked Tabby loudly.

"Better. A little disappointed though. I had made so many plans . . . I wanted to see a bit of Delhi."

"India is an experience," Dev said from behind her chair, making her jump. She hadn't heard him come up. "The moment you stop planning and let life happen, you will start enjoying your stay."

He leaned over her shoulder and filled a cup with coffee. He was waiting for the waiter to bring a chair for him.

"When are we leaving for Dehradun?" Tabby asked, trying to ignore his sculpted arm hovering close to her flushed cheeks.

"The men, Maya and some of the kids will take the flight tomorrow evening," Mrs Mansukhani answered Tabby. "Gayatri, Meena and I have booked a private bus for rest of the women that departs tomorrow morning at six. My mother doesn't like flying, so some of us decided to go by road."

"How much is the flight?" Tabby whispered in Maya's ear.

"Two hundred pounds," Maya whispered back.

Tabby paled. "And the bus?"

"Free. Nani, that is my Grandma, is paying for it."

"Can I join you on the bus?" Tabby asked Mrs Mansukhani.

"All the young ones are taking the flight," Gayatri Aunty objected. "What will you do with us boring ladies?"

"She can see a lot more if she goes by bus," Baby Aunty shot back. "And who says we are boring? Speak for yourself."

"But she is still recovering," someone else objected.

"I'm fine now," Tabby replied hurriedly. She wasn't completely, but she would rather suffer the six-hour journey on a bumpy road than spend on a flight she couldn't afford.

Chapter Fifteen

The early morning light filtered into the room through bamboo blinds, creating horizontal shadows on the floor.

Tabby smoothed her hair and looked under the bed to ensure she was leaving nothing behind. She spotted a purple hairband fallen next to the bedside table and tucked it into her furry brown handbag. The bell boy had already taken the suitcase down.

Sweeping a final glance around the room and bathroom, she stepped out into the hallway and softly closed the door behind herself.

When the elevator pinged open, she found Dev standing inside sporting a faint stubble and talking to someone on the phone. He barely glanced at her when she stepped in.

This was her chance, she realised, to thank him for helping her that day during the monkey incident. He may be a criminal, but she had been brought up right and wouldn't forget her manners.

How should she frame it?

Thank you very much for not thinking I am a looney bin?

No, that sounded wrong.

Thank you, for believing in me? Gross. That sounded sappy.

Thank you for helping me—

The elevator slid open, and Dev walked out. He was no longer on the phone.

She raced after him. They had walked half the length of the long, carpeted hallway when she decided to suck it up and just say thank you. Two words and no more.

She opened her mouth, but before she could speak, her head butted his broad chest.

"Watch where you are going," she exploded.

"You," he jabbed a finger in her direction, "banged into me."

Her eyes skittered away from his face. She knew he was right.

He looked down at her, his face sporting an insufferably patient expression.

She had half a mind to forget about thanking him and storm away.

"Hmm?" he prompted.

"I-You are blocking my way," she muttered.

"Why don't you say it?" he asked silkily.

"I don't have anything to say."

"So you make a habit of following people around for no reason?"

"I'm not following you. I'm going to meet everyone near the bus—"

"The bus is on the ground floor. I got out on the fifth floor, and you followed."

"Oh, I didn't realise I got out on the wrong floor." Bloody detective, she fumed inwardly.

A shadow of a smile crossed his face.

"Dev," a high-pitched girlish screech came from her right. She winced as two young girls shouldered their way past her to get to him.

"Autograph please," the girls begged.

Tabby frowned. She had noticed a lot of people asking him for an autograph or a picture. What did he do? Had he followed in his father's footsteps and become an actor as well? Maybe done a couple of Bollywood movies? He was good looking enough—"

"Miss Timmons?" Dev prompted. "If you have nothing to say to me, then why are you still waiting?"

The girls were gone.

"Thank you," Tabby finally blurted out.

Surprise widened his eyes briefly. He inclined his head. "You are welcome."

She turned to go.

"Wait," he said. "I wanted to tell you that day but didn't get a chance to . . . You should dress carefully."

Her shoulders stiffened. She turned back around and looked at his face. She found no sign of humour.

"Excuse me?" Her voice had gone dangerously quiet.

"Your skin," He cleared his throat and looked away. "You look different. People will stare at you on the streets. You can become a target. Wear long pants or jeans and full sleeves until you—"

"How dare you?" she blazed. She knew she was alone in a long empty corridor with a criminal who had probably murdered someone. She knew that if Dev wanted to, he could slit her throat and then get the sleazy manager to destroy all evidence of the fact.

She also knew that she should walk away right then and there, but her anger drowned out the sensible voice in her head. "I will wear what I please and when I please. You are nobody to tell me what to do. This is not the eighteenth century."

"Miss Timmons," he growled, "learn to hear the other person out before attacking them. I was thinking of your comfort. I have had a few foreign friends feel awkward in the beginning. It took them a few days to get used to being stared at. And the manager . . . he had been harassing you deliberately. I learned he looks for easy targets. Anyway, he has been fired—"

"Are you saying his disgusting behaviour was my fault because of the way I dress?"

"No. I am asking you to watch your step. You can wear what you like, but it might be easier to deal with hundreds of eyes raking your body when you are covered—"

She moved her handbag to her right shoulder. Her fingers were trembling. "Narrow-minded men like you should be . . . should be . . . oh! Something horrible should be done to people like you. You are the sort of man who wants a woman chained to the kitchen. You are a chauvinistic pig."

His jaw tightened and his eyes flared with a dangerous light.

Tabby closed her mouth and swallowed nervously. What in the world had gotten into her? She was never so irrational, bubbling with so many extreme emotions. She never objected like this when Chris told her what to wear. Did Delhi Belly infect the brain as well?

"I think it's best if you leave," he said abruptly.

"I think it's best if *you* leave," Tabby repeated, but this time her voice had lost its strength.

His lips quirked at her childish response and he took a step towards her.

That was all he had needed to do, for she promptly told her pride and dignity to lump it and fled back down the corridor.

Water bottles, thermoses filled with tea and coffee, bags of crisps, chocolate, sweets, sandwiches and *parathas* were being loaded onto the bus. Some of the women had already claimed their seats.

Tabby entered the dark grey air-conditioned bus and looked around. The seats looked comfortable with plenty of leg room. Even the backrest tipped back a good bit. She chose a window seat right at the back.

An old lady in a plain white cotton sari sat in the front of the bus shouting orders. She clutched a stained silver box in her bony hands, and every now and then she would open it up and pull out a betel leaf, put all sorts of funny little condiments on it, wrap it up and give it to whoever walked by her.

Tabby had been given one as well. She had taken one bite of it and almost choked. It was definitely an acquired taste.

"That's Maya's maternal grandmother," Baby Aunty said, twisting around in her seat to look back at Tabby. "The silver haired woman in the white sari. You can call her Nani. She has an awful temper, but when we stop for lunch, she will be the one making sure that the driver eats well."

The roar of the engine filled the air momentarily ending all talk, and Baby Aunty turned back to face the front.

The bus lurched forward and inched out of the narrow driveway.

Tabby quivered in childlike anticipation.

Once they had left the residential colony behind and joined the main road, the silence gave way to the ebb and flow of gentle chatter.

Tabby kept her eyes glued on the view outside. This was the first time she was truly seeing the country.

The traffic was sparse, and the sun was just beginning to brighten fully. The roads glistened with the early morning's rainfall. School children waited at bus stands and a few families were beginning to make their way to work.

Tabby spotted a family of five huddled together on one scooter. She watched them whizz away, praying they would arrive safely at their destination. Further on, steel shutters groaned as shopkeepers yanked them up to get ready for the day. Fruit and flower sellers whipped away brown and grey rags draped over wooden carts to reveal their wares.

The noise, too, was slowly but steadily increasing to a deafening roar. Trucks carrying sugar canes, bricks or hay thundered by. Tankers plodded along dripping water on the street, cars hooted just because they could, buses weaved through the traffic disregarding every traffic rule in the book.

It made her feel exhilarated and frightened. She was suddenly aware of her mortality and how fragile her body was. One dangerous turn and their bus could tip over and fall into the murky Yamuna River flowing beside them.

This was the India she had read about. Busy, chaotic and noisy. Bustling with life and energy. It was also stressful. Her heart was often in her throat as pedestrians ran in front of cars to cross the roads.

Their own driver sped down the highway, believing that since he was driving a big vehicle, he could rule the road. If there were an accident, the smaller cars would be squished. At the same time, he respectfully gave way to giant trucks. It seemed to be an unwritten rule.

The only rule.

It was in Meerut, a small town on the outskirts of Delhi, that Tabby first encountered a beggar.

The bus screeched to a halt at a traffic light, and Tabby, whose nose was pressed against the window, watched a thin young woman wrapped in a brown sari swiftly approach her side.

The young woman caught Tabby's eye and slowly lifted her hand to her mouth.

"Look away," Baby Aunty muttered from the front seat. She wore headphones and had her own head ducked low, her eyes resolutely fixed on her lap.

But Tabby couldn't look away from the haunted, hungry face. Her eyes grew large and wet. Her hand automatically scrabbled for change in her bag.

"If you have to give them food, not money," Gayatri Aunty said. She had arrived to hand over a plastic cup filled with *masala chai* to Tabby.

"You can't feel sorry for all of them," Baby Aunty added gently. "Or you will never be happy. How many times will you cry when you see a beggar? This is what we live with every single day. For our own mental peace, we need to harden ourselves."

"Help by donating to a good charity instead," Mrs Mansukhani said, coming up to them. She was carrying a plate of warm onion *bhajis* with green chutney on the side.

Tabby's eyes went back to the beggar. She didn't care what they said. She dug into her purse and pulled out a hundred rupee note, intending to give that as well as the cup of tea to the woman, but before she could open the window, the light changed and they sped away leaving the woman looking after her in heart-wrenching disappointment.

"You have homeless people in England as well," Gayatri aunt said. "And people who die of drugs and disease. And in America poverty is not novel. So why do you only feel sorry for the poor in India? Are your American ones not good enough?"

"Gayatri," Mrs Mansukhani said coldly, "shut up."

The sharp response, it seemed, touched a nerve. "You should learn to keep your future daughter-in-law under control. Look at her clothes," Gayatri Aunty snapped back. "If she were my daughter, I would have put some sense into her by now. Sniffling over a beggar. You are ruining her just like you ruined Maya. What are Maya's in-laws going to say when she answers back to them? She will be sent packing within a month."

"At least my children spend time with me and listen to what I have to say. Yours have met you four times in the last two years. Scared them away with your bitter tongue, have you?" Mrs Mansukhani asked cruelly.

"She gets like that whenever anyone dares to say anything about her children," A delighted Baby Aunty whispered to Tabby.

Tabby didn't smile back. Her mind was too full of the disappointed face. Why hadn't she acted quicker? Her eyes became misty, and she blinked furiously.

Nani, a vision in white and silver and smelling of cloves and Pear's soap, appeared next to her. She offered Tabby a swig from a bottle which turned out to be champagne. Champagne at nine in the morning along with fried onion *bhajis*— Tabby almost smiled as she took another sip. The bottle was passed around and plastic glasses filled up.

"One person cannot change the world, Tabby. Don't cry," Mrs Mansukhani patted her back.

"Grow a thick skin, or you will be depressed all your life," Gayatri Aunty muttered.

Word reached the bus driver. He decided to do his bit to cheer Tabby up. He turned on the radio, and soon a peppy Bollywood song blasted out from the speakers.

"Don't be sad o' lovely maid, for your lover awaits in Doon's green glade," Baby Aunty translated in a sing-song voice. "Paint your lips, don't be blue, Chug, chug, chug chug, the train rumbles through."

"Wipe away the tears, throw away the curry," Nani joined in. "He is here, he is here. Oh, he is here to kiss away your worry."

"Don't be sad o' lovely maid," chanted everyone on the bus. "He is here, he is here. Oh, he is here to kiss away your worry."

"Once again," Nani hollered.

Don't be sad, o', lovely maid
For your lover awaits in Doon's green glade
Paint your lips, don't be blue
Chug, chug, chug, the train rumbles through.
Wipe away the tears, throw away the curry
He is here, he is here,
Oh, he is here to kiss away your worry.

"Now the chorus!" Nani screeched.

The bus driver flipped a switch, and the ceiling split wide open, disco balls fell out and began rotating and flashing in time to the music. The bus twinkled and glittered in colourful lights and aunties leaped up on their seats, threw their hands in the air and began shimmying as if their life depended on it.

Shake your booty up and down
Rotate it left, right, round and round
Shake your booty, shake your booty
SHAKE IT all over town!
Oh yeah!

The sight of Nani rocking it like a star while bouncing on her seat and all the aunties' boogying while wrapped up in saris coaxed a smile out of Tabby.

Baby Aunty pulled Tabby up and made her join in teaching her a few quick Bollywood steps.

Tabby giggled and began dancing along with them until the song ended. They collapsed into their seats breathless and laughing.

Soon a new song came on the radio. This time a sad one. Tabby didn't know if the words were effective or if it was the wine that made everyone so sentimental, for every eye on the bus was moist by the time it ended.

The next few songs seemed to grow slower and slower and the

lyrics sadder and sadder until everyone was blubbering and howling in despair.

Beer bottles took the place of champagne by late morning. And it was only after lunch that the mood changed.

They were now passing fields of wheat, sugarcane and patches of wild rural landscape.

The women had begun playing *Antakshri*, a fun musical game. After many good-natured arguments, the game was scrapped although the singing did not stop, and everyone continued to sing and dance all the way up a mountain and down into the valley of Dehradun.

Chapter Sixteen

It was late evening when they drove into Dehradun. The sun was just setting and the sky had turned a fetching pink. The air felt clean and fresh and smelled of green trees, raindrops and wood smoke.

In the distance, the mystic Himalayas surged upwards piercing the dark grey clouds. The mountains appeared purplish grey and shadowy, as if made of mist and smoke, while Dehradun seemed to be lifting its bright little face up towards the magnificent snow-capped mountains looming over it.

Tabby took a deep, satisfying breath.

The bus came to a standstill outside a large red and white bungalow cheerfully perched on a hill. The house was owned by a retired couple, Mr and Mrs Khanna, who were old friends of Nani's. They had lots of spare rooms and had insisted on hosting all of them.

Tabby heaved her handbag further up her shoulder, grabbed the handle of her suitcase and followed the rest of the party through the large green iron gates.

Chris's father, a few uncles that Tabby had met in England and Baby Aunty and Meena Auntie's husbands were standing in the driveway. They seemed to be shouting instructions or asking questions in Hindi.

"Where are Maya and Chris?" Mrs Mansukhani asked worriedly.

"Off to the shops," replied Dev. He was reclining on a chair placed under a large, leafy tree, his eyes were closed and exhaustion was etched in every line on his face.

"What is going on?" Tabby asked Baby Aunty, who was standing next to her.

"A snake has entered the house. A maid saw it in the corridor. The servants are trying to catch it," Baby Aunty replied.

Tabby turned pale. "A snake?"

"A poisonous one," Meena Aunty said happily. "One bite and you would probably die. Isn't this thrilling?"

"We couldn't have asked for a better welcome," Gayatri Aunty remarked dryly.

Someone shouted from within the house.

Tabby tensed. Had anyone got bitten?

Another shout and everyone started talking at once in Punjabi.

"It's been caught," Baby Aunty translated for Tabby. "Don't worry. The people here are used to such incidences. They know how to handle it."

Tabby smiled weakly trying to put up a brave front, but she lingered back and was the last one to enter the house.

It was a lovely, big house decorated in the style of an old hunting lodge. Big fat beams of exposed wood ran along the high ceiling. Deer antlers, long rifles and colourful oil paintings depicting men in hunting gear dotted the walls.

"You don't mind sharing a room with Maya, do you?" Mrs Khanna asked in a soft voice.

Tabby smiled down reassuringly at the grey haired woman. "I don't mind at all."

The lines smoothed on the gentle face. "Then here is your room," she said opening the door with a flourish.

Tabby stepped in and almost clapped her hands in glee. The room was huge. The twin beds were placed so far apart that they might as well have been in separate rooms. The walls were painted cream and the fireplace in the corner was made of marble, but it was the view that filled Tabby with joy. She could see the mountains from the large French windows, and the private balcony seemed to dip into the middle of a tropical forest.

"It's perfect," Tabby sighed.

"Don't open the windows or the snakes and other creepy crawlies will get in. The iron bars on the window should keep the leopards and other big cats out, but the balcony has no bars. So be careful and make sure it remains locked all the time," Mrs Khanna warned.

Tabby deflated.

"The bell on the side table rings in the kitchen. You can press it whenever you want something or call from the phone. The direct number to the kitchen is 102 and . . ." Mrs Khanna hesitated.

"And?"

". . . and" she continued, "if you want to speak to Chris, then you can dial 203 and you will be connected to his room."

"Thank you," Tabby said.

"If you need anything else, let me know," Mrs Khanna said before closing the door behind herself and leaving Tabby alone in the room.

Tabby skipped up to the bed near the window and sat down. The bed near the bathroom had Maya's purple shawl and brown leather backpack on it. She wondered if Maya had given her the bed with the stunning view to be nice to her or because if some dangerous animal crept in through the window, it would get Tabby first and give Maya a chance to escape.

She decided it was the latter reason, since Maya didn't strike her as the sentimental sort.

The door opened and Maya strode in.

"Wassup?" she jerked a chin in Tabby's direction and then without waiting for a reply pulled out her sleek silver laptop and put on pink headphones.

Tabby ducked her head and hid a smile. Nope, not sentimental at all.

After a noisy dinner, Tabby slept well that night. Even the thought of wild creatures lurking outside her bedroom window did not keep her awake. The bus journey had tired her out more than she had realised.

She woke the next morning to the sound of Maya pottering about in the room.

"Good morning," Tabby said sleepily and then blinked. She rubbed her eyes, "Maya?"

"What do you think?" Maya asked twirling around. She was wearing an Indian *salwar kameez* in soft shell pink, sweet little bell-shaped pearl earrings, silver bangles and sparkling slippers. She had a matching pink dot in the middle of her forehead, and her hair, which was braided in a simple style, hung over her shoulder, reaching her small waist. Best of all was her smile. She looked happy, a tiny bit shy and completely unlike the cold, perfect Maya.

"Beautiful," Tabby said sincerely.

Maya grinned. "I love Indian clothes."

"I can see why. It suits you."

"Hurry up and get ready. We are going shopping."

"Didn't you go yesterday?"

"Yesterday I needed to get away from all the old men. Besides I can't smoke in front of the family. They would throw a fit if they caught me with a packet of ciggies. So, I dragged Chris along, and we went and sat in a coffee shop."

"What time do you want to leave for the shops?"

"Eleven?"

"What time is it right now?"

"Eight."

"Ok," Tabby yawned and stretched. She could have easily slept in for another few hours.

Maya chucked her braid over her shoulder so that it hung down her back. She observed the effect in the mirror. "The men are sitting on the veranda in front of the house talking about cricket, elections and the budget. The women are having breakfast in the back garden, next to the servant's quarters."

Tabby stifled another yawn, "Be down in a moment."

After Maya had left, Tabby pulled out her diary and began writing about everything that had occurred the day before.

It wasn't to keep up an appearance of a writer that she put pen to paper. It was a way to record her memories of the trip, and she found she enjoyed the process. It gave her clarity.

She got dressed soon after. She wore long khaki coloured pants along with a bellowing cream shirt. She emptied some of the contents of her handbag into a drawer to make it lighter and departed in search of breakfast.

She had just closed the room door behind herself when she spotted Dev approaching her. She tensed.

"Is Maya in the room?" he asked stopping in front of her.

She recalled the argument they had had back in Delhi.

He seemed to be thinking similar thoughts, for he raked a glance over her clothes, noting that her limbs were covered. He did not gloat.

Feeling annoyed for no discernible reason, she moved to get away.

His palm slammed the wall next to her head, blocking her exit. "I asked you a question. Have you," he asked pronouncing each word loudly and slowly, "seen Maya?"

Her heart began thundering in her chest. He was so close, she could feel the heat radiating from him. Her head started feeling a little dizzy, and her eyes sprang to his lips and traced their shape.

What would it feel like to have him kiss her?

Frightened of the intense emotions coursing through her, she jerked her head to leave from the other direction. She was madly attracted to him. She had never felt this kind of chemistry before in her life.

His other hand shot up and hit the wall blocking her escape route once again.

"What is your problem?" he asked, a spark of anger flared in his dark, almost black eyes.

"She is not here," Tabby told his chin. He had a faint stubble. She wondered if it would tickle her palm if she caressed it. She dropped her gaze to his shoes. Shoes were safe. Nothing sexy about shoes . . . unless you begin wondering what the size of the shoe said about . . . Oh, god, she desperately wanted to get away. He was standing too close, her brain was getting scrambled. Another moment of this and she would—

"You are one strange woman," he said, dropping his arms. He was eyeing her like she was a curiosity in an Indian museum.

Tabby ducked her head and walked away as fast as she could without it looking like she was outright running.

Once her heart stopped thundering, she tried to analyse what had happened back there. She must have eaten something funny which had made her brain fog up. This kind of head reeling attraction did not happen in real life. It wasn't possible.

How could a man steal your breath and your thoughts just by standing close to you?

She shook herself until she felt somewhat normal again and joined the women in the back garden.

It was a fairly large garden filled with lush looking mango, banana, and guava trees along with emerald green patches of red and green chillies, lime, tomatoes and many others she couldn't identify.

She took a seat next to Meena Aunty, and no sooner had she sat down than Nani complained that she had left her spectacles in her room. Tabby knew Nani's knees bothered her so she volunteered to fetch them.

"Since you are going, please get me the book I was reading," Baby Aunty requested. "My room is right next to Nani's."

When she came back, it was to find everyone reminiscing about the times they had encountered a wild animal.

"Wild elephants are the worst," Mrs Khanna was saying. "They always sit on the train tracks, and the passengers have to wait, sometimes for hours until the elephants decide to walk away. We were caught once in our car for four hours because an elephant decided to have a nap in the middle of the road. No one dares to shoo them off."

"Once," Meena Aunty said, "we were going to Ladakh. It is up in the north of India," she added for Tabby's benefit. "And we were driving down this dark, treacherous road. We had to go slow since the path was thin and slippery with snow. And then, all of a sudden, the headlights of our car illuminated the glowing eyes of a large animal waiting at the edge of the road. The driver tried to accelerate but the animal, which incidentally turned out to be a snow leopard, leaped with lightning speed and landed on the bonnet of our car. It sat there for a good fifteen minutes before getting bored and stalking off. I have never been so frightened in my life."

"Pity it didn't eat you," Gayatri Aunty muttered under her breath.

"Tabby," Mrs Mansukhani whispered so as not to disturb Baby Aunty, who had launched into a story about her motorcycle journey across India, "can you take this up to Chris? He is not feeling well and seeing you might brighten his mood up a bit."

Tabby took the tray loaded with a cup of coffee, porridge, a bottle of cough syrup and vapour rub.

"Thanks," Mrs Mansukhani patted her back.

The rooms had numbers etched in gold on the doors. Mrs Khanna said this place had been a functioning guest house before they bought it, and she had decided to leave the etchings since it looked quaint.

Tabby balanced the tray on her knee and knocked on the door of room no. 203.

"Come in," came a hoarse order.

Tabby entered the room. It was similar to her own, except it had a lot more blue in it. She set the tray on the table.

"Good morning," she chirped.

"Tabby?" he groaned.

She froze near the doorway. "You are wearing your underwear on your head."

The said garment was quickly whipped off and tucked under the blankets.

"I had a good reason," he said flushing red.

She helped him sit up in bed. "I'm all ears."

"My head was cold."

"You could have worn your clothes."

"They are on the couch at the other end of the room. I didn't want to get up."

"Covered your head with a blanket?"

"Not likely. My chest is congested, my nose blocked, and the thought of smothering myself under this quilt. . . ." He shook his head looking horrified.

"But wearing boxers on your head?"

"They were nice and toasty," he replied sulkily.

"Ingenious," she grinned and handed him the porridge.

He turned his face away.

"Come now, a few bites," she coaxed. She held a heaped spoonful near his mouth. "Open up."

"Will you rub Vicks on my chest and back?" He asked pushing away the food and reaching for the coffee instead.

She nodded and set the tray aside.

He gulped down half the coffee and then lay back down.

Gingerly, she pulled the blanket down and opened the tub of Vicks. She coated her fingers with the stuff and began rubbing his chest in circular motions. His chest was very hairy.

He kept his eyes closed and his hands under the back of his head.

She wondered if she could use this moment to seduce him. They were alone, the rooms had thick walls . . . Her fingers slowed becoming more of a caress.

But he was ill. Surely he wasn't in the mood . . . or was he? Was this his way of initiating things?

"Pass me the tissue. I wanna blow my nose," he wheezed.

Definitely not in the mood, Tabby thought, as she handed him a box of tissues.

He blew his nose a few times, mopping up the snot, and coughed up a goodly amount of phlegm.

"This bloody place is going to kill me. So many allergens. I have to take seven big fat pills every morning to keep my immune system in order. Have you tried sea buckthorn pills? No? Good stuff. And thank goodness for chamomile tea. I brought a giant box from England. Let me know if you get too stressed; I will let you have a tea bag or two. All the smog, the pollution and the dust. And the food! You need an iron stomach to ingest the stuff . . ."

Tabby's eyes glazed over as he continued ranting for a few more minutes. She only came alive when she heard him say he wanted to sleep.

She bent over and kissed him on the forehead. "Get well soon," she whispered. He looked so sweet, like a grumpy child. She did like him a lot, and she wished they could use this trip to learn more about each other. Set a strong foundation before marriage so to speak.

"Don't come close to me or the germs will hop from me to you," he said gruffly.

"I don't mind," she replied.

"You should," he snapped irritably.

She took a steadying breath. No point in getting mad at him. He was ill. "I will come and see you in a few hours."

A snore was her only answer.

Chapter Seventeen

Tabby and Maya departed shortly after eleven and arrived at Paltan Bazaar.

The market turned out to be teaming with people, even this early in the day. There were shops selling brightly coloured plastic buckets, tubs and crockery. Some stalls had heaps of colourful clothes piled on top of long wooden counters with handmade price tags dangling from them. Electronic, furniture and toy shops with bright neon signs leaped out at them every so often.

Maya headed towards one of the clothing shops that had a mannequin standing on the doorstep dressed in a vibrant fuchsia and gold sari.

"Good price, good price, madam," the shopkeepers yelled the moment they spotted Tabby walking by. "Come, come, I show you," screeched another eager vendor.

The shopkeepers were not the only ones who were noisy. Rickshaw drivers tinkled their bells as they sped by, cars honked, customers chatted and bargained, cows mooed, and somewhere someone rhythmically hammered metal.

Maya moved Tabby out of the way as one of the men walking by almost rammed into her. "Don't mind the looks," she warned.

Tabby bit her lip. She understood now what Dev had been trying to say. She felt as if every eye on the street was on her. Some of the men continued to stare even after she made it clear that she had caught them looking. They remained unembarrassed and continued to ogle. She would have felt worse in a short summer dress. And it wasn't just her that they were staring at. They were also staring at Maya, who still had on the *salwar kameez*.

"You will get used to it. They mean no harm. Be careful, though, when walking around in crowded areas," Maya said, smoke trickling out of her mouth and nostrils.

They were standing outside one of the few shops that were air-conditioned. Maya finished her cigarette, and they went inside.

They sat down on the stools placed in front of a long glass counter. A round-faced shopkeeper with an impressive pot belly and a number of solid gold chains strangling his neck greeted them.

"Tea or coffee, Ma'am?" he asked.

"Coffee," Maya said, and then pointed at one of the shawls wrapped in clear plastic placed on the shelf behind him.

"Tea," Tabby responded to his questioning look.

"The hot drinks will keep us here for longer, and we may buy more than we intend," Maya explained under her breath. "Marketing tactic."

Tabby opened her mouth to respond when a familiar laugh sounded behind her. A deep, rich, rumbling chuckle that made her stomach flip.

She turned around and searched the shop. It was a large shop but empty, save one other man minding the counter on the opposite end.

The laugh rang out again.

"I agree," Dev chuckled somewhere.

Tabby followed the eyes of the other shopkeeper and found him staring at a small TV mounted up on the wall in one corner. Dev's handsome face filled the screen.

She shot a glance towards Maya, who was engrossed in masses of wool, lace and pashmina shawls. She turned her attention back to the TV.

It appeared to be a news channel. The volume was low, but if she strained her ears and moved forward in her seat, she could catch a few sentences.

Dev was sitting on a chair facing two other men. One had shocking white hair and was smiling good-naturedly, while the other looked menacing.

And from what Tabby could make out, Dev was not the one being interviewed but was the one conducting the interview.

"If you continue your line of questioning," the sour-faced man was telling Dev in English, "then you will prove yourself to be a terrible journalist and lose your job soon enough."

Dev grinned in amusement. "Really, Mr Chopra? And who would throw me out? Your research team has let you down. They failed to

108

inform you that I own this channel and I *can* and I *will* ask whatever questions I damned well please."

Maya touched Tabby's shoulder. She dipped her head towards the TV. "It's a repeat telecast of a very famous interview that occurred a few years ago. The one with white hair is the current prime minister, and the one next to him is the opposition leader. Getting the two together in one room to debate on national topics before the elections was a coup for Dev. No other journalist had managed it before in Indian history."

"He is a journalist?" Tabby asked in disbelief.

"Well, he owns two national news channels and a few smaller newspapers and publications. But he prefers to be known only as a political journalist," Maya replied. She stood up and went to the full-length mirror. She draped a cream lace shawl over one shoulder and a black lace one over the other.

Tabby pointed to the black. Her mind was working furiously.

Maya picked up an olive green shawl with a pink paisley border next and tied it around her neck like a scarf.

Tabby made a face at the colour. "Why do people treat him like he is a celebrity?"

"Because he is one. A celebrity journalist. It all began when he had been working for a news agency. He was sent to cover a disastrous flooding that had occurred in a rural district of Bihar. While all other reporters were faithfully covering the footage and gathering sound bites, Dev threw his camera down and began helping the rescue team which was clearly shorthanded. He put his life at risk again and again and helped save many, many lives. It was unheard off. Another cameraman recorded the entire thing, and it was later broadcasted nationwide. Next thing you know Dev is being hailed as a hero."

Tabby stood up and walked over to a rack of saris. She stroked the lovely silks thoughtfully.

"That was not the end," the shopkeeper, who had been listening to them, spoke up. He had a thick Indian accent, but his words flowed naturally and without any hesitation. "Dev Sir has continued his good work. He has built up an empire based on the fact that people know he is honest. He has put himself in danger over and over again for the good of our country."

"But he was in jail," Tabby mused aloud.

The shopkeeper snorted. "They found a dead body in his house.

But the post mortem proved that when the man died, Dev Sir was in Japan attending a conference. He had been in Japan for that entire week while the dead body lay in his living room. His cleaner found the corpse. His passport as well as footage from security cameras in the hotel he stayed in proved his innocence. Someone was trying to frame him and did an awful job of it. Dev Sir was released from jail in less than two weeks."

"Why would someone try and frame him?" Tabby asked.

"He has unmasked many dishonest politicians, creating many powerful enemies in the criminal world," Maya replied. "Many people would benefit from his death." She dropped the bunched up pashmina shawl on the counter as if her appetite for shopping had been killed.

"I worry about him," the shopkeeper confessed.

The raw emotion in the man's face, a man whom Dev had probably never encountered in his life, touched Tabby. And just like this one man, millions of Indians felt the same for Dev.

It was strange, but even when Chris had told her Dev had murdered someone, somewhere deep in her heart, she hadn't believed it. There was something intrinsically good about Dev. She knew her behaviour towards him was nothing to do with the fact that he had been imprisoned, but to do with the electric chemistry that shimmered between them. She was running away from that chemistry. It wasn't right to feel it, not when she was engaged to Chris.

The sound of Maya opening the zip on her wallet broke the moment. The shopkeeper snapped back into mercenary mode and efficiently convinced Maya that five shawls was no big number and, in fact, she must buy one more to even things out.

"I love shopping here," Maya said dumping the packages on the backseat of the car. "Now for some *chaat.*" She led Tabby towards a guy standing on the side of a road with a portable stove frying little pancakes in oil. She asked him for two plates of *aloo tikki.*

"I will get sick," Tabby objected.

"Oh, shut up and live a little," Maya dared. "You can't stop doing fun stuff just in case you fall sick, and if you do, then pop a few medicines. I won't let you die."

"You are different here," Tabby observed. "Freer. Happier."

Maya shrugged. "It's where I belong."

Tabby understood. She felt the same about America.

The man behind the stove offered her a heaped plate.

Tabby flashed him a nervous smile and took a reluctant bite of the *chaat*. It turned out to be a fried potato dish topped with yogurt and generously sprinkled with tongue-tingling spices. It was like an explosion of flavours in her mouth. Her eyes widened in delight. It was spicy but at the same time very moreish.

"I have been thinking," Maya said, licking yogurt off her lips, "about a plan."

"Cuckoo Singh?" Tabby guessed.

Maya bobbed her head in agreement. "When I initially learned about Daaji's proposition, I decided to discover as much about Cuckoo as possible. One day his mother let slip that before I had come into the picture she had put an advertisement in the national paper looking for a bride for him." At Tabby's shocked expression, Maya shook her head." That's not the intriguing bit. A lot of Indian families look for brides and grooms through advertisements, matrimonial websites and now social networks. What was intriguing was the ad itself. I found it in my future mother-in-law's suitcase."

"You rooted through her stuff?"

"Of course. I had to find out for myself what I was getting into. What if they turned out to be psychotic criminals?"

Tabby stuffed her mouth with another spoonful of the *chaat* to save herself from replying.

"In the matrimonial ad they had mentioned that they wanted an educated, fair, light-eyed girl, who was also . . . pure. And the pure bit is key."

"Pure?"

"Virgin," Maya smirked. "It's a conservative mindset where people think a girl should be 'untouched' before marriage."

"And you think Cuckoo Singh thinks like that?"

"Yup. He doesn't drink, disapproves of parties and even objects to women wearing jeans."

"Huh," Tabby said. She wondered if Chris believed in the same thing. Was that why they had never made love? She took a deep breath and asked, "Do all Indian men think like that?"

"No, only the dumbasses."

"So," Tabby mused, "when you meet Cuckoo Singh next, you are going to regale him with your sexual exploits?"

"He is coming tonight. I am going to take him up to the terrace and confess a whole lot of naughty things."

"This I can't wait to see."

Maya smiled an evil little smile. "It should be fun."

That evening Cuckoo Singh and his parents joined them for dinner. They were staying at a nearby hotel, so Maya had to work quickly and get him up on the terrace before they returned.

Maya began fluttering her lashes at Cuckoo when the salad arrived. By the time the main course, consisting of *paneer makhani*, *tandoori chicken*, *naan*, *biryani*, *daal makhani* and pickled onions was served, she had progressed to looking at the door and then looking back at him.

Mrs Mansukhani shot worried glances at her daughter. No one else seemed to notice Maya's odd behaviour.

Cuckoo Singh devoured three *tandoori* chicken legs before getting the point. He looked scandalised.

A laugh escaped Tabby, and the rice she had been eating went down the wrong way.

Maya was out of her chair and beside her in a trice. Mrs Mansukhani came up to her and patted her back to help dislodge the morsel.

Tabby looked towards Chris. He looked at her once with a frown on his face as if her coughing fit had interrupted some important discussion.

Tabby's chest eased and she stopped coughing, but her eyes continued to water. And the tears weren't entirely the result of her choking fit.

Maya grabbed at the chance that Tabby had unknowingly given her. She went up to Cuckoo's chair, discreetly pinched his flabby arm and jutted her chin towards the door. She glared at him for good measure.

After an agonizing ten minutes, "Bebackfromwashroom," Cuckoo Singh muttered quickly to no one in particular and headed out the door.

Maya didn't bother giving any explanation. She winked at Tabby and then slipped away silently.

Tabby waited a few moments before following Maya out. She

tiptoed up four flights of stairs until she reached the rusted door right at the top.

The door was ajar, and she could hear low, urgent voices talking rapidly. A faint yellow light from the terrace was filtering out to illuminate the landing, and as promised, Maya had left an empty glass in one dark corner.

Tabby picked up the glass, placed it on the wall and stuck her ear to it.

The voices became clearer.

"This is not how women from good families behave," Cuckoo Singh was scolding Maya.

"But I have to tell you something important. Before it is too late," Maya replied firmly.

Tabby felt someone come up behind her. The glass slipped from her startled fingers, but before it could hit the ground with a crash, a large, dark palm shot out and caught it.

She looked up and found Dev frowning at her. He mutely held the glass out to her and placed a finger on his lips.

She nodded, her heart still thundering from the brief fright he had given her.

He put a hand in his jacket pocket and pulled out another glass. He tipped his head towards the wall.

Again Tabby nodded, replaced her own glass on the wall and resumed eavesdropping. It was a difficult task considering his proximity was once again fogging her mind. She couldn't blame the food this time.

She took a deep breath and forced herself to focus.

"I am not who you think," Maya was saying.

"You are not Maya?" Cuckoo asked, a hint of confusion in his voice.

"No, no, I am Maya, but I am not what you think I am. I mean my nature . . . I am not that."

"Explain."

"I wanted to tell you before . . . before you discovered it for yourself on the wedding night. I don't want to be accused of lying later on."

"Wedding night? Oh . . . You mean you are not a woman. You are a man . . . or is it both?"

A short silence fell after that. Maya appeared to debating if she should agree with Cuckoo Singh's bizarre analysis.

It could work, Tabby thought. Nothing better to send a straight man running. She glanced over at Dev, wondering what he was thinking.

She didn't have to look far since he was standing just a few inches away from her. The landing was so cramped that it was remarkable that the two had even managed to stand next to each other.

She gazed at his long lashes shadowing his face. He smelled clean, warm, and intensely earthy. His face was turned towards her, his pose identical to her own, one hand cupping the glass, ears straining to hear the conversation.

He was just so . . . *manly*. She always thought of Chris as cute, boyish and good-looking, but Dev . . . Dev could never be a boy. She couldn't imagine him ever being young. There was an intensity in his face, a certain controlled manner in the way he held himself that spoke of a raging passion simmering under his skin. Her fingertips tingled with an urge to reach out and smooth the single deep line near his brow.

He caught her staring.

She dropped her gaze, her face flushed.

"No," Maya spoke again, "I am a girl."

"Thank God," Cuckoo giggled weakly. "You had my good internals all knotted up."

"But I am not a typical Indian girl. I have no values. I am bad."

"Bad?"

"Very bad. Awful."

"Do you have a boyfriend?"

"Not a boyfriend per se . . . but I have had a few flings," Maya dropped her voice to almost a whisper.

Tabby squeezed her ear as close to the glass as possible.

"I see," Cuckoo Singh said. "Only, I must say I am not surprised. After all, you did grow up in England. The negative influences of western society must have rubbed off on you . . . but I can see now that you are very sorry about your morals running loose in the past. Still, I am willing to forgive you and marry you—"

"No, no, you can't," Maya's objected loudly.

"But I want to—"

"No, see you don't understand. I have been bad. I have . . . you know . . . warmed lots of beds."

"You have had, I mean done . . . I mean, WHAT?"

"Precisely."

"You have lost that sacred part of yourself?"

"Right!" Maya responded in relief. "That sacred part of me went bye, bye long ago."

"How old were you?"

"Seventeen."

"And you only . . . that one time?"

"Oh, nooo, many more times. Many, many more times."

"I see," he said thoughtfully. "Is this a problem of yours?"

"It is," Maya replied clearly thinking that the worse it sounded, the better her chances of getting rid of him.

"You mean you go off and do the hanky-panky with anyone?"

"Yes," Maya's voice came out all funny and strangled. "I am insatiable when it comes to . . . hanky-pankying."

Cuckoo Singh fell silent mulling over all he had learned. After a few tensed moments, he spoke, "I appreciate your honesty," he said, his voice trembling with emotion. "I admire a woman who can share her flaws so truthfully, that is brave enough to admit her worst traits. You have won my heart," he gushed. "Now, I would like to share with you an encounter I had once with a Thai ladyboy—"

"Eh?"

"I know you are the one for me. I can share my darkest secrets with you since you have done the same—"

"Why are you unbuttoning your shirt?"

"I am willing to offer myself to you to satisfy your desires. You can do what you want to me as many times a day as you like. I shall not object. I will make sure you are satiated. You will never have to seek out another man's arms. And afterwards I will tell you all about the ladyboy—"

"Don't! Oh, god you must need a mini lawn mower to get rid of the hair on your chest. No, no, not the pants. Please, not the pants . . . Tighty whiteys? Really?"

Tabby snorted and tried to stifle the laughter bubbling inside her. She looked over at Dev and found that he too was trying to bite down on a smile.

He felt her eyes on him and looked in her direction.

It was a mistake.

They caught each other's eye and it set the two of them off. They dissolved into helpless laughter.

Tabby snorted again, which further tickled them both. They tried to stop laughing, to be as silent as possible, but the more they tried, the harder they laughed.

Finally, Dev grabbed Tabby's hand and yanked her away from the wall. Between fits of quiet chuckles, he gestured down the staircase.

She nodded. It was best to get away before they lost complete control of themselves and made a noise loud enough to alert Cuckoo Singh.

They hurried down the stairs and turned into the corridor that led to Tabby's room.

Tabby collapsed outside the room door and finally gave in to laughter.

Dev slid down next to her, his shoulders shaking with uncontrollable mirth.

"We shouldn't be laughing," Tabby wheezed.

"Poor Maya, Cuckoo—" He broke off to start chuckling again.

Tabby had never found the name Cuckoo this funny before, but the way Dev said it . . . She clutched her stomach, willing herself to get a grip. "Foo, foo, foo," she spluttered unable to get coherent words out of her mouth.

"Finding this funny are we?" Maya's cold voice sliced through the laughter.

Chapter Eighteen

"We weren't laughing at you," Tabby sat up, all amusement gone from her face. She spotted a tear glittering on Maya's cheek.

Maya whipped around and banged open the bedroom door.

Dev caught the door and held it before she could lock it behind herself.

Tabby quickly scrambled into the room, and Dev followed.

Maya ignored them. She went and sat cross-legged in the middle of the bed. She opened her laptop and tried to stick the headphones into the socket, but her hands were trembling too hard to manage it. She cursed when the wire slipped from her fingers for the third time.

Tabby extracted the laptop and the headphones from her hand and put them on the ground next to the bed. Before Maya could open her mouth to demand it all back, Tabby hugged her.

Maya's shoulders tensed for a moment before she relaxed and allowed the embrace.

"I'm sorry," Tabby whispered.

Tabby felt the bed dip as Dev came and sat down next to them. With another heartfelt squeeze, she let Maya go.

"We were laughing at Cuckoo, not you," he said, reaching over to kiss the top of Maya's head.

"It didn't work," Maya sobbed. "I was hoping that it would be all over today. Tomorrow we meet Babaji and then leave for Punjab where my wedding preparations will begin. I will be officially engaged next week and married in just over a month."

"We won't let that happen," Dev said.

"You are not even coming with us," Maya snapped at him. "You hate Daaji so much that you are willing to overlook my feelings. You won't stay with us in Punjab because Daaji owns the house or attend my wedding because he is paying for it. How are you going to help me get out of the marriage when you are not even there?"

Tabby saw Dev's jaw clench. "I can't let him think he has won," he said looking away. "If I stay in his house, eat his food . . . that is what he will believe. That finally he has got me under his thumb. And just like the rest of the family, he will think he can control me as well."

"Is your ego so large?" Maya asked. "He is an ill old man. How does it matter what he thinks? Let him win."

"He threw my parents out, left us to starve and turned his backs on us when we needed him most," Dev bit out. "Our independence is hard earned, Maya. I cannot live under his roof. He will think I have come crawling back, and he has earned his right to lord it over us once again. I will not let him win."

"He loves you, Dev. He always speaks well of you," Maya pleaded.

He rubbed his temple, his face lined with exhaustion.

Tabby looked from Dev to Maya. They seemed to share the sort of brother-sister bond that was lacking between Maya and Chris. She chewed her bottom lip, wracking her brains to think of something that would solve both their problems.

"I have an idea," she offered hesitatingly.

Dev's dark eyes locked on her face.

"Why don't you come to Punjab—she lifted her hand to stop him from speaking, "listen for a moment. Come to Punjab, stay in Daaji's house but don't let him know. Your problem is that Daaji will think he has won some sort of a battle for control if you agree to stay under his roof. But if he doesn't find out, then he doesn't win."

Maya slapped the pillow in excitement. "The house has plenty of rooms. Daaji can't go up the stairs, so he will never discover you. You can help me stop the wedding and have the added satisfaction of tricking Daaji."

Dev's mouth twitched, but his eyes still looked hesitant.

Maya grabbed his hand. "Dev," she wheedled. "You have to help me or I won't get the money Daaji promised to give Chris and me. Please, please, please, Dev. Say you will come to Punjab."

"He promised to give Chris a quarter of million as well?" Tabby asked. Her voice sounded odd as if suddenly her ears were filled with air.

Maya turned stricken eyes towards Tabby.

"You didn't know?" Dev asked.

"I didn't," Tabby replied.

Dev dropped his long dark lashes but not before Tabby caught the pity shimmering in his eyes.

She took a sharp, painful breath. The air suddenly felt thick and viscous, as if it no longer wanted to slip down into her lungs.

"Tabby," Maya caught her wrist. "Listen—"

Tabby gently peeled off her fingers and stood up. "Excuse me," she said in a voice that shook.

"Wait," Maya called.

Tabby kept walking until she reached the bathroom. She locked the door behind herself and slid down to the cold marble floor until she sat with her back to the wall. She hugged her knees and tried to block out the sound of Maya and Dev talking softly in the bedroom.

After a few deep calming breaths, the dark fog clouding her eyes lifted and the gilt mirror hanging above the wash basin came into focus.

She stared at her reflection.

Her eyes appeared overly large and dark in her pale face, her hair had begun to frizz, and the baby hairs were standing straight up on top of her head forming an unattractive halo. The cap sleeve of her bottle green dress had slipped off revealing one freckled shoulder and the black lace strap of her bra.

A pale gecko with beady black eyes poked its bald head out from above the mirror, distracting her.

She watched the gecko inch forward, marvelling at how it managed to stay glued to the wall.

Its entire body now emerged. It was missing part of its tail.

She felt a tear trickle down her cheek.

The gecko—she named it Larry—suddenly shot its impressively long tongue out and caught a little fly.

She decided to call the fly Barry. She wondered if Barry had had any family. Any baby flies? A wife? Would Barry the fly be missed?

Another tear dropped from her eye and splashed onto the back of her hand.

She tilted her head back until it rested against the wall. She watched Larry prowl across the bathroom wall probably looking for more Barrys to snack on.

Soon another gecko appeared from behind the mirror. Mrs Larry.

She squeezed her eyes closed. Even lizards had partners that loved them.

The bedroom light clicked off behind her.

She opened her eyes and peeped under the door to ensure that the light was truly off.

She gave Maya another half an hour to fall asleep before she bid Larry goodbye, tiptoed out of the bathroom and climbed into bed.

She pulled the quilt over her head and lay there until the sun came up.

"Tabby?" Maya called softly.

Tabby kept the grey blanket firmly over her head.

"Are you asleep?" Maya tried again.

When Tabby still didn't respond, Maya gave up and left the room.

Once the footsteps faded away, Tabby emerged from under the blanket. She had not slept a wink, and the circles under her eye were now dark enough to rival a newly born zombie's.

She crawled out of bed and headed straight to the balcony. She slid open the glass door and stepped outside.

The sharp, fresh morning breeze, scented with damp wood, moss, and night jasmine, wrapped around her like an exotic perfumed cloak.

She took a deep, refreshing breath and stared out at the panorama in front of her. The clouds seemed to be hanging pretty low today, and the forest spread out in front of her as far as her eyes could see. The top of the dark, green trees were engulfed by a mist so thick that she felt she could reach out a hand and break away a fist full of it and keep it as a souvenir.

The unfamiliar flora and fauna and the dark, vibrant colours of the landscape seemed more foreign to her today than they had ever done before.

She wondered if Rudyard Kipling had ever visited Dehradun, for she could well imagine Baloo jiving in the jungle, Shere Khan prowling in the shadows and Mogli swinging from tree to tree.

The strange, intimidating beauty surrounding her intensified the emotions roiling within her. The sweeping expanse of the wild forest and the towering snow-capped Himalayas made her feel small, alone and insignificant.

She gazed at the faint outline of the mountains shimmering through the misty veil. Her skin pebbled from the morning chill, and she shivered and briskly rubbed her arms.

In the grand scheme of things, her troubles seemed petty.

Perhaps, facing her sister and Luke's smug and artificially concerned faces wouldn't be so bad. Even her dad's pity would fade with time. In fact, her dad might even be pleased to have her back home.

A pretty blue bird landed on a branch that was scraping the balcony wall. It cocked its head and eyed Tabby curiously, its dark beady eyes bold and unafraid.

Tabby squeezed her eyes shut and rocked on her heels. She had to be brave like the little bird. She would have to suck it up and return to America.

"Chai latte?" Maya chirped.

Tabby looked back over her shoulder and found Maya holding two large white mugs.

"You mean *masala chai*," Tabby responded.

Maya stepped onto the balcony and handed Tabby a steaming mug, "Its proper chai latte. The sort you get in England. I bullied the chef in the kitchen into making it for us."

"Thanks," Tabby took a sip.

"How is it?"

"Fine."

Maya swallowed a mouthful of tea. "I am sorry," she blurted out.

Tabby shook her head. "I'm glad you told me."

They listened to the screeching parrots in silence for a moment. A rustling in the bushes under the balcony made Maya scuttle back from the railing. "Mrs Khanna had warned me about standing here. She said a poisonous snake or a large hungry cat could attack us."

"Oh, live a little." Tabby threw her own words back at her.

Maya obediently shuffled back to her original position. "Chris wants to talk to you about it . . . the money thing. He said he will come and fetch you in an hour for a breakfast date."

Tabby dipped her head and took another sip of the hot, sweet chai.

"You will go, right?" Maya prompted.

"Oh, yes, I will," Tabby replied grimly.

"Yeah, I am not too fond him either."

Tabby drained the cup. "I need to get ready."

"Right. I will leave you to it then."

"Right."

"Sorry again."

"Bye."

Chris took her to a coffee shop located on the bustling upmarket Rajpur road. There was only one other couple in the cafe seated near the window. He led her to the other end of the cafe away from the couple and towards a comfortable looking red sofa.

"I will be right back with the drinks," he said and headed to the counter.

Tabby pulled down a magazine placed on the rack next to her seat. She flipped through an Indian version of Cosmopolitan while she waited for Chris. She wondered if he would bring coffee for her, and if he did, then should she dump it on his head and walk off?

Just as she had guessed, he returned with . . . two cups of coffee.

Her fingers slowly curled around the cup and she lifted it.

He smiled at her.

Reluctantly, she set the cup back down. "I don't drink coffee, never have. I despise the stuff."

Chris blinked at her, "You never said—"

"I have. A number of times."

"Right. What do you want to drink then?" His voice was still hoarse from the cold he had caught a few days ago.

"You should know," she snapped.

"Why are you being so rude?"

"Why do you think?"

"You never behave so unreasonably," he said looking genuinely baffled.

"You haven't tried to use me before."

"Look, Tabby, I can explain."

"Then explain."

"But first I need you to act normal. Listen with an open mind—"

"I may be easy going, but I'm not stupid or a doormat. You can't walk all over me and get away with it."

He opened his mouth and closed it again. He stroked his temple, sniffed a few times and coughed delicately into a tissue. He peeked at her after the performance.

She picked up the magazine and flipped over a page.

His chair scraped back, and she heard him leave. Had he abandoned her here?

A few minutes later he returned with a tray.

"I bought one of everything on the menu," he informed her as he set sandwiches, pastries, cookies, tarts and rolls down on the long table.

He went back to the counter and once again arrived with another laden tray. This time he had brought every drink on the menu.

He picked up a pink smoothie and took a sip through the straw. His eyes, over the rim of the cup, were apologetic and a tiny bit scared.

She wanted to smile in spite of herself. This was the Chris she had fallen for. The charming, generous Chris.

"I'm not hungry," she said and turned over another page. Her mind, though, was not on the model's portfolio plastered all over the glossy pages. Instead, she was wondering how she had failed to see it. The sudden proposal, the insistence on a quick wedding, the lack of love or passion in his eyes whenever he looked at her. He had bought a ring, but that ring had been for the first girl who agreed to his crazy proposal. And she had been foolish enough to fall for it.

"Two months ago, Daaji called Dad up," Chris began.

Tabby dipped her head until her dispassionate nose grazed the smooth pages of the magazine.

Chris pushed on, "He said he was certain he was going to die next year. Dad obviously panicked and asked if the doctors had said anything. Although, they hadn't, Daaji is touching eighty, and we couldn't help but take his fears seriously. He said he wanted to see Dev, Maya and me married off before he died. Dev refused outright, but Maya and I couldn't get away so easily. Initially, my family used all sorts of emotional arguments to convince us, and when that didn't work, they resorted to bribery. Half a million pounds is a lot of money. It means independence. I can have my own place, live away from my parents, and I don't have to go begging to Dad every time I need extra spending money."

Chris's upper-class British accent was becoming more pronounced as he spoke. She absently picked up the drink closest to her and sipped. It turned out to be bitter green tea.

"So Daaji found a suitable match for Maya," Chris went on. "All her objections were silenced. Dad even threatened to cut her off completely if she didn't agree to the deal. As for me . . . Daaji had found a girl for me as well."

Tabby finally looked up at him.

Pleased, he had her attention, he pulled out his phone. "Here. This is her photo."

Tabby stared at the photo of a smiling dusky Indian girl wearing a black and silver sari. Her heart sank. She could never compete with such perfection.

"As you can tell, the girl is not very good looking," he said.

She frowned. Not good looking? What was he going on about? The girl was stunning.

"Not my type," he said. "I refused to get married to her no matter how much money they threw at me. Finally, Daaji said that he would not budge on his desire to see me married, but he was willing to take a look at my girlfriend."

"How kind of him."

"Don't be angry, Tabs. Understand our situation. It is very difficult trying to keep a senile old man happy. I told him about you. He said he was willing to give you a chance."

Tabby scowled. She wasn't sure if she wanted this chance anymore.

"Do you understand now why I have rushed this engagement? I really, really like you. I don't want to marry some girl I have never seen before in my life. I would rather spend my life with you. I know you. You are fun, sweet, kind, and most importantly modern. I don't know how I can ever live with a conservative Indian girl. I can't."

Tabby ran a finger around the rim of her cup. She wasn't sure what to say.

"I did not know any of that," she said evenly. "You should have been honest with me."

"I don't think I am explaining things properly," he said running his hand through his hair in frustration. "Look, I want to marry you. I did not want to do this so soon, but circumstances are such that I have no choice. But, I am not unhappy with the situation. In fact, the more I think about it, the more I like the idea."

"You lied to me," she accused.

He took her hand and pressed her fingers, "Tabby, look at me."

She looked at him.

"I love you," he said simply. "That is why I want to marry you."

Her heart started pounding. He had never said that before. This is what she had been hoping to hear since he had proposed. And now that he had said it, she wasn't sure she believed him.

"I was going to tell you the truth right after we met Babaji. I swear. Please, Tabby give me another chance."

She shook her head. "We have no chemistry. Maybe it isn't meant to be."

He looked taken aback but didn't deny it. "I was attracted to you when we first met, but after that we just fell into a comfortable rhythm. You make me laugh, you are a good listener . . ." He shrugged. "I suppose the physical aspect of our relationship took a backseat. I want to talk to you more than I want to rip your clothes off . . . but that does not mean I wouldn't enjoy ripping your clothes off."

Her lips quirked. "I don't think it will work."

But he saw the hesitation in her eyes and quickly pressed on. "Look, you need time to make alternate plans. You have nowhere to go and even your finances are shaky. What if you stay until Maya's wedding? We can spend some time together, get to know each other better and then you can decide whether you want to walk away or stay."

He reached over and caught her hand. "Stay, Tabby. Give me another chance. As for the physical chemistry . . ." He paused and then continued with a determined look, ". . . I won't lie. It is an area we need to work on. I find you very attractive, but perhaps I haven't been able to express it enough."

Tabby stared down at their entwined hands. Deep in her heart she wanted to believe him. She was almost certain she was in love with him. Why else did the thought of leaving him fill her with such misery? Why else did she overlook his faults again and again hoping he would change with time?

"Can I give you an answer in the evening?" she asked.

"Before we go and meet Babaji?"

She nodded.

Chapter Nineteen

Tabby picked up the cell phone she had borrowed from Maya. Her finger fluttered over the dial pad for the sixth time, but once again she didn't press the call button.

What could she say to Becky? That her life was spiralling down a hell hole and she was alone in a strange country with no money and for the moment completely dependent on Chris and his family.

She gripped the phone in her hand, her knuckles turning white from the pressure. Had she purposely turned a blind eye and refused to look at his proposal too closely because she hadn't wanted to return to America as a failure? Or was it because Chris appeared to be an ideal husband? On the surface of it, he was everything a girl could want.

She knew she liked him a lot, but what about the lack of chemistry between them? Was that her fault? Was she cold? A small voice reminded her of her attraction to Dev. She quickly squelched that thought.

But she had never lied to Chris. She had been honest about her situation from the very beginning, while he had hidden the truth and used her financial problems to his advantage.

She moaned softly into her hand, her head pounding from all the questions crowding around in her brain. It was her own stupidity that had led her to this place. How was she going to get out of it? Even if she bought a ticket back to England, where would she go? She had no place to live, no money for rent.

She took a deep breath and finally pressed the call button. She would have to swallow her pride and ask for help.

Becky picked up on the first ring.

"Hey, Becky."

"Tabby? What's wrong?"

"Are you busy?"

"Kind of. My client, you remember the cute one . . . he has a gun trained on me."

"Do you want me to call the police?"

"Nah, just call me back in five minutes?"

"Sure."

After five minutes . . .

"Hey, Becky."

"Hey, Tabs."

"Is everything ok now?"

"Yeah, he has been arrested."

"You are fine?"

"I had already pressed the panic button before you called. Murderers tend to have these long winded conversations before shooting their victims. It would have been a good half hour more before he would have shot me dead."

"I thought that happened only in movies."

"Nope, it's all too common. Now, what's eating you?"

"Chris's granddad promised to give him a quarter of a million pounds if he got married before December. That is why he proposed to me and is in a rush to get married."

"You didn't know this?"

"No."

"He tried to convince you that he loves you, right?"

"Right. But only after I learned the truth."

"Divorce him in a year and take half the money?"

"Not an option."

"Shame."

"Hmm."

"Dump him then?"

"I . . . I'm confused."

Becky sighed. "Tabby, you need time to sort out your feelings. What if you do love Chris and lose him because you were too blinded by your insecurities to see it?"

"Ouch."

"I'm not going to lie to you or sugar coat things. That's why you call me every time you are in a crisis."

"I call you because you are my best friend."

"Then listen to your best friend. Take a month to decide. Make no promises. Watch his actions, watch what your heart does around him and use the time to make an alternate plan for your future if needed. Do you have enough money in your account to buy a ticket back to America?"

"No."

"I will transfer some money to your account. That will take some time processing. Until then you have to stay where you are."

"I agree," Tabby sighed. She had come to the same conclusion. "And thank you for the money. I will pay you back."

"Things will fall into place, love. Give it time."

"I will call you again soon with an update," Tabby said, and after a few more minutes of conversation where Becky tried to cheer her up, she disconnected the call.

They were on their way to meet Babaji.

Tabby kept her nose pressed to the car window, her face turned away from Maya. She was wearing a white cotton *salwar kameez* with a muted neon pink and green floral border. It was the first time she had worn Indian clothes but what with all that had happened, she couldn't enjoy it.

"I am glad you are giving him a chance," Maya whispered, ignoring Tabby's body language.

Tabby smiled politely. She kept her eyes on a giant statue of Ganesha that loomed up in front of them. It was beautifully made and painted in jewel tones. The god's almond shaped eyes were lined with kohl, and his long gold trunk gleamed in the sunlight. An old man was feeding apples to an emaciated cow standing near the idol's big toe.

"Chris is lucky to have you," Maya said bitterly.

Tabby glanced at Maya's tensed profile. The tendons in her neck were stretched and protruding from stress. Chris and she *were* lucky. They had a choice, whereas Maya was being forced to marry a man she despised.

She set her own troubles aside and focused on Maya's more urgent one. She racked her brains trying to come up with a new plan that would send Cuckoo Singh scampering.

"Almost there," Mr Mansukhani called from the front seat of the car. "Babaji's Ashram is at the end of this road."

They passed the statue and turned left. Tabby's eyes widened as

128

the fast moving Song River came into view. The evening light cascaded down tinting the surface of the river in gold, orange and pink shades.

It was breath-taking.

She wound her window down, and the sound of rushing water and the fresh, sparkling breeze filled the car.

"There it is," Mrs Mansukhani pointed, silver bangles clicking together on her wrist.

The Ashram was built on a small green hill facing the river. At first glance, it resembled a club sandwich. The top and bottom part of the building were painted white and were slightly oval in shape, while nestling in the middle was a long, thin row of terracotta coloured doors and windows.

The car moved uphill and soon came upon a busy parking lot. A teenage boy came running towards the car as soon as he spotted it. He had a short conversation with the driver in Hindi, and then the boy guided the driver into an empty parking space.

They waited until the other two cars carrying the rest of the family and friends arrived as well. Once everyone was accounted for, they followed the same boy who had guided them to the parking spot up towards the Ashram. The path they took was narrow but smooth and surrounded by jacaranda, fir and lychee trees.

As Tabby got closer to the Ashram, she noticed a walled garden at the front of the imposing building. The boy pushed open a small, squeaky gate and ushered them inside.

The garden had a well-maintained lawn, a marble fountain sprouting from the centre, and narrow steps that led up to a porch. The walls surrounding them were covered with deep red bougainvillea, blooming in such abundance that the fallen petals formed a thickly carpeted border.

They were not allowed to linger but ushered still further indoors. They went up the steps and turned right towards a door marked 'Meditation Hall'.

Tabby was curiously calm.

"You have the money, right?" Chris whispered in her ear.

Tabby nodded and hugged the brown furry handbag closer to herself.

"If he doesn't agree on two hundred, then offer him the lot," Chris said.

Tabby elbowed him. Mrs Mansukhani was staring at them.

Their guide, the same boy from the parking lot, asked them to remove their shoes and slippers at the entrance. Tabby took off her grey sandals and handed them to an attendant sitting outside the door. She was handed a numbered token in return.

She tucked it into her bag and walked into the meditation hall which turned out to be a brightly lit room with a giant fan rotating above their heads. A pleasant scent of copal and Red Sandalwood lingered in the air.

Their footsteps echoed as they shuffled further into the room.

Babaji was sitting cross-legged on a raised platform at the front of the room. He was wearing white robes and no slippers. His hair was long and streaked with grey, falling well past his shoulders. His dark, lush moustache merged into his beard that formed an inverted triangle shape below his chin. His one eye was smaller than the other giving him a wicked air. In different attire, he would have looked at home on a pirate ship.

Tabby and the rest of her party mimicked the few other people present and sat down on the carpeted area of the floor to wait their turn.

They watched as a young man walked up to Babaji and offered him a plate of Indian sweetmeats.

Babaji took the plate and handed it over to a man sitting behind him who was wearing similar white robes.

The young man then knelt his head and touched Babaji's feet.

Babaji took hold of a long gold slipper and whacked the man on the head in return.

Tabby gasped in shock and then recalled Maya telling her that he was called Chapal Wale Babaji because he gave his blessing by banging slippers on people's heads.

The procedure was repeated with a few more people until Mr Mansukhani went up to Babaji and whispered a few words.

"Please get ready for the *Aarti*," Babaji spoke in English. He projected his voice expertly and without using a microphone.

Everyone departed except Tabby and Chris's family. Babaji had a whispered conversation with Mr Mansukhani for a few more minutes before whacking him on the head with a slipper as well.

Mr Mansukhani left Babaji and came up to Tabby. He rubbed his head as he spoke, "Tabby, he wants to meet you alone first."

"Can't Chris stay?" Tabby asked.

"No," Mr Mansukhani said shortly. "Come on," he said turning to the others. "We will wait outside."

Chris patted her shoulder and smiled encouragingly, but his eyes gave him away.

He thought she couldn't handle things herself? She straightened her shoulders, lifted her chin and walked towards Babaji.

Babaji watched her approach. His small eye narrowed even further to form a slit.

Tabby's fingers tightened on her handbag's strap, and she knelt in front of him.

"So," Babaji asked. "You want to get married to Krishnamohan?"

"Chandra Mohan," Tabby corrected. Belatedly, she recalled Mrs Mansukhani's advice of keeping her eyes downcast, scarf on her head and to answer only in yeses and nos.

Babaji gestured to his attendant to leave the room.

Tabby nervously watched the man leave through a side door hidden behind thick red curtains hanging near the stage.

"Now," Babaji said, his voice soft and low, "Krishnamohan called me earlier today."

Tabby didn't correct him this time but kept her eyes on the well-worn maroon carpet.

"He told me," Babaji continued, "that he had an offer I couldn't refuse. He wanted to bribe me. I was offended, but since his family and I share a long history, I have overlooked it."

Tabby bit her lip, thinking furiously. After a moment she said, "I will be honest. Chris did give me two hundred pounds to pay you. I'm sorry about that." She peeked at him from beneath her lashes, watching his reaction.

His eyes brightened momentarily before he resumed his look of disapproval.

"Two hundred pounds . . ." He shook his head. "What will I do with worldly goods? All I need is two sets of clothes, some plain food and a pair of slippers. I desire nothing else."

"Surely your Ashram could do with a donation," Tabby tried again.

"Yes, but for a donation I will not lie," Babaji replied.

"How about four hundred pounds?"

"What does your father do?" he asked, ignoring her offer.

"He is retired. He stays at home in America."

"What did he do before he retired?"

"He used to manage the local grocery store."

A veil seemed to fall over Babaji's face. His eyes narrowed and he made a disapproving sound. "My dear child, you can leave some money as a donation, but please don't expect anything in return."

Tabby's heart sank. "Am I not good enough?"

"You are better than good, just not for Krishnamohan."

"Chandramohan. Why not?"

"You are a foreigner. You know nothing about our culture. You wouldn't be able to fulfil your wifely duties. Apart from differences in culture, there is a financial gap between the two families. Marriages should be made on an equal footing—"

"How about a thousand pounds?" Tabby asked desperately. That was all the money Chris had given her. Surely it was enough?

Babaji's eyes glazed over. "A thousand pounds," he murmured to himself.

"Cold, hard cash. I can hand it over this very minute," she nodded fervently.

"Hmm." His long, bony fingers tightened on his knees. After a few meditative breaths, his hands relaxed and he regretfully shook his head.

"I have no more money," Tabby pleaded.

He picked up the *chapal* and beckoned her to come closer. "I am sorry, but all I can give you is my blessing."

He raised the *chapal* and brought it down towards Tabby's head.

Tabby instinctively lurched forward to save her head from being ceremoniously whacked. Her hand landed on the tiger skin Babaji was sitting on and her fingers accidently nudged the material aside.

What caught her eye made her gasp in shock.

Babaji was warming an impressive collection of currencies consisting of dollars, pounds, euros, Georgian lari, Honduran lempira, Malagasy ariary and even the Vanuatu vatu. Wads of notes formed a neat layer under the tiger skin. No doubt he took the money offered by his devotees during the day and squirreled them away under his yoga toned buttocks.

This did not seem very spiritual, and from the guilty look on Babaji's face, it probably wasn't legal either.

Tabby's eyes began to sparkle. She didn't wait for Babaji to recover and come up with an excuse. She whipped out the cell phone Chris had given her for the day, pointed the camera at Babaji, and clicked.

"Don't you dare," Babaji sprang towards her.

She hadn't expected an old man to be so quick.

He came at her like a squinty hyena, his head bent low, his small eye almost disappearing in his angular face. His hand shot out, and he grabbed her wrist and twisted.

He was strong, but undeterred, Tabby brought her leg up and kicked him in his sensitive round bits.

He squealed, but did not let go.

Tabby tightened her grip on the phone and at the same time reached out to grasp a handful of his hair and yanked with all her strength.

The result took them both by surprise. Babaji's hair peeled off his scalp in one smooth movement.

Tabby stared at the black and white wig in horror.

Babaji flickered like a confused light bulb for a moment. His pupils swung from the cell phone to the wig, clearly wondering which one to rescue first.

Materialistic and vain, Tabby grinned to herself as she slipped out of his startled grip. A couple of photos of the bald Babaji and the pile of cash would soon have the wily fellow agreeing to all her demands.

"Let us negotiate," Babaji growled, circling around her like an enraged wrestler in a ring.

"Smile." Tabby took a picture, ducked under his outstretched arm and ran.

Babaji hurtled after her.

She scampered away.

He chased her.

She scampered some more.

She circled the meditation area twice.

He circled it four times.

He bounded and sprinted and flew.

She darted and flitted and galloped.

"I will agree to the wedding," Babaji finally wheezed, giving up all pretence of being high and mighty.

Tabby leaped on top of the stage to avoid him. She was trying to send the photos to Becky or Chris's email in case Babaji managed to grab the phone off her and delete them. Trouble was, she wasn't familiar enough with the phone to be able to do it quickly. She worked furiously, scrolling, searching, tapping and sliding.

The distraction cost her.

Babaji pounced.

He was on top of her like an offended cat with claws.

Tabby was knocked to the ground. She gripped the phone and the wig in one hand while trying to fend him off at the same time.

"Get off," she screeched.

"Give me the phone," he snarled.

"Won't," she grunted and caught his ear and twisted it.

"Ow, ow, ow! Let go, lego, legoooo!" he squealed.

"Tabby?"

"Not now Chris," Tabby snapped back and then froze. She turned towards the door and found Chris, Maya, Mrs Mansukhani and the parking attendant staring at them in horror.

Tabby released Babaji's ear.

Babaji sprang to his feet, swiftly rearranging his face to look dignified, offended and splenetic all at the same time.

"I can explain," he said. "This woman is possessed by a demon. I was getting rid of it."

No one believed him.

After that, it was a matter of a quick, discreet meeting between them where Babaji agreed to tell Daaji that Tabitha would make the best wife ever. Mrs Mansukhani insisted that the money under the tiger skin be given to a good charity, and in return they would delete the photographs and give him his wig back. Babaji had no choice but to agree.

Maya wanted to unmask him. She wanted to call the press and let everyone know what a fraud he was.

Chris disagreed. He thought this was an excellent weapon to have. They could use Babaji in the future if Daaji ever became difficult.

Mrs Mansukhani decided not to mess with faith. What if the naughty Babaji truly had supernatural powers?

Finally, Chris won and they decided to keep this whole Babaji business a secret.

They left the meditation hall and joined the rest of the family. Tabby headed to the porch and sat on a wicker chair while one by one the rest of the family visited Babaji.

It was a good half an hour before everyone was done. After that, they once again returned to the meditation hall to listen to Babaji's *pravachanam*.

Pravachanam turned out to be an hour-long speech on wide range of topics including the importance of yoga, meditation, abstinence, and religious teachings. Babaji spoke well, giving amusing examples from day to day life to clarify his point. He had recovered speedily enough from the hiccup earlier.

Tabby enjoyed the talk in the beginning, but sitting cross-legged on the floor for so long was difficult for her. First, her back began aching, then her waist, then her butt, and finally her legs began tingling like crazy. She wriggled her toes trying to get some feeling back into her numb legs.

The *pravachanam* ended, Babaji departed and everyone else began heading towards the river bank for the evening's prayer.

Tabby watched enviously as the people surrounding her stood up and departed.

She couldn't because her poor limbs, unused to sitting still for so long, had fallen asleep so deeply that they appeared to have gone into a coma.

Chris, Maya and the family arrived. They poked and prodded her feet. Chris even caught Tabby by the waist and lifted her up.

She rose in the air, but her legs remained frozen and twisted together like underbaked pretzels.

Chris chatted away with his father, discussing the next plan of action. He schmoozed on for a bit all the while holding onto Tabby's waist.

Tabby squeezed her eyes shut, pretending this was a horrid nightmare and that she was not currently suspended in mid-air like a levitating guru.

The number of people in the Ashram seemed to have tripled, and Tabby felt every one of those eyes on her when she was tossed into the back seat of the car. The three of them drove off to the hospital while the rest stayed back for the *Aarti*.

"Why me?" Tabby asked the statue of Ganesha when they flew past it. "Why do things like this only happen to me?"

Chapter Twenty

The plans to depart for Punjab were shelved since the doctor advised Tabby to avoid long journeys for the next two days. The injection and muscle relaxants had unfrozen her legs, but she was still stiff and needed to stay mobile to keep the circulation going in her legs. Tabby was apologetic, but the others didn't seem to mind the delay. It gave them a chance to plan a trip to Haridwar.

Haridwar turned out to be an ancient holy city located forty-five minutes away from Dehradun. The evening before their departure to Punjab all of them piled into a car and whizzed off to attend the *Aarti* at Har ki Pauri ghat.

Nani was most excited, and she insisted that Dev should come along even though he had to wear dark glasses and a thick scarf to disguise himself from the public.

By the time they reached Haridwar, it was almost dark. They took off their shoes in the car to prevent them from being robbed and walked barefoot down the warm, slick and treacherous stone steps.

Tabby paused to look back at Nani.

Nani, wearing her usual plain white sari, was carefully making her way down the steps. She was leaning heavily on Mr Mansukhani.

Tabby's hand shot out to prevent Dev from going past her.

He eyed her rakishly over the top of his sunglasses. His mouth was stained with beetle juice as part of the disguise.

She wanted to reach up and wipe the vermillion stain off his lips.

He waggled his eyebrows when she continued staring at him.

She mentally shook herself.

"Can you help Nani? I think Mr Mansukhani is having trouble," she said, jutting her chin up towards the top of the steps.

Dev didn't waste time on conversation but raced back up, sure-footed and balanced, even on slippery stones. He reached Nani and said something to make her laugh and then reached down and swept her up in his arms. She squealed, and the aunties surrounding her giggled.

Tabby smiled. She hadn't expected him to carry her, but now that she thought of it, it was a good idea. She turned back around and once again began her own descent towards the banks of the river Ganges.

She reached the bottom step and found Maya, Chris and Mrs Mansukhani waiting for her.

"We need to stick together," Maya said.

Tabby looked wide-eyed at the sea of people surrounding her.

There were well over two hundred people who had come to witness the *Aarti*. And it wasn't just Indians but foreigners, too, who were making their way towards the bank.

A group of sadhus wearing orange robes singing Hare Ram, Hare Krishna, danced past her. A small boy caught her by the waist and swung her around as he tried to escape from a girl slightly younger than himself.

"Is the river far?" Tabby asked, feeling out of breath.

"No, the river is only a few steps away. People are blocking the view," Chris told her.

Tabby strained her ears to hear the sound of rushing water, but the chaos around her was too loud.

Someone blew on a conch shell, and the sound trumpeted out and over the buzzing human voices, jingling bangles, and tinkling anklets.

As the sound of the conch shell faded away, the first beats of a prayer song blasted out of a loudspeaker.

The *Aarti* was about to begin.

There were little stalls near where they stood where shopkeepers were selling an assortment of things.

The shopkeeper's voices became more urgent as they quickly and efficiently handed out round silver plates called *thalis* filled with flowers, sweets, idols and burning clay lamps.

Chris and Maya braved the crowds to buy a few of the *thalis*. They handed one to Tabby when they returned.

Tabby stared down at the bunch of yellow marigolds, a pile of soft red powder, strings of red threads and other bits and bobs prettily arranged on a *thali* in confusion. She had no idea what to do with any of it. The scent of burning oil floated up to her nose from the clay lamp sitting in the middle of her silver plate. It was a pleasant smell.

Once Nani and the rest of them had arrived, they moved as one towards the river bank. They skirted around a buffalo meditating in the middle of the path and narrowly avoided stepping on a sleeping dog's tail.

The music picked up as they neared the edge of the river. The song was catchy and repetitive with plenty of drum and bass. It sounded too happy, too thrilling for prayer music or so Tabby thought until she spotted the saffron-clad priests.

The priests sat on makeshift stages glowing under the blazing light of burning cressets and torches. They held incense sticks that they waved in the direction of the river in time with the music.

The world suddenly plunged into darkness as shopkeepers switched off their store lights in preparation for the *Aarti*. The only thing now visible were the flames and the smoke around the priests.

People swarmed forward to set their clay lamps afloat. Soon thousands of little burning wicks bobbed along on the river making everything twinkle, shimmer and gleam.

The priests began chanting. It was lovely, haunting sound. Their deep synchronized voices seemed to reach deep into her core. She felt as if her heart were filled to the brim, and her throat choked with unshed tears.

The priests continued to chant, and the music blaring out of the speaker changed to another prayer song. This time the people surrounding her began singing along in soft melodious tones that ebbed and flowed like the Ganges.

Tabby didn't know how long she stood there. In that brief moment, she forgot her desires, her ego . . . her past, present and future. Her soul was caught up in the magical moment. She felt as if she were formless, like a peaceful, joyous, swirling mist drifting away with the music.

The strong scent of camphor brought her back to earth. The priests were now waving multitier lamps, and the flames flicking out from the tiny brass bowls rose up and merged together until it seemed as if the priests were holding roaring flames in the palms of their hands.

Nani had tears running down her eyes. Even Maya's eyes were moist, and Tabby was not surprised. It was an experience of a lifetime.

As the *Aarti* came to a close, the music stopped, along with the chanting. The sound of voices and shuffling feet grew louder as people turned to go back.

A priest recognised Nani and came up to them. He was a lean muscular man, with shining eyes and a pleasant face.

"Dad has paid for a *puja*," Maya said in Tabby's ear. "Do you want to participate?"

"What do I have to do?" Tabby asked.

"Nothing, just set the *diya* afloat—that's the clay lamp—when you are told to," Maya replied. "It's like writing a letter to Santa and sending it up the chimney. Here you are sending your wishes down the river instead."

"It means a little more than that," the priest said overhearing their conversation. "Ganga," he said affectionately waving at the river, "symbolises purity". She weaves down Lord Shiva's dreadlocks and then through the Himalayas to cleanse all evil in her path. You could offer the *diya* to her as a manifestation of your faults, bad habits or past mistakes, and she will cleanse it." He turned back around to look at Tabby, and his eyes were soft and kind. "Or if you have lost someone close to you, the *diya* will take away your pain and loss. Help you grieve, let the hurt go until you are left with only pleasant memories."

Tears pooled in Tabby's eyes. Did he know about her mother? How could he . . . and yet his eyes continued to shimmer with understanding.

"Will you do it?" Maya asked gently.

Tabby nodded and wiped away a tear. She didn't think it would work. She didn't think she could ever come to grips with the fact that her mother was no more. Any day she expected her mother to return, to tell her that it had all been a lie. That the hospital, the illness had never happened.

It was quieter now. A lot of people had departed, including boats that had been filled with eager spectators.

The priest led them closer to the bank and began the *puja*, which turned out to be a mini version of the *Aarti* but personalised.

Tabby stared out at the dark, flowing river, her mind no longer on the events around her but on her mother. She didn't know if she imagined it, but the scent of tobacco and vanilla enveloped her as if her mother was standing right next to her. Goosebumps formed on the back of her neck and arms and she shivered.

"Your turn," the priest said.

Tabby started and realised that everyone was staring at her. They had set their *diyas* in the water. She was the last one.

She gripped the plate in her hand, not wanting to let go, and yet with so many eyes on her, what choice did she have? She had agreed to do this, after all.

No one hurried her.

She felt as if someone had put weights on her feet and she had to drag her leg forward to come closer to the rapid, flowing water. A fine soothing mist sprayed her face as she kneeled down.

With trembling hands, she picked up the *diya* balanced on a leaf boat and nestling amongst fragrant white rose petals. "Be well, mother," she whispered and set it afloat.

The tiny lamp caught the rapid current and began moving further and further away until it mixed with thousands of similar hopes and dreams glittering on the Ganges and was lost to sight.

"She is here," Maya called down the stairs.

Tabby looked away from the midges swarming around the yellow light bulb and focused on the metal door.

Maya and Dev appeared on the terrace a moment later.

"Is it dry?" Maya asked, indicating the floor.

"Damp," Tabby said. She sat with her back to the wall, her knees drawn up and hands curled around her leg.

"We brought blankets," Dev said, showing her the pile he was carrying. He shook one open and laid it on the ground.

Tabby moved over to the warm, dry cloth. Maya dropped down next to her, and Dev, after a brief hesitation, joined them as well.

"I wish we had wine," Maya remarked after a moment. "We could lie here all night, staring up at the star filled sky and drink till we pass out."

"Sounds divine," Tabby muttered. She wished the two of them would leave her alone.

"Eek, eek, eek!" Maya squealed and leaped over Tabby and into Dev's arms. "Lizard!"

"Where?" Dev asked trying to push Maya back on the ground.

"There. By the water tank," Maya shoved her face into Dev's shoulder. "Get rid of it Dev."

"No, don't. That's Larry. And the one on that wall next to the chipped paint is Mrs Larry," Tabby said.

Maya let Dev go and crawled back towards Tabby on all fours. She placed a cool palm on her head. "Nope, doesn't have a fever."

Dev leaned over and encircled Tabby's wrist with warm fingers. "Her heart is beating a little fast, but otherwise she seems fine."

Tabby snatched her hand away, "I'm fine."

"Right." Maya raised a disbelieving eyebrow. "You named those disgusting lizards."

"They are cute," Tabby objected.

Maya threw her hands up in the air and leaned back against the wall. Dev lay down next to them, his arm a breath away from Tabby's leg.

Maya's light floral perfume faded away and a masculine scent laden with boozy caramelized spices filled the air.

Tabby shifted closer to Maya.

His eyes were closed, but his lips quirked up as if he noticed the change.

"You should go to your room and sleep," Tabby said. "We have to leave at six in the morning for Chandigarh."

"We should," Maya agreed. "But we won't."

"Why not?" Tabby grumbled.

"Dev is not coming with us," Maya said, instead of answering the question.

"This could be the last time we meet," Dev murmured sleepily.

Tabby felt a slight tremor go through her. He looked younger with his eyes closed, brows smooth and mouth soft and relaxed.

"Do you want to talk about it?" He opened one eye and shot her a piercing look.

"About what?" Tabby asked, looking away.

"Your mum," Maya said gently.

"No," Tabby replied and then without ceremony burst into tears.

She felt Dev slip his arms around her shoulders and pull her close, while Maya threaded her fingers through her hair.

They sat like that for a long, long time.

It was well past seven when the fleet of cars left Dehradun on its way to Chandigarh in the state of Punjab. It was a five-hour journey to Chandigarh where they were planning to rest for a day at a guesthouse. The day after that, they would leave for Daaji's house which was located in a small village on the outskirts of Amritsar.

Tabby sat near the window as usual, while Chris squeezed in next to her with Maya on the other side.

"This is kind of hot," Chris whispered, running his finger up her arm and nuzzling her in the ear.

"It is very hot." Tabby fanned herself, deliberately misunderstanding him.

The driver was watching them in the rear view mirror. Not wanting to cause an accident, Tabby inched away and plastered herself to the car door.

Chris rubbed his sweaty arm against her shoulder and waggled his eyebrows suggestively.

She leaned forward, uncapped the water bottle and took a drink. Why did he want to work on this in public?

He scowled, pulled out his phone and began playing a game.

She sighed in relief and turned her attention back to the view. They went down a mountain, past a dark jungle and onto the highway. Cars and trucks sped by with no regard to traffic rules. They flew past fields of sugarcane factories billowing smoke, and green farmlands.

They stopped at a traffic light in a small, busy town. A group of sari clad women walked by carrying bundles of wooden sticks on their heads. They were talking and laughing amongst themselves, animatedly waving arms filled with colourful, shiny bangles. A man walking ahead of them turned around and shouted something. A few women rolled their eyes while the rest chuckled, but they all quickened their steps.

Did these women have a choice when it came to marriage, Tabby wondered? Probably not. And yet they got on with life, making the best of it.

Tabby rested her head against the glass. A lot of women, she knew, were like her. They wanted to find a wonderful man, get married and live happily ever after. But perhaps it wasn't a smart thing to depend on a man. Maya would give anything to avoid marrying Cuckoo Singh and have the sort of freedom Tabby had.

Perhaps, it was time Tabby, too, appreciated her freedom.

The sun was high in the sky when they crossed into Punjab. The landscape changed and fields of wheat and mustard rose up on either side of the road. They sped past a few conical shaped medieval milestones. Mrs Mansukhani informed them that they were called Kos Minars, erected by Sher Shah Suri to mark the royal route in the past.

Chandigarh turned out to be a well-planned, beautiful city. They arrived at the guesthouse, which was uncannily similar to the one in Delhi. Even her room seemed to be about the same size.

After a quick lunch consisting of *Aloo parathas*, yogurt and mango pickle, Tabby crawled into bed. She had barely slept the night before, and the long drive had further added to her exhaustion.

She slept almost immediately and began dreaming a familiar dream.

She was racing down a seedy street. Slap, slap, slap, her old, trusty sneakers echoed in the eerily silent night as they rhythmically hit the ground.

She reached the base of the building and right on top the neon sign blazed in the darkness. The door was locked, but she could see the beginning of a scaffolding next to it. Without wasting a moment on thought, she grabbed the lowest board and pulled herself up. She hoped he didn't know how to climb or better still, the boards would turn out to be weak, unable to carry such a heavy man.

A cloak flapped below her.

He could climb.

Her hands grasped the slats and she moved upwards as fast as she could. She didn't know why, but she had to reach the sign.

Two more feet and success. Once she reached the top, she would be safe from him.

He chuckled behind her. A dark, dangerous sound. As if he could read her mind and found her logic amusing.

She trembled at the sound, her foot slipped and she fell from fifteen feet above the ground.

He caught her around the waist, his warm, calloused hand splayed on her bare sensitive back.

"Tabby," he whispered softly.

She opened her eyes and gasped. They were suspended in mid-air rotating below a glittering moon and a star filled night sky.

They were flying.

She woke struggling for breath, her heart pounding in fright. Her vision cleared and she clicked on the bedside lamp. She opened her diary, wrote the entire dream down, and then flipped back a few pages to compare it to the similar dream she'd had before. The two

143

dreams turned out to be not similar but exactly the same, except that this time the nightmare had gone on for longer.

She closed the diary and stared up at the rotating fan. Who or what was she running from? She had never had such vivid dreams before.

"Come down for Dinner," Maya called, knocking on her door.

"Coming," Tabby yelled and tucked the diary under the pillow.

By the time Tabby arrived downstairs to join the rest of the family, dinner was on the table. She sat down next to Chris and pulled the basket of *naan* bread closer.

"Are you ready to meet him?" Nani asked. She was sitting cross-legged on the seat, cracking beetle nuts with a hefty silver nutcracker. She dropped the quartered pieces into a silk pouch, uncaring of the annoyed looks the waiters were throwing at her.

"Meet who?" Tabby asked, through a mouthful of fresh cottage cheese.

"Daaji," Chris said.

The cheese turned to dust in her mouth, and she bared her teeth in a pained smile and shook her head.

"You will be fine," Nani said and offered her a beetle nut.

Tabby popped it into her mouth and promptly choked on it.

Chapter Twenty One

The next morning they were on the road again. They bobbed along dipping into potholes, dislocating jaws, veering side to side to avoid strolling farmers, cows, pigs, buffalos, elephants, sheep and camels.

They flew down smooth, empty roads or crawled along behind sleepy trucks taking up most of the lane. They screeched in fright when adventurous auto rickshaws hurtled past them and had mini heart attacks when motorcycles zipped by, recklessly weaving through the traffic. They skidded and swayed and shuddered their way through small towns and farmlands until all of them were rattling against each other in fright.

Finally, eight hours later, when the sky was filled with ominous clouds and thunder was roaring in the distance, they arrived at Daaji's house.

Tabby stared up at the dark looming mass of brick and stones. Lightning flashed illuminating the *haveli* that looked more like a sprawling mansion than a farmhouse.

They were ushered in just as the rain drops began to fall on the dry ground creating puffs of dust. A woman wearing a shiny purple sari with a maroon backless blouse, tons of glittering jewellery and heart-shaped sunglasses greeted them at the door.

"You can call me Dolly Aunty," the women greeted Tabby. She had lipstick on her teeth.

"Tabby," she replied with a tired smile.

"Quickly freshen up," Dolly Aunty told her, "you have to meet Daaji at eight sharp in the drawing room."

Tabby nodded obediently and followed her up the stairs. The house was massive, airy and just as opulent as she had expected. Large intricately designed statues of elephants and camels decorated the hall, the walls were dotted with paintings and tapestries, and every now and then carved cream pillars unexpectedly rose up in front of her awestruck nose.

Her room turned out to be just as beautiful. It had a four-poster bed with deep red cushions and an intricately embroidered cream and gold throw. A billowing white mosquito net dropped down over the bed from a silver hook suspended from the ceiling.

"Water," Dolly Aunty led her to a large copper pot placed on a blue and yellow painted stool. She took off the small lid covering the mouth of the pot and showed her the dipper inside. A copper glass sat next to it. "Don't worry. The water has been boiled," she said.

"It's got flowers in it," Tabby said, staring at the white petals floating inside the copper pot."

"Jasmine flowers. To scent the water. Try it," Dolly Aunty said, holding out a glass.

Tabby took a sip. The water tasted cool, fresh, floral and wonderful. She smiled in delight.

Dolly Aunty didn't smile back, and since her eyes were hidden behind the sunglasses, it was hard to tell what she was thinking. "Come down at eight," she said again and left the room, her bangles jangling as she went.

Tabby had a quick cold shower and changed into a white georgette *salwar kameez* that had delicate silver flowers embroidered on the wrist and neckline. She added silver hoop earrings, a silver dot on her forehead and sparkling faux diamond bangles. She had just covered her head with a cherry blossom pink scarf when Maya burst into her room singing a Bollywood song.

She took hold of Tabby's hand and spun her around.

"How do I look?" Tabby asked.

"Like a dream," Maya responded.

"Truly?"

"Indian clothes suit you far more than western ones," Maya said.

Tabby turned back to the mirror. She had to agree with Maya. The fabric skimmed her form, hugging her in all the right places, while the draped *dupatta* flattered her skin tone.

"Desirable," Maya grinned.

Tabby blushed and looked away from her reflection.

They went back down the stairs and Maya led them to the drawing room where Daaji sat in his wheelchair sipping whiskey.

Daaji eyed Tabby above the glass like she was a piece of spinach stuck between his teeth or a worm in his otherwise good apple.

Tabby bravely moved forward like someone battling gale force winds. Her hair blew backwards, her body strained against the resistance, and finally in triumph she drooped like an angel's trumpet and touched his feet.

"Hurr hurr," Daaji made an odd sound in his throat. The people in the room gasped, and Chris moaned behind her.

Tabby hurriedly straightened up wondering if Daaji was having a fit.

Her face paled.

There are a few things that universally annoy men who drink. Whether it is Punjabi, Irish or American men, young, middle-aged or ancient men . . . They all despise someone coming along and ruining their alcoholic beverage.

A man just wants to cuddle on a sofa, watch a bit of telly and have a little tipple. He wants to relax, unwind, and feel the warm and delicious alcohol racing down the oesophagus. Not a drop of the precious Manna should be wasted. He guards the glass as if it were a newborn babe, a Kohinoor diamond, or the last cigarette.

Daaji was no exception. He glared at Tabby and her whisky soaked hair ends.

Tabby had made that one mistake. The mistake of ruining a man's first real drink of the day. When she had bent over to touch his feet, a good fistful of her hair had landed in Daaji's whiskey glass.

And now . . . droplets of the precious fifty-year-old single malt were dribbling down the tips of her hair, splattering her *kurta* as well as Daaji's pristine cotton pants.

"I'm so sorry," she exclaimed in horror and taking her *dupatta* she began attacking the wet spots on his pants.

"Hurr, hurr," he roared in panic when her hands inched a little too close to his sensitive bits. "Stop, stop!"

Tabby stopped.

"You were supposed to approach at eight sharp," he said coldly.

"I was two minutes early," Tabby said. Surely that was a good thing?

He tapped his fat gold wrist watch. "The sun transits at eight sharp. You arrived at the wrong time when Saturn was in retrograde. Hence," he tapped a wet spot on his knee, "the accident."

147

Tabby ducked her head and stared at the ground. She hadn't understood a word of that.

"Sit," he ordered.

This she understood and obediently sat on a chair next to him.

He stared at his watch once again and a minute ticked by in silence. Finally, he looked up and said, "Now, the auspicious time starts. You may speak."

"Thank you for inviting me," she said.

Daaji smoothed his moustache and tweaked the ends upwards, rolling them between his fingers to form a point. "Babaji thinks this union is a good idea."

She nodded.

"Do you know how to knit and sew? Can you make *daal*, *roti*, rice, *lassi* and other Indian dishes?"

"I can sew and make rice and *roti*," Tabby said, choosing to focus on what she could do rather than what she couldn't do.

"Do you know any Indian prayers, sentences in Hindi or Punjabi? If you had to, would you be willing to live in India, have your children grow up here?"

Tabby adjusted the scarf that kept threatening to slip off her silky head. "I'm willing to compromise," she said. "I wouldn't mind living in India."

"What do you miss most about England?" he continued his rapid-fire questioning.

"Cheese," she replied without thinking.

That pulled him up short. "You miss cheese more than anything?"

Tabby nodded. "You have so many cows and goats here but nothing except cottage cheese."

"Cheddar, gouda, stilton, brie, camembert," he agreed, visibly softening. "A cracker with a slice of cheese and onion marmalade is heaven. I used to go to England just for the cheese. It's been a long time . . . I remember bringing home stinky cheeses and chasing my wife around and around the garden with it. She used to despise the smell."

"Once, I tried to age a piece of cheese at home," Tabby confessed. "Left it wrapped up in a muslin cloth nestled amongst shoes."

"Did it work?"

"It turned green all right and had enough mould on it to win a ribbon, but it didn't taste so good."

"Pity," he said.

"Yeah," Tabby responded.

After a moment of meditation, he said, "I would love a grilled cheese sandwich right now with a layer of blackberry jam."

"I haven't tried that."

"You must."

"I like a grilled cheese sandwich with a layer of salsa sauce," she said.

"I haven't tried that."

"You must."

Again they sat in companionable silence. Cheese had broken down some barriers between them and brought them closer. He was looking at her in a far more kindly way than he had when she had almost whacked his boy bits with her *dupatta*.

Finally, Daaji raised his whiskey glass at her and said, "Welcome to the family."

"Thank you," Tabby replied, and since no more seemed to be forthcoming, she got up from the chair and Chris came and took her place.

That, she thought, had been anticlimactic. Who could have imagined cheese to be such a remarkable bonding agent?

Nani and Mrs Mansukhani had arrived while she had been chatting with Daaji. She walked towards them now, her steps slow and measured. She had a curious feeling that she was entering a trap. As if the walls around her were closing in and her one escape route had been shut off. It was a strange feeling, and she didn't have long to dwell on it, for right then a petite young woman snuggly wrapped in a lime green sari arrived at the door.

Tabby froze, and her eyes widened in shock and recognition.

"Ma," the girl addressed Dolly Aunty. "Dinner is ready."

"Table is laid?" Dolly Aunty asked, getting up from the sofa.

The girl nodded, her eyes flicked towards Tabby and away.

Maya planted herself in front of Tabby cutting off the view of the girl. "Get a grip. Everyone is staring at you. Didn't Chris warn you?"

Tabby stared at Maya mutely.

"Gunjan," Maya hissed, grabbing Tabby's arm and leading her out of the room, "is Dolly Auntie's daughter. Dolly Aunty is Daaji's neighbour. She spends most of her day here taking care of Daaji or, rather, ordering his servants about."

"I see," Tabby said, not really seeing.

"That is why Daaji wanted Chris to marry Gunjan. He is fond of the girl."

"So that girl was the same whose picture Chris showed me. The girl Daaji wanted him to marry?"

Maya nodded, "Thank God he told you that much at least. You will be seeing a lot of her. Daaji is close to that family, and it would be rude to suddenly tell them not to come over anymore or attend any of my wedding functions."

"I don't think I'm hungry anymore," Tabby muttered.

"You will eat and smile and pretend that you are the happiest girl in the world," Maya growled in her ear, "and then we will go up on the terrace and cry the night away."

"Terrace again?"

"It's the best place to plot without leaving the house," Maya said, dragging her into the dining room.

Chapter Twenty Two

Dinner was painful. Gunjan fluttered around the dinner table like an enthusiastic fruit fly. She knew the right things to say and cracked jokes in a language that Tabby couldn't understand. She was lively, beautiful, and genuinely fond of Daaji.

At one point, Nani asked Tabby to pass the rice. But before Tabby could so much as touch the dish, Gunjan was out of her seat and serving Nani.

"You are our guest," Gunjan told Tabby sweetly. "We can't let you lift a finger."

"She is not a guest," Mrs Mansukhani crushed the poppadum between her fingers. "She is engaged to Chris, and that makes her family. Tabby, pass the potatoes."

Gunjan popped a carrot stick into her mouth and crunched. Her expression was unreadable.

Tabby was touched. No one had stood up for her before. Not even family.

The rest of the dinner passed without incident, and after dessert Maya led Tabby up to the terrace as promised.

"I have the supplies here," Maya said pausing to pick up a plastic bag hidden behind the stairs. "I went up to the roof to investigate earlier and realised that the light bulb had blown a fuse. I got one of the maids to get me some candles."

Tabby peered into the plastic bag. Apart from the candles and a lighter, Maya had added a notebook and a small portable radio. She closed the bag stifling a yawn. She was exhausted from the long drive, but sneaking up like this while the house slept made her feel like she was on an adventure.

It was the same sort of feeling that she used to get as a child when she and Maryanne would sneak down to the kitchen pretending there was a thief in the house.

Their imagination would take flight, and they would begin to believe that they truly heard the sound of furniture moving in the sitting room, feet pattering across the wooden floor board and a stifled sneeze.

They would carry an assortment of weapons like dad's golf stick, matchbox, an empty beer bottle and a dozen safety pins. The late hour, the fear that mom Might catch them, and the thrilling rush that they were going to become local heroes after stuffing a thief in a sack and presenting him to the incompetent police department had been indescribably wonderful.

She felt much the same now, slithering up the stairs with Maya in tow while the household snoozed.

She reached the topmost step and froze.

"Are you sure the bulb doesn't work up here?" Tabby called down softly.

"Yes," Maya whispered back.

Tabby stared at the light filtering through the cracked terrace door. It was too soft, too yellow, to be coming from the moon. She turned her head towards the stairs to warn Maya when a hand closed over her mouth and a strong muscular arm circled her waist, lifted her up and pulled her onto the terrace.

A familiar warm and spicy scent enveloped her.

"Shhh," Dev whispered in her ear. "It's me. I am letting you go now. Don't scream."

Tabby nodded.

Dev dropped his hand and stepped away from her.

Tabby stuck her head out of the door, "Maya," she warned. "Dev is here."

"Don't lie," Maya said. Her footsteps increased in speed and echoed louder than they had before. She emerged on the terrace seconds later and at the sight of Dev burst into happy, relieved tears.

Dev smoothed the dark head attached to his shirt button, "Don't worry, little sister. You are not going to marry that idiot."

Maya sniffed and stepped back. "Where are you staying?"

"In the room next to your mum." He grinned down at Maya. "I told her I wanted to attend the wedding but didn't want Daaji to know. She took care of the rest."

Maya turned and hugged Tabby, "You are a genius," she said.

"You gave him that idea."

His fingers tweaked a few nobs on the small radio Maya had brought up. "Any update?" he asked.

A static sound filled the air, which soon changed to a woman crooning a soft, sweet Punjabi folk song. He placed the radio on the ledge and turned towards Maya.

"I tried something this evening," Maya replied. "Cuckoo and his family came over for dessert, and during that time I stole a watch from his wrist and made sure he noticed me stealing it. I also swiped his mother's ring when she passed me the ice cream. I slipped it on my own finger and waved it under her nose."

"And?" Dev prompted.

Maya took a deep breath and let it out slowly. "When Cuckoo and I were left alone for a few minutes, he took the watch and the ring back and assured me that he knew all about kleptomaniacs. He said he didn't blame me and knew I couldn't help it. He said he knows someone who can help me. He promised to take me to her as soon as we returned from our honeymoon."

"That plan of yours could have gone very wrong," Dev frowned. "You could still try to convince your parents."

"They will tell me to sacrifice for the sake of the family," Maya responded sourly. "That's what most Indian girls are told to do."

"You won't know until you try," Tabby said. "At least tell Mrs Mansukhani that you are unhappy."

"I know Mum. She won't go against Dad. And Dad is as conservative and narrow-minded as they come. He has already threatened to cut me off if I refuse to marry," Maya cocked her head. "Do you have another plan?"

"I think so," Tabby grabbed a lit candle from Maya's hand and tilted it until some wax pooled on the ledge. She placed the candle on the molten wax and held it until it stuck. "I think we should catch him flirting with another woman. Take a video recording of it and show it to Daaji."

"Another woman . . . You mean you?" Maya's eyebrow shot up. "But what if Daaji thinks you were the one flirting?"

"We will edit out her part," Dev's spoke reluctantly. Candlelight bathed his face making his dark golden skin gleam while his eyes narrowed in disapproval. "I think this—"

"—is a bad idea," Tabby and Maya chorused and burst into

laughter.

Maya sobered and leaned her back against the ledge. The dark ringlets framing her face fluttered in the warm breeze. "Who will take the footage?"

"I can't unless you bring him up to the terrace," Dev said.

Maya pursed her lips thoughtfully. "I could climb the custard apple tree at the back of the house and record the whole thing with my phone."

"I will lead Cuckoo towards the tree, flirt with him until he becomes bold enough to try something and then throw a massive, indignant fit," Tabby finished.

"Can you flirt?" Dev turned his piercing eyes on Tabby. "Show me."

Tabby blinked up at him. "Err," she said squirming under his gaze. "Err . . . I'm so sexy. I can make your fantasies come true. Oooh, look at me—"

Maya slapped her forehead in disgust, "You can't tell him that. You have to do something to entice him. I once heard a photographer tell a model to look constipated to fake a sexy look."

Tabby tried to look constipated.

"No, no," Maya growled. "You look really constipated now. Not sexy at all."

"Imagine you are kissing a rabbit," Dev suggested.

Tabby imagined a giant fluffy bunny cuddling her. Her face softened, and her lips puckered as she leaned in to kiss his pink nose.

"Now, imagine lots of rabbits," Dev prompted softly.

Tabby arms came up to hug a dozen invisible fluffy bunnies, and her lips began kissing the air around herself.

"Now imagine you are standing on one leg," Dev continued.

Tabby stood on one leg, hopped twice and froze. She glared at Maya and Dev doubled over and laughing.

"You are so cute, Tabby," Maya giggled.

"Adorable," Dev grinned.

Tabby scowled. "I don't need to practise. It is hard acting flirty in front of—I will manage."

A hand shot out and pulled Tabby into a store room.

"Chris!" Tabby coughed as dust blew into her face.

"I don't know what it is about you in Indian clothes. You look so damn good in them," he murmured in her ear. "Like a beautifully frosted cupcake."

She looked over his shoulder at the long, dusty wooden shelves laden with pots, pans, giant metal tins and jars of pickle and stifled a sneeze. Her eyes widened in fright when she noticed the cobwebs draped over rusted fans, lampshades and broken furniture piled up in one corner. She felt as if she had been transported to a scene in a horror film where at any moment giant spiders, eerie ghosts or flesh eating zombies would leap out and attack her. . . .

"This place is giving me the creeps. Let me go, Chris." She squirmed in his grip. "You know I don't like spiders, and this place must be full of them—"

"It's romantic," he protested and chewed on her earlobe.

She sneezed. All those times when she had wanted to cuddle him, he never did. And now when Maya was perched upon a dodgy branch of a tree waiting for her to arrive, he was in a romantic mood.

"Not now, Love Muffin," she pushed his shoulder.

He licked her cheek.

"Don't ruin my makeup," she protested. She had spent a good hour getting ready to entice Cuckoo Singh. She had never worn so many layers of mascara before.

"You look beautiful," Chris murmured.

She softened and allowed him to kiss her.

She melted into his embrace. His lips felt nice and warm. She had just begun enjoying herself when someone slammed a door in the house.

The moment was broken.

"Go," he breathed huskily into her neck.

She didn't want to go, but the thought of poor Maya waiting for her in the heat forced her to duck under his arms and leave.

In less than five minutes, Tabby had Cuckoo Singh padding after her towards the fruit orchard at the back of the house.

It was a hot day, bees buzzed along importantly, flies floated about listlessly, flowers hid under broad green leaves away from the burning rays—

"Where is the box you wanted me to help you lift?" Cuckoo Singh asked looking around in confusion.

Tabby let her tongue slip out and lick her bottom lip. "I . . ." She paused.

"Yes?" he prompted.

She fluttered her heavy, sticky, mascara coated lashes. "I wanted to tell you that the toothpaste you gave me, blooming fresh—"

"Yes?" he breathed, his eyes fixed on her moist bottom lip.

"It was awesome," she confessed.

"I knew it!" He pushed his shoulders back and thrust his chest out. "It's a secret ingredient that makes it so good. Open your mouth."

"What?"

"Wider," he requested. "See, you still have a piece of food stuck between your bicuspids. A good quality water pick will take care of that. I will give you an excellent mouthwash—"

"What was the secret ingredient?" she hurriedly cut in.

Cuckoo Singh's eyes narrowed. "Why do you want to know?"

"Just," she tittered, dragging her toe back and forth on the muddy ground.

He continued to look wary, as if a rival company had hired her to seduce the big secret out of him.

She batted her lashes and let a soft smile play on her lips.

His long, droopy moustache quivered.

Pleased, she batted her lashes harder, and her small white teeth snuck out to flash him a naughty invitation.

He brightened, and the tips of his moustache began quivering like mad. And Tabby was certain that they would have curled up in excitement had her mascara coated lashes not decided to glue themselves together just then. They fused themselves together so well that she panicked.

"Are you all right?" he asked taking a step close to her.

Embarrassed, she unpeeled her lids in one swift desperate motion, losing a couple of her lashes in the process.

He took another step closer to her.

She stilled, her eyes trained on his shuffling feet. Her brain began working overtime.

He lifted his hand, and his eager fingers began moving towards the top of her shoulders.

This was perfect. This is what she and Maya wanted—his grubby hands on her—and as soon as Maya got the shot, she could karate chop him and escape. Now all she had to do was to lure him in further and he would fall right into their trap.

"Are you OK? May I be of assistance?" he asked.

She firmly closed one eye and frantically shook her head. "My eye," she squealed. "Oh it hurts, it hurts. I think I have something in my eye!"

"Let me look." He eagerly wobbled even closer. Concern and lust bloomed in his pink, sweaty cheeks.

"Ooooh! No, no, it hurts. Oh, I'm going blind," Tabby roared, while watching him approach in delight. "I am dying! The pain, I can't bear it!"

He poked her good eye.

"The other one," she moaned, and then let out another shout when he brushed against her eyelid.

Maya clambered off the tree and came racing to her rescue.

"Tabby, Tabby, what's wrong?" she asked shoving Cuckoo Singh aside and making him tumble to the ground. "Did a bee bite you? Are you allergic to bees? Did a mosquito get into your eye?"

Tabby closed both her eyes and leaned into Maya's shoulder. "Idiot," she growled into Maya's ear. "I was luring him in."

Maya reeled back, conflicting emotions flitting across her beautiful face. Finally, she decided to look disapproving.

"You didn't have to overact. The way you screeched, I thought you were going to drop dead," Maya whispered back. Aloud she said, "Tabby is not feeling well. I am taking her to her room."

Cuckoo Singh spat out the mud and grunted something indistinguishable in reply.

Chapter Twenty Three

Tabby sat in front of the air conditioner, letting the breeze blow her shaggy hair back like a long haired sheepdog sticking its head out of a moving car.

Usually during the day, the giant windows let in plenty of hot, bright sunlight, turning her room into an oven by mid-afternoon. But today it was hotter than ever. The room was too big for the air conditioner, and she had to sit directly in front of it to cool her flushed, overheated skin.

It was a miracle she hadn't turned into *Tandoori* Tabby by now.

When she had first arrived in India, she had wondered how anyone could wish for rain. She had never thought she would. But here she was hoping for a heavy thunderous rainfall, accompanied by cold stormy gale force winds and a dark, grey sky.

She repositioned her feet and stretched her neck towards the icy blasts. The air conditioner was placed above the dressing table and to get to it she had to stand on a wobbly stool.

It wasn't long before she became bored of just standing there.

She turned her attention to the mirror hanging above the dressing table and eyed her blurred reflection. She was wearing a thin white dress that floated around her knee. The only colour in her outfit was the ropey turquoise straps digging into her tanned, freckled shoulders.

She also wore her sister Maryanne's round glasses even though it rendered her almost blind.

She wasn't wearing the glasses because she missed the grown up, evil Maryanne. No, she wore it because she missed the younger Maryanne. The one she had loved with all her heart as a child.

Thinking of Maryanne reminded her of poor miserable Maya who was sulking in her room. Things had not gone according to plan.

Again.

What could Tabby do to cheer her up? The answer was easy enough. She would take Maya shopping.

She jumped off the stool and sat down on it instead. She fingered the thin cotton material wondering if she could go shopping in the dress.

If not this, then what? She couldn't bear to cover her arms and legs in this heat.

But what if her dress attracted shady men like mould to cheese? What could she do?

Not be helpless, that was for certain. She straightened her shoulder and lifted her chin.

Sure, she looked like a mid-priced breakable vase, but she only looked it. In truth, she patted the non-existent muscles in her arm, she was pretty strong.

She leaped off the stool, brought her fingers together and took up a karate pose.

"Yeeeaah!" she screeched and dropkicked and punched an invisible assassin.

Next, she shot into the air, zoomed a few feet forward and landed next to the sofa.

She rolled onto the cold stone floor imagining a swarm of men wearing black masks and flowing robes come towards her from all sides.

She oozed upwards, her eyes darting hither and thither.

Her fingers curled into a claw and she struck. Another assassin went down, his head exploding on the wall behind her. The skull cracked open confirming her suspicions. It was completely devoid of brain matter.

"EEEEE!" she cried, rotating on the spot with her left leg sticking out, kicking each one of the evil blobs in the face.

Her glasses flew and clattered on top of the dressing table.

She ignored them and bent over, stuck her head under her legs, reached out and grabbed yet another miscreant by his cuff and flung him across the room. He splattered on the wall in a bloody, gruesome mess.

She had finished off eight men all on her own.

She executed a few more moves impressed by her own flexibility. She had never contorted her body in so many ways before. It was remarkable what a human body could do.

This, she decided, was a new fighting art form. She called it Kyoga. Karate meets yoga.

She dusted off her hands, lifted up an invisible collar and turned back to the mirror.

"You," she blew on her finger and pointed at her flushed nose, "are a weapon of mass destruction."

A male chuckle sounded behind her.

She whirled around and found Dev leaning against the door frame.

"You are incredibly entertaining," he observed.

"You didn't knock," she accused, her face flushing in embarrassment. How long had he been in the room?

"I did. You didn't answer. You seemed . . . engrossed. Besides, your door was open."

"Right," she said and looked away from him.

"May I come in?" he asked.

"Yes, of course," Tabby said and gestured towards the small sitting area in her bedroom.

He sat down on the chair while she sat on the sofa facing him.

"Water?" she asked, leaping back up.

"Sure."

She went over to the copper pot, vaguely noting that her limbs were suddenly stiff. She pulled out the ladle and jerkily poured water into a glass, splashing some on her wrist.

Dev and she had spent a lot of time together, but Maya had always accompanied them. Now, in her absence, a strange awkwardness seemed to have risen between them, or was she the only one feeling it?

"Here," she said, holding out the glass to him.

He reached to take it from her. Their fingers touched.

Her eyes flew to his in shock.

He stared back, his dark eyes locked on her face.

After a long moment, she looked down at her fingers still holding the glass, the tips still touching his.

"Tabby," his low voice wrapped around her, pulling her deeper into the strange hypnotic moment.

A cloud parted in the sky, and a ray shot through the window and struck the diamond on the poo ring. It flashed bright and hot.

She jerked back guiltily. The glass clattered to the ground, spilling water and white flower petals on the grey stones.

"Sorry," she mumbled and raced to get a cloth to mop it all up.

"It will dry," he said, watching her scrub the floor harder than necessary. "Please sit."

She gripped the rag in her hand and sat back on the sofa.

"I wanted to talk to you about Maya," he said. His voice was steady and indifferent.

She felt some of the tension leave her shoulders. They were on safe ground.

"I wanted to do something to cheer her up," he continued. "I thought we could go on the terrace tonight and drink some wine, eat some good food and chat, or watch a movie on my laptop."

She shook her head, "the terrace will be baking today."

"Maybe some other time then," he acceded with a nod. "What do you suggest?"

"We should take her shopping," she replied.

"And it's cool enough for that?"

"The car and the shops will be air conditioned."

"Not the shops, not here. But I doubt Maya will notice the heat once she spots the clothes."

"We could leave by four. It would be cooler by then."

"I will meet you near the car," he said standing up.

She walked him to the door.

"And Tabby?"

"Yes?"

"Don't wear that dress to the shop. It's a small town and—"

"I will wear what I want," she bristled.

"But—"

"No."

"As you wish," he said in a voice that sent a shiver down her spine.

This was the tone he used to frighten off hardened criminals and bad politicians. For a moment, she wondered if she should give in.

He didn't give her a chance to change her mind. With a final look that would have petrified the bravest of men, he departed.

"I will see you at four," she called after him.

He raised a hand without turning around.

"You don't scare me," she muttered at his disappearing, sculpted back. "Not one bit. And I will wear a short, strappy sundress, just you wait and watch."

Tabby chickened out and wore a pale lilac maxi dress. Sure, it wasn't short, thin or skin tight, but you could call it a sundress. It was strappy, and it had watermelons printed on it with one of them placed in a naughty spot.

She ran a brush through her hair that hung limply on her bare shoulders. She hadn't bothered with makeup, since the heat would melt it away in minutes.

She reached the car park and looked around for Maya and Dev.

A broad man wearing a red turban, white *kurta*, blue jeans and tan slippers was leaning against one of the cars. His moustache and beard were dyed with henna and his dark eyes were gazing at her lustily.

She rubbed her arms uncomfortably and turned her face away. She prayed Maya would hurry up.

The man pushed away from the car and slowly approached her. He said something in Punjabi, his voice deep and guttural.

"I don't understand." She lifted up her hands and shrugged.

His right hand shot out and gripped both her wrists while his other hand closed over her mouth.

It happened so fast that all she could manage was a surprised squeak.

Once the seriousness of the situation sank into her brain, she panicked and began struggling. Her hands flailed, her legs contorted in positions her kindergarten ballet teacher would have applauded, and she even tried the old knee between the legs trick.

He evaded her every move.

Her heart began thumping so hard it hurt.

He raised his eyebrows, waiting for her to struggle some more.

Did he intend to tire her out? He was just standing there holding her wrists. Shouldn't he drag her off to a corner or steal her bag and run—

A soft, warm breeze blew just then carrying his scent to her. The deep, heady aroma wrapped around her causing her head to spin in a familiar way.

Her eyes widened.

Shock was replaced with anger.

Now that she knew to look, she wondered how she had missed it.

It was a good disguise. But he looked broader—ah, he had his legs spread further apart than usual, his chest was thrust out, and the flowing *kurta* added to the illusion of him appearing wider than he was.

He noticed the shift in her expression and stepped back with a smile.

"Dev!" she glared at him. "That was not funny."

"Wasn't meant to be," he replied. "I wanted to see if you really had those fighting skills. The ones I witnessed earlier in the room."

She scowled and rubbed her wrists. He was right. Annoying but right. She didn't just look like a mid-priced breakable vase. She was a mid-priced breakable vase. And as for her muscles . . . yeah, they were probably rolls of fat.

"Here," he said, taking a can out of his pocket and handing it to her. "Wear what you like, but keep this with you at all times."

She read the label, "Pepper spray?"

"Keep it for my mental health," he coaxed. "At least I won't worry."

"You worry about me?" she asked. The anger whooshed out of her.

"About everyone. I worry about everyone," he clarified. "I gave one to Maya earlier in the day—Here she comes."

Maya arrived wearing a blush coloured *anarkali* and a god awful scowl. Tagging along behind her was Gunjan.

"We don't know the shopkeepers," Maya said gruffly. "So, Daaji insisted we take this creature along." She didn't bother lowering her voice but then Gunjan didn't look too perturbed by the hostility rolling off Maya either.

"Let's go," Dev said.

"Who is he?" Gunjan asked suspiciously.

"My mother's second cousin's eldest son," Maya replied promptly.

"I have never seen him," Gunjan tilted her head like a wary sparrow.

"He is my mother's relative, not Daaji's. How would you have met him? Have you met everybody's relative? Do you remember every face that you see at weddings?" Maya growled.

"But—"

"If he bothers you, then don't come along," Maya cut Gunjan off.

"The car is this way," Gunjan responded calmly.

Tabby was impressed and confused. She was impressed with Gunjan's self-control. If anyone had spoken to her in such a rude tone, she would have burst into tears or whacked the person on the head.

And she was confused because she couldn't understand why Maya was being rude in the first place. Dev's disguise was excellent, and Mrs Mansukani would back up their story about the cousin bit. Then what was bothering her friend?

Maya yanked open the car door. "Tabby will sit in the back with me and D—"She froze for a heartbeat and then smoothly continue, "Dumpy here. Gunjan, sit in the front with the driver."

"I want to sit at the back," Gunjan objected.

"You know the way. It will be easier for you to guide the driver," Maya said.

"Dumpy," Dev grunted in Maya's ear.

"Suits you," Maya giggled.

Dev glowered at her.

Maya giggled harder. "Dumpy, Dumpy, Dumpy," she teased.

"Pinky, Pinky, Pinky," he teased back.

"Don't you dare go that low, Dev Mansukhani," Maya whispered in horror.

Dev crossed his eyes and stuck his tongue out.

Tabby smiled seeing Maya's eyes light up in mischief.

Half an hour later they reached a bazaar bursting with colourful shops. Tabby whooped in delight at the visual delight in front of her.

The early evening light cascaded down to illuminate a neat row of men sitting on their haunches on the pathway. Placed in front of them were old fashioned measuring scales and sacks overflowing with turmeric, dried red chilies, star anise, cinnamon sticks, black cardamom and plenty of other spices.

Further on, women were dipping cloth into buckets filled with dye, ringing them out and hanging them on ropes. Some of the dry, vibrant scarves rippled in the gentle breeze while heavy jewel-toned saris hung quietly on makeshift racks on the footpath.

The bazaar had plenty of stores and stands, but not many customers. Only a few people were loitering around, probably due to the scorching heat.

Gunjan led them towards a red brick *bindi* shop.

Bindi, Maya explained to Tabby as she marched purposefully down the road, were the little stickers that women stuck in between their brows. This particular shop was famous for its designs.

Suddenly, a man materialised in front of them, feigned tripping up and lurched towards the three girls with his arms thrown wide open, but Dev quick on his feet intercepted him and firmly steered him away. After that, even Gunjan slowed her steps and stuck close to Dev.

Tabby was having her own private set of problems. She had thought she was being smart by wearing a maxi dress.

But women with pale skin, bare shoulders, wearing maxi dresses were uncommon in rural Punjab. She was relieved when they entered the *Bindi* shop and the glass door clicked shut behind them blocking out the stares.

Dev left them, declaring the place was too boring.

Gunjan watched him go wistfully. "Is he married?" she asked Maya.

"Happily married with six lovely children," Maya replied without missing a beat.

They spent a pleasant hour browsing through stacks of beautiful *bindis* and pots of *kumkum*. The shop even had some hand woven materials that the locality was famous for. Maya slurped on a bottle of Thumbs Up while Tabby guzzled lemonade as they were shown rolls and rolls of gorgeous material.

A good while later, Maya finished paying and they were ready to go. Dev arrived as if on cue.

"I bought presents," he smiled and held out a lovely cream and gold scarf towards Maya.

Maya squealed in pleasure and hugged him, scandalizing the shopkeeper who promptly swooned, fell off his chair and disappeared behind the counter.

He offered a deep turquoise one to Gunjan, who took it after a few token protests. She stepped back, and her heel 'accidently' landed on Tabby's toe.

"And this," Dev flicked open the last one, which turned out to be a soft lavender, "is for you."

Tabby elbowed Gunjan aside and sent him a pleased look. Her eyes met his and she silently thanked him. Not just for the scarf but for understanding her and giving her a choice. He had noticed her discomfort, bought her a scarf and left it up to her to decide if she wanted to wear it or not. He was no longer dictating to her.

She smiled at him, and he dipped his head slightly, his expression unreadable.

By the time they stepped outside the shop, the sky was tinted orange and a strong, cool breeze had started up.

Maya chattered all the way to the car, describing her purchases in great detail to Dev.

They threw the bags in the boot and sighed in relief when the car began zipping down the road and the windows let in fresh gusts of breeze. Everyone was heartily sick of stale air-conditioned rooms.

The car halted at a traffic light. A young girl wearing an old frock whose colour was indistinguishable with layers of dirt approached the car. She ignored the other passengers, her eyes locked on Tabby. She had a basket balanced on her head, full to the brim with jasmine flowers.

The young girl, who could have been no older than ten, grinned at Tabby. She had a happy, cheerful smile with a spark of mischief in her eyes.

An older boy tried to push her out of the way, but the flower girl gave him a good strong kick that sent him howling away. She chuckled in delight, turned her dirt-streaked face back to Tabby and said something.

"She says you are more beautiful than Bollywood actresses," Maya translated.

"Thank you," Tabby said, her hand already busy fumbling in her purse.

"Tan koo," the girl copied cheekily.

Tabby felt her heart clench. The girl was so young, so filled with life. She wished she could take her home, dress her up and send her to a good school.

"Ten rupees," the girl said, and held up one tiny, brown finger.

"She means ten rupees for one string of flowers," Maya explained.

Tabby held out five hundred rupees and handed it to the girl.

The girl was first shocked and then delighted at the fortune in her small hands. She took hold of the basket and tossed the flowers into the car.

Hundreds of little white flowers cascaded all over Tabby's hair and clothes.

"Tan koo," the girl laughed and, clutching the money in one hand and the empty basket in the other, raced toward the boy she had kicked a moment before. She showed the money to him, and he grinned and draped an arm around her thin shoulders.

Tabby watched the flower girl disappear as their own car sped away laden with the exotic scent of little white flowers.

Chapter Twenty Four

Maya got engaged that evening. Tabby watched her shove a thick gold ring onto Cuckoo Singh's stubby finger and cringed.

The dining room had been chosen for the occasion, though the dining table itself had been taken out and replaced with two giant red velvet chairs and placed in the centre of the room. Maya, in a dull gold sari, sat perched on the edge of one of them while Cuckoo Singh, in a maroon and gold *sherwani*, lounged on the other.

Mrs Mansukhani had told Tabby that this would be a small gathering with only close friends and family invited.

The 'small gathering' turned out to be over a hundred people jammed into one room and everyone was dressed up brighter than a lit up Christmas tree.

Tabby wore a beautiful moss green *lehenga* that she had borrowed from Maya. She shifted uncomfortably as the short brocade blouse dug into her ribs. The tailor had done a good job shortening the length of the skirt, but he could loosen the top only so much. A tight bodice meant that most of the men had chosen to have a conversation with her chest rather than her face the entire evening.

She moved closer to the large standing fan that whirred behind her and watched Chris—looking particularly handsome in a blue and cream *kurta*—laugh at something Gunjan was saying.

Gunjan looked stunning in a yellow and gold sari. Her hair was wrapped in a dark glossy bun that wobbled when she moved closer to Chris. A tiny diamond nose pin jammed in her left nostril sparkled seductively up at him.

Tabby turned away and went to fetch Daaji a plate of snacks.

The next day, relatives began to arrive in earnest for the upcoming wedding.

Aunties arrived from New York, uncles from Sydney, *bhaiyas* from London and *didis* from Spain.

Once all twenty-five rooms were occupied in the house, mattresses were laid out on the dining room floor for the children and teens to sleep on. They loved this arrangement as it allowed them to giggle and chat away till the wee hours of the morning. The whispered shut ups and warning growls from adults tickled them even further and added to their merriment.

One afternoon, fed up with the noise and the chaos, Tabby escaped up to the terrace. It was a cloudy day with the breeze pregnant with rain. Green fields stretched out on three sides of the rooftop. A few bright red tractors rolled by leaving giant tyre marks in the dark, moist mud below.

She chose to sit on the side overlooking the orchard.

She gazed unseeingly towards the clustered guava, mango, and apple trees. She pulled open her diary and began pouring her heart out. Half an hour later, she read what she had written, sighed and tipped her head up to the sky.

In England, the sun, when it was out, blazed white and hot, while here the sun seemed to emit a golden light. She didn't know if she was imagining such things, but right now with the sun glowing like a yellow light bulb through an amoeba-shaped cloud, it sure seemed like it.

She realised she didn't miss England, and here, in spite of the dirt, chaos, noise, madness and smelly cow poos, she felt at home. She felt as if she were slowly falling in love with this vast, mystical country.

She wondered why that was. She closed her eyes, letting the sun bathe her face with warmth.

Perhaps, it was because India made her feel more than she ever had. It yanked out her passionate side, made her experience things in such a strong fashion that it shook her soul.

She hated it when men stared at her on the streets. The noisy traffic grated on her nerves, the beggars on the street made her heart hurt, while the heat and humidity made her want to scream in frustration.

At the same time, she loved the explosion of flavours in her mouth when she ate the local food. Her heart warmed at the affection Nani, Mrs Mansukhani, Dev, Maya, the aunties and so many other people showed her. She loved the fact that everyone sat together at dinner time and sang songs until late in the night. She loved the monsoon rain, the storms, the colourful bazaars and a hundred other little things.

She felt as if she had lived all her life looking at the world through pale, watery vision, and now she had put on a pair of spectacles and could finally see everything in its true, frightening, exhilarating colours.

Her philosophical daydream was very rudely interrupted by a crow cawing somewhere up over her head.

She closed the diary with a reluctant snap and moved to go when she spotted a flash of red from the corner of her eye. She jerked back around and stared down at the little clearing where she had tried to lure Cuckoo Singh not too long ago.

Maya had chosen that spot deliberately, since the trees surrounding the clearing offered privacy and no one looking out from the house could see what was going on.

Unless they happened to be standing up on the rooftop like Tabby was.

She shaded her eyes and watched Gunjan and Chris kissing like two desperate people starved of love. His hands were running all over her back while she was clutching a fist full of his hair and standing on her tip toes. Chris detached himself from her greedy lips and pulled her top aside to rain kisses down her neck and exposed shoulders.

Tabby's knuckles turned white as she clutched her diary in a painful grip. She turned away from the sight, straightened her back and made her way towards the little clearing in the fruit orchard.

Tabby walked right up to the couple. She noticed how Gunjan was wrapped around Chris like a cling film on a hot potato. She could practically see the steam coming off their clothes.

She was curiously detached and wondered how come he had never kissed her like that. She waited for them to notice her, and when they didn't, she tapped Chris on the shoulder.

He extracted his lips and looked up. The expression on his face would have made her laugh had she not been hopping mad.

Gunjan blushed and adjusted her top.

"You could have told me you had changed your mind," Tabby said in a calm voice.

Chris sprang away from Gunjan putting an impressive four feet between them. "I haven't! She threw herself at me, I swear. She was kissing me, and I was trying to find a way to get rid of her. She," he pointed at Gunjan with a shaking finger, "is a succubus. A horny devil."

Tabby raised an eyebrow. She was proud of that raised eyebrow. She had never before managed to lift it on command, no matter how many times she'd practised in the mirror, but right now when she most needed it to, it flew upwards forming a perfect, disbelieving arch.

Chris swallowed nervously, "Look, you know she is not my type. She can't speak a straight line in English. She has such a thick accent I can't understand a word she says. I can't marry her, what will people back home think—"

Gunjan swung back her fist and punched him in the stomach.

He doubled over in pain.

"I may not speak like a Londoner," Gunjan growled, "but I can punch like a proper Punjabi girl. And trust me, I would rather know how to punch."

"I think she speaks pretty well. Her accent is charming," Tabby observed, inclining her head towards Gunjan.

Chris emitted a sound extraordinarily similar to a sheep's bleating.

Tabby grabbed his hand and turned it over. "Keep the poo ring. It's over."

Tabby sat on a stool placed directly under the air conditioner with the vent pointing towards the top of her head. She was attempting to cool off her frazzled brain. This time, she didn't even think of calling Becky to solve her problems.

The reason she had gotten into this mess was because she had not bothered listening to her own heart in the first place. It was time she made her own decisions and took responsibility for her own actions.

"You can't leave until after Maya's wedding," Chris spoke from the doorway.

She plucked a brush off the dressing table and began unknotting her hair.

He kneeled down next to her and looked up into her face.

"Tabby," he said softly, "I am sorry. I didn't think . . . didn't plan the kiss. It just happened."

She refused to look at him.

"You are not in love with me," she said. "You don't have to explain anymore."

"But isn't marrying your best friend the right thing to do?" he pleaded. "We understand each other, get along well enough. I made a mistake. It won't happen again."

He didn't deny that he did not love her. And he was right, she realised. He did treat her more like a best friend than a lover. Why had she not seen it before? Tabby squeezed her eyes shut. She, too, had been attracted to Dev but never acted on it. Never thrown herself at him. Even thinking about him had made her feel guilty.

If every time someone cute came along, Chris was swept away in the moment, then how could they ever have a serious relationship? How could she ever trust him?

"We could have an open marriage," he offered hesitatingly.

Her eyes sprang open, and she stared at him in horror. She suddenly felt like she didn't know Chris at all. Who was this man?

Chris took a breath and launched into a rapid, rehearsed speech, "Fine. I agree we should call off our wedding, but I don't want our problems ruining Maya's special day. Think of her, think of my mother. They would be shattered. And all those horrible relatives will begin asking questions if they see you missing. I may not care about what people here think, but my parents do. Stay for their sake. They have been nothing but kind to you."

Tabby had not been planning to leave. She was hurt, yes, but she was not selfish. She knew Maya needed her help. She also knew that she couldn't abandon the family at such a sensitive time and leave them to face awkward questions. She would have to bury her pain and paste a smile on her face.

"Tabby," he prompted.

"I'm not leaving," she replied.

He smiled in relief and held out the poo ring, "Will you wear this until the wedding?"

She shook her head.

"Can't we?" he began and then stopped at the look of rage on her face. He held his hand up and slowly backed out of the door.

Tabby flung the brush across the room knocking over the copper pot. It fell with a crash spilling sodden flowers all over the floor.

"Are you all right?" Maya came charging into the room. "I heard a crash."

Tabby looked up at her mutely.

Maya's expression softened. "You need to get out of the house?"

Tabby nodded.

"I know just the place."

Maya and Dev took her to a Gurudwara. They didn't go inside but sat on the steps facing a crystal clear lake where the reflection of the gleaming white temple rippled gently in the water.

"Isn't that the flower girl?" Tabby asked staring at a line of people, both rich and poor, sitting crossed legged on floor mats and eating food in the temple courtyard.

The delicious smell of hot *puris* floated over and hung like a cloud over their hungry heads. Maya's stomach growled loudly.

"Do you want me to fetch her?" Dev asked.

"Please," Tabby said gratefully. She felt a curious attachment to the young girl and seeing her bright face would lift her spirits.

"I will be right back," he said.

"Do you want to go inside?" Maya asked, tilting her head towards the Gurudwara.

Tabby shook her head.

As if sensing Tabby's desire to be alone, Maya stood up. "I am going to pray. You should be fine here. Just don't wander off."

Tabby didn't reply. She rested her chin on her knees and watched a grey duck stick its head under water.

Maya patted her head and left.

"Madamji." A man came up to Tabby. He was short, skinny and bald and looked oddly familiar. He held a few colourful glass bangles in his hand. "Good price," he said sticking the bangles under her nose and rattling them.

Tabby was about to shake her head when a pretty yellow and turquoise one caught her interest.

"How much?" she asked pointing to it.

"Fifty for six," the man replied.

The young woman, Sarla, who cleaned her room every day, would like it, Tabby thought.

"Twelve," Tabby said pointing to the bangle.

"You want twelve?" he asked.

She nodded, not surprised that he could speak English. A lot of Indians, she had noticed, could speak very well.

"Come," he said gesturing towards a row of wooden shops standing a few feet away.

Tabby glanced back at Dev. He was kneeling by the flower girl waiting for her to finish eating. He would take a while.

Tabby turned back to the bangle seller and nodded. She stood up and followed him.

The moment they stepped out of Dev's sight, the man pulled out a knife and dug it into her ribs.

"No noise," he hissed at her.

She paled but did as she was told.

He led her to the parking area, where another man was waiting. He was tall with rolls of fat that jiggled when he moved.

The fat man was barking into his phone repeatedly while scanning his surroundings nervously. They seemed to be waiting for a car to come and pick them up. The car was apparently late.

The two men spoke in urgent tones in Hindi . . . or was it Punjabi? She wasn't sure. She heard Dev's name often enough to know that this was planned. Badly planned, she amended when she noticed droplets of sweat trickle down the fat man's forehead. His chubby fingers gripped the phone so hard that she was surprised it didn't shatter.

Finally, the fat man departed leaving her alone with the skinny one.

Tabby eyed the fellow from the corner of her eye.

He warily eyed her back.

Becky had often told her not to suppress her feelings, especially anger. She had always encouraged Tabby to bare her soul, vent her rage and never let it fester or it would become puss filled and dangerous.

Tabby meditated on the thought for a while and finally decided to squeeze the festering boil so to speak. She decided to share her feelings with a stranger and unburden her sorrow.

"My fiancé cheated on me," she announced, breaking the silence.

The knife jabbing into her ribs eased a bit.

That surely was a positive and encouraging sign. Pleased, she decided to unburden some more.

"I was falling in love with him I think," she continued morosely. "Then he went and kissed this girl."

The fellow tsked sympathetically.

"You should never love anyone," she told him.

He nodded in agreement.

"It's terrible. They either die or hurt you or go off with someone else." She stopped as her voice caught on a sob.

"Love is very bad," he agreed. "My wife went off with my brother."

"My sister went off with my ex-fiancé!" Tabby squealed.

They high-fived each other. This was the kind of stuff that made strangers bond.

The knife vanished into his pocket and he leaned back on the bonnet of the car.

"*Daru* helps," he mused.

"*Daru?*"

"Bhiskey, bheer."

"Alcohol," she nodded in understanding.

"Good stuff."

"Got any?" she asked.

He took out a flask and handed it to her.

She took a swig of the rotten tasting drink and felt it burn down her throat and pool in her stomach.

"Hashish?" he asked, pulling out a joint.

She shook her head.

He lit up anyway and a sweet, smoky smell filled the air.

She inhaled deeply and took another gulp from the flask. On second thought, it didn't taste too bad. More like stale coconut water spiked with vodka.

"Good stuff," she smiled dreamily.

"Good stuff," he agreed, blowing puffs of smoke into the air.

"Your wife is very bad. You are a good man. You deserve better," she said.

"Same pinch," he said, feeling too lazy to repeat it all back to her.

She giggled.

"Tabitha!" Dev strode towards them.

The fellow flicked the joint away, pulled out the knife and stuck it on her throat.

"Sorry," he whispered in her ear.

"It's your job," she said comfortingly. "I don't mind."

"Thanks," he replied.

The fat man came racing back, his belly bouncing so hard that Tabby feared it would detach and roll away.

"Let her go," Dev said in a soft, dangerous voice.

"Won't," the skinny fellow countered.

"Good job," Tabby praised.

"Did you drug her?" Dev asked, his eyes narrowed in fury.

"Nope. They did nothing of the sort," Tabby soothed him.

"Sir ji," the fat man squeaked.

"What do you want?" Dev turned towards him.

The fat man shot a desperate glance towards the road and said something in reply.

"Give us money and get girlfriend back," the skinny fellow translated the conversation for Tabby.

"Fifty lakhs," the fat men said.

This number Tabby understood.

"Fine," Dev said.

"No," Tabby said at the same time. "I'm not worth fifty. How about five lakhs?" That was reasonable, and she wouldn't feel guilty asking Becky for that amount. Fifty was too much. She would have to work an entire lifetime to pay Dev back.

"Forty-five and no less," the fat man argued.

"Look, mister," Tabby growled. "I'm not his girlfriend. I have a fiancé."

"She does," the skinny fellow backed her up.

"Fine, forty," the fat fellow barked. "And that is final."

"Why would anyone pay forty lakhs for me?" Tabby argued. "I don't even have a job. I have barely a few hundred pounds left in my bank in England. Be reasonable now. I think seven is a good number—"

"Tabitha, shut up," Dev snapped.

She closed her mouth.

"Now," Dev turned to the fat fellow. "I am not carrying that much money, but there is an ATM close by. If one of you will come along, I will take out what I can—"

No, he will not, Tabby thought in irritation. She was sick of owing people money, tired of depending on everyone. She did not need a saviour. She was an independent woman in the twenty-first century.

She could take care of her own damn self!

"Sorry, buddy," Tabby muttered and rammed an elbow into the skinny fellow's stomach and at the same time grabbed his wrist and twisted until the knife fell with a clatter on the road.

Dev caught on quick and punched the fat man, who fell to the ground with a moan.

Tabby twirled away from the skinny fellow and landed right into Dev's arms. He grabbed her hand and they began running. She turned back to find that the fat man had pulled out a gun.

A shot rang out.

Dev pulled her behind a car, and crouching low they began shuffling towards the Gurudwara.

Tabby peeked through a car window and noticed the fat man slapping the skinny man on the head. Repeatedly.

That was the last they saw of them because Dev gripped her arm and forced her to sprint the last five minutes until they were once again in the safety of a crowd.

They stood under a tree, gasping for breath, surrounded by people going up and down the steps of the temple.

They stared at each other for a moment, and then Dev leaned over and pulled her into a tight hug.

Her ear was plastered to his chest and she heard his heart beating fast and hard.

He pushed her back and glared down at her. "What were you thinking? Bargaining with the kidnappers. Have you lost your mind? How idiotic are you? What if something happened to you? I would have paid them off. Why did you have to hit that man—?"

She held up a finger and placed it on his lips silencing him. "Shhh . . . The skinny one? He was the same man who almost knocked us over when we had gone to the *Bindi* shop. They knew who you were even though you are in disguise. They didn't want money, they were waiting for a car to take me away. They wanted something else. The fat man was buying time until his ride came along."

Her finger was still on his lips when she finished speaking. She pulled it away and swayed on her feet.

"Did they drug you?"

"I had *daru*," she said. Her head had begun to spin.

"The local stuff?"

"Sh'pose."

"No wonder you can barely stand straight. Here, put your arm around my shoulder."

"Nope. All along I have been good and loyal. Loyal and good. Kept all naughty thoughts at bay."

"What?"

"What what?"

"Put your arms around me, Tabitha."

"Tabby. Put your arms around me Tabby," she corrected.

"Tabitha," he said slipping his arm around her waist.

"Tabby," she slurred.

"Tabitha," he muttered and began dragging her along.

"Tabby," she said, her voice now just a thread.

"Miss Timmons," he replied.

" . . . Abitha will do," she sighed, rested her head on his shoulder and closed her eyes.

Chapter Twenty Five

The women had assembled in the courtyard to watch the youngsters practice for the *Sangeet*. Someone handed Tabby a small clay pot filled with sweet and spicy *masala chai*. She absently sipped it, her fingers curling around the warmth of the pot.

She knew she should feel worse about the break up than she did. Mostly she was confused. She hadn't known what her heart wanted. She still didn't know what it wanted, but this time the unknown gave her a sense of freedom. Instead of being terrified of an uncertain future, she was excited.

The world around her moved in a set pattern. When she had been in school people asked her what she wanted to be when she grew up. When she was working, people asked her when she would get married. When she became engaged, people asked her when she was planning to have babies.

She had broken free of that pattern and it gave her an exhilarating feeling. All her life, she had done what she thought everyone expected her to do. Gotten engaged to a man who had seemed almost textbook perfect. Good looking, wealthy, educated, with a wonderful, caring family, and yet she had felt something was missing.

But now she no longer felt the need to appease the world around her. For once, she wanted to find out what her heart wanted.

The only trouble was that her heart was difficult to decipher. It seemed to emit feelings in a mysterious coded language.

"You need your chakras aligned," Meena Aunty said coming up to her. "I can see a grave agitation in your solar plexus."

"Eh?" Tabby blinked. "Solar plexus?"

"Here," Meena Aunty poked Tabby's abdomen.

"I had a few dodgy *samosas*," Tabby offered.

"No, no. This agitation is on a spiritual plane not the physical."

179

"I see." Tabby blinked in confusion.

"Your third eye is fogged up," Meena Aunty continued.

"And yours is sewn shut," Nani came and sat down next to Tabby. "Never mind her." She patted Tabby's hand. "Watch the dance."

Tabby obligingly turned back to watch the little kids hop around in the front garden. They were practising for the Sangeet, a musical function where the bride's and groom's family try to outdo each other. The performances were taken very seriously and Maya's cousins had been practicing for months since they first learned of the wedding.

Girls ranging from fourteen to eighteen were ordering the young children around. They roared out instructions over a Bollywood song pumping out of the music system. The kids obligingly twirled and bounced and shook and dipped.

One little exhausted fellow lay down on the ground and began throwing a tantrum. He beat the ground over and over with his small fists while his legs waved in the air in distress. That set off the rest of the children, and the howling lot were quickly ushered indoors for a nap.

The girls turned their beady eyes on Tabby.

"Oh no, I can't dance," Tabby objected.

"You are going to be Maya's sister-in-law. You have to dance," one particularly stern young lady admonished.

"But I don't understand the lyrics—" Tabby began.

"You don't need to. Just follow us. It's easy," another young girl begged. She pulled on Tabby's hand.

"It's going to rain," someone shouted.

Tabby sank back in her chair in relief.

"So?" a girl yelled back. "Just place the music system on the window sill away from the rain. We are going to continue practising."

"In the rain?" Tabby asked weakly.

"It's the best time to dance," a girl chanted, grabbing her hand and pulling her into the garden.

Warm droplets splashed on Tabby's nose and eyelashes. She was wearing a *salwar kameez* again. A plain white cotton one that Maya had given her as a present. Her *dupatta* was tie-dyed red and yellow.

She blinked through the drizzle trying to follow the steps of the young girl in front of her. The music was fast paced and the steps intricate and unfamiliar. She felt like an awkward giraffe waving her long stiff limbs about.

"Not like this, like this." One of the girls came up to her to correct the way she was jerking her hips.

Tabby forced her movements to become slow and fluid. Bangles moved on her wrist, bells tinkled on her ankles, and her silky *kurta* swayed as she twirled around the garden feeling soft, fragile and feminine.

The girl smiled in delight and moved back to her place.

They kept dancing even after the sky erupted in torrents of rain and all of them were soaked to the bone. The aunties, Maya and Mrs Mansukhani cheered from the porch and clapped in time to the music. Maya was shouting and whistling the loudest.

"Brides don't act so bold," Nani scolded Maya. "Dip your head, stare at the ground and look shy."

Maya whooped louder in response.

As the minutes ticked by, Tabby began to enjoy herself. The warm rain was not unpleasant and the dancing was fun. She laughed in delight when the thunder roared and the monsoon rain became heavier still.

After an hour of practising, she lost her shyness and flung her limbs about in abandonment, no longer worried if she looked foolish or made mistakes.

A cool breeze started up suddenly chilling Tabby.

The air around her seemed to grow thick and charged. A shiver ran down her spine, and she paused midstep as if the wind had blown magical dust her way and turned her into a statue.

The girls, in pinks, whites and blues, continued to swirl and skip around her unaware of the change. Her skin prickled, and she slowly raised her lashes and looked up at the house.

Her heart was beating fast as if she knew what she would find. . . .

Dev was watching her from the second story window. His expression was unguarded, his eyes full of heat.

She became aware of the way her clothes clung to her like a second skin. She blushed and yet couldn't wrench her eyes away from his face.

They stared at one another as if enchanted, and the world around them ceased to exist.

Her skin felt raw and sensitive and her heart began beating a thousand miles an hour.

Something deep and stormy rose up between them. Something chaotic, wonderful and frightening.

The feeling was so intense that Tabby couldn't bear it any longer. Panic welled up inside, and she wrenched her gaze away from him.

"Tabby, it's raining too hard now." One of the girls shook Tabby's arm to get her attention. "We are going inside. Practice is over."

She looked back at him one last time and saw him move away from the window and disappear into the house.

Tabby bit her lip and followed the girls.

That evening, a shop seemed to have opened up in the middle of the dining room. Sari, shawl and bangle sellers had set up their wares while all the women in the house crowded around inspecting the stuff.

"Your aura is shooting confused sparks," Meena Aunty said materialising next to her. "Your heart chakra," she shook her head sadly, "is in one big mess. Meditate." She patted Tabby's arm. "Meditate, my child, and all will be well."

Mrs Mansukhani called Tabby to her side and asked her to choose a couple of saris for herself.

Tabby sorted through the pile of colourful materials trying to find something cheap.

Mrs Mansukhani left her to it and went to consult the *mehendi wali*.

"Don't you think you should let Gunjan marry Chris?" Dolly Aunty asked, sitting down beside her.

Tabby pressed her lips together and flicked open a sari.

Dolly Aunty pasted a smile on her face and hissed between her teeth. "You don't know anything about our culture, Daaji is unhappy with the match, and you walk around with this stupid and confused look all the time. Save yourself some pain and go back to England."

Tabby kept her head down, her eyes glued to the gold shot silk cloth in her hand.

"You can find plenty of other rich men to trap," she continued coldly. "I don't understand what he sees in you—"

"A lot more than he sees in Gunjan," Gayatri Aunty said. She towered over Dolly Aunty, her expression harsh. "I think he has made an excellent choice. Tabby is far more genuine, respectful and well-mannered than that malicious daughter of yours."

Tabby was stunned. Gayatri Aunty, who always insulted everyone, was coming to her aid?

Dolly Aunty pushed her heart shaped sunglasses back up the bridge of her nose and scowled.

Gayatri Aunty reached down, plucked a pretty rose gold sari from the pile and pulled Tabby up on her feet. She thrust the sari into Tabby's hand and nudged her towards Mrs Mansukhani, who was bargaining with the bangle seller. "Go, I will deal with Dolly."

Tabby walked away in a daze.

When had she won Gayatri Auntie's heart, and how in the world had this miracle happened?

Chapter Twenty Six

Tabby sighed and continued plodding up the stairs. Her love affair with Chris had come to a tragic end. Her engagement was off. And even though she was not too badly hurt, she was still lugubrious enough, considering the circumstances, to want to curl up on a couch with a giant box of gooey dark chocolate, tubs of sardines and mountains of colourful macaroons.

She wanted to watch sad, romantic movies, howl into a pillow or shriek like a lobster in a hot pot.

She paused on the top most step and dug her nails into the wooden railing. Most of all, she wanted to be in bed and asleep for the next sixteen hours.

She just wanted some time or privacy to properly mourn the end of her relationship.

And yet here she was once again dragging her juiceless body up to attend a meeting with Maya, and what with only two weeks remaining until the wedding . . . things were getting desperate.

Her head ached from all the confusing emotions raging inside her. She was relieved she wasn't going to marry Chris and sad at the same time for losing his friendship. And along with him, she would lose Maya and the rest of the family as well. Once they found out, she doubted they would want to stay in touch with her. It was for them that her heart was truly breaking.

She glowered at her blue and white striped ballet slippers. The crux of it all was that no one loved her. Not a single human being loved her. She was like an old dog in an animal rescue home that no one wanted. Her father had opted to let her go instead of stopping her, her sister had stolen the man she had loved, and Chris had slobbered all over Gunjan.

She pushed away from the railing and forced her tired legs to move towards the terrace. The door was slightly ajar, and she spotted Dev fixing a candle on the ground. The flickering flame bathed his face in a flattering golden light, and she sighed softly.

As if he heard her, he looked up and smiled.

Tabby swayed on her feet. In spite of her recent heartache, she realised she still liked men. Chris had not turned her into a bitter, man-hating cynic.

"Aren't you coming in?" Dev asked appearing at the doorway.

She took a step forward and found the tip of her nose almost touching his shirt button. Her heart began the now familiar dance, and she tilted her head up and stared at him.

He was so close . . . She could smell his clean, masculine scent. Her vision became slightly foggy and she swayed on her feet.

His expression changed, and his eyes became alert and watchful as if he, too, could feel the roiling attraction between them.

She swallowed, suddenly aware of the damp breeze on the back of her neck, the way her thin, silky pyjamas felt on her skin—the very same pyjamas that had white bunnies frolicking in pink and lilac fields with a few of them doing something deliciously naughty.

If only they could be those carefree bunnies. . . .

"Squeeze me," she said and froze. *Had she said what she thought she had or was her tired mind playing tricks on her?*

"What did you just say?" he asked.

She had said it! Kill me now, she prayed to Zeus silently. Throw down your thunderbolt and tandoori me ASAP.

"I think you said—"

"Yes?" she asked defiantly. "What did I say?" It was best to pretend it had not happened.

"You—"

"Yes?" she prompted.

He frowned. "Did you say anything at all?"

"Do you think I said anything?"

"I think you did."

"Are you certain I did?"

"I am pretty certain you did." He crossed his arms and peered down his fine nose at her, looking more British than Indian at that moment.

"I don't think so," she looked back bravely.

"I think so."

"You are imagining things."

"I am imagining that you didn't say anything?"

"I did say something."

"Ah, ha! What was it?"

"I said ex-squeeze me." Her fingertips flew upwards to pinch her lips together. *Shut up Tabby, shut up for goodness sakes, her brain yelled at her.*

He grinned. "You said it again!"

"I said excuse me."

"No, you did not."

"Yes, I did."

"No, you didn't."

"What's going on?" Maya asked. Her eyes moved between Tabby and Dev.

Tabby imagined tick-tock sound effects accompanying Maya's oscillating pupils.

When no reply was forthcoming, Maya asked, "Shall we begin the meeting?"

"Sure." Dev moved away from the door and went back on the rooftop.

Tabby shuffled after him.

Soon the three of them were sitting on a large yellow yoga mat placed on the ground.

"Here," Maya said, putting two whiskey bottles and a small packet on the ground. "We are getting drunk tonight."

"What's this?" Dev asked picking up the packet and sniffing the contents.

"Bhang," Maya replied. "We are going to get Cuckoo Singh stoned."

"No!" Tabby and Dev yelled at the same time.

"Shhh," Maya growled. "It's the only way."

"Maya," Tabby sniffed. "You are drunk."

"Only a tiny bit," Maya snickered. "Was drowning my sorrows."

"I think we should call it a night," Dev said sternly. "You are in no state to plan anything."

"Changey mindey after drinky," Maya chuckled unscrewing the top of the whiskey bottle. "One sip, come now. Itty bitty sip," she said tipping the contents down his throat.

Tabby grabbed the other bottle and took a few generous gulps before Maya could do the same to her.

Another few swigs from the bottle had them all feeling a lot more relaxed.

"It's nice isn't it?" Tabby asked staring up at the star filled sky.

"This is what I wanted," Maya agreed. "Passing out on the rooftop on a starry night."

"I feel like singing," Dev confessed.

"Don't," Maya begged.

"I don't like whiskey," Tabby mused thoughtfully. "Too bitter."

"Like Gayatri Aunty," Maya agreed. "I couldn't find anything else in Dad's cupboard."

"Gayatri Aunty is not too bad," Tabby responded recalling how she had stood up for her against Dolly Aunty.

"She would have been pretty nice if Daaji had not ruined her life," Maya said.

Dev's fingers tightened around the bottle.

"What happened?" Tabby asked.

"Well, Daaji got her married to a fairly rich man when she was seventeen. After that, her husband lost all his money and expected Gayatri Aunty to restore his finances by asking her father. Daaji refused to give his daughter a penny. He said his wealth was for his sons and that she should make peace with her destiny. Once a daughter is married, she is her husband's responsibility."

"And watching her brothers enjoy the wealth that she couldn't have simply because she was the wrong gender turned her into a bitter woman." Tabby guessed the rest feeling a pang of pity.

Dev lay on his back and placed his head on his arm. "What were you planning to do with the bhang?" he asked Maya.

"Mix it with *laddu*, feed them to Cuckoo Singh and then bring him to Daaji or bring Daaji to him. Daaji doesn't approve of drunk people or people who do drugs. He will never allow me to marry such a man," Maya replied.

"Daaji, Daaji, Daaji," Dev said his name bitterly. He grabbed the bottle and took a few generous gulps.

"He loves you. It breaks his heart to see you reject him so," Maya said.

"He broke mine when he rejected my parents," Dev said coldly.

Tabby burst into tears.

"He broke my heart not yours, Tabithas," Dev soothed.

"Tabitha," Maya wagged a finger at Dev, "not Tabithas."

"What about the other two Tabithas? Won't they feel left out?" Dev asked in an adorably confused voice.

Tabby began chuckling and crying at the same time.

"You are losing it, Tabby," Maya patted her back. "Now out with it."

"With what?" Tabby sobbed.

"Why aren't you wearing your engagement ring?" Maya asked.

"I'm allergic to metals," Tabby lied.

"Right," Maya frowned. "That's possible. Is that why you are crying?"

"No, no, I'm crying because he is so . . . you know?" Tabby howled.

"We know," Dev and Maya nodded hurriedly.

"He just is, you know?" Tabby continued.

"He is," Dev and Maya agreed.

"I mean, since I have arrived in India, I have been all alone. If it hadn't been for Maya, I would be even more alone. More alone than alone," Tabby explained.

"Very alone," Maya agreed.

"When I had the Belly Dug—"

"Delhi Belly," Dev corrected.

"Yes, that. Well, he wasn't even there," Tabby cried.

"I would like to be a fashion designer," Maya said out of the blue.

"And then he lied. And then he lied again and was bad again," Tabby continued.

"I think I like this guy in London," Maya mused. "He is cute, but a year younger than me. Is that a bad thing? He has red hair with itty bitty golden bits. I like men with red hair . . . and golden bits."

"I don't know why I agreed to the whole thing in the first place," Tabby said. "It is never smart to depend on a man."

"Yeah, that," Maya pointed a lazy finger at Tabby. "Men suck."

"Men suck," Tabby agreed.

"I object," Dev said sleepily.

"Except you," Tabby gazed at him dreamily.

"You are falling in lurve with Dev," Maya giggled. "You go all moony-eyed around him. Tabby is in lurve, Tabby is in lurve—"

"Am not," Tabby giggled back

"Are too," Maya teased.

"Am not," Tabby laughed, failing to notice Dev's clear, intense eyes fixed on her face.

After a few moments, Dev asked, "Are you really going to marry Chris?"

"What's it to you?" Tabby asked sullenly. "We don't talk to boys."

"Except red haired ones," Maya said.

"Cept those," Tabby agreed.

"Red-haired men with golden bits," Maya sighed and closed her eyes.

Tabby crawled out of bed the next morning. She felt like someone had played ping pong the entire night—with her being the poor battered ball. She lurched around her room like a newly born calf desperately trying to find her bearings.

Maya stumbled into the room looking just as Tabby felt.

They stared at each other sourly.

"Sup," Maya jutted a chin at her.

"Don't know, don't care," Tabby groaned.

"Here," Maya tossed a packet of painkillers towards Tabby.

Tabby didn't even attempt to catch the box and let it skitter across the floor. She wondered if standing still for a few hours until the pain went away was better or bending over, picking up the medicines, moving towards the copper pot, filling a glass with water, struggling with the medicine packet to take out the pills, popping them in her mouth—"

"Dev brought you back to your room last night," Maya whispered.

Tabby was grateful to Maya for whispering. Her poor throbbing head could bear only so much.

"I am going to tell everyone we were out in the sun too long," Maya went on in a low voice, "and we both fainted."

"Isn't that a little dramatic? Why can't we say we are hung over?" Tabby asked just as softly.

"Nope. Daaji will lose it. He doesn't mind men drinking as long as they remain within limits, but women . . . He would have a fit if he found any of the women drinking alcohol."

"Can't we tell your mum the truth?" Tabby asked.

Maya barely shook her head. "I don't think she will be happy about it either. Dad, you see, takes after Daaji, and Ma doesn't like keeping secrets from him."

"Never mind," Tabby moaned. She was in no mood to argue.

"Just pretend you are ill," Maya said, shuffling towards the door.

"I *am* ill," Tabby swayed.

"Remember, you have a heatstroke," Maya warned before leaving her alone once again in blessed silence.

Tabby emerged from her room sometime in the afternoon wearing a soft powder blue tea dress with cap sleeves and silver sandals. She peered out at the bright yellow world through her thick, unruly fringe and winced.

Perhaps food and water would make her feel alive again.

Nani accosted her outside the kitchen.

"Tabby," Nani said and then began speaking Punjabi.

Tabby stared at her blearily. Had Nani gone mad?

"Tabby?" Nani shook her arm gently.

"Eh?" Tabby managed.

Nani slapped her head, "I am sorry, I forgot you don't speak my language. I am so used to you now that I keep forgetting you are not Indian."

Tabby felt a strange, bittersweet feeling sweep over her. She felt terrible that she was lying to Nani and the rest of the family about Chris and her engagement. First Gayatri Aunty had accepted her, and now Nani was looking at her with eyes full of affection—"

"Go to the storeroom." Nani's words brought her back to the present. "It's a big white and blue ceramic jar filled with mango pickle—"

Tabby scrunched up her forehead. "You want me to go to the storeroom and fetch a pickle jar?" she asked.

"Right. It should be at the back of the room. Be careful of the cobwebs. The servants are busy with the lunch preparation or I would have asked them—"

"I don't mind," Tabby assured her.

"Do you know the way?"

Tabby remembered Chris pulling her into what looked like a storeroom once. She nodded, "I think so."

"Good girl," Nani smiled in relief and hobbled off.

After a quick drink of lemonade and a bite of *roti*, Tabby went in search of the storeroom.

Her steps were light and had a skip to them. She was feeling better.

She found the storeroom easily enough and pushed open the door. She stared into the darkness, and her nose twitched as a musty, metallic smell wafted towards her.

Her hand scrabbled around the wall looking for a light. Something soft brushed against her fingertips, and she almost screamed in fright.

Was that a rat's tail?

Being more careful, she resumed her search, found a switch and pressed it. A yellow light illuminated the room. The light was so faint that she feared the bulb would go out any minute.

She sped towards the back of the room where a line of ceramic blue and white jars sat on a rusted metal shelf. It was like an obstacle race. Her feet moved between barrels and boxes, and her arms were tightly folded taking care not to brush against anything.

In spite of all her precautions, she managed to bump into a shelf. The wooden shelf rattled alarmingly, the glasses placed on it clinked together while a nest of Russian dolls threatened to topple off. She lurched forward to hold the dolls steady, and once they stabilised she sagged in relief.

Her relief was short-lived. In her hurry to save the dolls, she had walked into a giant cobweb, and now she stood covered from head to toe in sticky webbing.

She froze in fright and wondered if along with the cobweb a spider or two had also attached itself to her dress?

And was the spider poisonous? Would it bite her and send her into a shivering fit until she was frothing at her mouth and—

A faint scream escaped her as she felt something move against her back. She squealed again as this time she thought something raced up her leg. Suddenly she felt like creatures were crawling all over her body. She wanted to rip off her clothes, but the thought that any movement may startle the spider into biting her kept her frightened limbs locked into position.

"Hello?" Dev called from near the door.

"Over here," Tabby whispered.

"Tabitha?" Dev asked moving towards the back of the room.

"Hurry," Tabby squeezed her eyes closed, her lips pale in terror.

He was with her within moments. "I heard you scream. What's wrong?"

"I ran into a cobweb and I think I have spiders crawling all over me," she replied through chattering teeth. "Black widow, Fringed

Ornamental Tarantula, Yellow Sac, Redback, Brazilian wandering spider—"

"Tabitha," he carefully took her hand and squeezed it. "Breath."

She breathed. In and out, in and out, and out and in and repeat.

"Good girl. Now, I am going to slowly brush off the cobweb. I don't think you need to worry even if a spider bites you—"

She squeaked.

"*If* I said. *If* a spider bites you, but it probably won't," he soothed. "I am going to start with your arm. Is that all right?"

She barely moved her head.

Taking that as a yes, he gently began picking off the sticky webbing from her skin. When he had finished one arm, he moved to the other. His fingers were brisk and gentle, barely touching her skin.

"Do you know of anyone who was bitten by a spider?" he asked conversationally.

"A boy in my neighbourhood used to collect spiders and chase me around with his specimens. I was six years old when I was bitten by one of his finds. I shivered for three nights, nothing would make me warm—"

"Your mother must have been worried," he commented.

"Yes, and the strange thing was that even she had been bitten by a spider as a child. The bite had left an amoeba-shaped mark on her leg . . . ." Her voice lost its tremble as she continued speaking, and he kept up a series of mundane questions.

She almost jumped in fright again when his fingers brushed against the nape of her neck.

"Sorry, I should have warned you," he said huskily.

She pressed her lips together suddenly aware of his fingers lightly skimming across her bare skin.

She also realised that they were alone in a dark storeroom and standing close . . . too close.

A different sort of fright took hold of her limbs.

He seemed to feel the change. His hand slowed as he moved down her neck to the middle of her back. His breath was warm on her sensitive nape.

The silence turned deafening and the air electric.

His fingers continued to dance over her clothes, her hair, and bits of her bare skin, brushing aside the web.

She could barely stand still. She longed to speak, to break the spell, but some unnamed emotion kept a hold on her voice.

"Are you still afraid?" he asked, his voice low and deep. His hand was now at her waist, and she could feel the heat from his fingers seep through the fabric of her dress.

Her skin tingled, and she felt an urge to lean back into him, to close the gap between them and let herself dissolve into his arms.

"No, I'm not afraid," she finally replied. Her voice sounded odd to her ears.

"Then why are you trembling?" His fingers dug into her waist and slowly turned her around.

"Am not," she said and shivered. She was finding it hard to stop her body from swaying towards him.

His fingers brushed over her stomach, the tops of her shoulder and then moved across her collarbone.

She wasn't sure if it was to remove the remnants of the cobwebs or . . . he just wanted to touch her.

He tilted her chin up and studied her face.

She closed her eyes, shielding them from his piercing, knowing gaze. Her heart began racing, bumping painfully against her ribs. She felt much like a helpless animal caught in a hunter's snare.

"Tabitha?" He caught her hand and brought it to his chest. She felt his heart beating against her palm—quick, rapid— just like hers was.

The bulb flickered out. The sudden darkness broke the heady spell. She wrenched her hand out of Dev's grip and leaped away.

"Careful," he said dryly as he heard her knock against something in the dark as she hurried to get away.

She didn't respond but moved as fast as she could towards the door. Spiders were no match for the threat that was Dev Mansukhani. She didn't choose to examine that thought any further as she rushed back into the sunlit hallway.

"Tabby, where the hell have you been?" Maya stopped her outside her room door. "You have to help me steal the *laddus* from the kitchen and fill them with bhang. Have you forgotten our plan? We have to get Cuckoo Singh high."

Chapter Twenty Seven

"Here," Maya pushed a piece of paper into Tabby's palm. "Cuckoo gave this to me a few minutes back."

Tabby opened the crumpled paper and smoothed the wrinkles out.

Wanna Boink?

She read the words, blinked, and then read them again. Yup, it still said 'wanna boink' in cursive handwriting.

"I'm sorry," Tabby patted Maya's shoulder sympathetically.

Maya leaned her head against the door frame, her posture reminiscent of an unhappy 1940's starlet. She opened her mouth and sang a sad Bollywood song in a pathetic voice.

A perfectly timed tear trickled down Maya's left eye as the notes faded away.

Tabby wanted to applaud. She wasn't surprised that Maya had burst into song. Maya secretly believed she was a Bollywood film heroine; hence, all her actions were planned to have the most impact on an invisible audience.

They resumed their gloomy walk towards the kitchen where they were going to steal *laddus*.

"Maya," Mrs Mansukhani planted herself in front of them and thrust a tray laden with tea, *samosas* and *pakoras* at them, "Dev's parents are here. Go and meet them."

"Tayaji is here?" Maya asked in shock. "But Daaji?"

"Daaji has gone to give your wedding card to a close friend of his," Mrs Mansukhani explained.

"Why are they here?" Maya asked.

"They wanted to give you your wedding gift. They won't be able to attend the wedding," Mrs Mansukhani replied, ushering them towards the living room.

Maya visibly brightened and she skipped ahead.

Tabby followed at a slower pace.

Dev's parents turned out to be gorgeous. His mother was slim, willowy and beautiful. She wore a long white dress, turquoise beads and lots of diamonds. Unexpectedly, she had blue-green eyes that stood out in a dark, intelligent face. Tabby later learnt that she was part English; hence, the exotic colouring.

As for Dev's father, he seemed to take up the entire room. He was muscular with not an ounce of fat, and his face was full of laugh lines. "Hello, old man." He whacked Maya's father on the back almost sending him sprawling on the floor.

Tabby tried to disappear into the sofa and hoped no one would notice her presence. They were just so distinguished. She felt frumpy in front of them.

Dev's mother had a different idea. She insisted that Maya and Tabby come and sit next to her. She then proceeded to shell pistachios and offered the meat to them in turn.

Tabby automatically popped the nuts in her mouth and chewed, all the while answering a string of questions. After a few minutes, she became comfortable enough to slouch on the sofa. Dev's mother looked intimidating, but she was, in fact, warm, friendly and eager to please. An hour later Tabby was laughing along with the rest of them, feeling as if she had known them for years. Dev's father loved telling jokes, and the moment there was a lull in the conversation, he would come out with the worst one-liners possible. It left everyone groaning and chuckling at the same time.

"Daaji is on his way," Gunjan popped in to tell them.

The mood immediately shifted and the atmosphere became strained.

"We have to go," Dev's father announced. He dropped his lashes—long, dark and curling just like Dev's—but not before Tabby spotted the pain in his eyes.

Dev's mother did not hide her sadness. She hugged Mrs Mansukhani, clinging on for a bit.

"I need to use the washroom before we leave," Dev's father requested.

"You know the way," Mr Mansukhani said gruffly. "This is as much your house as mine."

"Tabby, can you bring the basket of vegetables? It is on the side table in the lobby," Mrs Mansukhani asked. She turned to Dev's mother. "It is fresh from the farm. I knew you were coming, so I—"

Tabby didn't hear the rest as she hurried out of the room to fetch the basket. She spotted it immediately, but right next to it, lurking behind a large elephant statue, was Dev having an intense conversation with his father.

Tabby didn't want to disturb them. The talk seemed emotional.

"I am not going to forgive him," Dev was saying in a low, intense voice.

"He is your grandfather. The fight is between him and me. You don't have to get involved," his father argued.

"I have to go," Dev replied stubbornly.

"Don't be childish. You cannot carry around so much anger. It can't be healthy."

"He hurt you and mum."

"I am sorry I let our anger colour your emotions towards him. He loved you . . . still loves you. You used to spend hours playing with him when you were a child—"

"I don't want to talk about this."

"You are living here, aren't you? Perhaps, you are beginning to warm up to him again—"

"I am staying here for Maya. I leave at five in the morning for work. If I ever come back in the afternoon, I stay in my room and work on my laptop. Only Mrs Mansukhani and Maya . . . and Miss Timmons know I am here."

"Miss Timmons?"

"Tabitha."

"Miss Timmons is a bit formal, isn't it?"

Dev didn't respond.

His father sighed. "Call me later. I wanted to talk to you about this land deal in Papa New Guinea. They have a lot of gold—"

Tabby slipped into the library and waited until the whispers and the footsteps faded away. Dev's father was right. The fight was between father and son. Dev shouldn't get involved.

As for Daaji, true he was old fashioned in his mindset and at times painfully controlling, but he wasn't a bad man. He loved his family and was only trying to do his best for everyone.

Both Dev and Daaji were losing out by continuing this cold war. Dev couldn't attend Maya's wedding, and God only knew how many other important occasions he had missed out on, while Daaji must feel incomplete without his son and grandson in his life.

She wished she could do something about it. Bring them closer somehow. . . .

"What are you doing?" Dev asked.

Tabby squished the *laddu* in her hand in fright.

"Making *laddu*," Maya replied defensively. "Aren't you supposed to be at work?"

"*Laddus* are meant to be round. These are oval," Dev said sitting down next to them.

"We are not experts," Maya mumbled. She adjusted her *dupatta* in such a way that part of the pink cloth fell on top of the packet of hashish lying on the ground.

A cool evening breeze swept across the terrace pushing Tabby's hair forward and hiding her burning face. She had not forgotten the incident in the storeroom. She wondered what would have happened if the light hadn't gone out. Would he have kissed her? Did she want him to kiss her? Maybe she shouldn't think about him and kissing in the same sentence.

But what would happen if they did kiss? She had never felt such an intense chemistry before with anyone. Why, at this very moment, she wanted to leapfrog her way onto his lap. It was taking a lot of her will power to sit still and keep her hands wedged under her thighs.

Should she try kissing him for experimental purposes?

"Can I help?" Dev asked, his deep, rumbling voice sending a shiver down Tabby's spine.

"Sure," Maya said brightly.

Tabby frowned. They had already made the four spiked *laddu* they needed. They didn't need to make any more.

Dev took a dollop of the sweet lentil paste and rolled it between his palms. He seemed to have forgotten Maya's plan of drugging Cuckoo using *laddus*. They waited in breathless silence for him to recall it all. He didn't. Instead, he made a perfectly round *laddu* and showed it to them.

"This is how you do it," he said proudly and proceeded to remake the ones they had already made.

Tabby and Maya sat very still, their brains furiously memorising where the spiked *laddus* were placed on the tray.

Dev worked quickly, and within minutes he had made twelve gorgeous *laddu.*

Was there anything the man couldn't do? Tabby wondered. He was very good with his hands. The way his long fingers gathered the paste and placed it in the middle of his palm and then rolled it with just the right amount of pressure. Round and round and round—

"Do you want to wash your hands?" Maya asked. "Mine are all sticky."

"Sure," Dev answered, standing up and stretching.

Tabby threw a dishcloth over the *laddus* while Maya gripped the remaining hashish, no doubt eager to flush it down the toilet.

Tabby was the first to reach the terrace door. She thought she heard footsteps scuttling down the stairs, but she couldn't be certain. Still, she paused with her head cocked for a moment before going down to her room.

Ten minutes later Maya and Tabby were back on the terrace. The trouble was, Dev joined them as well.

"Shall we try them?" Dev asked.

"Try what?" Maya started violently.

"The *laddu,*" he frowned.

Words burst forth Tabby's lips. "I'm so hungry. It is a pity we eat so late in India. Why, in London we would have already had our dinner by now. And I love *laddus*—"

Maya pinched her, and she obligingly closed her mouth.

Dev looked at Tabby for the first time that evening. He studied her face as if mentally putting together a jigsaw puzzle.

"*Laddu?*" Maya planted herself in front of Dev and offered him one.

He absently popped the entire thing in his mouth, his face still thoughtful.

Maya turned to Tabby, her eyes wide, trying to silently communicate the safety of the *laddu* in her hand.

Reassured, Tabby took it and nibbled a bit. It was pretty tasty, so she ate it all.

After the three of them had finished eating, they stared at each other, wondering what to do next. Maya and Tabby had planned to accost Cuckoo and feed him the *laddus*, but with Dev around they couldn't do that.

"I had a pet turtle once," Tabby remarked thoughtfully.

Maya and Dev stared at her.

"I was seven," Tabby continued broodingly. "I called her Slinky Noodles. She died. We had a lovely funeral for her. All the children from the neighbourhood came to pay their respects."

Maya started laughing.

"What's so funny?" Dev chuckled. "Her pet died. That's sad."

"It is sad," Tabby giggled.

"We should make you feel better," Maya said, "'cause your pet died."

"Okay," Tabby agreed.

"How about we do something mean to Cuckoo Singh?" Maya asked. "That will make you feel better."

"Like feed him spiked *laddus*?" Tabby burst out laughing.

"What's so funny?" Dev asked again. "What spiked *laddus*?"

"You look shooo shweet when you are confused," Tabby pinched his cheeks.

He blushed. "Miss Timmons," he admonished, "you really *shouldn't.*"

"I know what we should do," Maya announced. "We should frighten the life out of Cuckoo Singh and hope he really dies of fright."

"Oddly, that sounds like a brilliant plan," Dev frowned.

"How?" Tabby asked.

Maya's forehead scrunched up, and her face took on a look of a mathematically challenged person trying to do a complicated sum. "See, you are white. As pale as a ghost. Sometimes you are so pale that you glow in the moonlight." Maya tapped Tabby's nose. "So, we will dress you up in a white sari and hang you upside down from a tree. I will bring Cuckoo Singh, and he will take one look at your ghostly, cackling figure and die of fright."

"How will I hang upside down? I'm very bad at acrobatics. I can't even summersault," Tabby brooded.

"I will hold your legs," Dev comforted her.

"Now that's decided, let's go," Maya grinned.

"Go where?" Tabby asked stumbling after Maya.

"To my room to dress you up like a ghost, silly."

"I think you mixed up the *laddus*," Tabby said as she tried to climb an old gnarled Neem tree. The sari kept getting in the way or threatened to come off altogether.

"The spiked ones were on the right. We ate the ones on the left," Maya objected.

Dev made an impatient sound, caught hold of Tabby's waist and deposited her on the lowest branch.

"I think you made a mistake," Tabby insisted, rubbing the spot where Dev's hands had been. "I'm feeling foggy."

Dev climbed after her and helped her moved to a higher branch.

"Shut up and keep climbing," Maya growled. "Now, I am going to get Cuckoo Singh. Don't forget, when I hoot like an owl, Dev, you will grab her ankles and hang her upside down. Swing her around a bit. Now, Tabby, don't forget to laugh like an evil creature when you see Cuckoo."

"Your brain is working pretty well for someone who ate spiked *laddus*," Tabby commented.

"The *laddus* were not spiked," Maya snapped.

"Ooh, spiked *laddus* made you grumpy," Tabby grinned.

"Shut up. I am going to get him now. Be ready," Maya stormed off.

Dev caught Tabby's waist and once again helped her move higher up the tree.

"You have to stop that," Tabby complained.

"Stop what?"

"Touching me," she wailed. "It makes me want to do very bad things to you."

"Oh," he said, and after a moment added, "Same pinch."

She made a kissy face, and he groaned.

"Not now. We are on a mission," he scolded her.

"It's dark," she fluttered her lashes. "No one can see us."

He pulled out a flashlight and gave it to her. "Shove this in your bra and make sure the light is pointing at your face. It will make you look even scarier."

"You said bra," she gasped.

He rolled his eyes. "Let's test this out."

Tabby turned away, shoved the flashlight into her bra and turned back around.

He nodded approvingly and pulled her forward until she was straddling his thigh. Before she could object to the undignified position, he clamped a hand down on her right knee and pushed her shoulders with the other hand until she dangled upside down.

She started giggling and thrashing. "Your hands on my knees tickle," she complained.

He moved his hand higher placing it on her thigh "And now?"

She stopped laughing. The heat from his hand penetrated the layers of the sari and petticoat and reached her skin.

"It's fine," she said, her voice sounding thick and far away.

He noted the change in her and lightened the pressure on her thigh.

She panicked and reached for him, "I'm going to fall!"

He pulled her back up and into his arms. "I got you," he murmured soothingly.

Her heart was beating very fast now. She was straddling his thigh again, and he was rocking her back and forth in an attempt to comfort her.

Instead of being comforted, she became even more agitated as other baser feelings started taking over her body. She clutched his arms. "Don't," she said, her voice trembling.

He didn't stop the rocking. He knew, she realised, her eyes widening. He was doing this deliberately.

His lips quirked up, his eyes sparkling with mischief.

An owl hooted loudly, or rather Maya attempted to hoot like an owl.

The next moment Tabby felt herself being pushed until she was once again dangling upside down. Her face was still flushed, and it took her a few shaky breaths to calm down.

"And here," Maya's voice swirled in the dark night, "was the place where the young woman used to wait for her husband. They had spent just one night together before he disappeared. She would sit under this tree, waiting for him to return. She waited for years and years and years, and then one day she died at this very spot. Some sensitive people claim to see her ghost still—"

"I can see something," Cuckoo cut in breathlessly.

Tabby cackled loudly on cue.

"What can you see?" Maya asked in a low voice.

"Chris's fiancée swinging upside down like a monkey. Has she gone mad? It is the middle of the night." Cuckoo Singh frowned.

"That's the spirit of the widow. Not Tabby," Maya replied urgently.

"Nah. That's Tabby. We should take a video of this and put it up on Joochube. She makes a pretty convincing ghost."

"Not convincing enough for you, though," Maya said sourly.

"Where are you taking me?" a voice complained loudly.

Maya grabbed Cuckoo Singh and dived into the bushes. At the same time, Dev yanked Tabby back up into his arms. He placed a finger on his lips as a twig cracked loudly in the night. Tabby fumbled in her blouse and switched the flashlight off plunging them into darkness.

"Gunjan, I am warning you. This better be worth it," Daaji's voice rang loud and clear in the still night. He wheeled himself and stopped where a shaft of bright moonlight cascaded down to the ground.

Tabby dug her nose into Dev's neck in terror. What was Daaji doing here and that, too, in his nightgown and floppy cap?

"I swear, Dev is here. And Maya and Tabby were doing drugs. I saw them putting hashish in the middle of *laddus* and eating them," Gunjan whined.

That bitch, Tabby thought furiously. Every bit of sympathy that she had for the woman fled. For the first time that evening, she felt the effects of the drug wearing off and her brain began working clearly. Gunjan had spied on them and probably turned the plate around when they had gone to wash their hands.

"Tabby was here," Gunjan insisted, searching the ground. "I saw her come this way with Dev and Maya. This was all her plan."

"I don't see anyone," Daaji said disapprovingly. "Gunjan, I know you want to marry Chris, but this is taking things too far. You are getting desperate. I have been ignoring your hints as to how Tabby is not right for the family, but this is not the way to prove it—"

"But Daaji, wait. They are here somewhere. Give me a few minutes to search. Maybe they have hidden themselves up in the tree—"

Dev and Tabby froze.

"I don't want to wait. I don't care if the entire family is smoking chillums up on that tree. I am tired. Go back to bed, Gunjan, and stop this nonsense," Daaji's voice became fainter and fainter as he wheeled himself away.

"Daaji," Gunjan wailed racing after him.

Tabby sagged into Dev in relief.

Dev made a strangled sound, caught her chin, and as if he couldn't help himself any longer . . . kissed her.

Stars exploded in Tabby's brain, the earth moved beneath her feet, and her body tingled with a hundred thousand feelings.

His lips moved over hers urgently, passionately, and she clung to him, her nails digging into his shoulders.

"Come on, we have to go," Maya's sober voice floated up the tree.

Chapter Twenty Eight

It had been the classic case of getting drunk or high and using that as an opportunity to kiss a boy. Tabby cringed into the pillow. How could she have been so bloody stupid?

"Tabby," Maya oscillated into the room. "Call for you. It's Becky."

Tabby reached out an unhappy hand and took the phone.

"Lo," she mumbled.

"Tabby!" Becky shrieked. "Where have you been? I haven't had an update from you in ages. Is everything all right?"

Tabby burst into tears, "It should have been my father calling me to ask me that. I haven't spoken to him since I left London, but he hasn't bothered to find out if I'm alive or dead. If I did die, no one would know or care or look for me except you. I love you so much, Becky. You are my best friend, my soul sister, my family—"

"What did you do?" Becky asked warily.

"I kissed a boy."

"Not Chris?"

"No, his cousin."

"And now?"

"Well, he thinks I'm engaged to Chris, and I still kissed him. And he kissed me knowing I'm engaged to his cousin, so it makes both us very bad human beings. Except I know it wasn't wrong because I'm no longer engaged to Chris, so it was all right if we kissed. But he didn't know that I had broken up and he still kissed me. It was very good—"

"The pot was good?"

"No, the kiss. It was—"

"You are no longer engaged?" Becky cut in.

"No, he was kissing Gunjan."

"I thought he was kissing you?"

"He was, but then he went and kissed Gunjan—"

"But he is not engaged to you, so he can kiss anyone he likes."

"No, no, you are getting all confused."

"Tell me about it," Becky groaned.

Tabby blew her nose and started again. "Chris kissed Gunjan and I caught him. We broke up but decided not to tell anyone until Maya's wedding is over to keep people from asking the family embarrassing questions and ruining Maya's day. So we are technically not engaged. Then last night Dev and I were trying to scare Cuckoo Singh. We were high and not thinking clearly and we kissed."

"Hmm."

"It was the best kiss I have ever had in my life. I didn't want it to end."

"Tabs, listen to me. I have transferred money into your account. You have enough to fly back to America. It's time you stop thinking about offending Maya's random relatives and think about yourself instead. You need to leave, Tabby, and come back home. You are no longer engaged to Chris. You don't owe them anything."

"Maya is my friend, Becky. I won't do this to her and her family. It is different here. You won't understand."

"I understand that you are a soft-hearted fool."

"I would never do anything to hurt you and just like that I won't do anything to hurt Maya," Tabby argued.

Becky breathed loudly, her disapproval moving swiftly across countless oceans and lands to smack Tabby.

Tabby sighed. She realised that she never argued with Becky. She always let her make most of the decisions and went along with them. This was the first time Tabby was refusing to do as Becky asked.

"I'm sorry," Tabby softened her tone. "I know you want what is best for me, but I think it's time you let me make my own decisions."

"You have changed," Becky said finally. "I think for the better. I'm just so used to protecting you . . . but that is my problem, not yours."

"Thank you." Tabby blinked away her tears.

They said goodbye. Becky still sounded disturbed, but Tabby knew her friend would come around.

"So you are no longer engaged to my brother?"

Tabby flipped around on the bed and found Maya standing by the door. She had heard the entire conversation.

"I . . ." Tabby swallowed at a loss for words.

They stared at each other for a minute. A hundred expressions crossed Maya's face as she adjusted to this new revelation.

"I would have liked to have you as my sister-in-law. It would have been fun having you in the family," Maya said coming up to sit next to her on the bed. "But if it isn't meant to be, then so be it. I am just upset that my brother, that bloody muppet, cheated on you."

"It was for the best," Tabby mumbled.

"I really am sorry." Maya reached out to grip Tabby's hand. "I am sorry my brother put you through this. And in spite of all that you are going through, you are still here helping with a smile on your face." Maya swallowed and looked away. "You stayed for me."

"It wasn't your fault," Tabby said embarrassed.

"I should have told you," Maya muttered.

"You couldn't have known."

"He has done this often enough. But when he decided to marry you, I thought—"

"He has cheated on his girlfriends before?"

Maya bit her lip. "Let's not talk about that plonker anymore."

"But—"

"Miss Tabitha Lee Timmons," Maya leaped off the bed and kneeled on the ground. "Will you be my best friend?"

Tabby laughed. "That dramatic Bollywood heroine in you never fails to surprise me. And yes, I will be honoured to be your best friend, Miss Maya Mansukhani."

"Miss Maya Rosey Mansukhani."

"Rosey?"

"It was Dev's grandmother's name. The one who was British."

"Ah," Tabby said. "You are taking this really well."

"He is a git and never deserved you. Also, I knew something was wrong the day you stopped wearing your engagement ring. I think even Mom suspects." Maya suddenly brightened. "You could still be a part of the family you know."

"How?"

"Leave that to me," Maya said cryptically. "Now get ready. We are going on a helicopter ride. I convinced Dev to take us on one of his work trips this morning."

"I'm not sure—"

"Don't be silly. It's just the sort of thing you need."

"I really think—"

"We leave in an hour. Wear the green and blue *salwar kameez*. As for Dev . . . I am sure he was too high to remember the kiss. This morning I found him fast asleep wrapped around a tree branch that he had broken off sometime in the night and carried to bed."

Tabby wondered if he had slept hugging the tree branch thinking it was her.

She pushed away the delicious thought and spoke firmly. "I did not listen to Becky, I won't listen to you. I'm an adult. An independent woman. I can't face Dev right now—" She stopped talking when she realised there was no one in the room.

Not completely independent yet, Tabby scolded herself an hour later as she pushed a hand through the cotton *kurta*. If it wasn't Becky dictating to her, then it was Maya. She pinned up her fringe and stared at herself in the mirror. She could have said no . . . but Maya had not given her the chance.

And it wasn't like she wanted to see Dev again. She patted lipstick onto her lips and applied concealer under eyes. She wasn't even curious to see him in his work environment.

She stood back and inspected her face in the mirror. The fringe swept to the side looked better. She added silver hoop earrings and a tiny blue stone *bindi* that sparkled between her brows every time she moved her head.

He would probably be busy with other people all through their trip. She added a dot of gloss to her bottom lips to make it look more juicy and kissable. He wouldn't even have time to look at her. . . .

Dev remembered the kiss. She knew he did because he pretended that she did not exist all the way into the remote abandoned field where the helicopter was parked.

Tabby stuck her tongue out at his back as she followed him into the helicopter. Once inside, she froze in fright. The interior was smaller than she had expected. And the walls and the floor and the ceiling . . . they didn't look strong enough. Even a mild breeze would be enough to send the helicopter veering off towards a rocky hill. One bump and the metal walls would fall apart and then . . . Tabby gulped, forcing her mind away from negative thoughts.

Maya, she noticed, was already seated. Her long hair was pulled back and tied in a relaxed bun. Her face looked serene, like one of those yoga masters who had spent years perfecting the art of sucking in air and blowing it out. Not a worry, not a whisper of stress marked her brow. It was as if she made a habit of flying around in delicate looking helicopters.

As for Dev . . . He lounged next to Maya looking far more handsome than any human being should have a right to look. It was positively unfair.

Tabby scrunched up her nose and wondered if they would mind very much if she skedaddled, slinked away into the sunset, or as Chris would say . . . legged it. Surely they didn't need her. She half turned to go when the pilot switched on the engine and the blades of the helicopter began whirring.

Tabby, her nerves already on edge, hopped into the seat in fright. She didn't even wait to pick up the blue folder lying on it.

"Map?" the pilot yelled over the roar of the engine.

"It is in the blue folder. Maya, can I have it?" Dev shouted. His eyes were on Tabby.

Tabby smirked. He had seen her sit down on top of the folder. Now, if he really wanted the folder, he would have to ask her directly.

Maya, unaware of the situation, began hunting for the blue folder.

"Map!" the pilot screeched impatiently.

"Blue folder!" roared Dev.

"I am looking!" cried Maya.

Tabby twiddled her thumbs and admired the yellow mustard flowers swaying in the field outside.

Things got heated. Maya got even more flustered, the pilot fumed until smoke threatened to trickle out of his ears. Dev folded his arms and sulked while Tabby sat on the blue folder waiting for Dev to break and admit she was sitting on it.

Finally, after half an hour of the pilot and Maya scrabbling around the helicopter on all fours while Tabby and Dev stared out of opposite windows, Maya caught sight of the edge of the folder peeking out from under Tabby.

"You had it!" Maya pounced. "Why didn't you say so?"

"No one asked me," Tabby replied innocently.

The pilot grumbled under his breath and once again started the engine. The craft rocked and lifted off, hovering for a moment in the air before rising higher and higher, steadily moving towards the pretty white clouds.

Maya squealed in excitement, and Tabby couldn't help but laugh. She felt scared and exhilarated at the same time as if she were plunging down a rollercoaster. It was a good kind of scared. She caught Dev's eye for a moment before both of them looked away.

Tabby pressed her nose to the window and stared out at the yellow, gold and green fields of maize, mustard and wheat. She knew they were visiting a remote village but that was it. Dev had either been on the phone since they met him or working on his laptop. All his replies to Maya were given in unintelligible grunts.

Just when Tabby was getting used to riding in a helicopter, they began landing in a small clearing in the middle of a forest.

"Now, listen to me carefully. This is important," Dev said.

Tabby leaned forward. He was looking at her. Finally, he was looking at her and speaking. She would have whooped had it not been for the intense look in his eyes.

"Whatever happens—" Dev paused as his cell phone rang. "Hello," he growled impatiently into the phone. "No. I will be careful . . . Are you saying I am too old for field reporting . . . I did give them a chance. I sent two bright reporters before and you know what happened . . . I won't. How can I send the younger lot if I am not willing to take the risk myself?"

Maya and Tabby exchanged a glance. This did not sound good.

Dev cut the call and put the phone on silent.

"Right," he began again. "I am going to talk to the village elders. Meanwhile, I want both of you to stay put. The pilot has instructions to fly off without me if anything goes wrong."

"Gack!" Maya said.

"Are we in a war zone?" Tabby asked in a hushed voice.

He smiled reluctantly. "You can pretend we are. Whatever you do, do not on any account leave the craft. Is that clear?"

"Ok," Maya nodded, her eyes wide.

"Tabby?" he prompted.

"Do not leave the craft," Tabby said. "Got it."

"I can trust the two of you, right?" he asked again. "Maya, you insisted on coming along. I told you it would be dangerous. It is now your responsibility to see that—"

"We won't leave," Maya hurriedly assured him. "I swear it."

"I won't be long," he said, his eyes lingering a touch longer on

Tabby's face.

She smiled back weakly, trying to hide the terror she was feeling. Was his life in danger? Was he going to negotiate with some kind of extremists? What was going on?

"Do you have to go?" was out of her mouth before she could stop it.

"I will be back," he said gruffly, no longer looking at her.

"I wonder what happened to the other two reporters," Maya said once he had disappeared.

"They were stabbed. One of them almost died," the pilot said, chewing on the nail of his pinky finger.

Maya and Tabby jumped into each other's arms in fright.

"Don't worry. We are well hidden here," the pilot said, more to soothe himself than them.

"Do you know anything about this place?" Maya prodded.

The pilot thought for a moment and then said, "I suppose I can tell you. It is going to be all over the news soon enough if Dev Sir has his way. This village is pretty remote. They have no electricity and are lacking in many other basic amenities as well. They live off the land." He paused to dig some wax out of his ear. He eyed the wax thoughtfully as he continued, "They were doing fine until the local river dried up a few years ago. The government put in a pipeline, but the water was contaminated and a lot of the villagers died. The villagers were furious believing they had been poisoned so that their land could be taken over."

"Sounds awful," Maya said.

"And then?" Tabby prompted him to go on.

"The men broke the pipeline, refused to let anyone help them. They became suspicious of strangers, and the village chief insisted that the only way they could survive was to stay cut off from the rest of the world. Recently, this part has hardly had any rain which has increased their hardship. Three young men tried committing suicide in the last twenty-four hours. Trouble is, if something of the sort had happened in a city or a bigger town, it would have hit the headlines. But this village is too quiet and remote to be of interest to big media houses."

"Where does Dev come in?" Maya asked.

"He is always looking for human interest stories that others are unwilling to highlight. He hopes that doing something like this would get NGO's and charitable organisations interested and villages like these could be saved. He sent two other reporters before him to ask questions and speak to the elders. The villagers are so desperate and angry that they began attacking the poor men."

Tabby stared out of the window, thinking how sheltered and fortunate her life was.

"How do they get water right now?" Maya asked.

"There." He pointed at a group of sari clad women walking down a small hill that was visible through the trees.

Tabby and Maya moved closer to the window.

"They go to a small well situated two hours away. They trek down with clay pots balanced on their heads and bring it back filled with water," the pilot said.

Tabby watched in fascination as the painfully thin women carefully moved down the hill carrying three to four clay pots balanced on top of their heads. The pots looked heavier than they did.

Maya and the pilot went back to discussing the water situation in the village, but Tabby continued gazing at the women. Some of the women even had babies attached to their hips.

One of them stumbled and Tabby's heart lurched. It was a young girl right at the back. She looked no older than seventeen, and in shock Tabby realised she was also heavily pregnant. That poor girl had been walking in this heat for two hours to bring back water for her family. No wonder she looked shaky.

The girl stumbled again. Her face looked ill, and water sloshed from the side of one of the clay pots balanced on her head. Part of her brown saree became drenched. None of the other women noticed as they continued walking while the girl's steps became slower and slower.

When the girl stopped altogether, her hand clamped to her belly, her face wincing in pain, Tabby could bear it no longer. She saw the girl sway and knew she would fall any moment. She leaped out of the helicopter and raced towards the girl before Maya or the pilot realised what had happened.

Tabby caught the girl in time and made her sit down.

"Help," Tabby screamed at the women up ahead.

They looked back and gawked.

One of them tore her gaze away from Tabby and raced back up

the hill to help the girl. A few more women ran over while the rest continued staring at Tabby.

"Can you help her?" Tabby asked as the girl let out another moan of pain.

The old woman looked at her blankly and then turned back to the girl. She trickled a few drops of water into the girl's mouth and wiped the dust of her forehead. Her ministrations were gentle and loving.

"Miss Timmons, Maya," Dev's cold voice rang out over the hill. "What the hell are you doing?"

Tabby head jerked up. She found Dev standing a few feet away, blood trickling down his forehead while a few men with long sticks surrounded him. Her heart hammered in fear. His sleeve was soaked with blood. She instinctively moved towards him.

Maya placed a hand on Tabby's shoulder stopping her. "Tabby came to help this girl. If she had fallen, she could have hurt herself and the baby very badly."

"Go back to the helicopter. Slowly," Dev said, his voice quiet but firm. "Don't run. Walk."

"But the girl," Tabby objected.

"The women will take care of her," Dev bit out.

Tabby looked back at the girl uncertainly. She did look better and was sitting up. "And you, Dev? Are you all right?" she asked, her voice a faint thread.

"Maya," Dev turned beseeching eyes towards his cousin.

"Tabby," Maya took her hand and pulled her to her feet. "We better do as Dev says."

With a last worried look at the girl, Tabby allowed Maya to lead her away.

Maya began hunting for a first aid box the moment they entered the craft.

"It was just a small cut," Maya muttered. "He will be fine."

Tabby barely heard her. She felt numb and suddenly extremely exhausted.

The pilot kept one hand on the engine switch and one on a loaded pistol.

It was fifteen long, excruciating minutes before Dev burst into the helicopter.

"Wait," he told the pilot. "We are not flying yet."

Then he turned his eyes on Tabby.

212

Tabby shrank into the seat and wished she could disappear.

"You damn fool of a woman," he roared.

Maya gasped, Tabby squeaked and the pilot began praying.

Dev was always in control. He never lost his temper, and yet here he was, eyes blazing, skin taut and veins popping out of his gorgeous forehead.

"What the hell is wrong with you? Can't you follow simple orders?" he shouted.

"I'm not one of your employees," Tabby stammered back. "Why should I follow your orders?"

He scowled, unimpressed by her brave retort. "You have ruined everything. Months of work—"

"I was only trying to help—"

"Your help ruined an excellent report. A report that could have helped the entire village. A story that could save lives—"

"She had good intentions," Maya spoke up. "She doesn't have your sort of backing, nor is this her job, and yet, knowing the danger, she chose to run out there and help that girl. She was doing what you are doing. Saving a life."

"Had you been in her place, boss, I am sure you would have done what she did," the pilot added slyly. "In fact I recall when we flew into Kashmir—"

"Shut up," Dev said. He rubbed his face tiredly and in the process smeared blood all over his cheek.

"Scold me later," Tabby said, pulling him down on a seat. She moved his hair away from his forehead and let Maya inspect the damage.

A knock on the door made them all jump, and Dev was out in the open before Maya had the tube of antiseptic unscrewed.

Dev came back in. "That was the village elder who had asked me to wait," he said looking sheepish.

"What did he want?" Maya asked.

"He agreed to be interviewed," Dev replied.

"How did this miracle happen?" the pilot squawked.

Dev suddenly reached out and grabbing Tabby's wrist yanked her down to give her a hug. She ended up on his lap with him laughing into her hair.

"They thought Tabby was a supernatural being," he crowed. "They thought she was a sign of good things to come. And when she spoke to me, they thought she was giving me an order to help them."

"A supernatural being?" Maya chuckled.

Dev nodded. "They have never seen a foreigner in their lives. And seeing someone as pale as a ghost . . . the only explanation they could come up with was that she is not human," he grinned. "She saved me from being beaten to a pulp and possibly saved an entire village from destruction." He finally dropped his arms allowing Tabby to get off his lap.

Her face flamed as she adjusted her *dupatta*, and it took her a few moments of breathing shakily to be brave enough to push back his hair again.

Maya began cleaning his cut, carefully keeping her eyes averted from Tabby's blushing face.

"What are we waiting for?" the pilot asked.

"My crew is coming in to set up the interview," Dev replied. "I have to introduce them to the villagers. They are still a wary lot."

"I wish we could get water to them somehow. I am worried about that pregnant girl. What if her family sends her off again?" Maya said, applying an antiseptic to the cut.

"I already ordered the water tankers. They are nearby waiting for my go-ahead," Dev replied. "I had hoped, if things went well, I could offer it to them to tide them over until something more permanent can be done."

"You can't save everyone, boss," the pilot drawled.

"It's called corporate responsibility," Dev said. "The story will make me money. The least I can do is give a little back."

"What if no one takes an interest in the story?" Maya asked.

"That has happened before," he conceded, "which is why I had asked my researchers to find out about the water table in this area. It is high enough. We only need to get someone to dig a few wells and they will be sorted. I was also talking to this environmentalist friend of mine about rainwater harvesting . . ." Dev went on for a bit, becoming more technical. It was clear he was passionate about helping these people and had put a lot of work into finding solutions. If the villagers had refused to agree this time, Tabby was certain he would have found some way of convincing them.

Dev caught sight of Tabby's face and stopped speaking.

"Don't look at me like that." He cleared his throat.

"Like what?" she asked her voice all thick and funny.

"I am no hero. It's my job," he mumbled, flushing red.

It was his job to report, not to put his life in danger in order to help them. Most men would have done the interview and walked away from the village and not spent hours finding alternate solutions to the villagers' problems.

Tabby now understood why everyone in the country looked upon him with so much admiration and respect, and she also knew that her eyes were currently reflecting the same damn things.

"You are still pushing my hair back. Maya put the bandage on ages ago," he muttered.

Tabby dropped her hand, her heart too full to be mortified.

Chapter Twenty Nine

Back home that evening, Tabby was sober, thoughtful and utterly grateful for her life and everything she had. Her problems felt petty and no longer frightening.

If an entire village could survive such hardships, then her problems should be ridiculously easy to solve. She felt a strange sort of strength creep into her bones.

She pulled open her diary and began revising her priorities. She decided to look for jobs in Europe first thing in the morning. She would borrow Maya's laptop and send off her resume to as many companies as possible.

She didn't have to have ambition. She could drift through life hopping from job to job, frolicking with all sorts of handsome men. She would like to date a sensitive artist, a billionaire playboy, a Kamasutra expert . . . She would go through life like a happy hippie, wearing long gypsy skirts and dancing naked in moonlit forests.

It took her a while to sleep after that. The pleasant daydreams of a future where she had joined a witches' coven and trekked up Mount Everest with her traveller friends faded, and the face of that young pregnant girl popped up in her head. The villagers gaunt faces came back to haunt her. Tears she had held in all day escaped, soaking the pillow.

At half four in the morning, she finally drifted off to sleep.

Her hands grasped the slats, and she moved upwards as fast as she could. She didn't know why but she had to reach the sign.

Two more feet and success. Once she reached the top, she would be safe from him.

He chuckled behind her. A dark, dangerous sound. As if he could read her mind and found her logic amusing.

She trembled at the sound, her foot slipped and she fell from fifteen feet above the ground.

He caught her around the waist, his warm, calloused hand splayed on her bare, sensitive back.

"Tabby," he whispered softly.

She opened her eyes and gasped. They were suspended in mid-air rotating below a glittering moon and a star filled night sky.

They were flying.

She gazed up at his handsome, sensual face. Realisation dawned on her. She never had a chance. He would have won anyway.

She closed her eyes in defeat. Her body softening in his hard, iron grip.

"Dev," she whispered.

He smiled and dropped his hands from her waist.

Her mouth opened in a silent scream as she fell through the midnight sky, towards the rat infested street below.

She gasped awake and shot up in bed. She could still feel him wrapped around her, his breath caressing her face while her heart responded in tune.

She shook her head one more time to get rid of all thoughts of Dev. It didn't help.

She realised now what the dreams meant.

She was running from love. The death of her mother had been the hardest thing she had ever been through, and then Luke . . . He had shattered her, stolen her family, left her feeling bereft, miserable and helpless. She never wanted to feel that again.

She had chosen Chris because he had been safe. If he hurt her, which he had, she wouldn't feel quite as awful, which she hadn't. Chris was the kind of man she could be fond of but never ever love.

But Dev . . . Dev had won a million hearts. He was gruff, moody, and bossy, but he was also kind, gentle and compassionate.

She was scared.

She didn't want to fall in love with Dev or any man. She knew if she did, she would love with all her heart and this time . . . a bad end would shatter her.

No, she wanted to travel all over Europe, date all sorts of men and live a bohemian lifestyle. And when she was old and toothless, she wanted to own a pretty little cottage by the sea, adopt tons of dogs and cats and be best friends with a slightly eccentric neighbour.

She would dress in googly-eyed scarves, leprechaun hats and watermelon prints on her chest if she liked. She would sip on green tea all day, eat organic food and burn incense and sage.

Dev figured nowhere in her brand spanking new future. In any case, he still thought she was engaged to Chris, and even if he knew, he wouldn't date her. He would probably marry an activist or a social worker or a doctor. Someone who did something worthwhile for the world. Not jobless Tabby with no ambition or talent.

It was the day of the *Haldi* ceremony. The scent of burning sandalwood, cedar chips and citronella filled the air. Maya sat on a marble stool, surrounded by her aunts and cousins. One by one the women took a bowl of turmeric paste and slathered it on Maya's skin until she looked like a sickly monster from a badly made CGI film.

Tabby, being the future daughter-in-law, was given the important task of taking care of the guests, and in spite of the language barrier, she did quite well. She went around with trays of cold *lassi*, hot chai, *samosas*, kebabs, *kheer*, *laddu* and assorted *chaats*, coaxing even the most reluctant guests into trying a small bit. She made a special effort by smiling widely and racing to and fro from the kitchen as many times as was needed with not a complaint. She was grateful to be of help because she had been feeling guilty since morning.

Everyone was so nice to her. They were treating her like family. Even Gayatri Aunty had softened her tone when speaking to her. Nani kept talking to her in Punjabi forgetting she was a foreigner, and Mrs Mansukhani kept saying how glad she was to have her around to help.

And here she was pretending to be engaged to Chris. All this love and affection was for the future daughter-in-law, which she wasn't.

When the last of the guests departed, Tabby escaped to her room and turned on the air conditioner full blast. She began applying for jobs online, partly to distract herself from the guilt raging inside her.

After that was done, she still did not feel sleepy so she opened her diary and wrote a short story about a friendship between a happy polar bear and a grumpy penguin. She wrote it keeping the flower girl in mind. One day she hoped they would understand each other and she could tell her the sweet, heart-warming tale.

She snuggled into bed with that pleasant thought and closed her eyes.

"Tabby," Maya pulled open the curtains letting the sunlight stream in.

"Wha-What is it? Where are the bugs? Let me at them," Tabby shot up in bed.

"Wake up, Tabby. We are going shopping," Maya said holding out a cup of *masala chai*.

Tabby absently scratched her arm and took the cup.

Maya sat down on the bed. "You forgot to pull down the mosquito net. Your upper arm is full of spots."

"God, I look like I have measles," Tabby groaned.

Maya stared out the window at the green and golden field. "Dev spoke to Cuckoo Singh today. He met him at a hotel in Amritsar this morning and asked him to call off the wedding."

Tabby gawked at her.

"He should have warned us," Maya sighed. "But it was sweet and thoughtful of him to try."

"It didn't work?"

"No."

"How could anyone say no to Dev?" Tabby asked in surprise.

Maya's eyebrows shot up.

"I didn't mean it like that," Tabby hastened to assure her.

"Course you didn't," Maya grinned.

"Maya!"

"Tabby!"

"Stop it."

"Stop what?"

"Teasing me. You are getting it all mixed up."

"Getting what mixed up?"

"You know."

"I don't know. Enlighten me."

Tabby narrowed her eyes. "I have my future all planned. I'm going to get a job in Europe. Travel all over the world. Begin collecting travel cups from every country I visit and learn all about druids. I will date moody, artistic men or farmers or billionaires. Wear top hats and smoke cigars—"

"Enough, I get the picture."

"What's the plan today?" Tabby changed the topic.

"We are going shopping. The house is full of relatives. I can't breathe without being accosted and told how a bride should behave, how to impress my mother-in-law and how to keep my husband happy. The things these aunties tell me would shock most people. I mean the positions they get into with uncles—"

"Stop." Tabby stuck her fingers in her ears. "Don't want to know or I will imagine it every time I see them."

"Yeah, and you can't control your giggles," Maya grinned. "But I will leave you with something to think about. Aunty Meena discussed the lotus and the elephant pose with me for a good fifteen minutes."

"That doesn't make sense. What does it mean?"

"I am not going to explain but leave you to imagine the rest."

"That's cruel."

Maya stopped at the doorway. "Before I forget, wear something nice."

"Why? We are only going shopping. I thought there are no functions today—"

"Dev is taking us shopping. He is meeting us in the parking lot in an hour."

Chapter Thirty

Dev was leaning against a car wearing a pair of snug blue jeans, a grey flannel shirt and a short fake beard.

A wave of emotion swept over Tabby when she saw him, and she clutched the peepal tree for support.

He was just . . . so handsome. It took all of her mental strength to stay put and not race over and jump into his arms like a besotted Bollywood heroine.

Her eyes glazed over and an orchestra began playing a romantic ballad in the background. And if she listened hard enough, she could pick out the drum beats as well as the *shehnai*.

Soon, a deep, melodious voice began singing a song in Hindi while fragrant rose petals floated all around her. One of the petals landed on her plump bottom lip, and she ate it because she was hungry.

A soft cool breeze started up next and blew in her direction, playfully lifting her hair and caressing her hot cheeks. She smiled and her sunglasses fogged up with love.

"Cuckoo!" Maya's cold voice infiltrated Tabby's brain. "What's this?"

Tabby, with the goofy smile still playing on her lips, turned to look at what Maya was looking at.

She was glaring at a seedy-looking fellow standing a short distance away. He was holding a whirring fan aimed in Maya and Tabby's direction. Another young chap sat on a tree throwing fistfuls of rose petals in their general direction. As for the orchestra, there really was one, except instead of men and women dressed in classic black and white, there was a motley crew wearing bright orange, gold and red uniforms strumming and blowing various instruments.

"This is the band I hired for the wedding," Cuckoo said. "I wanted your opinion on them."

"And the rest?" Maya asked stubbing a rose petal.

Cuckoo nervously toyed with a white cricket hat in his hands. "I thought I should woo you. We will be married in four days." He peeked at his palm where he had scribbled some lines and continued. "I have the contamination . . . confession . . . no, I have the conviction that I can make you happy. I did not get a chance to court you. It is not too late—"

Maya squinted at him. "Did you memorise those lines?"

Cuckoo Singh's cheek turned salmon pink. "Yes. They were written by my good cousin brother who is an English professor at the University of—"

"Never mind," Maya said. She visibly controlled her temper and continued, "It is very sweet but unnecessary. We have to go now. See you on the wedding day."

Tabby looked back at a forlorn Cuckoo Singh as Maya pulled her away. She couldn't help but feel bad for him. She understood his feelings all too well.

They both had one thing in common—unrequited lust. And it sucked.

"I didn't need stitches," Dev told Maya as they strolled down the busy market. "It was a shallow cut."

"And the pregnant girl?" Tabby asked Maya. "How is she?"

"How is the girl?" Maya obligingly repeated the question.

"She gave birth to a baby girl," he smiled. "The villagers think the baby is blessed. They are taking good care of her."

"And the story? When will it be out?" Tabby asked Maya.

"Stop it," Maya swatted a fly. "She kissed you, you kissed her. Both of you were not in your senses. Now get over it and behave like adults and talk to each other."

Tabby's cheeks burned. "I will if he will," she said under her breath.

"I will if she will," Dev echoed her, albeit more loudly.

Maya glared at them. "I am going ahead. You two follow when your brains catch up with your ages."

"We should make up," Tabby said after Maya had stormed off.

He jerked his chin downwards. Once.

"You agree?" Tabby pressed.

He grunted in reply.

Tabby took that as an agreement.

"We could hug and make out . . . up, I meant make up properly," Tabby offered. She deserved one teensy hug from him even if it was gotten by unscrupulous means. After all, she didn't have much time left to spend with him.

He frowned. "Hug?" he asked as if it were an alien word.

"Forget it," Tabby blushed. "It was a silly idea."

"No!"

She looked at him in surprise.

He lowered his voice, "I mean, no. I think it is a good idea."

"So we should hug."

"Yes."

Tabby lifted an arm and dropped it.

He took a step forward and then backed up again.

"How should we do this?" He frowned.

"I don't know. Maybe, you could step forward and I will put an arm around your waist . . . or something."

"Just give me a hug," he muttered impatiently.

She obligingly stepped forward and leaned in. They did the awkward one-armed hug thing, trying to touch each other as little as possible. He patted her back like an old pal for added measure before they sprang back.

"I'm glad we did that," she said politely.

He slanted a disbelieving look at her.

She pressed her foot down on an old plastic packet lying on the ground and slid it around. Should she suggest they repeat the hug? They hadn't done it properly after all. Maybe the next time she could be bolder and hug him properly—

"Shall we go or are you planning to stay here and play with that all day," he asked.

Grumpster, Tabby thought irritably as she followed him into the jewellery shop.

"Did you two make up?" Maya asked.

Tabby nodded.

Maya smiled. "Good. Now, what do you think of this bracelet? It has uncut rubies and diamonds on a platinum and gold band."

"Gorgeous," Tabby responded obligingly.

"Dev, buy it for me," Maya ordered.

"Sure, anything else?" Dev shared a rueful glance with the

shopkeeper.

"These earrings or this bracelet," Maya mused.

The shopkeeper spoke up. "Madame, the bracelet is excellent. The blue balls are made from the finest turquoise."

Tabby began spluttering and giggling.

Dev eyed her in concern.

"Tabby is laughing," Maya whispered in Dev's ear, "because the shopkeeper said blue balls."

Dev smiled in spite of himself.

Tabby hurried away towards the other end of the store before she completely lost it. Still giggling, she went over to a large glass display case that had a small clearance sign hanging on it.

The stuff at this end seemed less pricey but still out of her budget.

A lovely silver rope bracelet caught her eye. It had a tiny winged cat charm carved out of an aquamarine stone dangling from the clasp.

She pressed her nose against the glass and sighed.

"Did you find something you liked?" Dev asked from behind her.

She jumped at the sound. "Is Maya done?"

"She will take a while," Dev replied. "You didn't answer my question."

"No, no, I didn't like anything," she lied.

He leaned over her shoulder and looked at the display. "Is that the one you were drooling over?" He pointed at the cat bracelet.

"How did you know?" she asked, her heart hammering. He was standing so close. His cheeks a few inches away from her cheek, his lips a few heartbeats away from her lips—"

"It was the only quirky piece in the display," he answered. "Let me buy it for you."

"No! Thank you."

"If I visit you in London, will you meet me?" he asked out of the blue.

"Of course."

"Will you let me take you out for dinner?" he continued.

Her heart accelerated, galloping now at sixty miles an hour. Was he asking her out on a date?

"As Maya's friend . . . my friend . . . After your wedding, we will be family," he hastily clarified noting her expression.

"I will go out with you . . . as a friend," she nodded, desperately hoping her disappointment didn't show on her face. How could she have forgotten he still thought she was still engaged to Chris?

"Will you allow me to pay for the dinner?" he pressed.

She hesitated for a moment and then nodded again.

He smiled. "The price of the bracelet is less than a decent dinner in London. Let me buy it—Fine, think of it as a gift for saving my life from the villagers."

She didn't know how to explain it to him. She didn't want anything permanent to remind her of him. When she left India, she wanted to leave everything behind and start her new life afresh. Having the winged cat would be a constant reminder of this moment . . . of him and his proximity.

He took her silence as an assent and bought the bracelet. He handed her the maroon velvet pouch, and her fingers automatically closed over it.

She wanted no reminders, and yet anything given by him suddenly felt more precious than anything in the world. Conflicted, she buried the bracelet deep into her furry handbag.

"Can I see the bracelet?" Maya asked when they were driving back to the house.

Tabby reluctantly dug the pouch out and handed it to Maya. Usually, she sat near the window, but this time somehow she had ended up sitting in between Dev and Maya. She kept her elbows tucked in, her knees together and sat as close to Maya as possible without ending up in her lap.

"It is a winged jaguar," Maya said admiring the carving. "Tabby, move a little on that side. I'm so hot and you have space."

Tabby's eyes narrowed. Was Maya matchmaking?

The car hurtled around a corner and skidded to a halt at a traffic light flinging Tabby sideways. She blew away her fringe and found her hands clutching Dev's shirt, her cheek pressed against his chest.

She looked up.

He gazed down.

"Blue balls was not that funny," Maya remarked. "Honestly, Tabby, sometimes you act like you are ten . . . Hey, isn't that your flower girl?"

Tabby extracted herself from Dev and sat up. "It is," she frowned.

"Is that a bruise on her cheek?" Maya asked pressing closer to the window.

"Hey!" Tabby yelled. She leaned over Maya and stuck her head out of the window. "Flower girl!" she shrieked.

The girl looked up, the flower basket was balanced as usual on her head, but something was different about her.

"Her eyes," Tabby whispered, "they look dead."

The girl smiled weakly and waved, but made no move to come towards the car.

The light changed, and they were once again speeding away.

"What was wrong with her?" Tabby asked Maya. "She knew I would have bought the flowers—Why didn't she come?"

"Maybe she didn't recognize you," Maya replied, avoiding her eyes.

"Is she in trouble? She had a bruise—" Tabby's bottom lip trembled.

"Oh, Tabs, she will be fine. Maybe she slipped," Maya pulled her into her arms and cuddled her. "Don't cry, love. We will find her again and fix whatever was wrong."

Tabby buried her worried face into Maya's shoulder. Had that been a bruise or dirt on her cheek?

A little later she felt fingertips run lightly through her hair. Once, twice and then they were gone. That brief touch soothed her and quietened her sobs. She knew that had been Dev.

Maya hugged Tabby closer in an almost motherly fashion. She gazed out of the window at the passing golden fields and villages and began warbling a sad song.

We saw a flower girl,
With lots of pretty curls,
Carrying a basket full,
Of flowers and cotton wool.

"She didn't have any cotton wool," Tabby hastily sat up.

"I couldn't think of anything else to rhyme with it." Maya continued,

She had a funny face,
That moved through interplanetary space,
And touched our hearts and souls,
Now let's go buy some poles.

"What on earth are you doing?" Dev asked, clamping his hands over his ears. "The lyrics, the tune, every damn thing about that song is ghastly."

"This is a moment where a Bollywood movie would insert a sad song," Maya replied. "So that's exactly what I am doing."

The family members were standing around Daaji in a semi-circle while the servants and the guests had attached their ears to doors and windows and floorboards.

Tabby shuffled into the drawing room and went and stood behind Mrs Mansukhani. Daaji had called an urgent family meeting sending everyone into a tizzy.

Once the room had settled, Daaji spoke. "Tabitha," he announced, "will get officially engaged to my grandson Krishnamohan—"

"Chandramohan," Mr Mansukhani interrupted.

"What?" Daaji asked.

"His name is Chandramohan."

Daaji scowled. "Now, Tabby and whatever his name is will be engaged two days after Maya's wedding. They will marry in a month from today. I had asked a renowned Guruji to draw up their kundalis, and according to him these dates are most auspicious for the couple."

"Isn't it too soon after Maya's wedding?" Mrs Mansukhani began nervously.

"I have decided," Daaji spoke over Mrs Mansukhani, "to give both the couples a gift."

Chris grinned, while Maya sent Tabby a panicked look.

"I am delighted," Daaji continued, "that London and western influences have not ruined my grandchildren. I have watched the two of them and realised that they are still obedient, respectful, and aware of their roots. Their hearts," he thumped his chest dramatically, "are still Indian. Which is why, instead of giving them a quarter of a million pounds, I will be transferring one million pounds each into their bank accounts the morning after Maya's wedding."

The room gasped, Meena Aunty and a couple of guests swooned, Chris whooped, and Maya burst into tears and fled the room.

"That was a bit of a shocker," Tabby murmured.

Mrs Mansukhani had organized a mocktail party in the garden. Maya once again sat on a throne, this time a silver one, while Tabby pulled up a white plastic chair with a green satin bow tied around it.

"Daaji, you mean," Maya whispered back. "I know. A million pounds each! I am almost tempted to marry Cuckoo for that kind of money. Almost being the key word."

"Chris must be gutted," Tabby frowned.

"He looks cheerful enough. I have never seen anyone happier," Maya said nodding towards the food table where Chris stood nibbling on fried king prawns. "Lucky duck. I am forced to sit here and nod and smile while he gets to scarf down the buffet. I am so hungry," she moaned. "I would kill for a measly Ginger Nut right now."

"You did say you fancied a red-haired boy," Tabby responded only half listening. She thought she had spotted Dev disguised as a waiter.

"Not that kind of nut! I meant the biscuit. Tabby, are you listening to me?"

"I thought I saw Dev."

"He is in Delhi," Maya replied.

"Who is in Delhi?" Cuckoo Singh leaned over to ask.

"Dev," Maya responded.

Cuckoo Singh leaned closer. "Do you want to leg it from here and have a little snog?"

Maya's mouth dropped open

Cuckoo frowned. "Did I say it wrong? I am learning how to speak like a Londoner. My good cousin sister from Birmingham—"

Maya grabbed a giggling Tabby and pulled her back into the house.

"Honestly, Tabby, I am not going to marry that man. I don't care about the money—Stop laughing!"

"I'm sorry," Tabby spluttered. "Are you sure you are not in a mood for a snog?"

"Haha," Maya growled. "Mother wants to take you shopping in the evening and buy you jewellery. Afterwards, she is planning to take you to a designer to buy you some clothes worth a couple of thousand pounds."

Tabby stopped smiling.

"Not so funny when you are in the thick of it, is it?" Maya asked smugly. "Now let's see you get out of that one."

"I can't let her spend that kind of money," Tabby said appalled.

"Mum thinks you don't have time considering the engagement is next week and the wedding in a month. She wants to get cracking as soon as possible."

"How will I get out of it?"

Maya shrugged. "Also, she wants your father's phone number. Daaji wants to have a chat with him and discuss the wedding details."

"What am I going to do?" Tabby panicked.

"Let her buy you the clothes and the jewellery?" Maya asked, softening at Tabby's pale face. "It's the least you deserve after my schmuck of a brother cheated on you."

"I can't let them buy me anything. I can't let them spend ridiculous amounts of money organizing the engagement party or have them invite all their friends only to find the bride to be has gone back to England for good. I can't take the clothes and the jewellery— And, oh my god, Maya, I will have to break the news and soon. I can't let your poor parents continue to think that I'm marrying their son."

Chapter Thirty One

"How is Maya?"

"Dev!" Tabby dropped her diary on the bed.

"Where is she?" Dev asked, looking around the room.

"Getting her hair done in Mrs Mansukhani's room. For the Sangeet."

"How is she doing?" he asked reaching down to pick up the diary.

Tabby snatched the diary away. "She seems fine. Cheerful even."

In one swift stride, he was upon her.

"Strange." His arm shot out and caught her wrist. "Let go," he said twisting her hand.

"You are hurting me. It's nothing important," Tabby said, her chest rising and falling in agitation.

"Then let me look at it," he said with a ghost of a smile.

Her eyes dropped to his lips, a breath away from her own. "I-It's personal."

"But not important?"

"Not important at all," she agreed foggily.

"Then I can take a look at it?"

"Hmm." Everything had become sort of swimmy around her.

"Give me the notebook, Tabby."

"K," Tabby sighed. "No, what? Hey, give me back the diary."

He held it out of her reach and quickly scanned a few pages.

She hopped around him tugging at his sleeves. "That's not fair. Did no one teach you manners? You can't read people's personal diaries."

He froze. "This is your personal diary?"

"Yes," she huffed.

"Why didn't you say so?"

"I did."

"What you said was that it wasn't important. I am sorry. If I had known, I wouldn't have read it."

"Couldn't you tell it was a diary?"

"People generally write 'Dear Diary' when they write in a . . . well . . . diary. You, however, don't stick to traditions." He eyed her up and down. "I suppose by now I should have expected that."

"What was that look?"

"You are wearing some very odd things. Did you raid Daaji's cupboard?"

"This," Tabby patted her tweed jacket, "happens to be my father's favourite jacket."

"Why is it with you then?"

"He couldn't wear it any longer. Bits of it in the back are moth-eaten." Tabby rushed on. "But this lovely vintage red dress was my mother's and is in pristine condition."

"The beaver hat?"

"My sister wore it in a play once. She loved it so much, she even slept in it that night."

"That explains the dent," he smiled.

"I was just missing the people I love," she said in a low voice.

"So everything you are wearing right now belongs to someone you love?" he asked.

"Even the shoes," Tabby nodded, showing off her white ballet slippers. "They belong to Maya."

"I see," he said and gave her back the diary. "You write well. Some grammatical mistakes, your spelling would make a lexicographer weep, but other than that . . . you are talented."

Tabby's mouth dropped open. A senior journalist, who owned DMTV, the largest English news channel in a country of one billion people, was telling her that she, Tabitha Lee Timmons, could write well. That she had a talent.

"You could be a travel writer," he continued, his eyes softening at the expression on her face. "A bit of practice and—"

"I want to write children's stories," she blurted out. She had never said that aloud, not even acknowledged it to herself before, even thought she would lie awake at night dreaming up children's stories about princesses and knights and dinosaurs and weevils. Dev's encouragement had given her the courage to wonder if she did have an ambition after all.

She clutched the diary to her chest and gave him a smile full of hope and joy. The sleeve of her jacket slipped revealing her wrist.

Dev frowned and took a step forward.

She saw what he was looking at and hurriedly pulled her sleeve down.

He grabbed her wrist. "Wait," he said.

"I have to go," she squirmed in his grip, her face bright red.

He took another step closer to her, and she had to strain her neck to look up at him. "You said you were wearing something from everyone you love."

"I never said that." She turned her face away from him.

"Don't lie," he said, lifting her hand and letting the sleeve fall back to reveal her wrist once again. His other hand circled her waist and pulled her closer.

"What's this, Tabby?" he asked huskily.

The aquamarine cat sparkled and glittered in the light.

She was having trouble breathing. If he didn't let go, she was afraid she would die from lack of air.

"You are wearing the bracelet I gave you. Does that mean—?"

"Nothing. It means nothing. It's all decided. I'm going to travel the world. Date moody artists, frolic with forensic experts—I really have to go wee now. Goodbye." She yanked her hand out of his grip and turned to flee.

He was too quick for her. He was at the door before she was.

"You have to wee?" he chuckled. "Date a forensic expert? And who says goodbye?"

"Lots of people say goodbye and everybody wees," she snapped, feeling foolish and embarrassed. She pulled off the bracelet and slipped it into his front pocket. "Here, you can keep it. It didn't mean anything. I wore it by mistake."

"I was worried about my poor cousin's heart for a moment," he said, all amusement wiped off his face. "Normally people don't date after marriage, and you are getting married within a month. You do remember that, don't you?"

"I don't need to be reminded."

"Are you sure about that?"

She looked away.

He glowered, "In our family, marriage means commitment. You cannot continue living in cuckoo land."

"Cuckoo land?" she spluttered. "You have some nerve talking about commitment and giving me advice about your family. You don't even speak to them. You only see everything from your side."

"You don't know anything," he growled in warning. "You don't know why Daaji and me—

"I know enough," she cut in. "Daaji gave an ultimatum to your father to join the family business or leave. So what? He didn't want your father to suffer or go through hardship while making a name for himself. You should be pleased you have a grandfather who wants to protect his family. But no, you want to sulk and gripe and moan and whinge. And the best part is, he didn't even do anything to you! Whatever hurt there is, is between father and son. You have no business interfering. Do you interfere when your parents fight? Do you take you mum or your dad's side? Then why are you sticking your nose into Daaji's affairs?"

He gripped her tweed coat. "Enough! Dressing up in your families old, moth-eaten clothes would be considered cuckoo by every sane person. You are like a cat or a dog who is given the master's old clothes to comfort them in their lonely baskets. What would you know of family or hurt? Half of your brain is in la-la land."

"I would have given anything to have a grandfather like yours," she hissed in anger. "Someone to look out for me, someone who would have at least tried to stop me from leaving America. No one asked me to stay even though my sister ran away with my fiancé. It was not my fault. It was hers, and yet I had to leave. Daaji tried to protect his son. I wish someone had tried to protect me. You have no idea how fortunate you are, and instead of appreciating it, you are throwing it away because of your big fat ego."

"Is everything all right?" Maya asked.

Dev whirled around to find her standing behind him, a curious expression on her face.

"I could hear the two of you at the other end of the corridor. I wouldn't be surprised if everyone knows that you are here, Dev," Maya continued when neither of them spoke.

"I have to go. Have fun tonight." Dev kissed Maya's head and with a final glare at Tabby strode out of the room.

"What was that about?" Maya asked.

"Not important," Tabby assured her. "What will you wear tonight?" I haven't seen the *lehenga* yet."

Maya allowed herself to be diverted, and the next few hours were spent in a hectic yet happy whirlwind of clothes, jewellery and perfumes.

The Sangeet took off without a hitch. The front garden had been transformed into an enchanted woodland. Fairy lights winked from amongst leaves and branches. Curtains of beads and crystals glittered in candlelight, strings of jasmine were wrapped around tree trunks, and bowls of white roses and tea light candles floated in water at the centre of every table.

They spent the evening dancing to various songs, sneaking cocktails past Daaji, and eating plates upon plates of kebabs.

Maya's cousins performed the dance they had been practising on stage along with Tabby. The alcohol helped boost her confidence, and since most of the people were tipsy they barely noticed her mistakes.

At one point, Maya leaped up on stage and joined them. It annoyed her mother in law, but she didn't care. She danced and danced and danced, her face reflecting a strange sort of joy that made Tabby uneasy.

The scent of delicious food, citronella, jasmine and roses made a heady perfume. And the alcohol snaking through her system lulled Tabby into a relaxed, happy state. It had been so long since she had truly enjoyed herself. She let go of her worries for one night and she and Maya popped, lindy hopped and freestyled the night away.

Chapter Thirty Two

Tabby emerged from her room, shoulders hunched, back bowed and head pounding. She blearily made her way towards the kitchen, scowling at the reflective mirrors as she passed by them.

By the time she had hobbled down the stairs and moved towards the back where the kitchen lay, she had progressed from wincing to muttering naughty words.

A young woman was sweeping the floor outside the kitchen. She rhythmically whacked the ground, blowing great clouds of dust into the air. She hopped aside with a squeak when Tabby lurched into view.

The cook took one look at Tabby's burning eyes and sour expression and produced an entire bottle of chilled lemonade and two painkillers. No words needed to be spoken. This sort of thing transcended the boundaries of language. A lot of the household was suffering from the same ailment, and the cook, with his years of experience, had the remedy laid out in a neat little row on the kitchen counter.

Sunlight streamed in through the kitchen window illuminating bottles of hydrating liquids, packets of painkillers and piles of salty, heavy food. The hangover cures seemed to glitter in the bright, golden light of the afternoon.

With a respectful nod, Tabby exited with her supplies and gingerly moved towards the stairs to head back to her darkened room.

Chris stood a few feet away from her in the hallway. He was not looking at her but at Daaji, who was sitting on the porch outside reading a newspaper.

Tabby watched as Chris nervously adjusted his collar, wiped the sweat from his forehead and shuffled outside.

Chris had been sufficiently dodgy for her to be intrigued.

Hangover forgotten, she pelted back to the kitchen and used the servant's door to sneak out and slither around to the front of the house. She found a large bush that was close enough to where Daaji and Chris were and crouched behind it. She parted two twigs and peaked out.

"Daaji," Chris was bleating, "are you listening to me?"

"Hmm," Daaji said, turning a page of the newspaper.

"As you know," Chris began in his best pompous voice. "I have been brought up in England, but that does not mean I have forgotten my roots."

"I appreciate that. Hence, the million pounds," Daaji said. The newspaper rustled as he smooth a hand over a particular column.

Chris cleared his throat. "Which is why, if you are unhappy with my engagement with Tabby, I am willing to break it off."

Daaji dropped the paper. "I recall asking you to marry Gunjan and you had flatly refused. Had you misplaced your roots then? What's changed now?"

Chris was silent for a moment. It appeared he had been thrown a googly that he had been unprepared for.

Tabby was suddenly enlightened. She realised that Chris was not very bright. Sure, he had swallowed a couple of intelligent sounding phrases and mentioned the science magazine a couple of times a week, but when it came to wit and common sense, he had none of it.

Daaji took pity on him. "I admit I had my qualms about Tabby. Even after Babaji approved of her . . . I was uncertain. But I have kept an eye on the girl. She enjoys helping people out, takes care of everyone's needs, tries to understand our culture and measures her words to avoid offending anyone. I don't see any malice or greed in her. She is honest, kind and a wonderful addition to the family."

Chris swallowed audibly. "But I thought you would rather I marry Gunjan—"

"I *had* thought. I don't think so anymore."

"But Tabby is an American. How will she ever adapt to our way of life?" Chris objected.

"Judge people on their own merit, not what country they come from. Our culture is no better than theirs."

"But Daaji, you are the one who has always been concerned about outward appearances—"

"When death is close at hand," Daaji cut in, "you become wise very quickly."

Chris changed tack. "I am glad you approve of Tabby. It is a weight off my mind. But I was wondering . . ."

"Yes?"

"I was thinking of buying Tabby a wedding present. An apartment," he said in a rush. "Could you . . . Could you perhaps give me the money before Maya's wedding so I can surprise Tabby on our honeymoon? The paperwork takes time, the transfer of deeds sort of thing . . ." he trailed off lamely.

Tabby gritted her teeth. *The rotten pig! He was trying to trick Daaji.* She wanted to storm out and confront him right then and there.

"Maya's wedding is in two days. Surely, that's not too long to wait?"

Chris's face contorted trying to reign in his frustration. "But, I will get the money on Maya's wedding day? For sure? There won't be any delay. You know these banks—"

"You will get the money the day *after* Maya's wedding," Daaji said staring at Chris. "Not a moment sooner or later."

"Thank you," Chris said avoiding his eyes.

"And Chris," Daaji stopped him from racing off, "I want Tabitha's father's phone number. It's high time we spoke to her family and formalised things. I want the two of you to get engaged as soon as Maya returns from her honeymoon."

Chris mumbled something incoherent and trudged away.

Tabby plucked a dry leaf off her sleeve and crumbled it to dust between her fingers. Daaji's words rattled around in her head. He liked her. He thought she was selfless, kind and caring.

She felt a wave of anger and disgust wash over her. She was angry, not with Chris, but with herself. She was a horrible human being. She had not been blind to Chris's faults. She had been aware of the lack of chemistry between them. She knew she did not love him, and yet she had continued with the relationship and decided to marry him.

Why?

Because she was a coward and a lazy, selfish human being. She had wanted the easy way out. She had wanted to marry him for security. Marrying him had meant gaining a loving family, freedom from financial worries and lifelong security.

And right now, even after knowing that it was all over between them, she was continuing to lie to his family. Continuing this charade, letting Daaji be cheated by his own grandson.

"Cobras are often spotted around here," Daaji voice made her jump. "One bite and you are dead."

Tabby screeched and jumped out of the bush.

Daaji's eyes danced as he watched her prance about trying to get rid of invisible insects and reptiles.

When she finally calmed down, she turned to Daaji, her eyes apologetic.

"Will you wheel me around the garden?" he asked.

She stepped behind him and began pushing his wheelchair. She was glad he could no longer see her embarrassed face.

"I have noticed your closeness to Maya and Dev," he said after a moment.

She froze. "You know about Dev?"

"That he has been staying in my house for days? Yes." His voice was a matter of fact.

"Does he know you know?" She began wheeling him around once again past the golden marigolds and red roses.

"No."

"Should I tell him?"

"No."

"Right."

After a few moments of peaceful silence, he said hesitatingly, "I had asked his father, my eldest son, to leave the house. I was angry that he wanted to work in a theatre rather than take his rightful place as the heir to the toothpick factory. I wanted to teach him a lesson. I thought he would realise how easy he had had it all his life, how much he had taken for granted. With time, I had hoped he would come to his senses. I never thought he would succeed in his career, become independent and never come home."

"Are you sorry?"

"No, I am not sorry that I threw him out. It helped him become the man he is. I am proud of him. My only regret is that in all these years I never reached out to them."

"You can reach out now."

"Do you think Dev will be willing to talk to me?" he asked.

"Not really," Tabby replied honestly. "If anyone even mentions your name, he turns into a sulking schoolboy. Unless you tie him up and force him to listen to you, I don't see any other way."

"I agree, which is why I think you can help."

"Me? What can I do?"

"Lock him up."

"What?"

"Only for an hour or two."

"I don't understand."

"It's simple. I will hide behind a bookshelf in the library. You send Dev to the library at the same time and lock him in. I will come out of my hiding place and confront him. He will be forced to talk to me. I want to sort out our differences. I want my grandson back."

Tabby felt overwhelmed at the responsibility she had been given. She was touched by the fact that Daaji trusted her enough to share so much . . . and yet, a shadow crossed her face, she didn't deserve the trust. She didn't have the right to know these family secrets. After all, she was continuing to tell porkies. Continuing to pretend she was engaged to Chris.

She wanted to tell him that she was no longer engaged. No longer a part of the family. That he shouldn't trust her but find someone else. But the bleak old eyes staring up at her tied her tongue in knots. She nodded once and was rewarded with a warm, affectionate smile.

Back in her room, Tabby mentally went over the things she had to do. Maya's wedding was in two days, and before then she had to find a job, book her flights to wherever she found a job, find the flower girl and make sure she was all right, lock Daaji and Dev up in the library, tell Chris she could no longer continue the charade and finally confess to everyone that they were not getting married.

She decided to face Chris first and tackle the rest later. She found him in the mustard field, next to an old abandoned well, chewing on a dried blade of grass.

"Chris?"

He whirled around, hand on heart. "You scared the poopies out of me. What are you doing here?"

"Looking for you . . . Poopies?"

"How did you know I was here?"

She bit her lip. "Gunjan told me."

He turned his face away hiding his expression.

Tabby wondered if he had fallen in love with Gunjan.

"Did you want something?" he asked, still avoiding her eyes.

"I'm going to tell everyone we are no longer engaged . . . on Maya's wedding day."

He looked at her, panic clear in his eyes. "You can't mean that."

"I do."

"Think about my sister. What will people think? You know how sensitive such things are—"

"I told you, I will wait until Maya's wedding day. I will wait until the ceremony is well underway. And I will be telling your immediate family, not announcing it on the loudspeaker."

His mouth twisted. "Are you trying to get some of the million pounds? That's it isn't it? You are blackmailing me. If I don't pay you, you will tell everyone and Daaji won't give me the money either."

"That's not true," she said shocked. "I didn't even think of that."

"Then why wait till Maya's wedding? Why haven't you already told them? Why discuss it with me first?"

"I'm telling you because we were once engaged. We were in a relationship and it is your family. It is only fair you know what I am planning to do. And the reason I held off is, as we discussed, I didn't want to worry Mrs Mansukhani and the family before the wedding. Have you seen how stressed they are? You mum doesn't have a minute to herself."

He took a step closer to her. His voice suddenly soft and coaxing, "I always liked that about you. The way you think about other people first. Wait for one more day, Tabby. Tell her a day after Maya's wedding. In fact, I will tell them myself."

Tabby smirked, "I may be soft-hearted but I'm not stupid. You want me to wait, not for your mum's sake but for the money. Daaji will transfer it in the morning, and once that's done, he can't take it back."

He glared at her. "So? It's my family's money, not yours. All you have to do is wait a few more hours—"

"No. I won't continue to cheat your family any longer. I'm only waiting until the marriage ceremony begins because once Maya is in the *Mandap*, Mrs Mansukhani will no longer be stressed. I can tell her—"

"Please," he interrupted, "for the sake of our relationship. We dated for a year, Tabby. You can delay the news for a few hours.

Daaji is not related to you. How does it matter if he is cheated or not—"

"I delayed it for so long for the good of your family. For their mental peace. I'm not going to undo it all by waiting and letting them be cheated."

"I will give you fifty thousand pounds—"

"No."

"One hundred thousand—"

"I have to go."

"Two hundred thousand pounds and not a penny more," he yelled at her departing back.

Her footsteps faltered. For a moment, she was tempted. All that money for simply keeping her mouth shut for a few hours. It would solve all her problems. She could live comfortably wherever she chose—No, if she relented, she would hate herself forever. She would never be able to enjoy the money. It would feel tainted, and the guilt would haunt her forever.

And Dev . . . What would he think if he found out about what she had done? How she had deceived him and his family and then taken part of the money and run?

She resumed walking.

"I am warning you. If you don't change your mind, then I will have to do something I don't want to," he threatened. "Stop, Tabitha! We can discuss this—" Chris raced after her.

"Discuss what?" Gunjan materialised next to Chris.

"Nothing," Tabby said, and used her arrival to escape.

Chapter Thirty Three

Once she was back in her room, Tabby powered up Maya's laptop and checked her emails. Her inbox was full of rejections from companies she had applied to.

A cloud of Nag Champa incense entered the room followed by Meena Aunty holding a smoking charcoal burner.

"I am cleansing the house," Meena Aunty explained. "Banishing all negativity. When happy occasions like weddings come around, jealous people cast an evil eye on the family."

"Now is not a good time—"

Meena Aunty pressed on. "I would suggest you allow me to burn some red chillies for you. Also, hang a few lemons and green chillies around your neck. Might as well—"

"I'm busy—"

"When your life is stagnant and you are in a rut, cleanse your space and yourself. Spring clean your soul," Meena Aunty rattled on. "It will put your life back on track. Here," she handed Tabby a rose quartz crystal, "you look like you have got the evil eye. Clutch that piece of stone and breathe deeply imagining all your worries being cleansed. You will have the answer."

Meena Aunty swept away in a whirlwind of smoke leaving Tabby open mouthed and clutching a pretty pink rock. She stared at the rock and then at the door. Her life was pretty miserable.

What the hell. It couldn't hurt.

She closed her eyes, breathed in deeply and imagined her worries whooshing out as she exhaled.

You write well, Dev's voice echoed in her mind.

A few minutes later, her eyelids sprang open.

She turned to the laptop and applied for still more jobs. But this time, she focused on emailing travel magazines, newspapers and freelance writing websites. She was at the lowest point in her life. Homeless, poor, lonely and miserable. This was the time to take chances. The only way forward now was up. Surely nothing more could go wrong.

Tabby got into the car and instructed the driver to go to Gulbaag, the closest town to Daaji's *haveli*. Once they were on the way, she realised this was the first time she had been alone since coming to India. Usually Maya or one of the aunties accompanied her.

She would have enjoyed her independence if she hadn't been so worried for the flower girl.

It was strange, but she had barely spoken to the girl, she didn't even know her name, and yet she felt as if she had formed a bond with her. She kept her eyes wide open trying to look everywhere at once.

The driver had circled the small market square four times before Tabby thought she spotted the girl or, rather, part of a dirty flower basket. She asked him to park near a *paan* shop and leaped out of the car.

Buses, trucks and dusty auto-rickshaws sped past her honking like agitated geese.

Without a thought, she stepped onto the road.

A cyclist cursed as he narrowly avoided hitting her, a cow mooed, a scooter wobbled and a wooden cart bumped into a lamppost scattering green guavas everywhere.

But it was the truck hurtling towards her that slowed down time.

She saw the driver's panicked expression, the horror on his companion's face, and yet her feet remained frozen in terror.

She closed her eyes and readied herself for an impact. She felt as if something slammed into her, and she was knocked off her feet and flying through the air. She frowned. Why was she flying? She should have been squished by the truck and feeling mighty flattened. Perhaps, her brain was releasing that stuff, what was it called . . . endorphins?

"You fool!" Dev roared.

Tabby opened her eyes and found Dev staring into her eyes. She smiled loopily. *Endorphins were awesome. Either that or she had died and gone to heaven.*

"What the hell is wrong with you?" Dev asked furiously. He

pulled her into his arms and hugged her tightly. She could hear his heartbeat hammering away in his chest.

She sniffed his neck and felt her head swim. She drawled, "Shouldn't say hell in heaven. Must be against the rules or something."

He shook her. "Why did you do such an idiotic thing? Raced into the middle of the road with no thought. What if something had happened to you? What would I have done? Don't you ever think about other people . . . ?" His fingers painfully dug into her waist.

She frowned. She was in pain. Surely in heaven, one didn't hurt. She closed her eyes and opened them again, allowing the fog to lift. She focused on her surroundings letting the sounds of the traffic once again assault her ears.

She widened her eyes.

They were surrounded by a group of dodgy men watching them hug in fascination.

She pulled away from Dev. "I'm alive," she said amazed.

He glared at her. "What were you thinking?"

"You saved me." She stared up at him. "You said if something happened to me—"

He looked away. "You are in shock. We should get you to the hospital—"

"I was looking for the flower girl. Wanted to make sure she was ok. The bruise—"

"Forget about her. She will be fine." He softened his tone.

"I thought I saw her across the road."

"You were imagining things."

"Was not."

"Tabitha, you need to go home and rest. You are in no state to go hunting for the girl."

She planted her feet and refused to budge. "I won't get another chance. I'm not going to go home until I have found her. I bought her a heart pendant the other day. I want to give it to her and see if she needs anything else—"

"Let's go to the doctor first. You are in shock—"

"Don't talk to me like I'm a dim-witted child. I'm perfectly fine."

"You won't go home until we see the girl?"

"Right."

He sighed. "If I take you to her then, will you go straight home right after that?"

Tabby nodded. "Do you know where she is?"

"Yes."

Tabby stared up at a beautiful red brick building with dozens of sparkling French windows.

On her right, a few girls were playing basketball while others screamed out instructions on a cricket pitch. On her left a group of students sat in a circle under a tree. They were attempting to sketch asters, roses and canna lilies.

Everywhere she turned, she saw happy young girls of all shapes and sizes living a typical school life. She frowned in confusion.

A pretty blonde woman came up to them and greeted Dev like an old familiar friend.

"Where are we?" Tabby asked.

The blonde woman answered in surprise, "Didn't Dev tell you? He is one of the founder members of the charitable organization that run this place. We attempt to educate homeless girls here. We give them a place to stay if they want it, food, books, medical aid, counselling . . . you name it."

"How is she doing?" Dev asked.

By she, Tabby assumed he meant the flower girl.

"I'm so glad you brought her to us," the young woman smiled up at him. "She is smart and shows a lot of promise."

"Thank you, for making room for her. I know you have more children than this place can handle," Dev said.

Tabby's heart swelled. She wondered when she would stop being surprised by his kindness. While she had been dreaming of helping the girl, Dev had already gone and done it.

"It's our job. You don't need to thank us." She shook her head, and her wavy golden hair rippled in the sunlight.

Dev smiled down at the teacher, his eyes warm and gentle.

Tabby felt a stab of excruciating jealousy. Unaware of her actions she stepped in between the blonde and Dev.

"Can you call her?" Tabby asked sullenly.

The blonde woman looked from Dev to Tabby, her eyes calculative.

"We are getting late," Tabby prompted.

"Please," Dev added, sending Tabby an amused look.

"Payal," the blonde girl called out to an old Indian woman, "can you send Chameli here?"

"Her name is Chameli?" Tabby asked eagerly.

"Yes." The blonde thawed at the transparent delight on Tabby's face. "It means Jasmine in Hindi."

"How apt. Do you know anything about her family?" Tabby asked.

"Not really. She was living with three old women who claim they found her bawling by the lake a few years ago. People are more sympathetic to beggars who have a child so the women took turns carrying her around while they begged. When she was too old to be carried, she started selling flowers."

"Won't the women mind that you have taken her away from them?" Tabby asked.

The teacher shook her head. "A shopkeeper had recently spotted her and wanted to employ her as a servant. When Chameli refused to go with him, he hit her. The old women love her like their own child. They understand Chameli has a better future with us . . . Ah, here she is . . ."

Chameli was unrecognizable. Her jet black hair was oiled, combed and pulled into two adorable pigtails tied with bright red ribbons. She wore a neat red and white uniform with not a speck of dirt on it. When she came closer, Tabby got a whiff of Jasmine. The delicate flowers were peeking out from the front pocket of her school shirt.

"Hello," Tabby said.

"Tabby," the girl grinned, her upturned nose scrunching up charmingly.

"How?" Tabby asked, her eyes prickling with unshed tears.

"I told her your name," Dev mumbled behind her.

Tabby held out a hand hesitatingly, and Chameli took it and held it.

They smiled at each other.

"Study hard," Tabby babbled, knowing the girl didn't understand a word of what she was saying but needing to say it nonetheless. "Write to me. I will send letters from wherever I'm. Let me know how you are. I hope one day we will be able to communicate without needing interpreters . . ." She paused as she choked and her eyes welled up.

Chameli squeezed her hand, the smile fading from her lips. Her eyes were dead serious and wise beyond her age when she said, "Thank you."

The dam broke and Tabby burst into tears. "She pronounced it perfectly."

"She has been practising." The blonde teacher patted Tabby's back. "First thing she wanted to learn when she came here. How to say thank you."

"Tank coo," Tabby smiled. "She used to say tank coo."

"Thank you," Chameli corrected, picking out the words she understood in that sentence.

"Thank *you*," Tabby said again with a nod.

"*Thank youuu,*" Chameli giggled and nodded back.

It was the silliest thing, yet they both laughed as if it were the funniest thing in the world.

They spent some time chatting after that with the help of the blonde teacher. There was so much to learn about the flower girl and so little time. What food did Chameli like? What was her favourite colour? Did she have any future plans? She said she wanted to own a flower shop, and Tabby was not surprised.

All too soon Chameli had to return to class along with the teacher. Tabby hurriedly pressed the heart locket and the short story she had written for Chameli into her hand and hugged her for one last time.

She watched until Chameli's back had completely disappeared from view before turning back to Dev.

Dev, it appeared, had been busy while she had been having her emotional moment. He was surrounded by dozens of children climbing all over him with familiar ease. They were demanding kisses, hugs, toys, sweets, cars, helicopters and whatnot. They pulled his shirt, yanked at his tie and almost took off his pants. Some had burst into tears from excitement while others laughed and shrieked around him. But one thing was common amongst all of them. The love and admiration for Dev shimmered in every eye.

And how could anyone not love him? Look at what he had done for her, for Chameli and what he was trying to do for Maya. Tabby could fight it no longer. This gesture from Dev had pushed her over the edge.

She, Tabitha Lee Timmons, was hopelessly in love with Dev Mansukhani.

Chapter Thirty Four

They were on their way back to Daaji's *haveli*. Tabby had somehow ended up travelling with Dev and sending her own car back. She kept her face averted from him trying to come to terms with the fact that she had been almost run over by a truck, found the flower girl and realised that she was in love with Dev.

"You are looking nuttier than usual," Dev commented. "Missing your family again?"

Tabby fiddled with her scarf filled with plastic googly eyes. "Something of the sort."

He asked curiously. "Is there any other reason you would dress like that apart from missing your family? You look like a greedy homeless person who is so protective of her belongings that she has decided to wear all of them."

"It's raining again," Tabby said ignoring his question.

"When do you leave for London?" he asked.

"Day after Maya's wedding," she replied.

"Two days," he mused. "But you will be back soon?"

"Why would I be back?" she asked in surprise.

"Your wedding is in a month," he responded. "Isn't it?"

"We broke up a while ago," she replied softly. "I was keeping it quiet until Maya's wedding."

He didn't look surprised at the news. "What have you planned for your future?"

"I'm going to go back to London. I had one positive email. An Italian travel magazine wants to start an English column. They asked if I could do some freelance writing for them . . . Let's see what happens."

"But you will continue focusing on writing a book for children, right?"

She nodded. "That's the plan."

"Don't you want to stay on in India?" he asked after a moment. "I could give you a job."

She shook her head. "I'm not going to take any favours. I have to learn how to be independent."

"You have been independent since you left America, Tabby."

She paused at that. It was true. She had been independent. In fact, she had been independent since she left school. She had even supported Luke for a while. Why hadn't that occurred to her before?

"Still," she said reluctantly. "It won't be right to take such a favour. I would like to get a job on my own merit."

"I respect that."

"I want to see the world, flit from job to job—"

"Date a forensic expert and a brooding artist," he finished. "You said so. Are you upset about the breakup?"

"Marriage is not everything. It is not the definite path to happily ever after," Tabby said thoughtfully. "Contentment comes from following your dreams, whether it is to be a mother, writer or explorer."

"You have been on quite a spiritual journey," he said, his eyes twinkling. "You have grown wiser in a few short weeks."

The driver pulled into the parking lot. The *haveli* loomed up before them, the rain battering its grey stone walls.

"*Dhanyawad*, thank you," Tabby said to the driver.

Dev looked at her in surprise.

"Chameli taught me how to say that," Tabby said. "I'm going to learn Hindi while she learns English. We promised each other."

His eyes turned warm making Tabby blush. She suddenly felt as if he would lean over and kiss her.

"You should solve your differences," she said in a rush. "Talk to Daaji. He really wants to mend things—"

"How would you know what he wants?" Dev asked icily.

She cursed herself for opening her mouth. The moment was gone.

"I want you to stay out of this, Tabby," he continued. "Please, don't meddle in my affairs."

"But what if I spoke to Daaji. What if he agreed to apologise to your father—"

"Stop right there. You will stay away from my family affairs, Tabitha, or you will consider our friendship over. I will never speak to you again, and I will make sure no one, including Maya, speaks to you either."

Tabby climbed out of the car after him. Her legs felt as if someone had tied giant rocks to them. It was a pity he thought so strongly about her meddling in his affairs. And it wasn't like she would stay in touch with him when she went off to Italy to work for the magazine company. Better to cut all ties than stay in touch and nurture the love until it grew and grew and grew.

But she *would* do something for him before she left. Something in return for all that he had done for her. She looked at her watch and gritted her teeth.

Daaji was waiting. It was time to lock the love of her life in the library with a batty old man and seal her miserable fate.

"I need a book," Tabby halted outside the library.

"You have time to read?" Dev asked her in surprise.

"I will be too tense to sleep tonight," Tabby replied. "If I have a horribly boring book, perhaps I can conk off."

"Ok," he said and began walking away.

"Dang it! I mean, wait," she yanked him back to her side. "Can you get the book for me?"

"What book?" He was beginning to look suspicious.

"Nineteenth century England and its eccentrics," she replied promptly. "I tried to get it the other day, but it is placed too high on the shelf for me to reach."

"Sounds interesting, the book I mean," he said watching her with narrowed eyes.

She kept her face carefully blank. She couldn't spoil it all now. They had come this far. . . .

Still wary, he stepped into the library. He moved to where the switch was, but before he could turn the lights on, Tabby slammed the door shut behind him and locked it.

"Tabitha!" He rattled the handle. "What stupid game is this? Let me out."

"Not until you speak to him," Tabby called back.

"Speak to who?"

And then there was silence. Daaji must have shown himself. Tabby slid to the floor and leaned her head against the wall. She didn't want anyone to come and open the door before Daaji had finished talking to Dev.

Minutes ticked by, and the loud, angry voices faded into soft murmurs behind the thick library doors. No one went by her. Everyone was presumably busy with wedding preparations. Someone had already decorated the hallway with marigold strings.

It felt like hours before she hear Daaji's voice at the door. "Tabby? You can let us out now."

Tabby lurched to her feet, her legs stiff and tingling. She quickly wriggled her toes and rubbed her thighs to get her blood circulating, and then she reached over, turned the key, heard the click and waited for Daaji to open the door just a smidgeon before she whipped around and fled.

Back in her room, she pulled out her suitcase and laid it on the floor.

"Tabby," Chris strode in. "we need to talk."

"I don't have time."

"Your hands are busy," he countered, "not your adorable ears."

"Stuff it."

"Look, be reasonable. You will never see any of us again. Leave the talking to me. Let me tell my family about our break up."

"Will you do it before Daaji transfers the money . . . ? I thought not. We have been over this, Chris. I'm going to tell your mother, and nothing you say is going to change my mind."

"I love you, Tabs. I cannot bear the thought of living my life without you. Marry me?"

Tabby smirked. "Nice try."

She folded a pink and black Sari and placed it in the suitcase.

Chris began pacing the room.

"Look," he pleaded. "Don't do this. I would like to part as friends. I don't want to do anything that is . . . unpleasant . . ."

Tabby eyed the black shirt wondering if it had faded too much. She threw it in the discard pile.

"Are you listening to me?" he growled.

"Hmm? Yeah, go on." She closed the suitcase and zipped it up.

The discarded pile was huge.

"You think this is funny? I am in debt, Tabby. I have spent the money that I thought was coming to me. If you refuse to help me, I will never be able to return to England. What will my friends say?"

She narrowed her eyes. "You shouldn't have spent the money, and if you did, then earn it like any normal human being by getting a job or working hard at your father's firm. Now, I would like my privacy. I have a lot to do."

Chris's face twisted and became unrecognizable.

She let out a breath she hadn't realised she had been holding when he finally left the room. For a minute there she thought he was going to do something horrible. Maybe kill her?

She scoffed at her overactive imagination and picked up the stuff on the floor. It was time to put Chris behind her.

Tomorrow was a new day and Maya's wedding. Life was not perfect yet, but happiness had boarded the train and was well on its way to Tabby land.

Or so she hoped.

Chapter Thirty Five

It was the day of the wedding.

Tabby spent all morning running to the shops fetching forgotten garlands, prayer beads or last minute altered dresses.

She spent the afternoon soothing aunties who had decided to bawl over the fact that Maya was getting married and going to a new home and leaving her old relatives behind. This befuddled her a bit. Sure Maya was lovable and everything, but to howl like a bunch of werewolves at full moon seemed a little overdramatic.

It took her a good half an hour of listening to the yowls, blubbers and shuddering sobs to get it. They were howling their hearts out because they were enjoying it.

She supposed it was therapeutic, crying buckets of tears at every happy and sad occasion.

By the time evening came around, everyone was busy getting ready. The wedding ceremony was meant to start at the auspicious time of nine o'clock and no sooner or later. Daaji had already wheeled himself into the courtyard where glittering waterproof tents had sprouted up.

Tabby placed a tiny gold *bindi* on her forehead and inspected herself in the mirror. She was wearing a beautiful peach and gold georgette sari sprinkled with crystals and delicate hand woven motifs. Her slim waist was visible through the soft lace pallu while her face glowed above the bejewelled neckline.

She wondered if people would think it odd if she continued wearing Indian clothes for the rest of her life. Would her employers mind?

She suddenly smiled at the thought. She had employers. The Italian magazine had hired her. They were not paying her much, and she would have to take another job on the side to make ends meet . .

. but it was a writing job. A proper, professional writing job. One more day in India and then she was off to Italy the next day.

She would miss it, this country, the people . . . Dev. Tears sprang to her eyes and she carefully dabbed it away with a tissue to avoid ruining her *kajal*.

"Tabby," Maya careened into the room. "Open the window and help me out."

"What?" Tabby spun around and found Maya standing in front of her in all her bridal finery. The red and gold *lehenga* looked like it weighed a ton, while the uncut diamond necklaces, strings of pearls, blobs of gold and rubies swathed her until she sparkled like a lit up disco ball.

Tabby squinted. "Where do you want to go?"

"I am running away, silly. My room is filled with cousins trying to make me feel special so I have to use your window."

"But we are on the first floor. It is quite a drop."

Maya produced a rope ladder from under her skirt. "It's a good thing the skirt is so voluminous. You wouldn't believe the stuff I have hidden underneath."

Tabby planted herself in front of Maya. "You can't do this to your family."

"What choice do I have? I left it too late to talk to mum, and now . . . now everything is ready to go. The groom is going to arrive any minute." A band started playing and drums rolled outside. "*That* noise means he has arrived. Cuckoo must be bouncing along on an elephant entering the gate—I have to go!"

"No. Not until you tell your mother. Trust her, Maya. Besides, where will you go?"

"You remember the helicopter pilot that took us to the village with Dev?" Maya blushed. "He is waiting for me. He had snuck his phone number to me when you were not looking, and ever since we have been talking. I have my flights to London booked. I will go and stay at our place and look for a job. I have enough jewellery that I can sell to tide me over for a long time. The moment mum and dad arrive back, I will move to a rented apartment. I have it all planned, Tabby."

A shriek of laughter sounded outside the door, and the drumming grew loud and more urgent.

Tabby clutched Maya's arm and shook her. "Your mum will be worried sick if you disappear like this. Trust her, Maya. Tell her the truth, and if she still wants you to marry him, then I promise to help you escape."

Maya began shaking her head.

"I know your mum," Tabby coaxed. "And think how much better you will feel if you tell her. Let me call her, talk to her. You can hide and listen. I will try to tell her in my own way about your plan. If she is completely against it, then once she leaves, you can slip out of the window."

Maya nodded reluctantly. "I am not trusting her, I am trusting you. You better not lock me in and have some of my cousins come and drag me off to the *mandap*."

Tabby pushed Maya into the bathroom. "Hurry and stop rambling. They will begin looking for you soon."

Maya obediently slipped into the bathroom. She pulled out a champagne bottle, an opener and two glasses from under her skirt and placed them on the counter.

Tabby raised her eyebrow.

"I need it . . . to face mum," Maya said. "And to celebrate my freedom. That is if mum leaves me alive. She won't kill me, will she? What if she has extra sensory perception and knows I am in the bathroom? I swear I think she is a supernatural entity, the way she knows things—"

Tabby closed the bathroom door and rushed out to find Mrs Mansukhani. Five minutes later she was back in her room along with Mrs Mansukhani.

"Really, Tabby, can't this wait?" Mrs Mansukhani grumbled. "The groom's family has to be looked after. I haven't even spoken to Cuckoo Singh's mother's sister's husband's brother yet. They will be offended if they realise I have snuck off to have a chat with my future daughter-in-law instead of doing my duty as the mother of the bride."

"Relax for a minute. Breathe. You have been running around all day. Everything is done, now only the ceremony is left." Tabby plucked a glass of champagne that she found on the side table and placed it in Mrs Mansukhani's hand. "How was Maya as a child?" she asked gently pushing her into a chair.

Mrs Mansukhani softened. "She was a lovely child. Just as naughty as she is now. Adored Bollywood. She would steal my clothes and makeup and dress up and practice Hindi movie dialogues in front of the mirror."

Tabby smiled. "You are so different from Mr Mansukhani. I wouldn't dare chat with him about Maya's childhood. How did the two of you meet?"

"It was an arranged marriage. I was eighteen and he was twenty-five. I saw him for the first time on my wedding night."

"That must have been horrifying," Tabby said. "You were so young."

"Not so young. My mum got married when she was fourteen. It was common to marry the girls off young at that time. Now things are different. Better."

"It is lucky we have choices today," Tabby agreed. "Although," she paused searching Mrs Mansukhani's face.

"Although?"

"Does Maya really have a choice?" Tabby asked.

Mrs Mansukhani's expression changed. She bristled and sat up straight.

"Ma?" Maya said from the bathroom door.

Mrs Mansukhani eyed her daughter for a long moment. "Maya had a choice," she replied finally. "She could have chosen not to marry Cuckoo and given up the money."

Maya shook her head. "You know father told me that if I didn't marry Cuckoo, then I would have to sit at home until he found me a new man. He said he would cut me off financially."

Mrs Mansukhani frowned. "If your career and independence are so important, then you could have gone and gotten a job in London. You are well qualified with an excellent education. Forget Daaji and your father's money. Make your own."

Maya took a step forward. "I want a career and independence more than anything but not as much as I want my parents in my life. Dad would have disowned me if I had left home, just like Daaji disowned Dev's family. And you, you always do what Dad says. I would have lost you, too. I love you both too much to go against your wishes. I want you in my life . . . always."

A tear rolled down Mrs Mansukhani's eye. She sat clutching her daughter's hand, struggling with herself. Finally, she lifted her head up, decision made, eyes ablaze.

"Maya," she said firmly. "I am giving you a choice. A real choice. You can either run away now— I will give you the money you need until you find your feet—or stay and be married to Cuckoo and take the money."

"But dad?" Maya asked. "He will never speak to me again."

"For a few years. But he will come around. He loves you, too, you know," Mrs Mansukhani replied.

Maya threw herself into her mother's arm. "You are the best mum in the world. Thank you, thank you, thank you!"

"Now, quickly here is my gold card. This should cover your accommodation. I don't want to be here when you escape. I want to be able to honestly say I don't know how you left or where you went."

Maya and Tabby nodded, both grinning like loons.

"I wish you had believed in me and told me all of this before, Maya." Mrs Mansukhani downed the champagne.

Maya brought out the other two glasses and handed one to Tabby.

"To freedom, "she cheered.

"To happiness," Mrs Mansukhani smiled.

"To family," Tabby said and downed the drink.

Once Mrs Mansukhani left, Maya turned to Tabby. "Thank you for pushing me to talk to my mother. If it hadn't been for you, I would have lost my parents for good."

"Don't go all emotional on me," Tabby pulled open the window and flung the ladder out.

Maya stepped on over the sill and expertly moved down the ladder. "And Tabby," she whispered just before darkness swallowed her, "it's time to tell the family that you and Chris have broken up."

Tabby stood staring out into the darkness for a few more moments. In Maya's honour, she opened her mouth and started singing a bittersweet farewell song.

"Sorry, Tabs," Chris said from behind her. "I have to cut your song off in the middle and ruin the moment."

Tabby turned around and found Chris and six beefy men crowding her bedroom. She frowned in confusion.

"You see," he explained, "you are being kidnapped. Only for a day, love. I will deposit you at the airport in time for your flight."

Her eyes widened in horror, and she opened her mouth to scream, but Chris was too quick for her. He slapped a rag soaked with chloroform to her nose and darkness engulfed her.

Chapter Thirty Six

When Tabby came to, she found herself tied to an old wooden chair.

It was dark. Frighteningly pitch black.

She desperately searched for a pin prick of light, her heart beating faster and faster in panic. She couldn't see anything. Had she gone blind?

After what seemed an age, her vision adjusted and she spotted the yellow light filtering into the room from under a closed door.

The faint light cast the room in shadows. She made out a few burlap bags leaning against the wall near where she was sat. One of the sacks had split and tiny yellow lentils had escaped to form a small mound on the ground. Unpolished brown rice peeped out of a tear in yet another sack, while the one closest to her feet was open at the top and filled with muddy potatoes.

The rest of the room was full of dark looming shapes . . . Anyone could be hiding in the shadows watching her. She shivered.

A few men laughed in the next room.

She could also hear the wedding music, albeit very faintly. That meant she was still on Daaji's land. Perhaps in one of the red brick storehouses dotting the field that she had noticed a few times.

She tested the ropes and found she was tied up pretty well. She struggled with the ropes for a few more minutes until her wrists started feeling sore. She gave up and leaned her head back feeling weak and dizzy.

When was the last time she had eaten? A banana this morning and nothing else all day. She had been too busy helping prepare for the wedding to eat.

A wedding that wasn't going to happen anymore.

Had everyone realised by now that Maya had run away? Would

Maya have already gotten on the flight to London or was she still on the way? She hoped Maya would reach home soon.

A wave of homesickness swamped her. She wanted to be home, too, back in America eating fresh, sugar dusted donuts from Charlie's bakery around the corner from her house. She wanted to sit at the dinner table with her father and sister and discuss school projects or fight over the last chicken wing. She wanted to—

Something crashed to the ground next door. A man cursed.

"Mum!" Tabby squeaked in fright.

No comforting hand came in the darkness, not a whiff of tobacco and vanilla trickled into the room to pull her out of her nightmare.

She realised her mother wouldn't come.

Never again.

Calling out to her mother, wearing her clothes or her father's or sister's old things wouldn't help magically manifest them in front of her when she missed them.

She shook her head wryly. How silly and childish her behaviour now seemed. Now when she was in real danger, she realised that even if she had been buried under her mother's old clothes, it wouldn't have saved her from the goons next door.

She balled her fist and gritted her teeth. The first thing she would do when she got out of this place was to throw away every single thing that belonged to someone from her family. Burn it in a bonfire or donate it. She would no longer keep her parent's clothes that she had been lugging around since her departure from America. As for her sister's glasses, she would gleefully chuck them into a bin.

It was time she relied on herself completely and wholly. It was time she healed old hurts, soothed her inner, tormented child, stopped grieving, was brave, went on a diet—but first, she had to get out.

"Help," she yelled.

Chris popped his head in through the door. "We are in a middle of a field. No one can hear you. Really, Tabby, if you were kidnapped by some big bad meanies, you think they would come and help you because you yelled 'help?' More likely they would knock you out. I, however, am a kind hearted person. Would you like some butter chicken and *biryani*?"

"Butter chicken and *naan* would be lovely," Tabby politely requested. "And some soft drink. I'm feeling dizzy."

"We didn't tie your wrists too tight, I hope," Chris asked in concern.

"A little bit," Tabby replied. "Loosen it a touch."

"Sure. Let me get the food first."

He arrived quickly with the food and sat down on a stool in front of her.

"I even got chocolate ice cream." He beamed at her and fed her a bit of chicken.

Tabby smiled, chewed, swallowed and yelled, "Help!"

"What in the world?" Chris reeled back and clamped his hands over his ears.

"It makes me feel better," she apologized. "Yelling every now and then. I feel like I'm doing something concrete to get out of this mess."

"Warn me next time," he grumbled and began feeding her again.

Tabby ate a few bites, and once she felt some of her energy returning, she opened her mouth and screeched, "Help, help, HAAAAAAAAALLLLLLP! I have been kidnapped!"

He winced but didn't complain. He offered her some more food.

She chewed and swallowed and yelled, "Save me from these inhuman monsters! Save me, save meeeeee!"

"Do you want more chicken?" he asked.

She shook her head and hollered, "SOS DAMMIT! SOS! I'm being tortured. Get me out of here!"

"Ice cream?" Chris asked.

"Yes please," Tabby said leaning back contently.

A donkey brayed somewhere outside.

"Did you hear that?" Chris paused near the door and cocked his head.

"The donkey . . . ? Yeah," Tabby replied.

"Strange," Chris muttered. "I'll be back in a moment."

"Don't forget my ice cream," Tabby yelled after him.

A moment later Chris came hurtling back into the room.

"My ice cream?" Tabby pouted.

"Later," he said distractedly. He appeared to think for a moment and then launched into action. He pulled out a piece of cloth and gagged her. "Sorry, I have to do this." After that he started piling sacks of grains in front of her as if he were trying to hide her from the view.

The donkey brayed louder, and men screeched in the other room. Glass shattered and something large crashed to the ground with a thud.

"Your darn hero is quick," Chris muttered.

Hero? Tabby's ears picked up. A hero had come to save her. She arched her neck trying to see the door.

Chris was about to put the last sack on top of the pile, which would have completely hidden Tabby from view, when the door burst open.

Tabby's eyes widened and then narrowed. The hero had arrived all right, but he had arrived astride a donkey.

"Dev," Chris greeting him. "I was about to save Tabby."

Tabby shook her head furiously and tried to tell Dev that Chris was a lying cheating scum who had kidnapped her.

"You are a lying cheating scum who has kidnapped her," Dev said.

Ooh boy, he was telepathic too.

"Let's talk about this. We are cousins. She is nobody—" Chris began but did not finish because Dev boxed him.

Chris reeled and collapsed on the ground.

Dev leaped off the donkey, pushed away the sacks and cut Tabby's ropes off with a knife.

"Thanks," Tabby said when he ripped off her gag. "Look out!"

Dev whirled around in time to see one of the goons holding something long and thin gingerly moving towards Dev.

"What is that?" Dev asked cautiously.

"It's a pencil. I want an autograph, sir. I didn't recognize you when you punched me the first time," the young fellow gushed. He touched his swollen cheek in awe. "I can't believe you gave me this bruise. I will cherish this moment for eternity, Sirji."

Dev looked confounded for a moment, but he recovered quickly and signed the man's shirt sleeve. "Help me load Chris on the donkey," he ordered the man.

The goon leaped to do Dev's bidding. "If you want the other boys to help you with anything, let me know. They would love to assist."

"Why were you fighting me outside then?" Dev asked.

"We weren't sure if it was you. By the time Chris sir yelled your name, you had already knocked most of us out."

"I don't blame them for not recognizing you," Tabby grumbled rubbing her raw wrists. "After all, you *did* come astride a donkey. Honestly, Dev, you should have chosen a horse or arrived in a helicopter. What will your fans think when they realised you saved your heroine on a donkey?"

"You have been spending too much time with Maya," Dev said. "I hope they didn't treat you too badly. Can you walk?"

"Not too bad. Novice kidnappers I'm guessing." Tabby stood up and took a few experimental steps. Her feet wobbled and she swayed

He caught her before she fell.

She gazed up at him.

He gazed down at her.

"Aww," the helpful goon observed.

Dev snapped to attention. "We have to get back home."

"How did you know where to find me?" Tabby asked.

He began walking, leading the donkey whose back was draped with an unconscious, incompetent criminal called Chandramohan Mansukhani. "Maya saw Chris and his hired men carrying you out the back door. She followed them for a bit and saw where they put you, but she was too busy running away herself to save you, so she called me and told me about it."

Tabby beamed at him. "Thanks again for saving me."

"I am not a hero, Tabby. Stop looking at me like that."

"You saved me, didn't you? Barging in, taking me out of the grip of evil bandits. That qualifies as heroic."

"Maya ordered me to save you."

"You would have saved me even if she hadn't ordered you to."

"That's not true."

"Liar."

"Can you two not argue?" Chris moaned. "I have a blinding headache."

They finished the rest of the walk in silence and arrived outside the *haveli*.

The house glittered prettily with all the fairly lights and marigolds strung on it. Torches burned at the entrance and a long red carpet lay on the ground making them feel as if they had travelled back in time and arrived at a Maharaja's house.

A sweaty Tabby with her lovely sari torn and stained, a bruised Chris hugging a bored donkey, and Dev, looking immaculate and handsome as always, took a collective breath and crossed the threshold.

"Eeee, *Hai Ram*!" A few of the aunties fainted at the sight of them.

Meena Aunty whipped out six strings of colourful beads from around her neck and began chanting prayers.

"Where is Maya?" Mr Mansukhani roared.

"Chris, what happened?" Mrs Mansukhani shrieked.

"Dev, what is going on?" Daaji wheeled his chair forward whacking people out of the way with his cane until he was right at the front of the assembled group of nosey guests. "Why are Tabby's wrists bleeding? Why is Chris on top of an ass?"

"Donkey, Daaji, not what you said," Dev muttered. "Can we discuss this inside? In private?"

Daaji scowled. "It is an ass. I have been farming for fifty years. I know what an ass is. Why, when India got his independence in 1942—"

"Bride has run away. There won't be any wedding," Dev hastily interrupted.

Cuckoo Singh burst into tears and launched into his mother's arms.

A sweet, plump girl emerged from the crowd and took a small, hesitant step towards Cuckoo Singh. Her eyes were full of tenderness, her lips quivered with unspoken emotion and her hands twisted her *dupatta* over and over again.

Tabby sighed in relief. It looked like Cuckoo Singh would have a happy ending just as soon as he realised that the girl loved him. And the way his mother was eyeing the girl speculatively, it seemed the happy occasion would occur soon enough.

The guests were politely asked to eat dinner and leave. Meanwhile, the immediate family retired to the dining room.

"Now, Tabby, let us start with you," Daaji said. "What happened?"

So, Tabby told him everything starting from the beginning. How her engagement with Chris had ended and how they decided to hide the fact from everyone and why he had kidnapped her. She went on to explain Dev's part in the entire drama and the fact that Maya had run away because she had never wanted to marry Cuckoo Singh.

Daaji heard Tabby out and was quiet for a long time. He finally spoke, his lips curving up in a slow, pleased smile. "I am glad Maya finally got the spine to rebel. Good for her. I may be old fashioned, but I am not stupid. What Maya did was brave, and bravery must always be applauded. True, she should have spoken up earlier than this, but after the way I threw Dev's father out," He shook his tired head, "I don't blame her." He looked them each in the eye when he continued next. "I am doubling my gift to Maya. She does not have to marry to get the money. Not anymore. The girl showed that being honest with herself and her dreams was more important than any amount of wealth. I admire that."

"But—" Mr Mansukhani began to splutter.

"And you," Daaji said sternly, "better forgive your daughter. Do not make the same mistake I did years ago. You will regret it for the rest of your life."

"Does that mean we can once again be part of the family?" Dev's father asked from the doorway. No one had spotted his arrival.

Daaji's lips trembled, "You were always welcome back."

"You never said so," Dev's mother said, not bothering to hide her tears, unlike the men.

"You don't have to ask if you can return home," Daaji retorted. "Home is a place you can come and go from without permission."

Tabby snuck a look at Dev and found his eyes were moist.

He caught her looking and smiled. A sweet, joyful smile.

"What about Chris?" Mrs Mansukhani broke in. Her worry for her son made her speak up and cut short the emotional reunion.

Daaji scowled. "Chris won't get the money even if he gets married tomorrow. Kidnapping Tabby was a disgusting thing to do. Falling so low shows he does not have the maturity to handle responsibilities. He should be in prison, and Tabby is free to press charges—"

"I won't," Tabby said immediately. "He didn't mean to hurt me."

"Nevertheless, he won't inherit the factory or any of my businesses—"

The room gasped.

"I had improved my opinion of Chris once I got to know Tabby. I had hoped her good sense would rub off on him, but now . . ." Daaji turned to look at his eldest grandson. "It is a pity, Dev, that you have your own fortune and need none of mine. I would have loved to bribe you with a million pounds just to get you to marry Tabby.

Chapter Thirty Seven

No one blamed Tabby for breaking up with Chris. The kidnapping fiasco had tilted even Mr Mansukhani in her favour.

Mrs Mansukhani confessed to her that she was going to marry Chris off to Gunjan. She thought Gunjan was just the sort of person her son needed. She would stand no nonsense from him and if he dared to stray . . . Gunjan would tie him up in so many knots that he would spend a lifetime unravelling himself.

On the day of Tabby's departure, her room was constantly filled with aunties coming to wish her luck and showering her with gifts and hugs. And through it all, Nani, with her eyes brimming with affection and warmth, stayed glued to her side.

Tabby felt overwhelmed with all the love and went through four tissue boxes. Maya called in the afternoon to tell her she had arrived safely in London. She was predictably thrilled at the news that she was getting two million pounds just because she had run away from her own wedding. She was even more delighted to learn that Chris had been disowned. She couldn't believe her brother could stoop so low. By the time the call ended, Tabby knew she had found a friend for life.

Thirty-five people saw Tabby off at the *haveli's* door. She had insisted on going to the airport alone. She didn't like goodbyes.

Laddus were stuffed in her mouth, a final round of hugs and kisses exchanged, and Daaji announced in his booming voice that Tabby should continue thinking of them as her family.

Chris was the last person to come up to her.

"I am sorry," he said. "I never had the intention to hurt you. I thought it was such a small thing . . . lock you away for a few hours and then set you free."

"I know," Tabby patted his hand. "I don't mind. You have given me such a wonderful family in return that it's all forgiven."

He beamed at her. "Friends?"

Tabby grinned and shook his hand. "Friends."

His face lit up like a boy with candy, "You must come over to our London house for Holi, Diwali, Christmas and whatnot."

"And you must make up to your family by working hard," Tabby replied getting into the car.

"They will come around," he said confidently.

Tabby knew he was right. His parents loved him too much.

She waved at all the aunties, uncles, Daaji, Nani, cows and water buffalos for one last time. Once the smiling, tearful faces disappeared as the car sped down the road, Tabby leaned back and closed her eyes. She was wearing a soft, flowing white crocheted dress, brown sandals and was carrying not a thing belonging to her family. Her luggage consisted of stuff she had received as gifts or things she had bought herself. She knew this trip had changed her. Made her more confident. Healed her.

The only thing . . . She swallowed a sob . . . Dev had not even come to say goodbye. His mother had said he had had to leave to cover some breaking news.

She dashed impatiently at her tears. She was footloose and fancy-free. She had had some amazing adventures. Been kidnapped twice, been shot at and fallen in love. . . .

The car screeched to a halt in the parking lot and she got out. She knew her heart would remain in India with Dev . . . perhaps forever. But she had to get away. Move on. Learn to live independently, fulfil her ambitions—"

"Hello."

She squeaked and dropped the suitcase right on her foot. "Dev, ouch! Sorry, I thought you wouldn't be able to say goodbye."

She was suddenly glad she had dropped the suitcase. Her eyes had welled up at the sight of him, and hopefully he would think she was crying because she had squished her toes.

"What are you doing here?" she asked when he continued standing in front of her, watching her face as if he was trying to dig right into her soul.

"I have to go abroad as well," he answered.

He hadn't come to see her off? She hid her disappointment, angry with herself for thinking he would consider her important enough to do something like that. She began wheeling her suitcase away when—"

Bang!

Tabby yelled and without a thought leapt in front of Dev.

"What are you doing, Tabitha?" Dev asked sounding genuinely intrigued.

"Didn't you hear that noise? Those men who shot at you near the Gurudwara must be back," Tabby replied, her eyes watchful, her arms out making sure as much of Dev was covered as possible. "You have to get through me first before you get to him!" she yelled at the invisible assailants. "Now, crouch low and get into the car, quick," she told Dev from the corner of her mouth.

He started laughing, "You are so adorable. It was a car backfiring. My life is not in danger. As for the men who shot at me that day, they were caught days ago. They were hired by a corrupt politician whom I had unmasked a few years ago. If you read the news, you would know."

"I don't like the news. It is always miserable," Tabby muttered in mortification. She ducked her head and moved to go.

His hand shot out and grabbed her wrist. His voice changed when he spoke again, all trace of amusement gone. "Why did you try to save me?"

"Your life is more important than mine. Millions of people love you and adore you."

"Did you save me for other people? Not for yourself?"

She ducked her head lower, even more embarrassed now that he had guessed her secret. She tried to wrench her wrist out of his grasp.

"Answer the question and then you can go," he said tightening his grip.

"It was for others," she said under her breath.

"Look me in the eye and say it," he murmured.

She tried, but her lids wouldn't lift. Her heart was thundering in her ribs, and something in his deep, dark voice was making her knees feel weak.

"Sir ji!" someone yelled.

Tabby's head jerked up, and a flash from a camera caught her right in the eye.

They were surrounded by a bunch journalists carrying notepads, cameras, mics and other fancy looking equipment. They were eyeing the two of them like sharks circling their prey.

"Sir ji," one of the journalists, asked, "how does it feel receiving such a prestigious international award for your work?"

Dev ignored him, his eyes locked on Tabby.

"You have done your country proud, sir," another young man said, his eyes darting from Tabby to Dev.

"Answer me, Tabitha," Dev pressed her wrist to get her attention.

"Tabby," she corrected automatically.

"Sir ji, what are your views on Bullu Gupta's arrest?" a beautiful young woman snapped. When Dev continued to ignore everyone, the young woman narrowed her eyes and continued, "Is it true you have moved back to live with your grandfather?"

"What was the reason for the rift in the first place?" another bold creature piped up. "Who is this young woman?"

The questions now came thick and fast.

"Are you too proud to answer to journalists when you began your career as one?"

"Is it true you have been giving younger journalists in your company tough jobs and taking the credit for them? I heard from a reliable source that you sent a junior to Jonpur, that village with water problems. Were you too scared to go and face them on your own?"

"He was not!" Tabby fired up. "I was there. He went all alone and even got hurt. He did his best to help those villagers. How can you people be so horrible to think that one of your own, someone so brave, kind and wonderful, who has proven himself over and over again over the years would sink so low?"

The journalists pounced as Tabby bit the bait. At the same time Tabby realised Dev was no longer holding her wrist. She was wondering if this was the time to make a run for it when suddenly the journalists gasped in shock.

She turned around to see what they were looking at and found . . . Dev kneeling on the ground with a ring in his hands.

"Tabitha Lee Timmons," he asked. "Will you protect me from imaginary bullets all my life?"

Tabby couldn't speak. Her heart was too full.

"Will you protect me from mean and cruel journalists?" he continued.

The journalists chuckled.

He smiled. "I know you want to write and become independent, but surely you can do that even after marrying me? I promise not to . . . well, only occasionally, pay your bills. Only if you ask. I won't interfere otherwise. I have an office in London. I can move there if you like, or Italy? We have a small office in Italy. I can turn it into the headquarters if you would prefer that. Or how about America?"

"But you love field work," she finally squeaked.

"I think it's time to give the younger ones a chance and trust them to do their job. I can run my company and continue to do interviews from anywhere in the world. Technology is advanced enough."

She made an odd sound in the throat.

"Are we live yet?" a journalist urgently whispered to his cameraman.

"Hush," someone snapped.

"Pan to the left. Close up. Close up on that tear trickling down the right cheek. Perfect."

Tabitha wiped away the tear on her right cheek.

"Tabitha," Dev coaxed. "Marrying someone does not mean you lose your independence. You can have both. Love and a career. It doesn't have to be either or. And as for you wanting to date a moody artist, I can be moody. And the forensic scientist bit . . . I could wear a lab coat and play detective."

She realised he was doing this in front of the entire world. He was willing to take a risk just like he always did when he thought something was important, even if it meant putting his image or life at risk. It proved to her how much he cared about her.

He winced and continued. "My knee is killing me, so let me ask you quick . . . I don't know if it is too soon." He stumbled over his words and cleared his throat. "I don't know if I should wait to give you the ring until you are—"

"Oh no, the ring is good." Tabby sprang at the ring. "Not too soon at all."

He started laughing at the eagerness in her face. "I love you so much," he chuckled. "Will you marry me?"

Tabby slid the ring into place. It was a perfect fit. She grinned up at him. "Yes. I mean, I love you too. And I will marry you."

His eyes blazed with joy, and he gathered her up in his arms and lifted her off the ground in a tight, warm hug.

The Journalists surrounding them whooped, sniffed, and hollered along with millions of people watching the live telecast of Dev Mansukhani getting engaged.

"Aww," the journalists sighed and then quickly went back into ruthless mode.

In Hindi, Malayali, English, Greek, Marathi, Punjabi, they began speaking into their mikes.

"Hearts are being broken around the world as we speak."

"We are bringing this moment to you live from the parking lot of the airport."

"The most eligible bachelor of the country has decided to get married. He has just become engaged. As you can see, they are kissing behind us."

"I am sorry, I have been told we cannot show the kissing, censor issues, but rest assured they are kissing."

"He has decided to marry a girl called—"

"The journalist paused and a wave of whispering began.

"What was her name?"

"What did he call her? Tubby"

"Tibby? Toby?"

"Let's stick with a mysterious foreign girl."

"What do you think, viewers? Do you think it will last? Will it be happily ever after?"

A bystander looked at the couple engrossed in each other unaware of the chaos around them. "Oh yeah, it will last." He grinned into the camera. "From the look of them it will definitely be happily ever after."

"Best love story ever." The journalists high-fived each other. "Brilliant breaking news."

Long after the journalists had got bored of waiting for the couple to stop kissing and answer a few more questions and had left the parking lot, Tabby looked up at Dev with love in her eyes. "We have to get married before we make babies."

I know," he groaned.

"It does take some time making babies. I mean we can begin trying now—"

"In the parking lot?" he brightened.

"No, no. Home?"

"Too far. The parking lot is good. Those bushes look thick—"

"Dev!"

He grinned and nuzzled her ear "I am sure the entire family has seen me propose on live TV. Why don't we skip going home and go on a short holiday to New Zealand instead?"

"Too far."

"Bushes it is."

The End

ABOUT THE AUTHOR

Anya Wylde lives in Ireland along with her husband and a fat French poodle (now on a diet). She can cook a mean curry, and her idea of exercise is occasionally stretching her toes. She holds a degree in English literature and adores reading and writing. Connect with Anya Wylde on Facebook, Twitter, Pinterest, or Google+ to be notified about her upcoming releases.

Website: www.anyawylde.com

Book   cover: goonwrite.com

Other Books By Anya Wylde

The Wicked Wager

Penelope

Seeking Philbert Woodbead

Murder At Rudhall Manor

Ever After

36413721R00174

Made in the USA
San Bernardino, CA
22 July 2016